Sons of Neverland

by

Della Van Hise

Eye Scry Publications
www.eyescrypublications.com

First Published: 1997 (as Ragged Angels)
Kindle edition: 2010 (as Ragged Angels)
Second edition: 2014 (Sons of Neverland)

ISBN: 978-0989693882

Many other Eye Scry Publications are available at a substantial volume discount to bookstores, libraries, etc. Please visit our website at
www.eyescrypublications.com

Sons of Neverland was originally published as a novella in TOMORROW MAGAZINE. It was released in novel form in 1997 as *Ragged Angels*. This current edition is released under the title *Sons of Neverland* – revised and re-edited.

Set against a background of contemporary culture, *Sons of Neverland* explores one man's grief as it plunges him into the realm of the vampire. There, Stefan encounters Dimitri and Miquel, one of whom is destined to become his maker, the other his brother. But the price of immortality is high, and as the vampire warns, "Through my blood you will learn a secret that will compel you to live forever, yet a secret so profane it will haunt you for that same eternity."

The secret will haunt you, too.

This book is dedicated to the quest for immortality and human

evolution, to the muses who make the quest possible

…and most of all, to Wendy.

Sons of Neverland

PROLOGUE

"Have you come to a decision in this matter, Stefan?" he inquired in a voice so flawless and clear it could have been the song of some mythical siren.

Dimitri was asking me to choose between life and death, yet all I could do was sit there listening to the clink of glasses and the din of meaningless conversation all around us. At a nearby table, Batman and Robin shared an order of french fries, thick red catsup bleeding toward the center of the plate in an erotic slow dance. In the buffet line, Captain Kirk and Mr. Spock chatted about the "prejudicially Terran cuisine here at Starbase One" as the Vulcan popped a fat black grape in his mouth. Hotel employees strained to maintain polite expressions in the face of a 200 pound Catwoman and an overly talkative Jean-Luc Picard whose skullcap was peeling away to reveal scraggly locks of auburn.

My head hurt from the wine. I was drunk on illusion. I was sick on grief.

And the creature sitting across the table just looked at me and smiled, revealing straight white teeth whose only peculiarity was the two small fangs where incisors should have been. It was no Hollywood make-up job, nor had this blond waif undergone dental alterations in order to personify some macabre fantasy.

No, *this* illusion was real.

Looking at the vampyre now, it was as if I'd known him always, though we'd met less than 24 hours before...

CHAPTER ONE

The 15th Annual MystiCon was well underway, but I didn't belong here among the starship troopers and the knights and ladies in their Arthurian finery. The huckster's room writhed, undulating with milling misfits and freelance vendors hawking everything from pointed ears to solid gold chess sets cast in the likenesses of Tolkein's hobbits.

Money traded hands, coins jangling. A bearded man broke into a raunchy folk song, strumming a battered mandolin. At the booth next to mine, a lady with long gray hair and one blind eye gave Tarot readings as a Celtic harp played _Greensleeves_ on a distorted cassette. Two aisles over, a young knave in a jester's hat extolled the virtues of the swords he was selling, proudly proclaiming in an affected English accent, "Guaranteed to sever the head of the nastiest dragon or your money back!"

There were two things any science fiction convention could guarantee: the atmosphere was chaos, the majority of attendees not plugged in to the reality most people would consider normal. So when I looked up to see a vampyre standing in front of my table as if he'd appeared out of dusk's early vapor, it never struck me as particularly unusual.

Dimitri was a face in a crowd of odd faces, though paler and more gaunt, with straight blond hair that would have fanned over his narrow shoulders had it not been gathered into a loose bundle tied with black satin bows. And while his costume was striking—a black velvet tuxedo and sable cape—his persona seemed nonetheless tame when compared to some of the others wandering the drafty exhibition hall at the L.A. Airport Hilton.

He arrived just after sunset, not long before the room was scheduled to close, and stood there looking at the _Star Trek_ mementos, movie posters and new age books which were all that remained of my daughter. Stephanie had been buried almost two years now, and while I would have preferred to leave her belongings enshrined in her room, the house had been sold to satisfy the terms of the divorce, and I couldn't bring myself to toss her favorite possessions in a plastic sack to be picked through by strangers at a thrift store.

No, it had to be _here_ that the ashes of her memory were

scattered, here that her spirit was returned to the other pilgrims who'd shared her visions of faeries and far-flung civilizations, worlds more real to her than life in the suburbs of San Diego had ever been. It had to be here, where she and I had come so often—I as a bewildered guest to sign copies of my books, Stephanie as my guide and my inspiration.

Ironically, had she been at the convention, she would've recognized Dimitri for what he was. She would have skirted behind me, whispering, "He's a vampyre, Daddy. Don't talk to him and don't look in his eyes!'

Wanting to indulge her as any father indulges a daughter, I wouldn't have replied when Dimitri first spoke, and I never would have known that he wore those mirrored shades to conceal more than just his identity.

But because Stephanie wasn't there, I was vulnerable when the vampyre began to make small talk. Charming and expressive in a manner not commensurate with his age—maybe 19 and tender at that—he tipped his head in greeting, then said in a voice so clear it could shatter entire realities, "I wish to thank you, sir, for making me believe in spirits and sprites."

I stared blankly before I realized he was referring to my first book, _Travelogue of the Underworld,_ rumored to be a factual account of the author's adventures into a shadow reality existing at right angles to our own. At gatherings such as these, it wasn't uncommon for people to believe my books _were_ the truth.

But those were stories I'd written to entertain Stephanie when she was a little girl, and now the room shimmered, more mist than substance, more past than present. Merlin walked by in a tall purple hat, Xena and Gabrielle not far behind.

'The world's not science, Daddy. The world's magic if you just look!'

But the words were spoken by a ghost, and any magic I'd ever known was buried in her grave.

"I wish I could tell you it's true, but fairyland's closed. There's no such thing as elves or trolls, no sorcerers, no magic. _Nothing,_" I concluded, sharper than I intended.

The vampyre gave a small smile, delicate and birdlike. "Oh, but there _are,_" he insisted with an expressive gesture of ashen hands. "They exist because you made me _believe_ they can, and belief is the first principle of magic, just as the ability to create belief is the mark of a true storyteller."

Oddly, his words didn't strike me as hollow flattery. Though I was now just another face in the swarm, the fact that Dimitri knew who I was after my two-year absence from the convention circuit gave me an unexpected sense of comfort, leaving me embarrassed for the way I'd spoken to him.

"Sorry, it's been a long day," I muttered, a polite social lie to conceal the grief still consuming me whenever I saw a girl in the crowd who looked like my Stephanie, whenever I looked at the empty chair behind the table and remembered when she'd sat at my side.

I turned away from the memories.

"So you're a vampyre," I commented numbly, hoping to lose myself for a moment in someone else's world. I motioned toward the clothes he wore, the dark glasses hiding his eyes. "Am I to assume you never drink—" here I paused for dramatic effect "—*wine*?"

"Ah, Dracula," he sighed, catching my eclectic reference which would have been lost on any normal human being. "A truly unfortunate stereotype that will haunt our kind for centuries to come."

Maybe it shouldn't have surprised me that he spoke as if from experience.

An uneasy silence dropped between us as he studied the articles on the table, the way one politely looks at something when he's really looking for a reason to linger. Picking up a dusty copy of The Lost Boys, he slowly turned it over in his hand until the harsh overhead lights glinted off the cellophane wrapper and time did a backbend—

—in my den, a prisoner to the clackety-rackety-click of a plastic keyboard as I pounded out another chapter of Lucas the Lizard. But I was startled from my thoughts when Stephanie burst through the door, excitement sparking in waves that were all but visible. "Daddy, look!" she exclaimed, holding up the spoils of her weekly allowance, a shiny new copy of The Lost Boys. Sun streaming through the window flashed off the shrink-wrap and bounced around the room, time taking a snapshot. "Watch it with me tonight? Okay, Daddy? Please?"

But I'd been too busy that night and every other night, and

now my throat tightened as Dimitri held that same old tape in his hand, a ruthless reminder of what I'd lost. Ghosts were strange companions, manifesting in the form of an old movie, an empty room, a song on the radio.

Oblivious to my grief, Dimitri set the box down, fingertips barely brushing the soft peach tablecloth as he looked up from his silence.

"The portrayal of vampyres has become quite an obsession in Hollywood," he murmured, clasping his hands together at his waist with an air of formality that seemed somehow natural. "Still, it's unfortunate that no film has ever captured the true essence of what it means to walk the Earth as a citizen of the night."

Strangely nervous, I laughed, not for what he said but for the manner in which he said it. After all, *I* was the word merchant— or had been before Stephanie died—and Dimitri had stepped on the untended grave of my muse with his eloquent manner of speaking and his aggrandized gestures that would have suited a character in a very old book. He belonged in another world and time, right down to the cloistering scent of his cologne, the brush of powder on his cheeks, the old world propriety of his conduct.

"So what *does* it mean?" I asked, not sure if I expected an answer or was only making fun of him.

He didn't respond, just twitched his lips in a smile that might have been real had I been able to see his eyes. Instead, I saw only myself in duplicate, his glasses throwing my reflection back at me as twins.

For an instant, I thought the images were tiny paintings on the lenses, for no mirror ever captured a man as he saw himself. Momentarily disoriented, I gaped at the distorted stranger, this man who always seemed too tall and too thin, this man who had peered back at me in mirrors for 34 years, an eerie doppelganger wearing my face. Stefan London was his name—*my* name—yet I knew nothing of the man behind it. It was only a symbol for the face who wore it, four syllables meaning absolutely nothing.

Only when the scream of a plastic phaser split the air did I jerk myself back to reality, embarrassed to be searching for my lost identity in another man's glasses.

"I—uh—sorry. I'm Stefan London—please, call me Stefan," I stammered, as if speaking the name out loud might cause it to have meaning again. I thrust my hand toward him, a marionette going through jerky social formalities.

He bowed slightly from the waist, far more graceful than my clumsy handshake. "I am deeply honored to make your acquaintance, Stefan. As for myself, I am called Dimitri, though it's only a word, as you already realize, a label incapable of telling you anything about me. Sad, really, that our entire lives are spent in such isolation from one another. Don't you agree?"

How could I answer that? While verbalizing the mental aloneness every human being experiences every moment of their lives, he seemed to be reaching inside my mind, speaking my thoughts aloud in a way that destroyed the isolation itself.

And even if it were nothing more than some inexplicable synchronicity, the confident aura with which Dimitri spoke sent a chill down my spine. This kid hadn't just crawled into the tuxedo and the black silk cape on a whim. He *fit* inside them, for unlike most human beings, Dimitri was more than just his name.

He truly saw himself as a vampyre, and the fact that *he* believed it intrigued me utterly. Instead of automatically writing him off as just one more deluded soul, a part of me I'd thought extinct broke free of its grief with a vengeance that was exhilarating and at the same time absolutely terrifying. A voice inside my mind burst alive, whispering, '*What if he is? What if he could be? How did it happen and what does it mean to be a vampyre? What if...? Oh, what if it could be real?*

It was a voice I knew well, yet one that had been silent so long I'd believed it mute. In short, Dimitri's very existence made me want to write again—a reaction I could not have predicted under any circumstances. I took a step away from him and would have bolted altogether had the wall not halted my retreat.

My words were no longer for sale. I had to keep them locked up inside lest they, like Stephanie, leave me forever, for although I might occasionally run across a ragged novel bearing my name in a used book store, the man on the dust jacket was dead.

Suddenly, I wanted to chase Dimitri away before he disturbed my living death. I'd grown comfortable in my mourning and was loathe to give it up. Yet it also occurred to me that perhaps Stephanie had known him. Maybe she'd spoken to him or flirted with him at some other convention years ago. Maybe he would remember her sad smile, her rare laughter. With an effort, I controlled my panic, forcing an unnatural calm.

"These things belonged to my daughter—Stephanie," I said, gesturing toward the table as I spoke her name.

Dimitri looked at me from behind his dark glasses for a long time. "She was a beautiful girl," he said at last.

My heart beat faster. "You knew her?"

Another long silence followed, as if he really did have eternity. Then he shook his head. "No, but because she lives so strongly in your memories, it's as if she still stands by your side, the stygian sprite of your early novels."

His insight left me numb, its implications chilling me through to the very bone. And yet, suddenly, it didn't matter *how* Dimitri knew these things. It only mattered that he *did* know them. It only mattered that, for one single moment, I no longer felt so completely alone.

Finally, blurry-eyed, I managed in a whisper: "Thank you."

I wasn't sure what I meant, but perhaps I was simply grateful to him for acknowledging my grief in a way most people never could. It made friends ill at ease, made them find reason to be someplace else.

But Dimitri didn't withdraw. Instead, he studied me as if coming to some profound decision while the two of us stood encapsulated together at a mystical crossroads existing apart from the rest of the world. Finally, in a gesture that was curiously intimate, he smiled ever so slightly and slowly removed his glasses, our eyes meeting for the first time.

My initial reaction was that he must have some medical condition which could account for the fact that his right eye was cobalt blue and flecked with gold while the left was a shade of green like summer grass. Animal eyes, predator sharp.

I should have known then that he wasn't human, or perhaps I refused to acknowledge it because those terrible eyes were penetrating the very core of my mind. But when he reached out and grasped my hand, pressing it between both of his own with a strength I could never hope to match, lightning flashed inside my head, obliterating whatever sovereign thoughts made a man unique unto himself.

The din of the convention was chopped off, and before I

could react, some supernatural force jerked me away to a place where the stars were black and the sky white, where the silence was as shrill a dying man's scream. I was falling then, plunging through infinite space and timeless void, a disembodied consciousness hurtling toward oblivion through the very nothingness which was both destination and annihilation.

My only thought was that the city had been struck by a nuclear blast and this was what it was like to die. But then, through sheer intuition, I understood that I had been miraculously transported into the alien environs of another man's mind, where I stood looking out through his monstrous eyes, seeing myself through his strangely intensified perceptions:

A man in the peak of his life with shaggy hair the shade of pine bark after a cool rain and eyes blue as tropical waters. Though willow thin from too much grief, he was also willow strong. And though he struggled to stress only the mediocrity in himself, the strength of the long distance runner he had been in his youth always crept past the nondescript clothes and downcast eyes. Stefan London was beautiful, his soul a veil of black lace torn in spots by sorrow, yet it was through those gashes that his crippled aura bled to draw people to him as flame was attracted to wick—

"Yo! Death Star to dealer! You okay, buddy?"

Darth Vader was shaking my shoulder, waving one of Stephanie's books under my nose until the scent of printer's ink and dust acted like smelling salts to shake me back to my senses. "How much you want for this?" he rasped from inside a black plastic helmet.

The jolt of being catapulted back into my own body was like a rubber band snapping, the pain of it causing me to gasp. I had no idea where I was, nor even *who*, and the world had become a merry-go-round churning out of control.

Then I saw. Still standing in front of me as if nothing were out of the ordinary, Dimitri just looked at me with those omniscient eyes which seemed to be saying, *You wanted to know what it's like to walk the night? Well, I can show you, my friend, things you can't even begin to dream. Oh, the things I can show you with these eyes...*

Bathed in an icy sweat, suddenly sick to my stomach, I yanked my hand away from him, yet before I could discover any answers in his face, he slid those mirrored shades back on and reality righted itself, not unlike an old film fluttering through the projector until the picture and the soundtrack were once again in sync.

In front of my table, a small crowd had gathered to gawk at Stephanie's collection, yet their expressions were vacant, their attention captured by plastic toys and paper worlds hidden inside out-of-print books.

"How much?" Lord Vader asked again.

He might as well have spoken High Martian. I could only stare into the distorted world the mask reflected back at me.

"I—did you see—?" I stammered, fighting the vertigo.

Dimitri placed a hand on my shoulder, warning me to silence with a oddly erotic gesture of one long finger laid discreetly over pale lips.

"Each of us sees only those things we allow ourselves to see, Stefan," he said in response to my thoughts. Then, leaning nearer, he added, "What _I_ see is a man whose grief is an unrelenting master but also a powerful muse—one that could serve us both well."

I pulled away, realizing in an awful flash that his lips never moved when he spoke.

"Who _are_ you?" I demanded, struggling to shake myself free of a dream that had turned dangerously real. "What do you want from me?"

And suddenly we were alone again. Darth Vader stormed off carrying his head under his arm and the others just drifted away, extras milling about at the whim of some unseen director.

"It's not a question of what I want, per se, but a matter of how we may be able to help one another," Dimitri explained in that crystalline voice. "True vampirism isn't based on the surreptitious control of your mind or the theft of your blood, but is instead a matter of give and take." Here he paused to give me an alluring smile, then concluded rather boldly, "I've shown you a glimpse of yourself through my very own eyes, so now I ask you: are you interested in seeing more? Are you interested in discovering who you are, who you _can_ be? Are you interested in evolving beyond this mortal life and into eternity itself?"

His questions unnerved me deeply.

It was hot in the room.

My mouth went dry.

In a matter of minutes, with a minimum of words, this

willful fiend had seduced my senses and burned my sensibilities. He had lured me to the very brink of madness and now I would be compelled to follow him over the edge—not only because he was clearly a magical being, but because he made me feel *alive* again, so much that the sensation was not unlike physical arousal, and *that* was the worst of all.

As if understanding my dilemma, he reached inside his jacket, pulling out a card which he handed to me with a flourish of pallid hand and lace cuff.

DIMITRI ALEXANDER KARROS
FREELANCE COMPUTER ANALYST
213-555-8267
Graveyard shift only

Dazed, I read it twice before he said, "If you should choose to pursue these feelings, Miquel and I would welcome you into our home this evening."

His speech was so formal and succinct it was altogether spellbinding. I had to blink to rid my mind of images I couldn't have described had my life depended on it. Wine thoughts. Gravestone musings. Mermaid etchings that flowed through my soul like black water and left me hallucinating.

Stephanie dancing with Mephistopheles high atop the Acropolis, spinning and seeming to fly as her long black dress flew out from her on the wind. Then I was cutting in—not to waltz with my beloved daughter, but to dance in the arms of the devil himself because the idea was as erotic as it was absurd.

These were the visions that came when Dimitri touched my wrist in a gesture of intimate familiarity. His fingers glistened with emeralds, rubies, a star sapphire that reminded me all too much of his one blue eye. He was casket satin, moonlight on baptismal waters.

And then he was just a man-boy in a vampyre get-up as my mind abruptly translated what he'd said. Mortified by the very feelings he referred to—taboo curiosities I might have found intriguing years before—I held out his card to return it.

"I'm driving back to San Diego tonight," I muttered, tripping on my words. "Maybe some other time."

16

The room was shrinking, the air thin. In the alley outside the building, dusk was luring night into the city.

But Dimitri leaned over the table and, in a brazen gesture, folded his card into my palm and closed my fingers around it until the stiffly laminated paper cut into me and drew blood. Our faces only inches apart, he smiled again as a drop of red squeezed through my fist and rolled down my wrist.

"A lie is a terrible way to begin eternity, Stefan," he sang to me, his breath a cemetery breeze, cool and eerie on my cheek. "Miquel will send a car for you at ten. It is best that you come willingly."

He brought my hand to his lips, and though I thought his intention was to kiss it in the fashion of a European gentleman bidding farewell to a paramour, he flicked out his tongue and darted it between my fingers to catch the flow of my blood. It happened so quickly I couldn't twist free, and my heart cramped as I saw the lips of this dreadful cherub stained red.

Before I could say another word, before I could parade my wounded pride around the room or hurl accusations at the boy, he was gone. A flash of burgundy, a sparkle of bejeweled hands, and he had vanished into the crowd, disappearing altogether.

My hand smarted. Somebody giggled. I couldn't breathe.

*

Within an hour I was telling myself it was all just a clever illusion by some trickster at a convention. I was afraid to believe, and I wouldn't have known *what* to believe even if I hadn't been afraid. From the sanctuary of my hotel room, I called my best friend, but when Charlie answered, I had no idea what to say. How does one describe being jerked out of body, propelled at indescribable speeds through a photo-negative-world, then looking at oneself through the eyes of another man?

But because Charlie had known me since we were children, she did exactly what I wanted her to do: she listened, she didn't say she was too busy to talk even when I heard her 4-year-old fussing in the background, and when I was done babbling like some bewildered mental patient, she laughed out loud.

"Damn, Stefan, nothing like that ever happens to me. I'm

17

jealous as hell," she said, robust and filled with life. "So, are you going?"

That was Charlie's approach to the world: meet it head on and beat it with a stick. I envied her tenacity.

Lying on the bed, I stared at the ceiling, my emotions warring between amusement and the melancholy which had been my constant companion since Stephanie's death.

"Why would I?" I grunted.

"You know, Stefan, it might do you some good to make some new friends now that you and Laurie are split up," she suggested without polite preamble. "What've you got to lose?"

"Charlie, this kid cut my hand and licked away the blood!" I protested, indignant. "He really believes he's a vampyre!"

"So what do *you* believe?"

I scoffed. "I believe he's a screwed-up kid who should get some help before he gets arrested. Or worse."

On the other end of the line, I heard Charlie rolling her big brown eyes the way she always did whenever I said something inane.

"Men," she commented, long-suffering. "Look, if you really thought so, you wouldn't have called me in such a dither. Face it, something incredible happened to you tonight and if you don't try to figure it out, you'll be crazy within a week. Regret's an ugly bedfellow."

A feeble smile crept up on me. "Chase the muse again?"

"*Catch* the fucker," she corrected with a chuckle. "Isn't that what writers are supposed to do?"

"Those who catch the muse die," I reminded her. And though I intended the comment as lighthearted prattle, it brought a sudden dread to the center of my chest. I wasn't ready to quest after fantasies. I wasn't ready to write. I wasn't ready to live again.

Without remembering how I fell in the quicksand, I was over my head, wanting nothing more than to be alone with my misery. Stephanie's face whispered across the blank screen of the television, a different muse of a distant life I'd once lived.

"God help me, Charlie, I miss her." *Why did I go up to the room while she was off with her friends? Why did she have to die?* "Why couldn't it have been me instead?"

I didn't realize I'd spoken out loud.

Charlie didn't answer for awhile, though I could hear the comforting shush of her breathing. "I know, Stefan... I know. But you have to stop blaming yourself. You have to go on with your life." She paused, gave a soft sigh. "God, that's a stupid thing to say. I'm sorry."

"Don't be. It helps." It didn't. We both knew it.

We were silent for a few seconds. "Maybe life doesn't make sense because we're missing the corner pieces," she offered just before we hung up.

Maybe she was right.

For a long time, I lay there staring at a spot where the wallpaper didn't quite match up, listening to the distant slamming of doors as other patrons on the 9th floor came and went. Where were they going? I wondered. For what purpose did they move about inside this skyscraper hotel, and what would happen if we all just stopped going through motions that had long since lost any meaning?

We scurried about like ants in a hive, but what was the purpose of the hive itself? Worse: *was* there a purpose, or was it only random happenso that society had come together as it had, and that Man served *it* far more than *it* served *him?* We worked at our varied tasks, gathering riches like ravens collecting bright objects, but what did we hope to accomplish when all was said and done? We raised our families and grew old sitting on wooden porches, but in the end it would always end the same way.

Why? I caught myself wondering. What did any of it mean, and if it really did mean nothing, why keep doing it? Why not just run wild into the world and suckle from it what pleasure we could before death finally caught up to us?

Where these thoughts came from, I do not know, but they sent me tumbling into a maelstrom. And though I might have believed reality-altering revelations should happen to pious monks on mountaintops in Tibet, my own came in a nondescript hotel room when I suddenly understood that my entire existence had been nothing but a series of aimless movements, common gestures, worn-out clichés.

I had to get on with life, Charlie said, but what the hell *was* my life?

I'd spent years staring at a cyclopsian monitor as if it were the Eye of Knowledge, transcribing the lies of my imagination to trade for bread and butter, but surely there was more than pushing paper, mowing the lawn and making sure the guy next door didn't get a bigger tv. than the one in my den. We were so busy with the trappings and the rituals that we'd forgotten they *were* just trappings and rituals, yet I couldn't have ventured a guess as to what might lie beyond the world we thought of as reality.

What were we supposed to *Do* with life in all its briefness?

Every bit as troubling as this unwanted apocalypse was the knowledge that my encounter with Dimitri had inadvertently spawned it. Something inside me was torn free at the instant he walked up to me, and now everything in the world somehow related to him, including the blue and green stripes on the bedspread that were like his mismatched eyes and the creamy flesh of the telephone that was the color of his sandstorm skin. And though the tv. from the next room droned through the wall, I could hear only his voice: *'Grief is an unrelenting master but also a powerful muse...'*

Like a lunatic possessed, I rose from the bed, pacing and muttering to myself, rubbing at a spot between my eyes where my head had begun to throb. Finally, finding no escape, I slumped into a chair by the window, yet there was nothing redeeming in the world beyond.

Two strip joints with flashing neon lights, an assortment of sleazy nightclubs, and the glittering runway of LAX luring the newest victims down from heaven. A ribbon of headlights twisted toward the horizon, an angry snake coiling around the city, choking it. The stars had flown away long ago, the sky was yellowed and spoiled with smog. The night which should have been black and seductive was instead grey and terminally ill.

It was a world with a ruined soul.

Suddenly sickened by it all, I rose from my chair and hurried into the bathroom, turning on the shower to drown out the unrelenting noise in my head. While the mirrors fogged with steam, I hastily removed my clothing, mesmerized by my own reflection as, for an instant, I saw myself as I'd looked through Dimitri's inhuman eyes.

Lithe. Strong. Masculinely beautiful.

'Are you interested in finding out who you are, who you can be?'

My hand was an ocean, my erection a serpent gliding through it as I collapsed to my knees and uttered a choked cry into the mist.

CHAPTER TWO

When my head cleared, I made the decision *not* to leave my room that night. Vampyres were nonsense! I wouldn't stand at the curb wringing my hands like some bride at the altar while Dimitri hovered in hotel shadows and giggled at the gullibility of a grieving fool.

Perhaps for that reason, it came as a shock when I found myself in the elevator, surrounded by several other con-goers. Their painted faces drifted by me, taffeta and lace costumes glittering in scattered light thrown by flickering fluorescent tubes. Stephanie's ghost danced in the shiny metal doors and spoke to me in a whisper that was only the rustling of Superman's cape.

The world had become my dream, solid yet not, molasses beneath my feet. A kid in Klingon garb pointed a plastic disrupter at my chest, but I had lost my sense of humor in the fall between floors.

When the elevator stopped, I could only watch myself walking through the revolving glass door that led toward the night and the darkness and the black stretch limo waiting in the portico. A somnambulist unblinking, I approached the car as a skeletally thin man with a lyrical Jamaican accent ushered me inside. It never seemed strange that he knew me on sight or that he called me by name.

As the door closed behind me, there was an odd sense of finality, a feeling that one world had just ended and a new one was about to begin.

Ah, but now you must make the choice, Stefan, for it's human perception that determines the reality of any reality. Will you choose to see this brave new world or stay stubbornly rooted in your own?

The thought was outlandish in that it wasn't my own, yet the partition separating me from the driver was closed, the other man only a silent silhouette as the car rolled forward. A chill fell helter-skelter down my back, but as I rubbed my eyes to clear my vision, it suddenly struck me that my first impression of a standard limousine was altogether wrong. Reality shimmered and glittered, just so much fog.

Black leather seats had transformed to crushed red velvet, the pile thick and soft beneath my curled fingers. Small interior lights above the doors morphed into white tapered candles, orange flames flickering inside fragile glass globes.

Terror rose up within me, yet it was accompanied by curiosity, too. A voice inside me whispered, *Quit fighting, just let go, let go.*

And it was then that I found myself in another world—a place that had been there all along, yet one I only began to perceive when I allowed myself to see it.

It was a world of opulent luxury, where the seats were littered with petals of a pallid pink rose and where a narrow bed that took up the entire rear of the car had its crimson comforter turned down in silent invitation. At first glance, it *was* a bed, but when I blinked, it was plainly a coffin, custom-made of mahogany and wide enough for two to share.

On one of the plush white pillows sat a plate of fruit— cherries, strawberries, raspberries, grapes—all things red, and wet as if with dew. On the other pillow lay a bottle of fine merlot, and on the seat at my side was a crystal wine glass bearing a folded note, written in perfect calligraphy and completed with a bold signature.

My dearest Stefan,

As the journey will take the better part of an hour, please be comfortable and accept these modest gifts if you find them pleasing. I have long admired your visionary work and look forward to having you in my home this evening.

Miquel Kaliq Constantine

My heart hammered, but these macabre visions didn't vanish to fulfill my wish to be back in the real world. Even if I'd had the presence of mind to flee, the car was already racing through the city, a sleek ebony projectile where all the troubles of the world

22

were only paintings playing on tinted glass.

I was a dazed prisoner in a speeding museum.

Nevertheless, I wanted to weep for the pain captured in those life-size canvases—for the vagrant preaching at a deserted public park and the tragedy in his life that had brought him to such humiliation; for the hookers selling flesh to support their habit while Death and Disease stalked them slowly; for the skinny yellow dog running wild-eyed and headlong through traffic as if he were there to symbolize every misguided, condemned soul on Earth.

I thought of Stephanie, for I knew we must be near the underpass where her body was found, and once again I blamed myself. She was barely 13, yet I'd let her run with her friends at these gatherings since she was 11.

Wanting to be her confidant as much as her father, I created fantasy worlds for her to inhabit, and when she outgrew them, I encouraged her to find her own or make them herself. But because my life was complicated, too, I'd patted her on the head and only half listened when she told me that the ability of the supernatural world to manifest was directly related to man's willingness to perceive supernatural manifestations. Anything was possible and the impossible was altogether likely, she said, and oh how much she'd believed it!

My failure as a parent and as a man was that I still didn't know *what* she'd believed or what she'd been searching for other than belief itself. I didn't know *her*, and never had.

Now I never would.

I stared at that truth in the limo's magical windows, and for an instant I saw her blood on my hands. Impulsively, I pressed them against the glass and gazed out, a lost child with my nose fogging the window.

"Stephanie," I cried, though no sound came from my lips. "Stephanie..."

What took my thoughts away from her right then, I don't know, though the depth of that pain was suddenly replaced with an equally profound separation from myself. A sign along the road announced we were leaving Los Angeles County, though some philosophical vagabond inside my head told me I'd left the city the instant I entered the car.

It all made sense in that none of it made sense at all.

I held the wine glass and saw that I'd drained it, though I had no recollection of opening the bottle nor any memory of how my fingers came to be stained with the sweet red blood of ripe cherries.

And then I was completely entranced, a participant in a waking dream as the limo thrust deeper into its night lover and left the world behind.

*

When the car entered a long circular driveway somewhere between San Bernardino and the Mojave Desert, the sound of tires transformed the whine of asphalt to the unique warble of cobblestone. Tremendous evergreens yearned skyward, the scent of freshly mown grass creeping through the vents to color the air green. By the dim light of a waning moon, the wrought iron gates through which we passed created prison bars across the constellation of Taurus, a cage to hold the stars themselves.

Completely surrounding the estate—nearly 25 acres in all—a 12-foot hedge had been painstakingly pruned to resemble a dragon, its countless spikes and ridges actually dappled ivy. On one side of the gate, the terrible head stretched upward, jagged teeth ripping the sky, red eyes really sensors on high-tech security cameras. On the other side, after wrapping around the grounds, the forked tail formed a delicate curl which was incongruously playful.

My face pressed to the window, I gazed out over what appeared to be sepulchers, yet what sent shivers through me were the humanesque statues atop those cold, grey markers. The entire front lawn was strewn with these life-size figures, men and women frozen in pose as the breath caught in my throat and the limo's lights split the darkness in two.

Atop one knoll, a wraith thin woman would waltz forever with an invisible partner. Nearby, a young man was held in an eternal pose of martial arts *kata*, one stone arm and one stone leg extended in perfect balance. In a corner of this eerie garden, twin brothers no more than 17 embraced, expressions of lust forever preserved in identical faces as one boy's hand cupped the other's buttocks in a gesture of incestuous foreplay.

But as the car cruised past this gathering of stone ghosts—

24

dozens in all—I caught a glimpse of the central courtyard and the even more unnerving statue standing watch over all the others. A full 8 feet tall, it stood with outstretched arms and black wings that bent longingly toward the garden of lifeless lovers. Instead of raw grey marble like the others, it was intricately painted—raven hair that matched the sheltering wings; lithe musculature shaded bronze and gold; full red lips parted in a sardonic smile. Its head tilted slightly to one side, a pose reminiscent of the Virgin Mother gazing with rapture at the infant Christ, yet the hunger caught in those savage eyes was far from holy.

So spellbound had I become that I scarcely noticed the car rolling to a stop. When the driver's shadow blocked the window, I must've startled at seeing him there, for he gave a chuckle as the door opened and the night rushed in to deliver me from my trance.

I stepped out onto the cobblestone driveway, dizzy and disoriented from the wine. A scent of jasmine filled the air, heady perfume painting the sky of this surreal world. Completely surrounding the drive and leading up the marble steps to the estate's double doors, tiny lights glittered like thousands of fireflies. Water rushed through a manmade creek, and frogs hidden within the lush gardens sang an off-key melody that was reassuring and yet keenly sad.

I do not recall being led up the cool stone steps to the entrance, my mind overwhelmed instead with candles burning from every multi-paned window, eyes of fire that threw my shadow behind me to create an army of willowy ghouls. Nervous, I turned to make some comment to the driver, but the Jamaican had disappeared and I caught only a glimpse of blood-red taillights when the limo vanished into what must have been a subterranean garage or the mouth of Hell itself.

With hesitation born of dread, I lifted my hand to the bell, but the doors abruptly opened of their own accord. Startled, I took a step back, confronted by a young man I imagined to be a servant. Little more than a boy, he flourished an elaborate bow that caused the tails of his coat to sweep the polished marble floor. His face was smooth and ashen, a porcelain doll incarnate, with a hint of powder on his cheeks and a glimmer of lipstick on his mouth. His gloved hands were inordinately fine, his movements deliberately exaggerated like those of a diminutive mime.

25

Without a single utterance, he led me into the foyer, closing the carved oak doors behind us.

Unnerved, I started to speak, but he laid a finger across his lips, then waved his hand like a magician conjuring a spell. In response, music began to play—Beethoven's _Fur Elise_. The boy looked at me with his head tipped dramatically to one side, then gave a frown which said the classical selection wasn't to his liking. A wave of his hand transformed Beethoven to Pink Floyd, and now the servant placed his hands together like a child praying homage to God, and smiled a smile of sheer bliss.

Then, with the grace of a dancer, he indicated I should wait while he turned sharply and retreated into the house, his boot heels clicking sharply behind him.

My heart beat faster, and for the first time since I'd wandered like a spellbound zombie from my hotel room, I came to my senses with a suddenness that caused me to gasp.

All the world was mad.

Suddenly alone in that high-ceilinged foyer with its ice-cream-smooth white walls and its two curved arches leading off left and right, I questioned the sanity of a man who would do the things I'd done that night. I had no idea where I was. I knew nothing of the waifish youth who had invited me here, less of the mysterious Miquel to whom Dimitri had referred.

Their limo was a hearse, their wine a drug, their servant a harlequin.

For all I knew, I had been brought here to die in some ritualistic murder. The house exuded darkness despite its fiery eyes. It smelled of decadence and the grave grim yearnings of the human soul regardless of the fresh white roses on the flower table and the painting of Botticelli angels hanging above them.

As the music abruptly stopped, a cuckoo clock sang its tick tock dirge, causing my body to jerk. I cast a rapid glance over my shoulder, and though I saw nothing, some eerie sixth sense warned me someone was there.

The air seemed to move, little currents drafting through the room, silent breaths of an unseen audience. A hint of cologne, faint yet undeniably masculine. And though I couldn't say I heard anything at all, there was a sense of cloth brushing cloth, the barest rustling that comes when a handkerchief drops to the floor or a cat

26

rubs against one's leg in a dark room.

I felt him there. Waiting. Watching.

And then my mind was out of control, conjuring images of maniacs and madness and my own blood spilling out to stain the polished hardwood floor. With a rough breath that came out as a garbled cry, I spun toward the door. I'd run back to the real world if need be. Or I would crawl.

When my fingers closed around the cold metal knob, I experienced a profound moment of relief—a split second *before* a hand appeared from behind me to press the door closed again. In that instant, I knew the dread of a man strapped in the electric chair waiting for a governor's reprieve, and the ironic sinking in the pit of the gut that came from a wrong number. I knew what it was to die a thousand times in the span of a single moment. And I understood what it meant to look death in the eye and come away with the knowledge that, in the end, there is never a reprieve for any living thing.

Frozen in time as an unnatural calm fell over me, I stared at that graceful hand for an eternity. The fingers were long and elegant, the nails carefully manicured. On the middle finger was a gold band etched with the Greek symbols for alpha and omega, on the fourth finger an oval cut emerald the size of a large almond.

His skin was olive-hued and dark, and as my head slowly turned, I saw on his wrist a band so smooth it shone like liquid gold. He wore a simple white shirt with the sleeves pushed up to the elbows and the three top buttons unfastened, and a pair of jeans so fashionably old they were more patches-and-holes than anything else. The scent of Eternity clung to his body—for he had a keen sense of humor about himself—and when I raised my eyes and looked into his face, I was inundated with the profound realization that Miquel wasn't human.

That was the first thought which assaulted me, though the assault was gentle and dangerously erotic. I knew his name. I knew what he was. And I knew that he *was* a vampyre.

He studied me with candid curiosity, keen eyes raking from my face to my toes and back again, and then he gave an unexpected smile that caused the color to drain from me completely. The front teeth were normal enough; it was the incisors that formed the exquisitely sharp fangs gleaming in his full, wet mouth.

"Such terrible anguish in such a lovely bottle," he murmured in a voice rich with the faintest accent. His words caused me embarrassment, though that was quickly forgotten when he extended his hand in a gesture that seemed trite under the circumstances. "My name is Miquel Kaliq Constantine," he said, his smile turning bolder. "At least it is the name I've adopted for a lifetime or two."

Perhaps I was too shocked to do anything but respond in the expected manner, or perhaps I was already so deep under his spell there could be no hope left for me. I offered him my hand, and when he grasped it in an embrace shocking for its strength as well as its chill, I could only imagine what other names had followed him throughout history. Eros, perhaps. And Pan. Don Juan. But I also considered Vlad the Impaler. Ivan the Terrible. Belial, Zamiel.

My breathing stopped. My heart tapped a crazy rhythm.

He stood at least six foot five, coal black hair brushing the tops of his shoulders in ragged layers and spiked bangs that would have suited a brooding model or a moody bass player in a rock and roll band. His features were angular, sharp, and so perfectly chiseled that he might really have been a Greek god or maybe a Hollywood special effect escaped from its creator. His lips were full and surprisingly pink, his strong chin sporting a two-day shadow which imbued him with an overall ominous look.

His face and body called him 30. His aura told a darker secret of his antiquity.

But what held me captive were his eyes, substantiating all myths of a vampyre's ability to mesmerize. Green as the emerald on his hand and flecked with lighter shades of brown and gold, a hundred flames reflected in those immortal mirrors—candlelight and history and secrets so profound no human could have known them and lived.

While Dimitri was alluring by virtue of his ashen innocence and ballet dancer grace which could be misinterpreted as fragile, Miquel wore his power in a far more imposing fashion, not the willowy body of a youth but the finely honed sculpture which was the epitome of all things male. If Dimitri were Gainsborough's *Blue Boy*, Miquel was the model for David—yet he was the paradigm whose true physical splendor couldn't be captured even by Michelangelo himself.

He was life and death and pure carnal force, and though I had always considered myself strong-natured, I knew I had encountered a creature to whose will I would inevitably bend. I had never been so drawn to another man, yet I stood before him practically swooning with the knowledge that this was how he wanted me to feel and there was nothing whatsoever I could do to change it. If Dimitri had briefly bewitched me, Miquel had stolen all my reason, and I knew in that instant that my life would never be the same again.

Without question, he was a vampyre—a being who could drain away physical defiance and moral inhibitions as easily as he could drain the blood from my body. With God as my witness, I tried to fight him. My fists clenched, fingernails digging in until my palms bled like the wounds of Christ, but even that tangible pain was inadequate to break his spell.

He made a motion that cautioned me not to resist, then took my hand and gently uncurled my fingers. And though I struggled to look away, I was paralyzed with sick fascination as he ran the pad of one long finger over my self-inflicted wounds. Then, never taking his gaze off of me, he touched fingertip to tongue tip, moist lips slowly closing over a single drop of red.

He drew a slow breath, his eyes closing in approval, and only then did I realize I had been droning incoherently.

"*Ohgod—ohmygod—godhelpme!*"

He gave me a look that might have held amusement or curiosity. Then, with a movement so graceful and quick I sensed more than saw it, he placed one hand behind my head, the other on my ribs, and drew me to him in an embrace as intimate as it was inescapable.

"My dearest Stefan, stop talking to God and yourself, for aren't they really the same?" he asked, his body a cage surrounding me. Fairy-tale eyes darkened, and when he leaned closer I noticed the gold cross he wore in one ear as if in defiance of his nature. "If your Heavenly Father were such a benevolent old man, you and I never would have met—and *that* would have been the real tragedy, don't you agree?"

Because he willed it, the strength had left me until I was nothing but clay, the raw material of life that could offer no resistance against the sheer potency of his magic.

"Please," I heard my voice saying, and hated myself for begging. "Please—let me go!"

He pinned me with those terrible eyes, and for a moment I thought he might—not because I asked it, but because he detested weakness and I was behaving like a child. But before I realized what was happening, he brought me so tight against his chest I could feel the hard, slow beat of his immortal heart.

A soft sigh came through his lips and, shaking his head in a gesture of tender reassurance, he forced my body against the cool white wall, compelling me with a thought not to look away.

The sensation I cannot describe except to say it felt as if the idea were mine rather than his. I wanted to look into his eyes and never glance away. I wanted to feel the heady detachment of his trance like a drug-induced euphoria. And I *wanted* to collapse in his arms, a dead weight caught between the world of the living and the world that belonged to the night.

My head had fallen back, and only now did I realize the ceiling was covered with mirrors through which I was compelled to watch the obscene sight of my own seduction by a vampyre. Miquel's reflection was remarkable, the mirror capturing the essence of him which couldn't be seen by human eyes alone. A noncorporeal radiance engulfed him, a silvery resplendence reminiscent of the ethereal glow attributed to the angels themselves.

But Lucifer was an angel, too, I thought.

And I began to weep.

Yet while I would have been loathe to give him any credit for compassion, I felt he wanted to make this easy for me. His arms went taut around me, the full length of his preternatural body pressing against me as if to shield me from what was to come. With a tenderness that was cruel somehow, he smoothed the hair away from my face, leaning in until his lips were brushing the curve of my ear.

"Ssshh," he whispered, rocking me back and forth. "It doesn't have to be like this, Stefan. It doesn't have to be so terrible if you just let go of your fear."

I knew it was going to happen then. He really would have me. A long feast of my blood. A little drink of my soul. Yes, he would have me, and there was nothing I could do to prevent it.

As that unshakable understanding came to me, his embrace

loosened just enough to let me breathe. And as if he'd heard my tortured thought, he said quite reasonably, "Yes, I'll have you, my friend, but if you give in to me without a fight, you'll find my kiss far more pleasure than pain."

Then, with that suggestion murmured against my throat, I felt the rapid sting of his teeth and the blade sharp rush that set my blood flowing. The pain of his bite was acute, that peculiar brand of anguish which raises the hair on the back of the neck and causes the body to go taut, then limp, then taut again, the pain that makes a man surrender instantly in some misguided hope that his surrender might somehow ease the torment or appease the tormentor.

His fierce fangs easily punctured my flesh to bring a stream of warmth pouring down my neck, a torrent quickly diverted by the vampyre's tongue, a crimson well tapped at the source with a ferocity that coaxed a needful moaning from his chest. Separate from myself, yet mercilessly more aware of my body than I had ever been, I became instantly weak as he began drawing hard on the wound, his suckling so intense I could actually feel the blood being pulled through my veins.

I must have tried to cry out, for a rush of wind came from my lungs that carried no other sound. My arms thrashed at the air. My legs were numb, and I would have fallen had he not held me.

It is impossible to say what went through my mind as he took me there in the foyer while Dimitri looked on from candle-carved shadows. Only then did I see the boy, a lanky blond waif leaning against the wall with a jealous grin as his master drank from me in what was, to vampyres, the most intimate of all experiences.

At the time, I would have denied it. I would have said the torment of Miquel's kiss was not something to be described as sensual. I would have tried to convince you that I found no pleasure in the eager suckling which drew the lifeblood out of me while feeding his wicked thirst. I never would have admitted that the sensation of his arms constricting around me as he fed was the most repulsive and yet the most comforting embrace I had ever known.

And never—absolutely *never*—would I have confessed to being overwhelmed with a yearning so excruciating that I fainted in his arms and became a believer in vampyres.

My squandered soul liquefied, flowing out of me in twin rivers: one was red, the other pale.

CHAPTER THREE

"You see, Stefan, the problem is that we've been glorified, vilified and crucified throughout history, yet other than brief glimpses ofhe truth by enlightened individuals, not a single work has ever come close to defining what it means to *be* an immortal."

Those were the words Miquel spoke as I regained consciousness in his bed, though their deeper meaning was lost on me when my eyes snapped open and I began frantically struggling to reassemble the pieces of my shattered world.

Candles burned on the sills of wood-paned windows, curtains thin and iridescent as butterfly wings rising and falling on the cool October wind—surreal and yet oddly nostalgic in a way I couldn't have named.

The room was awash with color, so brilliant and rich as to be disorienting. Walls the shade of storm slate sky filled me with longing for something I'd left behind in a childhood barely remembered—an imagined fairyland where little boys lay on a bed of pure white mushrooms and stared up at the heavens, blinking with wonder at every magical thing. In the four corners of the room, potted trees stretched leaves of ash and elm toward a cathedral ceiling covered with sunset purple clouds, a mural where painted night had already fallen at the peak of the tall roof.

The bed on which I found myself was far larger than any conventional bed. An antique that could have come from some baroque plantation in the south, the headboard was openwork wrought iron, filigreed with individual motifs representing the seasons—spring ivy climbing crumbling columns; flowers bursting in the primary colors of summer; muted autumn leaves falling from a skeletal tree; snowflake lace against obsidian winter night sky.

Like a Technicolor hallucination, two walls were painted with a moon dappled forest that seemed to extend into infinity; and when the wind came stealing through again, I could have sworn I saw the trees sway and bend.

My head swam. My pulse, rapid and shallow from loss of blood, fluttered in my ears.

I looked at the vampyre and wanted to weep—not from fear or anger or any other tangible emotion, but because I was overwhelmed with the notion that my blood now coursed through his veins and we were inexorably linked.

I had fed him from my heart and now that heart belonged to him.

The thought humbled me utterly. And yet, still in a daze, it didn't seem so terrible, this sense of belonging somewhere when I'd belonged nowhere in so long. At first, as I lay there with Miquel on one side of me and Dimitri on the other, all I could do was record the fact that they sat like mirror images of one another. Miquel was propped on his right hand, Dimitri on his left, both looking down at me as if I were expected to understand anything they were saying.

I groaned, my head thrashing, but as awareness returned with a vengeance, I bolted up in the bed and backed away from them until my shoulders were pressed against the cold iron headboard. Looking at them now, I was appalled, and before the rational man inside me had an opportunity to vote, the animal within my skin reacted.

"You son of a bitch!" I snarled at Dimitri, placing the blame squarely on his shoulders for luring me to this place where vampyres were real and blood was sustenance and sanity was a word without meaning. Clenching my fist, I was—

—*six years old when little Jason Haverhill yanked my pants down in front of the whole first grade. Embarrassed, I cried, but that made it worse, especially when Old Lady Marley scolded me to stop being such a baby. (But even she was laughing behind her frilly flowered handkerchief). When my snuffling stopped, I was filled with uncontrollable rage, a fury that could only be quelled as I lashed out at that toe headed, freckle faced Haverhill brat and beat my fists against his ugly mug until his shirt turned red and his bawling wail filled the halls of Patrick Henry Elementary School—*

Now my face burned again, and I would have struck Dimitri had Miquel not grabbed my wrists and wrestled them above my head, pinning me with his unearthly strength.

Dimitri never even flinched, but he did smile a little, and that only enraged me to thrash against Miquel in a battle I had no chance of winning. His hands were steel belts around my wrists, his legs scissoring my ankles, and yet his demeanor was one of complete nonchalance.

"So much bolder you are after your nap," he commented, amused. "But this foolish tussling won't change your fate, nor will striking poor Dimitri right the wrong you feel you've suffered."

I writhed, my body twisting on the bed until the strength left me. Only when it was gone altogether—a casualty of blood loss and vampyre magic—did I finally subside, falling back onto the white satin comforter. My chest heaved with the exertion. My ears roared.

Humiliated by a vulnerability to which I was unaccustomed, my eyes fixed on the ceiling, where a tiny spider was building her web in the corner, oblivious to the grim nature of these creatures with whom she shared the room.

Then, suddenly, I was calm.

"If you're going to kill me, get it over with," I said, the reality of my situation stabilizing around me. It would be all right. If I died then and there, I'd be with Stephanie again, the struggle would be over, and it would be perfectly all right.

Releasing my wrists, Miquel ran his fingers through my hair, an unexpected gesture which had the effect of making me tremble because it was so completely without inhibitions, and because I truly believed I was about to die.

"If I wanted to kill you, I would have drained your life away when I drank from you," he reminded me, though now his tone was unforgivably tender. "No, I haven't brought you here to harm you, Stefan, but to offer you a life that never ends."

I almost laughed at the absurdity of it all. Vampyres! And yet, my gaze remaining fixed on Miquel, my fingers dug into the comforter as I was again bombarded with the raw understanding of what he was.

This man—for he could have passed for a man if one didn't look too closely—*was* a vampyre, a being said to be only myth, yet a myth which sat at my side making a very real indentation in the bed and soothing me with a hand that was undeniably solid and alive, even if cool to the touch.

The word beautiful had been penned just to describe him, yet it was a word incapable of capturing the antiquity of him and the totality that exceeded the sum of the individual parts. He was *more* than this man, more even than the refulgent reflection I'd seen in his shiny mirror. He was an immortal with power over life and death, a vampyre with my blood still warm in his belly, a creature who could as easily destroy me as not.

He was *real* magic, and *that* meant the end of the world as I'd always known it.

When I groaned in acknowledgement of that awful truth, he attempted to placate me with a smile that was anything but reassuring when I saw his teeth. My neck hurt where those fangs had stung me and, stupefied, I raised a hand to the injury still moist from his lips.

"You—you bit me!" I blurted out, an ineloquent accusation.

Miquel's smile deepened and, running his fingers down my cheek, he said matter-of-factly, "Bite is such an ugly word, Stefan. I prefer to call it a kiss, and it seemed best to prove my authenticity with such a gesture rather than waste time attempting to explain with a thousand words what a single action could accomplish just as well." His eyes glistened as he leaned closer and lowered his voice to a whisper. "I meant you to find it enjoyable, you realize, though I'll understand completely if you prefer to pretend it wasn't."

At this, Dimitri gave a hearty laugh, then got up and moved to the window, where he stood with his back to us. Candles on the sill silhouetted him against the night, painting a halo of smoky gold above his head.

But he was no angel.

He'd approached me under the guise of a human boy in a vampyre suit at a gathering where identities were put on with a stroke of eyeliner or the donning of a Calvin Klein tux. I'd no more expected him to *be* a vampyre than I'd expected Superman to fly or Captain Kirk to whip out a communicator and beam up to the *Enterprise*.

Miquel sighed dramatically and gave me a probing look that sent flocks of demons skittering through my soul when I realized he really was reading my mind, when I understood he really *could*.

"Ah, poor Stefan, you need someone to *blame*," he surmised, psychically drinking in my chaos. Then, altogether congenial, he added, "I suppose you could blame *me*, though you realize I can't force you to do anything you don't want to do. I can make suggestions in your mind and soften your fears with my trance, but any decisions you make are ultimately your own. The only salvation which exists is within *you*, my friend." His voice trailed off, his smile turning suggestive as he spelled out a blasphemous truth. "Ah, but the only way *out* of your life that isn't a dead-end is through *me*."

Saying this, he once again soothed my brow, undoubtedly to soften the frightening implications of his words. And though I struggled to push his hand away, he slipped one arm behind my head and gathered me to his chest, where, like an infant, I was cradled. I tensed, distraught by his physical closeness, but he put one long finger over my mouth to silence me.

"Hush now, Stefan. Look at what I'm going to show you and try not to put up such a fuss," he said sternly, rocking me as a father might rock a child and lulling me into some altered state with the deep and metered cadence of his voice alone. "Just be still and let me tell you a story that has no words and no end, yet a story that begs to be told."

His body was warm now, heated by *my* blood. Stretching out next to me, he pulled my head down on his shoulder, and though I longed desperately to be free, there is no defense against vampyre magic, no hiding from the trance. His white cotton shirt pressed my cheek, bearing the scent of him that was muted cologne and wildfire out of control, anesthesia and aphrodisiac all at once.

Terrified that he would kill me, perhaps even more afraid that he wouldn't, I began to pray—for strength and detachment as he ran his hands over my back to calm me; for some glimmer of hope when there was no hope left; for salvation from knowing I was falling under his spell because I *did* find him altogether alluring. It was what he wanted, of course, the way I *had* to feel because it was his will.

But as an inexplicable telepathic union opened between us and he whispered against my ear, "Ssshh," I suddenly knew no one was listening to my prayers except the very devil in whose arms I was held.

"Hush now," he said again, seductive and terribly calm. "Just close your eyes, Stefan, so you may finally begin to see."

And my eyes closed as if I'd been drugged.

Perhaps Miquel's most terrible power was that of Truth—the ability to strip away the lies humans tell themselves and force them to look at reality for what it is. This seeing came as a tickle of thought, a trickle of an idea, a drop of awareness that quickly swelled to a rushing river. It came when he opened his immortal mind to me, pulling me inside that somber sanctuary which was both Tartarus and Elysium.

And though I struggled fiercely not to look, I beheld in his thoughts those higher truths humans could only imagine: the dreadful condition of mortal man, the futility of old age, the emptiness of an afterlife consisting only of casket satin and bone dust. I heard the wail of the void as the prayers of lost angels and fallen souls were screamed out into the night, unheard and unanswered, and I tasted the emptiness between galaxies which no words could ever describe.

It is one thing to acknowledge intellectually that Man is alone in the universe. It is another matter altogether to stand in the middle of that wilderness and *see* it for the wasteland it is. It encompasses no color, no sound. It permeates everything, yet cannot be touched.

It is a meaningless abyss in the center of the chest where human awareness got caught in a permanent spin and drain cycle. All of us have touched it at one time or another, yet for the first time I *knew* what it was.

That black hole at the heart of human consciousness was the blind eye of our manmade God.

Assaulted with the sensation of knowing rather than merely believing, I still *believed* life had meaning. Yet I *knew* it had none. Man had created God to create Man, and now the entire lot of them were stuck in an endless loop.

It was so simple it was blinding. This brief life was all there was and it was a life that always came to the same fatal end. The flaw in the program was that the program was irrevocably flawed, contaminated with a self-destruct virus that was intrinsic to the program itself. Death was death, certain and final, for although I had a human soul, there was nowhere for it to go except back to the oblivion that spawned it.

God wasn't sitting behind the grave with a catcher's mitt.

Oh, we were immortal, yet it was an immortality existing on a cellular level alone, the recycling of our atoms across a universe so vast it was inconceivable that two molecules from the same human body would ever find one another again. If we lived after death, it was as fertilizer for the flowers on our grave or dinner for the worms.

Valhalla was a fallacy, reincarnation a lie.

When I looked up into Miquel's eyes and saw my reflection captured there, I understood these things with a terrible and dark sobriety. Heaven and hell were only ghost towns with crumbling altars and unpaved streets. God and the devil were off playing cards for quarters and could no longer be bothered with the snivellings of Man.

Worse than merely lost, we were a lost cause, blasé.

A cry of despair tore from my throat, for though I had never been particularly religious, I had cultivated a firm belief in God. I *needed* my God, as most men did: someone to cry to with my suffering, some fanciful benefactor to pray to for things I neither needed nor wanted. But most of all, as Miquel had already noted, I needed someone to blame for the state of our wretched world and the death of my beautiful daughter.

But there was nothing out there—at least that is how Miquel perceived it—and the reality of that profound abyss devastated me utterly and sent me whiplashing back into my own body. I began to shake uncontrollably, convulsing.

"I'm sorry," the vampyre whispered against my ear, rocking me until my body stopped its shuddering. "I *am* sorry to end your world so abruptly, but isn't that how worlds always end, Stefan?"

What surprised me was his genuine sorrow, for I knew then that he was as alone in the universe as I was myself. His eyes were wet—wet with red tears that left a trail on his unshaven cheek, tears he cried for me because I was too afraid and too proud to weep for myself.

"Sometimes, knowing you *are* alone is worse than *being* alone," he barely whispered.

"Then why did you show me?" I demanded, my heart an unlivable desert, broken in two by the things I'd seen. "Why did you want me to know?"

He bent over me, and for a moment I thought his fangs would deliver me into death, but instead he placed his mouth close to my ear and spoke so softly I barely heard him. "Because truth is all we have, dearest Stefan, and the greatest truth of all is that I *could* be wrong, though I've no reason to think so." He paused, then added with a certainty that told me he'd already made up his mind: "I will show *you* some of these truths, and *you* will show them to the world."

When I stiffened, afraid of what he was asking me, his hand tightened on my shoulder. He tilted his head, the masculine stubble of his chin a shocking contrast to the softness of his lips moving over my neck as he spoke. "Humanity has lived in spiritual darkness and religious fear too long. It's time their eyes were opened, and who better to do it than you and I? My knowledge, your words, yes?"

He was seducing me with an opportunity to say something which had perhaps never been said before, and surely he knew it was a lure no writer could have refused. The ramifications caused me to bolt up off the bed, for while I was adamantly telling myself I couldn't be enticed into such a Machiavellian task, I had already begun falling into the mire of that dark seduction.

For that I hated him.

In a single evening, he'd torn down the walls I'd spent a lifetime building, making me see what I didn't want to know, and now there could be no going back to the sanctuary of writing children's books and drinking cappuccino with Charlie and driving off to church on Sunday to look for promises of salvation that were as hollow as my own heart.

'The only salvation which exists is within you...'

Crying out as I tore away from him, I staggered to the middle of the floor, disoriented and physically ill. What little blood remained within me drained to my feet and dragged me to my knees, and suddenly I was holding my entire life in my hands, looking at it for the tiny microcosm it was.

It was finite. It *would* end.

All I had held sacred was lost, reduced to ash as I stood apart and watched, yet Dimitri turned from his station at the window to regard me with a look which told me I was behaving inappropriately. With long, delicate arms crossed over his boyish chest, he sighed heavily.

"Really, Stefan," he chastised, his songbird voice a desolate melody to my ears now. "Nothing has changed except your perceptions. Life and death go on, but don't you think it best to finally *tell* these secrets so that men and women may live their lives honestly rather than on their knees? For after all, do you really believe nuns would marry ghosts or priests wed the solitude of their own sinful hand if they knew this book they've held sacred is only a myth written by ancient politicians to control an unruly population? Indeed, if people knew the truth about life and death, you'd see them finally come alive!

"It's time for Man to take responsibility for his own immortality, Stefan! It's time he starts to use that dormant portion of his brain to create his own heaven and destroy his cumulative hells so that—*perhaps*—he might find a way to transcend death on his own. As it stands, Man goes through his life thinking he'll live *again*, so he consoles himself with believing death is only a transition when, in reality, it is the end of his entire world."

How does one answer that? I couldn't.

And the world spun out of focus all over again, though for reasons altogether unclear to me at the time.

Miquel shot a disapproving glance which Dimitri met with a sultry stare and a subtle curling of his lip. Disapproval and disagreement synapsed between them, as if the kid had said too much too soon. Never speaking out loud, they argued, quarreled, tension crackling between them like a violent storm.

Something in their wordless exchange contained more history than in all the world's encyclopedias, yet attempting to translate it to language would be no easy task. It was, quite simply, an exchange of passions dating back centuries—an exchange that caught me in the crossfire, where the tempest in Dimitri's eyes revealed—

—a young boy alone on an foggy night shore, shrouded in heartfelt silence and sick with the disease of unrequited love. Greece, when tattered sailing vessels brought visitors from faraway lands and the music of shepherds' flutes carried down from rugged hills.

The boy wept into the ocean's basin, depending on it to carry his tears away in secret just as it had carried his love away to Italy. He never saw the shadows unfold nor felt the unnatural wind against his neck until it was too late. And he certainly never understood that it was his own melancholy which beckoned the vampyre from the belly of some dismal ship where he had hidden seeking passage out of the country.

When unrelenting arms closed around him and the cruel fangs found his throat, all Dimitri felt was the puncture wound through which his soul was greedily drained. As he lay dying, he thought of love and was glad to be released from it. And as he drew his fatal breath while cradled in the vampyre's possessive embrace, he smiled up into those rueful eyes and said in a diamond clear voice, "Thank you, sir, for taking my life so gently."

And then the boy was dead.

My head pounded as I was inundated with telepathic images so vivid it was as if I had *become* Dimitri, looking at the past through his perceptions just as I'd looked at myself through his eyes earlier that evening at the convention. I felt for him. I felt *with* him. I died with him in Miquel's arms there on the warm, soft shores of Piraeus.

But as I stared into Miquel's quicksilver eyes, he just sat there on his bed with his lips drawn back to a vicious snarl and shot me a look which catapulted me back through time itself, a vehement thought that proclaimed:

The boy mustn't die!

The blood singing through Miquel's veins fed more than his thirst and the outpouring of gratitude he felt while expecting the hatred reserved for one's executioner was so acute he wept. 'Thank you, sir, for taking my life so gently'.

What manner of creature was this?

He gazed at the ragamuffin in his arms and longed to join him in death, yet that was a voyage reserved for humans alone. Miquel could no longer remember when he had been mortal. He could no longer recall when he'd walked in sunlight or taken a lover to his bed.

He could no longer remember when he had felt love, and though the One who Created him had said he would never feel it again, he experienced that old stirring return with a vengeance now. Love, he thought. And the word became an obsession wearing Dimitri's face.

But it was too late, that unique force of life gone from the universe when the boy's mismatched eyes closed in death.

The unfairness of it overwhelmed Miquel, the very existence of death incensing him to the point of outrage, and it was that divine injustice which caused him to tilt his head back and wail a wordless cry of bone-splitting despair into the night. A keening shriek. A soul deep weeping to rival an angry siren's screech or a banshee's scream.

And then, looking down into the face of this mortal angel, he fell calm and coldly determined as a sensation such as he'd never known gripped him, shaking his very soul inside his body.

Though he had no real idea of what he intended to do, he tore away his shirt, and with a broken shell found in the sand, drew a wet line across his nipple until a trickle of red bled from him. His body shuddered against the pain and rapture of such a deep cut, and moving solely on instinct, he cupped the pale head and lifted the still warm lips to the wound.

Intuitively cradling child to breast, he watched those lips turn dark with his blood as the river flowed into the dead boy's open mouth. Frantically, desperately, he rocked the limp body in his arms, his only solace a far removed memory which told him he had once been suckled at his Creator's breast in similar fashion.

"Live again and live forever," he whispered, exerting the sheer force of his vampyre will to create the reality. A litany now, over and over: "Breathe because I bleed for you! Breathe because I need for you! Breathe because I am the only god I know and because I call on this immortal blood to make it so!"

Though he'd never spoken such words before, they fell naturally from him now. The blasphemy tasted sweet on his lips, an honest hatred for death, for the pious lies of a God who'd long ago forsaken him.

"Breathe... live... breathe..."

And because the blood was part of him, alive and vital as the paradox of those very words, Miquel accompanied it on its magical voyage. No longer a single entity, he was elaborately woven through the boy's empty veins. A caress of human heart, unbeating but still warm. A burn of needful lips now beginning to suckle on their own.

Though he had never experienced this holy thing before, the instinct to create another like himself was suddenly there as if it had been waiting for the sound of Dimitri's voice to awaken it. And for the first time, he knew he was more than just a vampyre. He was a Creator—one who could give life as well as take it. Of all the preternatural powers, this was the most sacred. Maybe one vampyre in a thousand possessed the gift of Creation. Maybe only one in a million.

The implications flooded him, spilling from him in a cry of sheer wonder. He was a Creator!

Waves broke hard against the shore as dawn slaughtered another night. The first sliver of silver tore the horizon at the same instant the boy's chest heaved with an unearthly cry. Like a newborn babe—and that he was—the child knew only its pain and its insatiable need. So with little regard for its father/mother/sibling/progenitor, it attached its newly formed fangs to the nurturing laceration and made known its demand for Life.

For years to come, all Miquel would remember was scooping the little progeny beneath his cloak as dawn came looking for them with accusation burning in her fiery eye. Running at full force, in awe of this fragile son of his blood, he barely made it to the darkness of the old ship,

42

and even then Helios singed the ragged edges of his vampyre soul—.

"Enough!" Miquel decided roughly, breaking eye contact and shattering the spell. "*Enough!*"

I must have cried out when I fell back to Earth, back into my body, on my knees in the middle of the floor.

Had I seen the visions only in Miquel's eyes? Had I tasted a vampyre's hatred of death only on his tongue? The stench of dead fish cloistered in my nostrils from a sailing vessel that hadn't existed in hundreds of years said otherwise. The pale white sand dusting my hands confirmed it.

Suddenly, it no longer seemed important that Miquel and Dimitri were vampyres. All that mattered was this transcendental experience which defied explanation and would have shaken mere science to its foundations. I had been there—on the shores of Greece in what I roughly imagined to be the 17th century.

Suddenly, I wanted to crawl to Miquel—for I was unable to walk—and beg him to show me more. How I craved this knowledge, this feeling of wonder that had been dead and buried since Stephanie left me. For the first time since I delivered her body and my soul to the care of worms, I was alive again—ironic, considering that it was vampyres who brought me back from the dead.

"Please!" I said to Miquel, feeling as a junkie must feel surrounded by an ocean of morphine just out of reach. I looked back and forth between the two of them, realizing I'd been trapped in their private mental war. A taste of vampyre magic. Bait I couldn't ignore. "*Please!*"

Whatever became of *me* was irrelevant. For the first time, I truly *knew* there was a reality beyond the five senses, and for an opportunity to photograph it with my words, I would do anything in all the worlds.

Miquel looked at me as if coming to some private decision, then turned his eyes on Dimitri and quirked a smile beset with those menacing teeth which now struck me as oddly attractive. An unspoken communication passed between them, then Dimitri shrugged with seeming indifference.

"If he plays with his food the way he plays with his words, he might prove an interesting distraction for a century or two," the boy said to his Creator, substantiating my suspicion that they'd been reading my thoughts all evening. He turned his head to study me with a fair amount of disdain, a twinge of jealousy. "But there are thousands of scribes in the world, Miquel, and while this one is somewhat intriguing, is he really worthy of the dark evolution? Is he worthy of being an immortal?"

What surprised me was my immediate and profoundly emotional outburst. "I'm worthy, goddamn you!"

But I had to ask: worthy of what? Of being a monster? A thief of human blood? But as I looked at Miquel now and recalled his vulnerability when he'd shown me how alone each of us is in the world, I could not attach the label 'monster' to him whatsoever.

He was, quite simply, another species. Not human. Not at all a "vampire" as mythology paints them. He was something else entirely, and he had shown me more about myself in a single evening than I'd learned in a lifetime.

More than any monk or priest or doctor or wizard, this creature despised death and had gone to war against it.

Now he was offering me a chance to live forever, yet I couldn't help feeling a bit like Adam pondering the outstretched apple. He wanted my words, which meant he was asking for all I had. He wanted me to tell the world vampyres were alive and God was dead, and it was a job I didn't want in the least.

And yet, it was a job I had to take because I needed—so desperately—to prove him wrong, and the only way I could do it was to live long enough to make a thorough search of all the nooks and crannies of the universe where the Almighty might have gone to hide.

Maybe that's why Miquel wanted me. He needed a fool who could argue both sides of any coin with equal conviction, a bumbling pilgrim obsessed as much with the journey as with the destination.

Oh, I wanted to find God, all right—but for all the wrong reasons. I didn't want to worship the son of a bitch. I wanted to slaughter Him for destroying my faith in Him.

In answer to that thought, Miquel gave a melancholy smile. "Mortals feed themselves on faith because they have little else to sustain them, Stefan," he said as if he really did feel sorry for them. "Indeed, when I was still a man, it was easier to believe in forbidden apples and a serpent in the garden as a means to explain Man's mortality than to believe our entire existence was random chance. It was even easier to believe the soul might exist forever in Hell's torment than to think it would not exist in any capacity whatsoever."

Truth again. That's how he gave it to me—in little doses of irony and pain.

Immortality, then, existed not in resurrection nor belief in any deity, but only in the tender mercy of a vampyre's kiss—the kiss of the Creator, the kiss of the black angel. Eternal life was to be found only in eternal death.

"You begin to understand, Stefan," Miquel told me as he got up off his bed and walked to where I still knelt. "But is it a life you would want? Most men would prefer to die simply because it's far, far easier than living forever, and this is not a choice to be made lightly." He placed a hand on top of my head and looked at me with an expression reminiscent of angels gazing on their mortal charges.

I knew then what the statue in the courtyard symbolized, and why it watched over all the stone ghosts in a moonlit garden. They were Miquel's human lovers, dead and buried and destined to be mourned forever by their immortal beloved who had gone on without them. I envied them such devotion. But I also envied him the eternity stretched out in front of him, his patient mistress.

"I don't want to die," I told him, realizing for the first time the truth behind those words. "I *don't* want to die!"

I wanted to weep for all the souls already lost throughout the scope of time, my Stephanie most of all. We were throwaways: replaceable, recyclable. And I suddenly despised Nature for making us in such a shoddy fashion. Perhaps, I thought deliriously, vampyres were more thorough than God—better creators than the Creator. They made their children to last, at least.

And so, in that moment of tumultuous revelations, I added blasphemy to my list of unpardonable sins, though it never occurred to me that such a sin or such a pardon would have required the cooperative agreement of something which did not exist. How much we depended on God. How much we depended on *nothing*.

I trembled, in awe of this knowledge and yet filled with dread at the thought of my *own* death. Even Dimitri had died. Surely Miquel had, too. But why must it happen to *me*?

My ethereal ponderings stopped cold, my knees aching from kneeling so long on the floor. Outside, even the frogs had given up their singing, and in his motionless silence, Dimitri had become a still life portrait framed by the open window.

I blanched, holding my breath. And I lifted my head to look the creature squarely in the eye, mentally asking the question I didn't have the nerve to ask out loud. *Are you going to kill me?*

"No one gets out alive, Stefan, not even us," Miquel warned aloud, oddly compassionate despite his threat. "If you choose to live forever, it is true you must first die in my arms."

I stiffened with anxiety, but he soothed me by tangling his fingers in my hair and slipping a thought inside me that transformed my worry to molten slag.

"It's just a small part of the price," he said softly. "And look at it this way, my friend. You will go to your death with *knowledge* of it! You will die with the certainty that you will live again—a certainty not dependent on hollow hope or fragile faith." He paused for a moment, offering a wistful smile. "I cannot promise you heaven, Stefan, but I *can* give you eternity if you're willing to accept it."

The cadence of his words was so hypnotic I wanted to be lulled into that new life by the sound of his voice alone, and it is my belief that had he simply told me to die I would have done it then and there.

"But—*why*?" I heard myself ask in a strangled, desperate whisper. "Why would you offer this to me?"

Miquel only looked at me, his unexpected empathy a tangible presence in the room. "I offer it to you, my grieving friend, because you burn with a thirst for life that will be reborn in your vampyre skin, surviving even the barrier of death. The pain within you can make the nature of life and death ugly enough and beautiful enough to peek through the words you'll write. People will come to you—frightened and impassioned and looking for answers—and *you* will bring them to *me*."

I started to protest, but he shushed me to silence. His voice softened to an awestruck whisper, and once again he caressed my face to mute the blow of what he was telling me.

"Together, Stefan, we will build a new garden with mortals who'll live forever because that's the way nature intended it before

Man lost his way and became a plaything of Death."

Now Dimitri turned from the window, locking his gaze on his master. "But is he *worthy*?" the boy repeated, sultry.

Miquel's wicked smile was his only answer as he knelt at my side and gathered me against his chest, an embrace so intimate I could have refused him nothing. Had he asked for my life, I would have given it. Had he taken it, I would not have resisted.

But he merely held me in those illusory black wings and rocked me back and forth as we knelt there in the center of his deep green world. It was another reality—a place where trees grew out of the floor and time was a forest painted on the walls and the sun was always setting on the ceiling. *Forever sunset*, my mind whispered, delirious. *Forever dusk and dawn's a million years away.*

Then, as if it really were a kiss, Miquel bent his mouth to my throat and sank the sharp points of his teeth into the wounds he'd left me with before. It hurt brilliantly, though I made no attempt to pull away from the euphoria that instantly overcame me. This time, I did not lose consciousness, and I can only describe the soft red suckling as a libertine union of pain and pleasure.

It lasted only a few seconds before Miquel drew back, and the additional loss of blood drained my strength entirely. My head collapsed on his shoulder as the breath flew out of me, and then the black angel brought his moist crimson lips to my pale dry ones and left a kiss on my mouth that tasted of my own blood.

It was a flavor both erotic and sweet, a taste of copper pennies and a little boy whose face I'd once worn running by the railroad tracks with autumn leaves and magic spells crumbled in his pockets. It was a brief taste of knowing my life *could* go on forever, and a deeper drink of the realization that I had a right to eternity. The dark evolution, Dimitri called it. Perhaps that's what it really was, a willful parthenogenesis whereby a man passed through death in order to evolve forever beyond its reach.

My head swimming as Miquel's mouth brushed over mine and lingered there, I wondered if this were the forbidden kiss that would forever transform me.

"Just a taste to whet your thirst," he whispered in response to my thought, and I felt him nurture my disappointment like preparing a complex cocktail. He was a vampyre all right, whether he drank blood or sorrow, laughter or tears. "Tomorrow is soon enough for eternity. For now, you must return to the dayshine world and make your peace with your mirror."

His proclamation stunned me utterly.

I tried to protest, to tell him my peace was made on my daughter's grave, yet he hushed me with a finger laid across my lips.

"It isn't only a matter of manners that I send you away to contemplate this grave choice," he said, so close I could count the fires dancing in his eyes from the candles' myriad reflections, "but this is how it is done, you see. You must offer me your life and your death willingly and of sound mind, and this you cannot do while weak from loss of blood and still half fainting from my spell."

I was afraid of thinking about it at all, afraid I *would* change my mind or come to my senses or simply give in to other responsibilities as I'd always done before.

The thought caused him to smile—compassion and darkness all rolled into a single paradoxical expression that embodied the sheer essence of him.

"If you survive the transformation," he told me in a tone which said these were the most important words I would ever hear, "you will learn a secret which will give you the strength to live ten thousand years and beyond. But I am constrained to warn you, the price each of us pays for immortality is high and filled with irony. You would be wise to turn me down right now."

I'd already paid the highest price of all. My daughter was dead. Eternity would never be long enough to mourn her. "I won't change my mind," I insisted, and a terrible resolve caused me to add coarsely, "just do it!"

But he shook his head and fastened those preternatural eyes on my soul. "You know I cannot, Stefan, for all of this is nothing more than a dream within a dream."

And with a hypnotic gesture of one bejeweled hand, he made it so.

CHAPTER FOUR

I came to in my hotel room, my cheek resting on the cold white tile of the bathroom floor. The water in the shower was still running, steam so thick the wallpaper had peeled away at its seams and started to curl.

My head ached horribly, and at first I recalled nothing of Miquel. Groaning as I struggled to consciousness, the only thing I remembered was Dimitri—the crazy kid from the dealer's room who'd gotten under my skin.

Clearly, I'd been masturbating and struck my head on the sink when my climax dragged me to my knees with images of the vampyre boy sneaking through my sick mind.

I did not recall turning off the shower nor crawling to bed, where I fell into a fitful sleep.

Dreams of red fruit and painful kisses haunted my dreams.

*

It wasn't until I went down to the dealer's room that the memories of the night before caught up to me. I was taking the covering off the display when a fat guy with a green dragon perched on one shoulder ogled me with a knowing grin.

"Looks like I'm not the only one who scored last night," he said, though he obviously hadn't scored his entire life. I recognized him as the vendor from the stall next to mine. The eyes of the latex dragon blinked, tiny red LEDs that gave me a start for the irretrievable image they stirred – a different kind of dragon and dappled ivy and images I both feared and longed for simultaneously.

Strangely light-headed, I gaped at him.

He just shrugged and pointed at my throat. "Looke like your girlfriend took a nice bite out of you." Snickering, he elbowed his partner. "Hey, Carl, get a load of this guy's hickey!"

Another hollow-eyed ignoramus with a Big Mac in his hand and a _Jurassic Park_ t-shirt stretched too tight over his belly stared at me and started to chuckle. Hercules and Indiana Jones sidled up next to them, gawking now, too. The tarot reader with the silver hair stood on her tiptoes and whispered in my ear, "Don't think of the man in your dreams as the King of Swords but call him the Magician. The path of least resistance always leads to the grave, so take the higher road if you dare."

Under normal circumstances, with reasonably normal human beings, I wouldn't have scrambled away so abruptly; but it was at that moment the memories came flooding back as if injected deep inside my brain with a dull needle and a hard, fast push.

In a flash, all of the night before was there—the limousine, the dragon hedge with its red eyes, Miquel and Dimitri and the things they'd done—laid out before me like a feast of rich desserts that left me nauseous until I fled the crowded room and burst through the emergency exit onto the loading dock with a breathless gasp. It stank there—rotting garbage and diesel and rat piss—but at least there was no hint of Eternity when I sucked in the foul air in an effort to clear my head.

I had to be alone and I had to be in the real world, in a place where daylight had chased away the shadows, where traffic and airplanes and sirens created a comforting uproar of human existence. And yet, the thing that had happened the night before caused me to suddenly wonder just how real any of it really was.

So is your entire reality only an illusion held together by the glue of society's consensual thoughts?

Strange ponderings again, uninvited cousins from another universe.

As I looked at the 'real world' now, it seemed an illusion, a thin shade pulled down to conceal an inconceivable reality beneath, a transparent overlay of stages and actors in one of Mr. Shakespeare's plays.

And though I'd never noticed it before, the edges of the set were a bit rickety, the colors faded and dull; and when a security guard walked by without asking what I was doing there, I realized some of the extras had forgotten their lines. Indeed, it was as if I started to see the world for the thing it was—a two-dimensional backdrop, a cheap painting on black velvet hiding a masterpiece beneath, a Hollywood set that could fold in on itself at any moment like—

"—a carnival!" Stephanie exclaimed, her nose pressed to the window as we sped down the freeway late at night. "Can't we stop, Daddy? Oh, please—just for a little while?"

At the edge of Del Mar's fluorescent sea, a double ferris wheel plummeted end-over-end through whirligig darkness. A tumbledown roller coaster labored up unseen tracks to plunge over the nothing into nothing more. The Tilt-a-Whirl spun, a magically illumined eggbeater stirring up a potion in the night.

"Maybe tomorrow, honey," I told my little girl, exhausted from the long convention weekend. Laurie would be waiting up at home, probably drinking again, and perpetually annoyed because we were late.

Stephanie just kept looking out the window, her head turning to stay with the lights as we left the carnival behind. "It won't be there tomorrow," she said with ethereal certainty. "It's only there for now because we see it, because we're creating it. As soon as we look away, it'll be gone forever."

She'd either be a quantum physicist or a writer. "We'll go tomorrow, punkin. I promise."

But as I looked in the rearview mirror, the carnival had already gone dark. When we returned the next night, there was nothing to indicate it had ever been there—not a drink cup blowing along the shore, not a half eaten corn dog crawling with ants, not even a faded funhouse ticket torn in half.

It was a thing of the night and to the night it had returned. That's what Stephanie said. I believed her just enough to begin fitfully scrawling notes for my fourth book, Tilt-A-Whirl Worlds—the diary of a mental patient who believed the key to other dimensions was a wobbly thrill ride at a phantom carnival...

Now I wondered what Stephanie had seen that I never could.

I would have given anything for one chance to do it over again, but there was no going back, and now I'd never know if those distant lights had been real or just a special effect, courtesy of Industrial Light & Magic. I sat down on the hotel's loading dock with my legs dangling over the edge, staring at the metropolis which had sprung up out of the earth just as that carnival had sprung up out of the ether.

Was L.A. any more real, or if I turned my back would it disappear, too?

Engrossed in my troubling reverie, I barely noticed the vagrant passing through the alley until his scuffling footsteps caused me to look up. Wrinkled green army fatigues folded in on his frail body as he caught my eye and shot me a mock salute accompanied by a toothless grin.

"You'll drive yerself crazy tryin' to figger it out," he slurred in my direction, clutching a paper sack with the neck of a whiskey bottle peeking out. He took a swig of amber amnesia and wiped at his scroungy beard with a dirty hand, tottering from side to side as he stood there in a stupor and began urinating in his pants.

The wind stopped whipping the dandelions that had fought their way up through a crack in the asphalt. The world went still. And though it had once been my nature to look the other way in circumstances such as these, I stared into the derelict's jaundiced eyes as if they held all the secrets of the universe.

And because I was already crazy, I said to this vagabond who could as easily have been a wizard, "Was the carnival ever there that night?"

He looked at me and chuckled. "The carnival's always there—'cept when it ain't."

His words sent an icy rush shooting through my veins, for I knew then he was as real as I was myself—not just some organic prop going through the motions of a random life. But he was already staggering away, as if he, too, had entire worlds to build before the sun went down.

"Wait!" I called after him, jumping to my feet. I hurried down the loading ramp, but a gust of wind burst around the corner and tossed a handful of grit in my eyes. Above the rushing howl, I could have sworn I heard the giggling of mischievous munchkins and the cackling of the wicked witch.

By the time my vision cleared, the dust devil had swept the stage bare and the drunk was nowhere in sight.

Trembling, lost, I clutched my arms to my chest, leaning heavily against the dirty block wall for a long time. *'For now, you must return to the dayshine world and make your peace with your mirror'.*

Miquel's warning came back to me, though I knew now he hadn't been referring to the looking glass above the sink. The world was my mirror, reflecting back at me whatever I put into it, whether carnivals from the phantasm or a hobo who was only a visiting zephyr.

The people and the dogs and the props *looked* real enough, but I was starting to suspect they weren't as solid as I'd once believed, and, indeed, they were probably hustled off at dusk to an abandoned factory where they slept a dreamless sleep until some other isolated traveler thought them back into existence. For when darkness came calling again, this whole vast stage would fold in on itself to be reborn as a carnival that existed only at night, complete with its own sun in the form of neon lights and kaleidoscope vampyre eyes.

During the course of that day, I convinced myself that the entire affair was nothing more than an hallucination brought on by bad hotel food, or some bizarre experiment with virtual reality for which I'd been the unwitting guinea pig. But in the end, when I felt that cold wall at my back and saw the sun crawling toward its ocean bed, a strangely euphoric calm came over me.

The understanding came easily when I stopped chasing after it—the realization that humans have little purpose on the Earth other than learning, and what greater thing was there to learn than the way out?

Like all men, I was afraid of death and I was most certainly afraid of change, so it stood to reason I was terrified of this thing Miquel had offered me, for it meant I would no longer have the luxury of looking at the world the same way. It meant acknowledging a fourth dimension of sorts, an underworld where vampyres walked the night and death was the blink of an eye instead of an endless black sleep.

It meant turning my back on everything I'd ever known, and *that* meant dancing a dangerous tango with a designer label known as insanity. Still, I couldn't help thinking that madness, like death, was a threat thrown in by the scriptwriter to keep the stakes elevated.

If we stripped away the social taboos and could ever confess what we truly believe, I doubt there would be more than a handful of souls who really believe in heaven, and those would be captured within the pale green walls of asylums or cloistered inside dank monasteries.

We all *pretended* to believe in some nebulous afterlife, but no one really did.

We hired gurus to search for our truths and doctors to find cures for our ailments instead of eradicating the source of the ailments themselves: the belief that we *would* die. We trusted priests to show us the way to eternal life because we were far too busy creating corporations and slinging hamburgers and raising our families to look for ourselves.

Death, therefore, had become an institution, nursed at the breasts of undertakers and all complacent fools. But faith could no more save my life than wine and wafers could raise me from the dead. There was no miraculous snake oil on the 6 o'clock news which would cure me of my mortality. There was no proof of reincarnation, no hint that even Harry Houdini had survived that final disappearing trick.

There was only Miquel and his red kiss. Take it or leave it. Live or die. Now or never.

Eat my body, drink my blood and you will never die.

A chill passed through my heart and caused my eyes to water. It was a sensation I'd known only rarely in the past, some eerie confirmation of a deeply hidden truth clawing its way to the surface. A niggling at first, an phantom itch, nagging.

When the epiphany did come, it snowballed into an assault, each realization more dangerous and soul shattering than the last.

"Oh, God," I whispered, and slid down the wall until I was sitting on the ground hugging my knees to my chest. "Oh, God!"

Eat my body, drink my blood and you will never die.

Had similar words once been intended literally but became warped over the centuries into mere symbolic ritual that had lost its meaning? Was this man Christ crucified in the noonday sun not because of his claims of godliness, but for deeds that could only be explained as witchcraft or vampyre magic? Was the wine really wine that night or were the disciples already Princes of the Blood— emissaries of eternal life set loose on the world to do battle with the brute with the scythe?

Had Jesus *really* been the submissive child come to do his Father's will, or was he the rebel son in disguise, determined to steal the secret of immortality from Daddy's blood and give that secret back to Man?

Eat my body, drink my blood and you will never die...

Was our entire Western society based on vampirism?

Jesus Christ! my mind protested, appalled and imploding as it tore loose the bonds of decent moral restraint. *Jesus Holy Vampyre Christ!*

Clever boy.

54

A voice in my head screamed *Blasphemer!* to scare my thoughts into obedient silence, but when I closed my eyes and took a peek beyond the veil, the only thing shouting in my ear was me. That was the truth which came to me while workers unloaded shredded lettuce as if it really mattered and two kids from the kitchen stood smoking a joint as if knowing none of it mattered

But I had to ask myself, *Is it worth it, Stefan? Is it worth giving up your humanity to defeat death?*

We're expected to keep a stiff upper and pray for an afterlife for some part of us that scientists can't find and mystics can't define and surgeons can't transplant into a corpse to give it life again. The ironic thing was this: the only way I could avoid dying was to die trying and trust the bloodthirsty devil to raise me up from the dead.

Faith.

There was that word again, that monosyllabic abstraction which stated that humans were in control of nothing, including our fate or even our faith.

But at least Miquel had held me in his arms and offered me immortality in a body I already knew and a location right here on Earth. God and his unmapped heaven had some catching up to do.

The city shimmered in the distance, a mirage in the corner of my mirror.

If this isn't your will, strike me dead now, God, I prayed in earnest, not because I expected an answer, but because I desperately needed one.

But the lightning didn't come. The building didn't fall on me. No embolism ruptured to stop my lungs.

I was almost disappointed.

Blasphemer! the little voice cried again, louder and more shrill as it took up the chant of well-worn clichés. *You'll burn in hell! All things die! God moves in mysterious ways! Blasphemer! Blasphemer! Blasphemer!*

"Shut up."

Imbued with total calm, I returned to the dealer's room, packed up my dead daughter's belongings and left them in a box for the cleaning crew to find. Inside the lid, I scrawled a note for Charlie, asking her to take care of my cat and telling her I wouldn't be coming home again.

Then, not really sure where I was going, I ambled into the

lobby where the convention's din was at its loudest and the bustle of chaos swam around me. It was there I saw Dimitri coming through the revolving door just as the last dim watercolor bled from the sky. His coat fluttered in brisk wind. His hair shone, a halo of pure light. He had come for me.

It was night and would be forevermore.

CHAPTER FIVE

"Stefan? Have you reached a decision in this matter, Stefan?" Dimitri repeated, tapping a fingernail on the wine goblet from which he never drank in an effort to regain my attention.

I snapped back to reality and tried to think of at least one reason why I should refuse him. Eternity courted me in his eyes as the world shrunk to hold us. Batman and Robin had gone away, leaving only an empty plate at an empty table. Kirk and Spock were tucked safely in bed.

My heart screamed in my chest. "If you had it to do over again, would you?" I asked at last. "Would you give up your human life to embrace what you've become?"

"Oh, yes! *Yes*—I would!" he whispered with a fervor that showed me a glimpse of the things he'd seen in his lifetime. He'd stood on the battlefield at Gettysburg. He'd sailed on the *Titanic* and gone down with her in dark waters. He'd danced with royalty and drunk from the veins of slumbering queens. "Any fool can die, Stefan, but it takes a brave heart to beat forever."

His passion made me want it all—that perfection, that dark evolution, that immortal life coursing through his body. I leaned closer, unintentionally conspiratorial as my stomach knotted with thoughts of Miquel, with details of what had to be done.

"What about you?" I asked, nervously running my fingertip through a drop of wine spilt on the table. "Why can't it be you who... why can't you be my... Creator?"

He grinned at my uncharacteristic lack of words. "You flatter me, Stefan, but I do not have the power to give life back once it is taken." His little fangs glittered as he smiled philosophically. "And besides, why would you drink from a peasant's stone cup when the golden chalice of the prince is pressed to your lips?"

56

Dimitri was good, a cunning and patient hunter who knew a net of pretty words would capture me faster and hold me tighter than any cage. If he really had been jealous the night before, it didn't show now, for he was open and casual in a way that put me at ease.

There was only one thing left for me to know, and that because I was still afraid of the dark. "Will it be terrible?"

His blue eye winked. His green one sparkled, reflecting the chandelier and all its little lights. "It will make you whole and enable your spirit to fly."

We left the restaurant together and, like two little boys, raced across the lobby to the limo waiting beyond glass doors.

*

My next awareness was of being in the great room of their home, where candles burned on the sills and the scent of smoke from the fireplace filled the air like pleasant anesthesia. Dimitri led me to an overstuffed sofa of soft burgundy leather and had me wait while he went to tell Miquel of my decision. He even told me not to be afraid, though he confessed he was glad he'd never had to make the choice himself.

As I sat there listening to the irregular pounding of my heart, it occurred to me to jump up and run. I was beginning to think Dimitri and Miquel had forgotten about me entirely when I heard the hushed padding of tennis shoes on the hardwood floor. I looked up, expecting to find some monster looming over me, but instead it was the young servant from the night before.

He stopped in the shadows of the stairwell, peering at me from a distance. Tight bluejeans hugged his athletic legs, and a green spandex top made it look as if he'd just come from the gym. His hair, which had been tied back before, now hung almost to his waist in glassy waves the shade of imported dark chocolate.

He was a vision, unreal, an album cover.

When I saw how exotic he truly was, I thought I'd been mistaken and this wasn't the same boy at all. But when he emerged into the light near the foot of the stairs, his porcelain doll skin and graceful movements were trademarks that couldn't be forged or inadvertently twinned in nature.

Seeing him better—firelight flickering over pronounced

cheekbones, narrow nose and defined chin—I realized he was older than I'd first believed. Twenty, perhaps. No more than 22.

"Hello," I said, sensing that any quick movement would cause him to bolt. He was a shy animal, wild, and I could only wonder what had happened to make him this way. I held one hand toward him. "I'm Stefan—Stefan London."

He nodded a wary acknowledgement, looking at me with wide brown eyes reminiscent of a deer.

"You came back," he said, coming no closer.

I'd almost decided he was mute, but his voice was even more clear and sharp than Dimitri's—not a human voice at all, but the plaintive sound one might expect from a merman or some fabled he-wolf crying to the moon. He cast a nervous glance toward the darker part of the house, then inquired in a fervent tone that sent chills through me, "*Do you know what will happen if you stay?*"

I was too scared to be scared anymore, so I sat there numbed to the bone by his voice, his extraordinary male beauty. "Yes, I think I do." I didn't, of course. How could I?

He crept a step closer, and as our gazes locked across the wide room, I felt sorry for him without understanding why. Uncomfortable with the silence, I started to say something, but a sound from the top of the stairs stopped me—a little bump, a soft thump, hushed male voices that sent a rush of dread through my gut. My head jerked toward the source, but the darkness sweeping down that curved stairwell revealed nothing.

There was a sensation of abrupt movement nearby, yet when I cast my eyes toward the young man, he was nowhere to be seen, the only thing that gave any hint to his whereabouts a curtain moving on the far side of the room. The window was open, and as I leapt from the sofa and hurried over to it, a shadow streaked through darker shadows at the farthest edge of the lawn.

I opened my mouth to call out, but the garden of statues and their watchful black angel stole my voice away completely.

Perhaps I should have gone after him or run away myself, but a writer's curse is to record events, often missing their significance at the time, so that he might mull them over at some later date. Returning to the sofa, I sat tentatively on the edge, struggling to quiet my ragged nerves.

The fire in the hearth was warm, a pleasant crackling filling the room, comforting somehow. The smooth white walls which stretched two stories high here in the great room were adorned with ornate tapestries and the hardwood floor covered with Persian rugs perhaps as old as Miquel himself. Overhead, a stained glass skylight depicted two enormous seraphim in frantic flight, carrying between them a third comrade whose head hung limp and whose broken wings trailed from his muscular back, lifeless.

Enthralled, I stared at it as the moon rose to illumine its fragile beauty. Then, when I could no longer bear the grief captured in the eyes of those stained glass angels, I drew my attention back to Earth.

What brought a smile to my lips was the large screen tv. and the elaborate stereo system with its 8-speaker surround sound tied in to the home theater. Two DVDs in rental cases sat next to the array, tagged with a common yellow sticky note which read: *Dimitri, return these on Monday. ...M.....*

For reasons I might never understand it was *that* silly detail which made Miquel human to me—sticky notes and memberships at the local video shop and a note written with plain black ink instead of blood.

For all his eloquent speech and his Ming vases gathering dust on a corner shelf and his undoubtedly authentic Van Gogh leaning against the wall as if he hadn't yet decided where to hang it, Miquel Kaliq Constantine was no Count Dracula imprisoned in a dreary castle. He could be just as comfortable at a rock concert as at the Bolshoi, and that was the thrill of him.

My stomach leapt unexpectedly – a rare premonition – and when I spun toward the stairs, it was to see the vampyre descending in all his glory. Whereas the night before had seen him in jeans and a plain white shirt, now he wore a tuxedo that made him appear even taller and darker than I remembered. He hadn't shaved—his scruffy countenance part of his vain self-portrait—and his glossy black mane crept inside his collar to nuzzle his neck, a curious pet. His eyes sparkled with mischief as he glided toward me and extended his hand in greeting.

I laughed nervously as we shook hands, halfway expecting him to say, *'Smile, you gullible fucking idiot, you're on Candid Camera!'*

Instead, completely at ease, he took my hand and pressed it firmly between both of his own, meeting my eyes in a steady emerald gaze that wasn't meant to mesmerize but nonetheless left me light-headed.

"You must forgive my protegé for not offering you something to drink," he said with consummate poise, "but I'm afraid he's run away into the night again. The act of creating a vampyre still scares poor Donny, you see, for he was made against his will— a struggle that almost destroyed us both." He smiled a little, sharp fangs glistening in his mouth. "Tell me: did he try to talk you out of it?"

I went cold to the bone when I saw his teeth, when I thought of what he was going to do to me. "Uh—no. But why—why did you—why against his will?" I stammered, taken off guard by the realization that the boy *was* a vampyre and the strong insinuation that Miquel wasn't above using force to get what he wanted.

He put an arm around my shoulder and led me to the window, and though I'd never been accustomed to such familiarity with another man, the strength of his embrace was reassuring. I tried to relax, knowing the time was past for changing my mind.

For a few moments, he looked at me as if trying to decide whether to answer my question. The creek gurgled, rushing through the flower gardens. Glass windpipes hanging beneath the eaves began a melodic chiming.

"Donny was my blood lover, you see," he explained in a voice that was barely audible despite our physical closeness. "When he fell ill, I had to bring him into this life or lose him forever." Taking his gaze from the window and fastening it on me, he added darkly, "I do *not* like to lose, Stefan."

These words he uttered with an arrogance that was palpable in its intensity. I could think of no appropriate response as he looked at me with a vulnerability which told me he really did want me to understand why he did the things he did.

"I have been acquainted with death for over a thousand years," he explained, and I knew then that the madness in his eyes was history. "I've seen him steal friends, obliterate families at a whim, annihilate entire civilizations. Normally I've looked the other way, ignoring him as he's ignored me. But when he came for Donny and singled him out of all the world, I took his audacity as a personal affront, and on that day death and I went to war."

His ardor chilled me. His passion moved me. And because I

wanted to understand, I foolishly muttered, "I understand."

Miquel turned his head to me, his scrutiny causing me to writhe inside. "Really?"

Knowing he'd seen right through my bravado, I gave him the truth instead. "I want to."

This made him smile, though somewhat sadly. "I believe you really do, Stefan."

Then, before I knew what was happening, he reached out to run his fingertips over my hand, a gesture that wasn't intrusive when I consciously lowered my walls in response to the telepathic presence of his will. And without the bulky burden of words, I suddenly knew—

—the April storm was unexpected, making the house damp and full of shadows even at mid-afternoon. By the open window, Miquel danced, naked and frenzied, grateful for the clouds yet resentful that the sun was hiding behind them, waiting to sneak out again. The windows fogged, frosty ghosts peering in at the corners. Music screamed—the same song playing over and over on speakers omnipotent enough to render even a vampyre deaf to the world's din.

The thirst aroused him, thoughts of drinking from his chosen blood lover causing his lips to part and his eyes to roll slightly upward. How long had he known Donny? A year? Or was it two? The kid shouldn't be dying. The kid shouldn't have AIDS.

"I shouldn't have to kill you just to make sure you will live." Though he said the words aloud, Miquel never heard them above the music and the pounding of his own crazed heart. Death was mocking him, challenging him to a duel for the soul of a dying man.

Donald Anthony Carrera—lead vocalist in a rock band that played weekend gigs at the local pub. The first time Miquel laid eyes on the kid he had to have him: a taste of his blood, a drink of his poetry. The first time he heard him sing, he was lost.

To make it perfect, Donny loved the blood bite, his entire essence surging every time Miquel drank from him. With this one, there was no need to hide the truth, no need to resort to sorcery to make him forget. With Donny, Miquel could openly enjoy being a vampyre again, partaking in the shared symbiosis as it was meant to be.

His body quickened. Neither God nor Satan could have the kid and that was that!

He visualized making it real: Donny climbing into his arms as he'd always done, accepting without fear or fight the sharp kiss that would end his life in order to chase away his death forever.

The magic wouldn't be quite that easy, of course. It never was.

From the cold gray fabric of the storm, Miquel gathered strength, knowing he would need every molecule of power he could conjure, and even then it might not be enough. The sting of mortal death was sometimes fatal, defying even <u>his</u> blood. Fear could destroy it all and plunge the kid into the sun, a failed Icarus.

He trembled, feeling terribly small. He had to be more than a man, more than even a vampyre. Could he be the Creator now, when it mattered more than anything?

He never knew, and that was the hell of it.

"You <u>must</u> fly – beyond the ability of Death to undo!" Miquel said to the empty room, the breath rushing out of him as he collapsed on the floor, his chest heaving from hours of exertion. He touched his body for magic, for luck, and to bring forth the power of Creation itself.

He closed his eyes, hugged his arms to his chest, and he wept. Soon it would be night—time to take the life of a love.

I was staring fixedly into Miquel's eyes when the trance dissipated. A small sound escaped my throat, and though I swayed dizzily in response to the clash of conflicting realities—what I'd always believed possible and what I'd always thought of as myth—the myth steadied me with a firm grip on my arm.

"I will not lose you either, my friend," he assured me.

The sheer force behind those words caused me to look away. Panic pressed close.

If this thing had to be done at all, it should be clinical, detached and quickly over, an awful thing to be gotten through like a trip to the dentist. I didn't want to hear him talking about mortal lovers and challenging death and making a man a vampyre against his will—an act that sounded obscenely erotic despite its more sinister overtones. I didn't want to watch the plays written in his memory, nor see him dancing like some savage warlock, naked and crazed by a storm.

To my surprise, Miquel laughed, then reached out a hand to tousle my hair. "But don't you see, Stefan?" he murmured with a little grin that caused my heart to miss a beat. "I've danced the day away for *you* this time—to prove to Death that my will is stronger even than his."

I tried to speak, but no words came as I took a step away from him. He had danced for *me*. He had danced a barbaric dance because it truly was his intention to kill me.

Suddenly it was all very real and sharply focused, and I was no longer ready to give up my life even for the prospect of living forever. Before, it had been an idle thought, a fantasy. Now, with him standing in front of me as we finalized some unholy pact, it became 3-dimensional and far too detailed.

Without volition, I stumbled another step backward, glancing toward the tall double doors, knowing I would never reach them.

"Oh, God," I whispered. "Oh, God!"

Instead of chastising me for my cowardice, Miquel followed after me and slipped an arm around my waist in an attempt to calm my fright. If I'd ever wondered how a prisoner felt on his way to the gas chamber, I knew. My body was numb, my mind detached, and my life was far too finite—measured in minutes and seconds rather than years. The air in my lungs had turned to fire because I'd forgotten to breathe, and I was on the verge of nausea when Miquel pulled me to his chest and forced my head down on his shoulder.

Without words, he held me there, swaying easily back and forth with his fingers tangled in my hair and my cheek pressed to the ruffled shirt of his tux. His chin rested against my forehead, his shadowy stubble coarse and entirely too physical, his clean scent filling my nostrils. Unable to bear the sight of our reflections in the mirror above the mantle, I clenched my eyes tightly shut, dancing with the instrument of my impending death.

An hour passed, maybe more.

Finally, when I could breathe again, he placed his hands on my shoulders and held me at arms' length as the room came back into focus. I do not know what our minds said to one another, but after a minute or two, he led me to the sofa and sat down at my side.

"I know you're afraid, Stefan," he told me with compassion, resting a steady hand on my shoulder. "But I've done this thing before and I know you'll make it through. So we'll speak with reverence of your death for a moment and then we'll simply do it. I think it would be best that way—without so much angst and contemplation, yes?"

It was so easy for him, so natural to seduce a mortal soul right out of the vessel that held it. All I could do was stare at him, at those feral eyes framed by the most exquisite features I'd ever seen.

He was both executioner and messiah. He was my fate and undeniably he was my faith.

I tried to reply, but my stomach cramped and my vision blurred. My heart went into an unearthly rhythm until I cried out in pain, ashamed of myself for an anxiety so acute it reduced me to this.

In the face of eternal life, I was about to die of a stroke.

Miquel squeezed my shoulder to calm me. When he gave an unexpected smile at my predicament, I saw his teeth and once again knew that special fear reserved for those who had looked their death squarely in the face. Meeting my gaze with an expression of real empathy, the amusement left him.

We were alone in the world then, and I believe he planned it that way—for time to stop, for the lights in the distance to dim, for the wind to stop stirring the chimes in the garden. All that remained were the songs of the frogs and the gurgling of the little creek, a miniature Styx winding its way past the window.

"All you need do is come to me willingly, Stefan, and I will do the rest," he assured me, holding his hands open as he spoke. Here he paused, fingertips brushing my cheek. "Can you do it, my friend? Can you surrender your life to me and trust me to make you whole again?"

I hated him for the images his words awakened—a savior offering me body and blood and telling me I would live forever if I were first willing to die.

I began to weep, for there was only one answer to his question, and with a gruesome effort that drained me, I whispered it before I could change my mind: "Yes."

His entire self surged in response, a burst of energy on my mind. "*Excellent*," he breathed darkly. "Perfect."

Then, meeting my eyes and compelling me not to look away as his trance engulfed me, he began to speak in a voice that was hypnotic and soothing unto itself.

"When you feel my lips on you, draw a deep breath and rejoice in knowing it will be your last as a mortal. You'll think you're drowning, but remember I'm with you in the waters, driftwood at your side. You'll want to fight me, but if you do, know you'll die the death from which not even my blood can awaken you again."

I couldn't breathe. I couldn't move. "I'm afraid."

He wet his lips with the tip of his tongue, as enraptured by this insufferable act as I was horrified. "Then come to me, Stefan, and let us take that fear away from you forever. Let me show you the way out."

Our eyes locked, passing candlelight back and forth in an endless hall of mirrors.

It *was* the only way out, terrifying and terribly seductive because of that very singularity. When I finally saw that, when I acknowledged that death was the only chance I had for life, I fell into his outstretched arms because there was nowhere else for me to go.

I believe I was speaking—whimpering and crying and begging him to let me live, I suspect—though I could not tell you for sure. It was a terror I would will on no other living soul, and had I known I would experience such an all consuming dread when his arms closed around me, I could not have gone through with it.

My world was ending and I was going to my death as if it were a lover.

My body surged in protest, survival instinct making me resist even his pleasing trance. But when he seized my wrists and forced me down with a strength I could never match, I could only look up into his eyes and accept as fact that I was already dead.

Releasing one wrist, he touched my face as his weight pressed me deeper into the dream. Then, as if he wanted to shield me from the hunger I read in his gaze, he brushed his fingertips over my eyes, forcing them to close.

"Driftwood, Stefan," he whispered as my head began to spin and I knew he really was going to do it. "I am driftwood."

I caught a shaky breath when he gathered me to him and his lips fell quickly upon my throat. My heart pounded, wild drums. My tears fell, a fatal storm. In a final act of resignation that begged for mercy, I threw my arms around his back and pulled him roughly to me, burying my face in the curve of his neck as I began to weep.

"Beautiful," the angel of death whispered, his thirst a palpable force in the room. "Your surrender is genuinely beautiful." His fingers caressed my throat, luring the blood to the surface, and then I began falling into a warm, sheltering faint. "Now let the world be gone, Stefan. Let the world go away so the night can come in."

And with that, he seized me with his teeth in a grip so fierce I felt the cramp of torment all the way through to my feet. My eyes flashed open for an instant, but I clamped them tightly shut, afraid I would see death in the room. Warmth poured down my neck, a rushing river caught by the devil's lips.

I panicked, surrendered, panicked again.

At first, I fought to shove him away from me, but when I remembered his final warning as my blood ran freely and I began to suffocate, I grabbed the driftwood to me and rode that hellish tidal wave straight on into the night.

The world went still then, and I stood apart from myself, a voyeur watching my own metamorphosis as I lay in the arms of a vampyre who drank my dying soul. It was all I'd dared to think it might be—my body conquered beneath him, my soul rising up to dance on the ceiling in a bid to escape the terrible pain.

The music of the spheres wasn't Lawrence Welk or Andrew Lloyd Webber or even Enya. It was rock and roll, with my own high-pitched scream wailing like an electric guitar.

The suffering was indescribable. The pleasure left me spent. I stopped breathing. And then, as Miquel suckled the blood from my world, I knew the gruesome serenity of death itself.

Though one might think it would be the most enigmatic experience of man, the actuality of it was altogether dull. For a moment, it seemed that whatever essence had made Stefan London a creature unique unto himself would merely be absorbed into the spongy black cloth of the cosmos, soaked up, finished.

The horror came with the realization that even this disintegration of the Self would have been acceptable, because the will to live was the first thing death stole away. In that way, it was an altogether flawless mechanism. Annihilation wasn't a process of defeat or surrender. It was, in the end, nothing more than nonexistence—a state of non-being which would triumph by default because one could not do battle with a vacuum while inside that very vacuum.

In one moment, I had been alive and vital and terrified that my life was going to end. Yet when that ending came, the heavy *blankness* obliterated even the realization that there had been a *me* to be destroyed in the first place.

For the first time in all of time, I did not exist and never had and never would, and that was the nature of death as I perceived it. There was, if Nothing can be said to exist, Absolute Nothing which could not even be perceived because the ability *to* perceive was lost in the Nowhere, swallowed whole. There was no blinding white light, no line of dead relatives welcoming me to heaven, no angelic choirs, and not a single deity or demon in sight. And yet, if there *was* a Hell, this was it: this profoundly empty and hollow void where Stefan London had once existed, this hole death created in the very fabric of space and time, this hole which was the annihilation of consciousness itself.

Adrift in that nihilistic state, I didn't see Miquel loosen his crisp black tie nor unfasten his ruffled shirt to reveal his neck to me. And though I have no recollection of him making a small incision below his ear, I was drawn to the scent of that scarlet milk as a baby instinctively seeks its mother's breast—the only real thing in the midst of the cold black mire.

Because I could not do it for myself, he lifted my head to the wound and held it there as I was overcome by a hunger so fierce it threatened to consume me. Abruptly, I was dragged back into my lifeless body—*too heavy, so small, so cold*—when I tasted the precious salts of his blood on my tongue.

Greedy for that flavor which I now recognized as the only cure for death's nonexistence, and gifted with sharp fangs that had replaced my own dull incisors, I bit down hard and sucked in my first immortal breath: a choking, gurgling reverse scream of vampyre evolution.

Miquel cried out when I was born, trembling beneath the suffering I caused him even as his arms tightened around me and a low groan of wicked bliss whispered across his lips. The anguish thrilled him as it thrilled me. We were two of a kind, he and I. We were cloud and rain. Pain and pleasure. We were flesh and bone.

At first, I knew only the security reserved for a newborn first set to its mother's nipple. But then, as his blood began threading its way through the veins and the capillaries of my death-still heart, something happened I hadn't anticipated. It came as a flash at first, a quick burst of images with no rational explanation.

A male concubine, groomed as a consort to the emperor, but arrogant and defiant in his youth, refusing to be subservient even to the highest lord of Byzantium. When he struck the monarch and would not allow himself to be taken, his belly was cut open and he was thrown out for the wild dogs to find.

But it was the king's odd son who found the beautiful creature first, the pale young prince who fed the dying man blood from his own body and nurtured him back to health in secret.

When Miquel was well again, he stole the vampyre's sword and plunged it through his heart—not because he believed it would kill Prince Leo, but because he desperately hoped the prince would be driven to kill <u>him</u> in a fit of rage and revenge. Leo, like his father Basil, had taken liberties with Miquel against his will. A vampyre now himself, he would not be sodomized like some common whore; and though he secretly wept when his maker cast him out into streets, he never saw the prince again.

But he would not let me linger there, giving me only the briefest glimpse of his past.

Centuries tumbled together in his mind, a haze of lost memories made dim by the will to forget. Before Dimitri, there was only the darkness. After Dimitri was born in his arms and he knew he was a Creator capable of building a new world, he no longer mourned the loss of the sun or cursed the thirst.

He was a vampyre, and now he held his head high as he smiled at the moon and admired his own reflection in pools of still water. Though barely 19 when Leo changed him, Miquel's magical body had settled into the maturity of a man in his early 30s—the prime of mortal life, the peak of strength and prowess, when a man was feared by powerful men and desired by beautiful women.

The images came hard and fast, mixed in his blood. The images *were* the blood, the culmination of all Miquel. I drank of popes and soldiers, kings and fools. I tasted Lord Byron on my tongue, and pressed the elixir of Shelley to my lips. I sampled the soul sick sweetness of Norma Jean and the final breath of Jim Morrison. There were the homeless urchins from the streets of L.A., whose blood ran strong and quick in anonymity. And there were the willing victims who had sought out the vampyres since the dawn of time in the hopes of finding immortality.

I suckled deep as his heart fed me, finally encountering my own familiar flavor running fast through his veins. The taste was narcissistically sweeter than all the rest, and I yearned for it so much that I released my hold and re-sank my teeth to gain a better view.

Railroad tracks slick with rain and tennis shoes pounding footprints into the mud. Wild pumpkins growing in an empty city lot, still green. A finger sliced open and the flood of blood in a little boy's mouth as he sucked it, secretly hungry with the need to know himself better.

Again Miquel writhed, fingers twisting in my hair as he held my head to him and encouraged me to feed.

"Yes, my child, take all you need and take it deep," he whispered, though I heard the words in my mind more than in my ears. He stroked my face, my throat. *The instinct is strong with you because you were born to the Blood.*

I floated in the soft, warm core of him and let its red waves gently rock me. But as my feast continued and I indulged this terrible hunger to the point of gluttony, something went skittering past my lips that gave me sudden pause. It was a presence half remembered, a face in an album of faded photographs, an old song playing on a distant radio.

"Drink deeper, Stefan," Miquel encouraged, though his voice had gone sad, resigned. "Drink it to the soul so you may understand it."

Because he was my Creator and I was compelled to obey his will, I drank deeper of this familiar essence. So perfect was the flavor on my lips that I never wanted to let it go, so dulcet and trusting I wanted to devour it as Miquel had once devoured it.

They moved together on the dance floor at the costume ball—the vampyre in his tuxedo, and the goth girl with the dyed black hair and skin paler even than his. Enamored of his physical radiance, thrilled when he lifted her in his arms and waltzed with her, she threw her head back and laughed with an abandon only an adolescent girl can know.

"Are you really a vampyre?" They'd courted one another all evening, covert glances across a crowded room. Finally, he'd asked her to dance.

"I really am," Miquel told her, and captured her in the folds of his cape.

She rested her head on his chest, for she barely reached his shoulder. A strange sensation such as she'd never known alighted in the pit of her stomach.

"I believe you," she whispered, and she did believe. A soft sigh pressed through lips painted red with her mother's borrowed lipstick. The

calm inside her grew. "Can you read my mind?"

"Yes."

"What am I thinking, then?" Her head was held high, chin beginning to tremble.

He drew her close, so close, caressed her hair. Emeralds snarled in ebony. "You want to die," he barely whispered, sucking that ghastly aloneness until her essence filled him. Other couples danced nearby, oblivious to the pact being secretly sworn.

Her eyes closed, cheeks suddenly wet. Her small hands clenched his back, shiny black fingernails digging in. "Nobody understands," she told him, her soul awash with the torment of growing up. "Nobody ever has."

"I understand, Stephanie."

God help me, I believe he did. He understood something about her I never had. He understood her pain enough to acknowledge it and, more, enough to make it stop.

And though I tried to tear myself away from him and run screaming into the night, I could never run far enough now. In a horrible flash that came through the blood, I knew how she'd died—*kiss of death, soft and fine and without fight or pain*—and I knew it had been as mystical for her as it had been for me because it had come at Miquel's skilled hands.

The bastard even made love to her before he pressed his teeth to her throat and gave her the release she desperately craved. As he stole her innocence, he liberated her from a life she'd never wanted: a mother addicted to therapy and booze, and a father more obsessed with trying to describe the color of her hair than with questioning why that color came from a bottle when she was only 13.

When I tore my mouth from his nurturing throat, my lips wet with her blood, I could only look into Miquel's predatory eyes and cry out when I saw my own iridescent reflection caught there. I would have killed him if I could, yet there was no denying he was already dead.

In shock, my words came out cold and ineloquent. "You godless, soulless bastard—you *murdered* her!"

But he shook his head and forced my head down on his shoulder, knowing I was too weak to resist. Worse, he knew I *wouldn't* resist, for he was my Creator whom I would love by nature, even in the face of a hatred equally profound.

70

It was a paradox for which no reconciliation existed, and by that very definition it was madness itself.

In defiance of nature, my body quickened as he coddled me, and that was worse still. Shame overwhelmed me, and I wept in denial as the river of arousal flowed from me in a rush that confirmed his intolerable power over me.

"You murdered her!" I shouted, twisting and writhing. My fists flailed at his face, his neck, the air, but the blows had no effect whatsoever. "You murdered her! You murdered my baby girl!"

With little effort, he stilled my protests, placing one hand firmly over my mouth and the other in the center of my chest until I fell back, unable to do anything more than stare up into his face.

"No, my dearest Stefan," he said with a degree of regret that astonished me, "*you* murdered her—you and your busy, busy world that had no time for a little girl with a melancholy soul." And as if I needed to hear it again, he leaned down close to my ear and repeated, "*You* killed her. I only gave her the ability to die.'

My mortal tears were drying as they fell, though my chest still heaved. "Then kill me, too!" I begged, so frail I could barely speak. I hadn't the strength to attack him again, yet I couldn't imagine going on with him in the same world—wanting him, needing him as a father, a friend, a teacher and more. Loving him more than I could have loved hatred itself.

I vowed to destroy him. But at the same moment, my immortal soul was swelling and shattering with the excruciating love a man feels for someone who has just saved his life.

That was the price, that was the passion, that was the motivation which would spur me to eternity itself. Damned to love the creature who had murdered my daughter, it was his blood mingling with hers in my veins that caused my vampyre heart to start beating.

"Kill me!" I demanded, appalled at the strengthening flutter in my hollow chest, yet secretly filled with a hunger that horrified me with its intensity. "If you have any compassion in you, kill me, Miquel!"

A jeweled hand stroked my head. "I already have," he whispered, and gave an ironic smile.

Then, rising from the sofa, he lifted me easily into his arms and, like a loving father, carried me up the stairs to his white satin bed. There he lay me down to sleep, curling his body around me, sheltering me in the down of his noble black wings.

Perhaps there was no God, but I knew then there was a devil. Not the Christian devil, to be sure, but colder still and far more brutal. Marble hearted. Not a fallen angel, but one who had deliberately flown away from the light because it offended him.

Is the coyote evil because he kills? No, he is only a hungry coyote, capable of compassion.

Because he left me no other choice, I fell into a cold and bottomless sleep with the kiss of the black angel on my lips and the blood of my Stephanie dancing The Mephisto Waltz in my veins.

CHAPTER SIX

"The only drawback is that the tale will have to be told under the guise of fiction," Miquel was saying when I first awoke as a vampyre. "But I suppose that's been the case throughout history. Tolkein and his elves. Bradbury and his Martians. Rice and her—" here he paused to give me a wink and a wicked grin "—*witches*! Ah, but those who yearn for immortality will seek us out regardless of how the story is presented, don't you agree, Stefan?"

The monster had taken my mortal life less than 18 hours before, yet as the new day broke, all he could talk about was how quickly I might be able to commit the story to paper.

In reality, it wasn't daybreak but nightfall instead, and my disorientation as I fought to hold my eyes open was as disturbing as any sensation I'd ever experienced. It had the same eerie quality as climbing up from anesthesia—the feeling of being lost, displaced, and acutely terrified.

Sometime during the night—the night which was actually mortal day—my shirt had been draped across a nearby chair, a faded blue rag stained with my blood, a surrender flag for my lost humanity. Though the room was pleasantly warm, I felt cold and exposed, and in response to my discomfort, Miquel drew the comforter higher on my chest.

Delirious, my head tossed on the pillow.

I was aware of him holding me and I was aware of *being*

aware of being held. I felt my fingers running through the slick silk of my hair, yet they were not my fingers, but Miquel's instead. When he breathed, air filled my lungs. When my heart beat, blood sang through his veins like water through distant pipes.

When he hugged me closer, saying, "Ah, Stefan, just relax and enjoy it while it lasts," his affection was a deep tickle in my own body, and *that* awakened the fury which delivered me from my stupor.

This *thing* had murdered my daughter! The images I'd found in his blood whiplashed through my mind, violently poison, and I understood that this creature who had transformed life into death and death into life had held my daughter in his arms and suckled the last breath out of her.

But for Stephanie, there was no getting it back, no magical kiss that returned her life filtered through his transcendental veins.

Stephanie was dead and I was dead and God was dead and that was that. Worse, it was no coincidence that the same bloodthirsty devil had annihilated us all—Stephanie through physical death, me through eternal life forever condemned to live with the knowledge of what he'd done, God through the dismemberment of my inadequate faith.

I drew a breath to throw accusations at him, yet the words died in my mouth. My fists clenched, but when I tried to strike out, all I could feel was the pain of that intended blow landing in my own mind.

To hurt Miquel—to even think of hurting him—was to hurt myself, for we truly were one entity in more than just a petty romantic sense.

But pain was of little consequence to me, so I scrambled to my knees and seized the fiend by the lapel of his tux. My fist doubled, sharp fingernails digging into my palm as I struck him on the jaw with a right cross that would have sent a normal man to the hospital.

The resultant shock caused me to cry out as if I had been the one hit, yet Miquel never even flinched. Instead, when I drew back for a second assault, he merely caught my wrist and flung me onto my back, his movements effortless and almost nonchalant. Holding me with one hand in the center of my bare chest—not unlike an insect is crucified to a board with a pin—he spoke without ever raising his voice.

"If you truly wish to harm me, there are more elegant ways for the deed to be done," he said, entirely untouched by my rage. "There is a stiletto in the nightstand with which you could sever my carotid artery, for example, and while the wounds would not be fatal, the gratification you would garner might be enough to wean you from this bitter nipple of revenge."

Horrified, I screamed—the wail of despair and the howl of denial—yet my lips remained mute, my body still as death as I was sucked down into the web of his trance, a prisoner of his will, utterly helpless.

He tried to assuage me with his thoughts, but with the last ounce of control I possessed, I slammed a telepathic door in his face. It wasn't any mystical power, but a side effect of having once been married that gave me the ability to bombard him with icy wrath while also shutting him out thoroughly.

It actually surprised him. For a minute or two, he just looked at me, studying me. Then a soft sigh pressed through his lips.

"I don't expect you to understand, Stefan," he said at last, the way a father might address a stubborn child, "but I do insist you listen. For while you are now impervious to old age, disease, and common accidents, you are far from invincible."

Fuck you! It wasn't creative or eloquent, but it was honest, and since his telepathy had stolen even my ability to speak, it was the only defense I had.

I wanted to kill him, yet he never showed me anything but kindness, and that was the worse thing he could have done to me.

"Very well, then, let us talk of my death," he murmured in response to my psychic outburst, and began speaking in a low and measured voice. "If you really are a perfectionist and insist on doing the thing right, decapitation is one way to execute a vampyre, or chaining him in sunlight for an extended period of time. Of course, I've always thought the latter highly overrated, since chaining a mortal without food or water in the noonday sun would have the same effect. Indeed, while we prefer darkness and thrive on the night, small doses of daylight are no more fatal than rain."

He sighed with indifference and began going down the list. "You'll find garlic, wooden stakes and crosses completely ineffective and even rather silly when you consider the lack of religious convictions of most vampyres, though the things which *can* kill us vary from one to the next, depending on our age and individual gifts.

"I wouldn't recommend rushing into a burning building or drinking the blood of animals in some noble attempt to avoid taking human life, for example," he explained. "Cats and rats and squirrels in the park have killed more vampyres than any modern-day Van Helsings, for while their blood may taste the same on your tongue, it can't sustain your vampyre body or nurture your vampyre soul."

I was mute and cold and full of hatred, but also full of unwanted questions which he heard as clearly as if I spoke out loud.

"Your vampyre soul?" he repeated, and smiled a little to show me his teeth. But despite his frivolous exterior, his aura was genuinely sorrowful, filled with regret he could never admit.

"It isn't only blood we drink," he was saying, his voice softening from the tone of a teacher to the soothing purr of a lover. "We suckle the very essence from those we feed upon—the memories of mortal life, the pains and pleasures of their existence, the unbearable questions all humans carry in their hearts. But most of all, Stefan—ah, most of all!—we take into ourselves whatever answers they may have found along the way, and that is the hunger which will drive us to hunt even when our bodies might not feel the thirst for months or years at a stretch."

He really did believe that history was written in human blood and stored in the vampyre heart, and that our kind held some cosmic obligation to record the social evolution and the spiritual deterioration of Man. Later, he would even tell me he saw it as his *responsibility* to drink blood as a means of understanding the human race on a level no mere human ever had or even could.

Settling down at my side, he slipped an arm around my back, and though an unearthly snarl tore from my throat in response to his intimacy, I could do nothing to break his controlling spell.

I will kill you, you bastard! I vowed as images of Stephanie came back to me. Miquel drinking of *her* life, *her* unanswered questions, and the pain intrinsic to youth.

Propping himself up on an elbow, he gazed down at me with a tenderness I neither expected nor wanted. "I understand your grief and anger, but they're only reflections from the mortal world, ripples on the sea of your memory," he said without animosity. And because his psychic shields were lowered, I knew he was speaking from experience that came with great age. In time, time would heal even *this*.

But I *wanted* my grief. I *needed* my rage.

And, oh, how I wanted him dead!

He stroked my face, fingertips barely brushing. "Yes, of course you do. But the problem with that is this, and I suggest you take it to heart: if you *do* succeed in killing me—whether now or in a thousand years—you'll be destroying yourself as well. You see, our lives are connected now, and when my blood no longer flows on Earth, *you* will know death, too. But when you die again, it will be to oblivion and it will be forever. That, and the knowledge that nothing is truly immortal is the price we pay for this illusion of eternal life. While humans may question if they will live again, for vampyres it is a certainty we do *not*."

Death was precisely what I longed for, but before I could speak the words, he'd already begun to reply.

"If you wanted to die, you would not have come into my arms last night," he reminded me. "You would not have allowed me to take your life so you might live forever."

In a sane world, a man could hunt down the monster who'd killed his daughter and break every bone in the fiend's body. But in this vampyre universe, I could do nothing but lie there looking up into the bastard's eyes. The hatred and the passion I felt for him were precisely equal, and as a result I was reduced to a mass of quivering flesh that no longer bore any resemblance to the man I'd once been.

He had made me, you see, and that was the trap. He'd *made* me—his son and his immortal love. There is no way to explain it beyond that. He was in my blood. *He* was my god now. He most certainly was my devil.

He was my *Self*.

Time came and went.

"Oh, God," I said, struck with the realization of what I had become. There I was: a fledgling vampyre praying in my Creator's arms, tears bleeding from my eyes like rain turned pink.

The room was spinning—potted trees and blues and greens

and clouds painted or the ceiling whirling in the cosmic drain. Through the window, stars glittered, but even those distant suns threatened to blind my eyes forever.

My mind could hold no coherent thought and raced at random from one thing to another. In one instant, I was cursing him for killing my Stephanie. Yet in the very next second, I was begging him to hold me because my body felt feather light, and I was concerned that I might float away and bang my head on the moon.

When he finally relinquished the trance that held me paralyzed, I made the mistake of taking one last swing at him, an action I regretted when he smacked me back on the bed with a clout on the jaw. Like a child, I cried against his disapproval far more than from physical pain.

My mortal life was over. My eternal life was just beginning.

The problem was reconciling the two.

As a human father, I *must* hate Miquel for what he'd done. Yet as a vampyre, I could look at my daughter's death with a sense of detachment that was both a comfort and a horror.

Stephanie would have died anyway.

Whether the thought was mine or his, I would never know, but it came straight into my heart as I lay there writhing and weeping, a bona fide lunatic. Then, as he stroked my hair almost absent-mindedly, I felt the vibration of his aura change to include a note of resonant wonder.

Time skipped, a rock over water, and I knew he was about to reveal something of vital importance.

"One thing you will discover as you grow into your new skin, Stefan, is that there are sacred moments in time—when a mortal will come to you, knowing precisely what you are, and ask you to end their life because it truly is time for them to die." He paused, brushing the blood of my tears away. "It is a rare thing, a sacrosanct pact, and if I had not taken your daughter's life at her bidding, she would have done so on her own, and in doing so, she would have damned her soul."

"Goddamn you, she loved *life!*" I cried out.

"She loved *you*," he countered. "How she felt about *life* was another matter altogether."

I was silent for a long time. "If you don't believe in God, damnation can't exist," I muttered, though why I was trying to reason with him, I do not know.

"What I believe isn't important. What mattered was that *she* believed it, and any reality is a self-created trap if belief is strong enough." He paused, and during the lengthy stillness, an unexpected clap of thunder brought clouds to obliterate the stars. "The only thing I know is that by giving herself to me, she brought you to me, Stefan—for it was through her blood that I first saw you and knew our paths were destined to connect."

My heart beat slower than death. My eyes clenched shut, but I could not close out his words.

"Bonds such as ours are sacred, my friend, even among vampyres," he stressed, saying the thing I desperately did not want to hear. "We *have* come together for a reason, but only time can show us what that reason is to be."

Saints save me, I could not deny it. A terrible clarity shook me and I saw things as they were instead of as I wanted them to be.

Stephanie would have died anyway.

Whether from Miquel's kiss or a bottle of Valium stolen from her mother's medicine cabinet, she would have died—for the simple reason that she no longer wanted to live. And though it would take an eternity to accept it, Miquel's telepathic sorcery enabled me to see that the manner in which Stephanie's life had ended was just Nature operating with her usual precision. At least her death had served a purpose. Her blood had nourished the vampyre, and in exchange he had given her a gentle ending where candles burned to light her way and warm her final night. He held her in his arms with affection when he took her life, and the *only* reason he took her life was because her time on Earth was finished and Nature had given him the ability to *see* that. Fate merely sanctioned their paths to cross on that day, at that hour, in that moment.

Life and death were a well choreographed ballet, everything beginning or ending as it was meant to. Both Stephanie and I had wooed the reaper, yet he had slaughtered the flower girl and married the best man.

The human I had been screamed, *Sacrilege!* Yet the vampyre I was becoming could only view the entire affair with an awakening sense of wonder. For after all, Stephanie and I were joined not once by blood, but twice—once by birth, the second time by death itself. I had tasted her on my lips, and through Miquel's blood she had played a part in returning to me the life I had first given her all those years ago.

It was all connected.

As these thoughts assaulted me, I struggled to tear myself from his embrace, but he held me firm and rocked me back and forth. "In a little while, I'll let you go," he promised. "But for now, while this world is new and my blood is still struggling to find a calmer path through your veins, you must lie here and let me take care of you, Stefan."

The thought disgusted me. The thought aroused me.

My stomach heaved and I tasted the blood I'd drunk the night before. His blood. My blood. Stephanie's blood. A few drops came up into my mouth as I lay there in a daze, but when it flowed over my lips to stain his white shirt, I found the sight not only alarming, but alarmingly seductive as well.

Mesmerized, I gradually began to quiet as he caressed my hair and kept repeating, "Easy... easy." And: "Be still, my little changeling. Just be still," and, "rest... Ssshh... rest your head on my shoulder and sleep."

Maybe he was controlling me, forcing me to bend to his will. Or maybe I just needed to think so. All I know is that I did begin to calm as I lay there staring at the ruffles on his shirt and the little smudge of bright red blood.

It drew me. It had forever changed me.

Now I was hungry—a primal need even more demanding than vengeance.

CHAPTER SEVEN

While I do not believe any mortal could fully comprehend the transformation from human to vampyre, it was that very change which enabled me to go with Miquel when civilized morals would dictate that I should have been finding some way to destroy him. I had been granted a merciful distance from mortal precepts, and while it would not be easy to forgive Miquel, there was a certain comfort in knowing it had been in Stephanie's nature to seek him out and in his nature to grant her request.

Each of them was a necessary part of the other's journey.

Miquel was surprisingly congenial as he helped me toward the stairs, and only when I began to move did I realize how profound the changes within me were.

An incredible strength coursed through my body. The colors of life were brighter. Green wasn't just a shade of grass, but as I looked through the window and realized I could see better in the dark than I'd ever seen in daylight, I understood that green was a symphony of mingled tones which tasted fresh and sharp to the eye. I could feel the texture of tires on the distant street. I could smell funeral dirges written in the minor key of black or taste the *chit-chattery* thoughts of spiders crawling in the ivy dragon's mouth. And most of all, I could know things without knowing how I knew them—such as knowing three Dobermans were prowling the perimeter and knowing Dimitri had gone into the city to hunt.

As we made our way down the stairs, Miquel with an arm around my waist to steady me, I couldn't help noticing that his movements were slower than before and not as graceful. His clothes were wrinkled and stained, and for the first time it occurred to me that I hadn't been the only one to make a sacrifice of blood.

My transformation had taken its toll on him, and in the dim light of the curved stairwell, with paintings of cherubs and still-life irises behind him on the papered walls, he was far paler than when we'd met. The hand gripping the mahogany railing trembled, and though I wanted the world to be black and white—with Miquel as the ogre and myself as the victim—this mystical creature had fed me his blood so I might live forever.

It was humbling.

We paused together on the landing, an awkward moment like some unrehearsed ad-lib, and for the briefest of instants, he stood psychically naked before me, revealing himself to me in a manner to which he was clearly unaccustomed.

I cannot tell you what I saw, except that I was inundated with the feeling that he wanted me to like my new life. And, like any father, he wanted me to love him as he loved me.

There was such dignity in his gaze, but also a terrible pain. He felt it all, Miquel did—all the angst, all the beauty, all the dread of all the worlds. He felt the perfection of a butterfly in flight and the anguish trapped inside the killing jar, and it shone as a light in his eyes that would inevitably draw lost souls to him—just as it had drawn Stephanie, just as it had drawn me.

Perhaps these realizations were nothing more than illusion, pretty pictures he gave me to play with. But *something* passed between us, some lightning-fast and lightning-bright exchange that left me leaning against the stairwell, dazed by the sheer presence of him.

But just when I would have questioned him about it, he began to smile with a sense of awe and absolute delight. That was his greatest secret, his ability to shuffle through human emotions and deal himself a hand suitable for any situation. One instant, he'd been vulnerable and sad somehow, yet now he was as affable as any child with a new toy.

"Come," he said, taking my arm and leading me down the stairs. "Before we take you out to face your first night as a vampyre, there's something you really must see."

When we reached the foyer, I thought he wanted to taunt me with memories which had surely been absorbed into the very glass of those overhead mirrors, memories of the first time he'd taken me to his lips, memories of a day or two before which were now as distant as centuries. Such a short time ago, I had been mortal, filled with mortal concerns, a prop in a mortal drama. Now, as I followed Miquel into the vestibule which smelled of yellow roses and floral clay—funeral parlor scents—I was forced to concede that nothing would ever be the same again.

But when he encouraged me to look up into the mirrors, I was terrified to comply.

"Don't be afraid," he told me. "Look—*look*, Stefan, and tell me what you see!"

The way he said it, I could not have refused him.

"The beauty of it is that it enhances whatever we are," he explained in a raw whisper. His lips bent into an impish smile, and with the arrogance of Rodin, he proclaimed in a louder voice, "With all due modesty, I have created a new masterpiece, Stefan!"

Forgive me, but I had to agree.

Shirtless and trembling, it was as if I had grown slightly taller and the muscles in my body had thickened just enough to make me athletic rather than bookish. The hair I'd always kept short now fell past my shoulders and had turned a richer shade of brown; and the face which had stared at me in mirrors for 34 years was no longer mine, but that of some ruffian twin who belonged in the slick pages of _GQ_. And the eyes... they were the dead giveaway that the creature who had once been Stefan London was now forever transfigured as if by some heavenly rapture acted out on the steps of Hell. Once a nondescript blue, the color had deepened to purple—a shade so brilliant the pupils appeared illumined. Animal eyes. Disturbing, yet disturbingly beautiful.

But more than this was the realization that I, too, seemed to glow from within, as if passing through death had imbued me with a lifeforce such as I'd never known before. Invisible to normal perceptions—for if I looked directly at my hand or Miquel's face, I could not discern this eerie illumination—it was a trait captured by mirrors alone, dispelling the myth that vampyres cast no reflection because they had lost their soul. Rather, the mirror _revealed_ the soul, the transformation having infused the human body with an inhuman effulgence.

Staring at this transmuted man, I smiled with nervous disbelief, seeing for the first time my strange new teeth. The little fangs glistened, sharp and alien inside my mouth; yet when I curled my lip into an unintentional snarl, I was struck with the thought that they were more honest than the dull, blunt teeth of mortals. Both were killers in their own right, humans and vampyres, but vampyres could admit they were predators while humans would try to disguise their nature with Sunday clothes and palliative psychotherapy.

Quite abruptly, I wanted nothing more to do with that life, for when I saw it for what it was, it was appalling to me. Humans were blind because they had deliberately plucked out their own eyes, choosing self-made gods and self-created delusions which they'd agreed to call Reality. Their minds were locked onto a single frequency of a vast cosmic radio, yet they'd been listening to the same song for so long that now they _couldn't_ change the station, couldn't even know there _were_ other options and infinite possibilities.

The entire world, it seemed, was nothing more than the lowest common denominator of all existence, the razor's edge between heaven and hell, _nothing_ in and of itself.

I didn't want to think such thoughts, but suddenly they were there—little apocalypses that came from nowhere and forced me to take a long and disturbing look at the world, at the man I had been and the thing I had become.

It's all chaos, a voice inside me whispered. *It's all just random chaos masquerading as social order.*

I must've made some sound of dismay at this unexpected revelation, for Miquel slipped an arm around my waist and led me to the great room, where he helped me to the sofa and sat down at my side.

"The transformation is like that," he said with compassion, running one hand up and down my arm. "It opens our eyes to deeper truths, but all too often we don't like the things we see. '

Embers in the fireplace glowed orange and black, jack-o'lantern eyes weeping tears of gray smoke that fell upward through the chimney. Candles blazed their silent vigil on the window sills, the scent of wax and wick oddly comforting despite the memories invoked by that burgundy couch where my mortal life had ended. When I realized where we were—full circle in so short a time—I fought the urge to jump up and run out into the night, a screaming vagabond.

On the one hand, I was confronting the understanding that my entire life had been a charade acted out on some trivial stage, but I was also beginning to see the macabre choreography behind the dark comedy. I was starting to catch glimpses of the strings attached to the arms and legs of every blind man and every blind woman who'd ever lived, yet try as I might, I could find no external force controlling those puppets, no gods or devils putting them through their paces.

They danced on wires entirely of their own making, running from home to office to church, and the fact that they had strung themselves up by choice when they could as easily have run free made me want to laugh and cry all at once.

That I saw it with such clarity is what devastated me most of all, for I was seeing myself as I'd once been. When I was a man, I had also chosen blindness and the security of strings. I had clung to the threads of responsibility, always doing what was right and wholesome because it was expected of me and for no other reason than that. I had been, quite simply, a machine fulfilling the program of another machine—society itself.

Now, as a vampyre, I made a vow to look at all the worlds—

the mortal world, the immortal world, and all the worlds in between—and to see things for what they were. Miquel and Dimitri were right: Mankind had lived in spiritual darkness and religious fear too long. I would reveal the truth. I would be the messenger between worlds, the long distance runner—

I was, of course, quite delirious to think such aggrandized thoughts, and so I let my mind wander to simpler things. Leaning forward with my head in my hands to stare at the Persian rug, all I could think was that this was where it had happened. This was where I had drawn my last breath as a human, my first breath as a vampyre.

The realization was such a tangible thing that I groaned at its enormous implications. Staring down the maw of eternity itself, I could almost envy mortals who wove their lines of hope and cast them up toward heaven in the name of faith. With them, they could fish for salvation and not care that the gods had all died or sunk to the bottom from sheer lack of interest. It was the fishing that soothed them, fruitless though it was.

Suddenly, I wanted to scream out to these frail creatures, telling them to claw their way out of the maze, to use that vast computer inside their heads to create their own evolution and their own resurrection, or at the very least look for it some place other than on the tube or the lips of the pope, who was, in the end, no different than the rest of them, just one more complacent, lost soul.

"Ah, but complacency is the human condition, and sadly necessary at that," I heard Miquel saying as if through a long tunnel. "For without the blindness from which you came, your new sight would mean nothing."

Perhaps no wiser words were ever spoken, yet I ignored them with all the idiocy I could muster, for I was far too busy feeling sorry for myself.

"And in self-pity, you risk driving yourself mad," he reminded me with a sigh.

Sensing a dangerous truth to his warning, I began staring at him instead, so intently that he gave a short, self-conscious laugh. "The answers aren't within me, but out there," he chastised, gesturing toward the window and the vast world beyond.

But the answers *were* in him. He was a mystical being, to be sure, yet he was more human than the automatons roaming the planet calling themselves men and women. He was alive and, more than that, he was aware of how fragile and precious life really is.

The sensation of his hand on my back was a sharp focus, and when he spoke it was as if I could follow his voice and climb inside him. I do not know where the urge came from, yet without volition, my consciousness snaked up his fingers and wound around his arm, and I was spiraling out of my own body and looking for a way inside his as if this were the most natural instinct in the world—the need to be *not-alone*. But just when it seemed I might be able to gain entry through his pierced ear or by sliding into the wounds my teeth had left on his throat the night before, he shoved me off the couch. I landed with such a *thud* that I was snapped to my senses and thrown back into my own body.

What surprised me was that it *hurt*.

He stood over me with his lip slightly curled, his eyes kaleidoscopes of hostility as he pointed an accusing finger in my direction.

"Don't *ever* do that, Stefan!" he warned, fury flying off of him in sparks only supernatural eyes could see. "You may play such tricks on mortals if you wish—stealing inside their bodies for a peek at the life you've left behind—but you must *never* attempt it with me, do you understand? *Never!*"

His anger was like a physical blow, so great I thought he might actually strike me. But as our eyes locked—he standing there in his rumpled tux and me on my knees—the rage suddenly left him to be replaced with compassion. Changeable as always, he knelt at my side, gathered his composure through a deep breath, then reached out to stroke my face.

"What a vampyre you shall one day be, Stefan," he marveled, seemingly to himself. "What a vampyre indeed."

"What?" I stammered. "What do you mean?"

He ignored my question, helping me off the floor and guiding me back to the sofa. This time, however, he went to a chair closer to the window and picked up a remote control from the coffee table. And though I thought it was his intention to watch television while I squirmed inside my new skin, he turned on the stereo instead.

It was a song I'd heard a thousand times, one of Stephanie's favorites. Something about never seeing the light. Something about vampyres and broken mirrors and blood stains on the bed. Perhaps she'd always known how her life would end. Perhaps we all do, to one extent or another.

Several minutes passed, and at least the music enabled my mind to focus. Now, instead of thinking ten thoughts at once, I could carry on a conversation without flying around the room or trying to climb inside Miquel's body.

"Better?" he asked.

"Yes—" *Sink-float-fly-thinkofblood.* "—better."

He shook his head with amusement. "All things considered, maybe it would be best for you to stay indoors tonight, Stefan."

"I'm hungry." I sounded like a spoiled child.

Seeming to understand my dilemma, he rose from his chair and came to my side. "We'll order in," he grinned, exotic eyes filled with devilment.

Giving my arm a reassuring squeeze, he moved to the window and stood with his back to me, resting his palms on the sill and gazing out at the darkness. Candlelight engulfed him, wrapping him in a golden aura that made up for the loss of the sun.

Miquel really did belong to the night.

And as he stood framed by the window—the royal portrait of the vampyre king surveying his kingdom—I knew he was a being of the underworld who had learned to enjoy his role in the scheme of things just as a banker or a truck driver or a minister enjoyed their standing in the mortal world. But while the mortal world would automatically despise Miquel for what he was, he had no such animosity toward them. Indeed, with his shields lowered, I could have sworn I heard his melancholy thoughts: *Neither day nor night can exist without the other, yet we are worlds apart and worlds asunder.*

Man created his own gods and demons, pitting them against one another by peopling heaven with angels and hell with vampyres. Worse still was the arrogant human notion that these divergent empires should be at constant war for possession of Man's soul when, in reality, immortals had very *little* concern for the human world at all.

Looking at Miquel, listening to his thoughts, I could not cast him in the role of monster *or* savior, god or devil.

His face was still water, so smooth it shone, the perfect

mirror into which mortals gazed as they gave up their blood to him. A compelling force surrounded him, and I could feel the presence of his will, a living entity which stood slightly taller and darker than his mere physical form. For a single moment, I beheld the black angel himself—the riddle, the power, and the seductive danger which were the very heart of the vampyre allure.

It was a musing both erotic and carnal. And though such thoughts might have troubled me once, the creature I was becoming could appreciate Miquel's beauty as easily as it could appreciate the beauty of a woman or the splendor of an extraordinary moonrise.

The music pounded louder, faster. The drumbeat heartbeat was consuming me until I was riding the waves kicked up by the lead guitar. In a bass rhythm, I bounced out the window and rolled across the front lawn—a sensation so real I could feel the cold, wet dew on my chest and smell the fresh green grass. In the percussion, I pounded my fist drums on the floor and throbbed against Miquel's feet through the house's very foundation.

I was lost, so when he turned and spoke, I couldn't understand a single word. Indeed, it was only when he focused those predatory eyes on me and willed me to listen that I was able to break the spell woven by the music. "If you don't stop that, you *will* die," he cautioned, his gaze turning black as the night itself.

"What's happening to me?" I asked, speaking the words that had been echoing in my head for hours. For the first time, I was genuinely afraid, for nothing was the same as it had been the day before—not my thoughts, not my beliefs, not even my body.

He came and sat at my side, taking my hand and pressing it between both of his own, compelling me with his will to listen. The control he exerted over me was oddly pleasing, even erotic.

"Sensualist," he pronounced, amused at my thoughts. But then he became serious as he squeezed my hand to the point of discomfort in an effort to hold my attention. "You're still changing, and for awhile yet you'll be all too vulnerable. If you go chasing after every thought that crosses your path, you could stray so far from your body you could become lost."

"Lost?" The word was ice blue and cut me like a blade.

He nodded gravely. "Now that you are a vampyre, the rules are different, you see. Though you are still an inhabitant of your body, you are no longer its prisoner. You can arpeggio over the grass to feel it tickling your soul, or pound on my feet through the floor because you think I don't recognize you in the drums. But if you lose touch with the physical shell entirely, your spirit will float away on the wind and I will be forced to destroy the empty vessel that remains." His expression turned merciless, taunting me as he smiled. "I wouldn't want to do that, you realize, for I *do* find the vessel almost as appealing as its contents."

I was sober in a hurry, not only out of embarrassment and an unexpected stirring awakened by his words, but because something warned me not to take the threat lightly. Miquel *could* kill me again, but this time it would be forever.

He gazed at me with an expression that might have been longing or loneliness or despair, then quickly looked away. And though I never would have admitted it, I was devastated when he stood up and returned to his vigil at the window, deliberately distancing himself from me.

"Soon you'll meet some of the others." His tone was lighthearted despite the bleak colors clinging to his aura, and I knew he was trying to distract me from the changes still going on inside my body. "Donny will come home to us soon, and Stygian will join us in a few days. By the time November comes, the Gathering will be well under way."

He had a hell of a way of changing the subject, but I knew it would do no good to protest. It occurred to me that it was late October already.

"The Gathering?" I repeated. Images of Stephanie tumbled off the shelf where I'd left them when I thought of Halloween, a little girl dashing through the night, begging for candy. I wept again, for a moment or two, for an eternity. There was no difference now.

Miquel turned to regard me, leaning against the window with his arms crossed over his chest. "You're part of my Family," he explained with a sense of genuine pride, "as precious to me as my own blood, for you *are* my blood now." He gave a tender smile, and had it not been for the fangs barely visible in his mouth, it would have been easy to mistake him for an ordinary man. "Mortal families live and die, Stefan, but your vampyre brothers and sisters will be with you always. The Gathering helps us remember that we alone are eternal."

88

Outside the window, a night bird was singing a song so lonely that I might have flown away on it, up to the rhinestone stars. Distantly, a horn honked. Storm clouds had commandeered the sky, stealing in from the west. Rain scratched at the window, seeking the company of vampyres.

I was conscious of Miquel speaking—a lengthy explanation about how his Family consisted of other vampyres he himself had made while a tribe or coven was comprised of members of several different families. The secrets he shared with me made me feel wanted, and that is what he desired for me—the beauty of being a vampyre and also the wonder. He wanted me to love what I had become just as he loved it, yet he also demanded I take responsibility for my new abilities, walking the razor's edge between life and death without cutting my feet.

All in one moment, I would see a larger-than-life figure looming over me like the black angel in the garden, but also a little boy—vulnerable and scared and feeling guilty for what he'd done to me the night before, for what he'd done to all of us who were brothers and sisters under his wings.

For though he really did love each one of us, he was keenly aware that we came to him only through death. To make us live forever, he first had to murder us with a kiss, and those were the memories I did not envy Miquel: killing his vampyre children and praying to an empty heaven for the strength to raise them up from the dead. Intuitively, I knew there were times he had failed. And I knew the toll it had taken on him.

But suddenly, the only thoughts in *my* mind were red thoughts. I looked at Miquel and felt real hunger and, consumed by an unfamiliar lust, I rose to my feet and moved toward him. The sensation of hunger became the act of hunting, and because he was the only person nearby, I staggered dizzily across the room us until I was looking up into his scruffy face.

I wanted.

I needed.

And I knew he felt my pain as our gazes locked and he reached out to steady me when my legs threatened to give way.

He quirked a grin, pure mischief. "Tell me, Stefan, what are you planning to do?" he asked, tilting his head until I saw the pulse in his neck, the slow, hard beat of him that kept rhythm with drums. He was teasing me, yet no matter how much I wanted it, I could not seize him to me and drink from him as I had done the night before.

"Because you are a vampyre now," he said in answer to my thought. "And though we do occasionally drink from one another, I assure you it isn't for nourishment, but to satisfy an entirely different kind of hunger."

Wanting to know everything at once, yet still too dazed to communicate properly, I blurted out the first thought that crept across my addled brain.

"*Can* we still make love, Miquel?" Perhaps I was still a human male after all, for *that* to be my primary concern among all the other questions in the universe I could have asked him.

He stood there looking at me for the longest time. Then, lips twitching, he shrugged one broad shoulder. "If you're referring to vampyres in general, perhaps the question shouldn't be whether or not we *can*, but why we would bother to get undressed for such a foolish bunch of grunting and straining." Looking me up and down, relentless in his torment, he added in a softer voice, "Of course, if you're asking from a more *personal* point of reference, the only way to be sure would be to make the attempt, no?"

My face heated. I looked away.

"Bastard," I called him, not for the first time. "You are a despicable bastard, Miquel!"

But the world was moving too quickly around me, sweeping me along through a stream of endless time.

On the stereo, Justin Hayward's glass-sharp voice cried out to _Nights in White Satin_. Casket satin, never-ending-night-love. The night that would go on forever was vampyre night, and I would be there to see the centuries pass. I would be a part of history itself, if nothing but a scribe.

It made my heart break and shatter.

It made me weep, more tears for the ages, for the nothing, for my own indulgence.

I would have deserved it had he made the decision to kill me then and there, for I was out of my mind and completely out of control as the full range of emotions whiplashed back and forth inside me. Intense compassion one minute. Overwhelming bloodthirst the next. And now tears of fantastical pain—the pain of knowing the stars were suns too far away to burn my immortal skin, the pain of hunger for spiritual knowledge and mystical answers, the pain only a vampyre could feel at knowing what an addictive drug pain itself could be.

I was pathetic.

"Pathetic," Miquel echoed, then reached out to brush my tears away, a gesture both suggestive and soothing. "But your thoughts will still after you've fed."

He looked toward the foyer and smiled darkly a split second *before* the doorbell rang. Then, placing his hands on my shoulders, he spoke with a gentle but deliberate tone of command.

"Though the act of feeding is intensely personal and best done in private, it will be easier if you allow me to help you these first few times."

Something inside me went completely calm while a new awareness was rising up from the dead. My senses sharpened. My mouth turned wet.

I heard a heartbeat neither mine nor his and smelled the molten metal scent of mortal blood.

CHAPTER EIGHT

There were no awkward introductions and no apologies. When the door opened to reveal a young woman standing under the portico, Miquel merely gathered her to him and pulled her inside.

The angels on the foyer wall covered their heads with downy wings. The roses turned their pale yellow faces away. The candles guttered.

I trembled, imagining what he would do to her.

Without knowing how I knew, I realized he had summoned her when he was standing at the window, and that she was a woman who lived nearby. Tonight, he had brought her to him as he'd brought her a hundred times before, and she had come without resistance for she had long ago yielded to his will.

Her name was Valerie Santana and she *was* pretty, with warm blonde hair and the healthy body of an athlete. Maybe 25, no more than 30, she wore only a t-shirt that fell almost to her knees, and dewdrops and grass blades which had collected on her bare feet.

And yet, despite her easy acquiescence to Miquel when he slid his arms around her and held her against his chest—clearly savoring her surrender as he would soon savor her blood—one look in her eyes told me she was a headstrong soul with a will of steel.

Miquel valued most those who fought him the hardest in the beginning, for he garnered as much satisfaction from the struggle as from the inevitable submission. It wasn't blind terror or even blind devotion he sought. Instead, it was that dangerously erotic fear which hit the solar plexus like a plane crash and could, under his control, bring mortals straight to their knees and straight to his bed.

Without a doubt, he had dined well on me, for now I could look back and understand that I'd wanted that first red kiss as much as I'd dreaded it. It had intrigued me as much as terrified me, and *that* was his diet of choice.

Son of a bitch.

As he led Valerie into the great room, I followed behind them in a daze. What amazed me most was that I could hear her heartbeat and through the very pores of her skin, I could smell her blood. She was, in that moment of my virgin starvation, the most wondrous creature I had ever seen, and because Miquel had stolen away her fears, she offered no resistance as he sat her down between us on the sofa.

And yet, it sickened me to realize I would destroy her because she *was* so unnaturally desirable to me. The hunger would drive me to it as it was driving me now. A demon alive inside me, it was an entity unto itself. It knew no compassion, no mercy.

It wanted her, and to get what it wanted it would kill.

But as my thoughts wailed with these things, Miquel regarded me with an admonishing frown. "You watch too many movies, Stefan," he declared. And his secret thoughts, known only to me, added, *I did not create you to be a killer. Any of us can kill, but only the best of us can not kill.*

Vampyres didn't need to take human life. And yet, as my body pressed against hers and my arm went around her, the instinct to sink my terrible new teeth into the soft throat and drink until there was nothing left of her was practically uncontrollable.

It hurt to want something so much.

"Valerie has come to offer you her blood, Stefan," Miquel told me, his stern voice a powerful focal point. "You must talk to her gently and entice the flow from her veins instead of calling it forth with violence, yes?"

I stared at him in a daze, caught up in the magic he was weaving on her mind because I wasn't yet strong enough to resist his trance, even when it wasn't intended for me.

Perhaps he understood my hesitation and wanted to show me the way, or perhaps he simply got tired of my awkward fumbling. Whatever the reason, he looked away from me and drew Valerie into his arms.

I know he was speaking to her, courting her as he'd courted me the night before. "Don't be afraid, my pretty Valerie," was one thing he said, and that more than once. "Just close your eyes and let me take you flying." Words to calm and seduce her into easy surrender. "Yes, like that, my love." And, mercilessly whispering, "You feel my heartbeat against your breast, no?"

Though I had believed her so deep under his magic that she could make no movement at all, her arms rose around his back with the passion of a lover; and when he eased his stubbly cheek to her throat—scraping his fangs over her neck, but not yet taking her— her jaw clenched in anticipation, raising the veins on her neck.

The abrupt realization of what I was seeing astounded me, leaving my hunger momentarily forgotten.

Not at all violent or in any way unnatural, it was a dance to them, well practiced. It was a seduction.

Valerie wasn't some dim-witted damsel-in-distress swooning under the powers of a monster. She certainly did not want to be rescued by any prince nor forgiven by any priest, for she was a willing sacrifice, in love with the raw power and the manifest allure of the vampyre who had bewitched her. It was Miquel's duty as a mystical creature to cast the spell and Valerie's obligation as a mortal to fall under it.

This was nature as *Nature* intended it—the age-old connection between human and vampyre—but acted out as it was meant to be, without Hollywood horror or Civilized Society to muddy the issues. It was perfect symbiosis, each species feeding the other with neither harmed and both benefited.

Mere sexual pleasure paled in comparison.

So when Miquel's breath quickened and Valerie crushed him to her, I could only look on with deepening arousal as he pushed her down onto that burgundy couch and shielded her beneath the weight of his preternatural body. Her head was in my lap, the heaviness of both of them on top of me. Valerie's mortal heat permeated me, causing my body to respond as it always had when I was a man. Her eyes smiled an invitation to me as my fingers tangled in her hair, and my thirst rose wild despite my vestigial human need to maintain some semblance of polite restraint.

Could I do this thing? Could I *not*?

Miquel's feral eyes encouraged me to act upon my need—*Do it, Stefan, just let go and do it*—yet he was so deep in the trance that even he seemed delirious as he bent his head and summoned the blood from her veins. Her body went taut, a cry of pain surging from her lips when his teeth cut into her and the stain of red came rushing over ivory throat.

So gentle it seemed. So, so easy the sinking of his fangs. So plaintive her tiny cries, so passionate the curling of her fingers.

At first, her discomfort was disturbing as I recalled the torment I'd experienced when he'd done this awful thing to me. But when the crimson drug poured over Miquel's mouth and he moaned with incorrigible satisfaction, I found myself looking at the play from the opposite side of the stage.

My vampyre heart fluttered. My soul went molten.

Then, as Miquel strengthened his hold and drew harder on her veins, she gave a whimper of protest—completely feigned, of course—and her eyes flashed open to meet my starving gaze. One hand tightened on my maker, fingers digging into his neck as she held him to her and encouraged him to feed. Her other hand flew up to grab my arm, her short nails cutting into me until I bled, too.

And suddenly I was flying with them, the sight of my own blood propelling me into the dance of madness. I have no memory of how the three of us came to be on the floor, a tangle of arms and legs, a symphony of scents and textures, a celebration of blood.

My first taste of it was like nothing I had known previously, far different from Miquel's blood because it was human still, laced with all the angst and obsessions that belonged to the mortal world. I could say it was warm and flavored with metals and salt, yet such explanations are inconsequential in comparison to the experience itself.

Perhaps the most accurate thing I could reveal was that it was like my first wet dream—hard and pounding and filled with satisfaction so primal the sheer force of it caused me to cry out. And just as a boy's first carnal dream symbolically propels him into manhood, my first drink of blood sent me reeling into another world: the underworld, the world of the night.

As my newly formed fangs cut into Valerie's throat— *effortless sinking, like swollen phallus into feminine mound*—the flow of her poured over my lips, a warm sea rising around me. I was aware of Miquel's embrace as we writhed together, and when I dared to open my eyes again, it was to find him looking at me while he fed on the other side of her neck.

Luminous emerald eyes glittered with amusement and, like a father, he tousled my hair to show his approval. Then, not at all like a father, he raised his head from the wound, leaning over to press his lips to mine as if we'd rehearsed it a thousand times. Too dazed to protest, I could only treat it as a lover's kiss, that wild dance of fitful tongues painted red with the mortal world and the cold steel passion of a vampyre's mouth.

My body thrashed, yet whenever I thought the sensations could go no further, whenever I believed I could fly no higher, the ceiling above me would split to reveal another level of heaven. I was weeping uncontrollably, but now for the beauty of humanity itself as I returned my mouth to this woman's neck and sank my teeth into the little holes again. She shrieked, riding the pain, nurturing it to grow.

In Valerie's blood lived summers at the beach with her family and winters at a ski lodge with college friends. The sno-cone from the circus when she was five left her lips blue, making her laugh. I knew the thrill of losing my virginity in a woman's body, the pinch and the pain of being taken by an older man who was both experienced and yet uncompromising.

I wanted to lose myself inside the fabric of her silk veins forever, living and reliving her life ten thousand times and more, for I had fallen in love with Valerie as I would fall in love with all mortals from whom I was destined to drink. But even as my sucking quickened and I greedily pulled her to me, I felt Miquel attempting to draw me away.

"Stop now, Stefan," he cautioned, an edge of mirth in his voice. "You've had more than enough for your first time, don't you think?"

I pushed him from me, shrugging away as I began to suckle harder and faster, as hungry for the memories Valerie could feed me as for the blood itself. Everything was new through her eyes, and I knew she was wanting me in return.

Don't stop, Stefan! Don't let him stop us! her junkie thoughts pleaded, craving the dangerous drug of her own bloodflow. She might die in the fall—and damn well she knew it—but the thrill of that terminal velocity would make the crash glorious.

It was as addictive for her as for me. She hungered for it— the pain of it and the elation. She climbed on it as if it were a trapeze. She flew.

A camping trip in the desert. Time to heal from the love blow dealt by a musician named Viper. Fuck the prick, he could rot in hell with that skinny little groupie and her silicon tits! All men were pigs, lacking only the curly tail to prove it.

She crawled inside the tent and sat there with the square whiskey bottle clenched between numb fingers as darkness fell around her. While the mountains would scare away intruders with midnight storms and arrows of lightning, the desert did it with wind that sounded like footsteps and phantom voices singing funeral songs in castrati soprano through the eerie rocks.

Dangerously drunk, she found it more amusing than frightening when one of the shadows dancing on the dome of the tent took on the shape of a man and crawled inside on his hands and knees. As she looked at Miquel in the moonlight, she knew the danger he presented was a threat to soul more than flesh, and since Viper had already torn her spirit from her body and ripped it asunder, there was really no danger at all. She had nothing to lose.

She drew a breath to speak, but he captured her in his arms and stilled her with a kiss fraught with controlling magic. She whimpered a little. And she fought a little (which she knew he wanted her to do because it thrilled him). But the truth was that she was whimpering with desire and fighting only because she'd seen it in the movies that one was supposed to protest when caught in a vampyre's embrace.

She knew what Miquel was—for he was enough of a gentleman that he wanted her to know the truth. And she knew what he would do— for he was enough of a scoundrel that he wanted her to know that, too.

So when he lowered his lips to her throat and his teeth cut into her, Valerie's greatest surprise came not from the pain of his bite, but from her own reaction. Her arms flew around him as if he were an old lover, and she tore at his clothes with the willful intent of making it so.

Within moments their bodies were fused, his teeth buried in her throat, his hands tangled in her hair, his manhood nestled inside her with a suddenness that propelled them both into a world of sensual—

Destruction!

A voice cried out, and only in retrospect did I realize the sound sprang from my own lips. I hurled myself away from Valerie a split second before her heart would have spasmed into real death. My own body clenched, trying to reject my very soul as I choked on blood wet with things I should never have known.

Throughout the centuries, mystics have said death and sex are closely related, and as I suckled those carnal images from her, I understood how true the analogy really was. Now I knew what bound her to Miquel as his willing blood lover: the threat of a sensual death, the promise of deadly sex, the hope that he would one day bring her into the night forever.

The razor's edge between one world and another.

Oh, God, how I envy you! I thought deliriously, looking down into her face.

But as Valerie stared up at me and the trance began to weaken, I saw the tears in her eyes, the regret which came from knowing that tonight wasn't the night when her life would end in Miquel's arms and begin there anew as a vampyre. She wanted it all—the mortal thrill, the immortal ride, the one thing Miquel had no intention of giving her: eternity itself.

"Not as much as I envy you," she said, weak from loss of blood and loss of faith.

I blanched and I squirmed, trying to forget the things I'd seen in her heart. Yet the memories were grown wild and dangerously spiced in a way that would always draw me back to feed. I was a junkie now, too, hooked on blood and mortal memories—*holographic-3D-reckless-virtual-reality-replay-replay-replay.*

It could just as easily have been me underneath Miquel in that tent. It *was* me, for I knew what he'd said to her, how he held her when he made love to her, the feel of his vampyre body. Not wanting to know any of it, I knew it all, and it came perilously close to destroying me as I looked up into the predator's eyes.

"You son of a bitch!" I snarled, knowing he could hear my thoughts, hoping he would listen. My heart soared for Valerie's beauty and her blood. My heart broke, for she was far better suited to eternity than I.

Miquel lay propped on one elbow, watching me with a lazy expression. "I warned you to stop."

My chest spasmed—horror and hatred and love and loathing—and not a single marker to delineate one from the other.

Desperate with the need to regain control over my life, not knowing what else to do, I impulsively brought my wrist to my mouth and bit down until the sharp fangs sent blood pouring down my arm. A terrible whimpering came from my own lips to fill the room as I grabbed Valerie to me, struggling to feed her as Miquel had fed me the night before.

'Live!', my mind screamed out to her. 'Live forever so I can love you forever!'

She pressed her lips hard to the wound, as needful for immortality as I was desperate to bestow it to her, but before she could even begin to drink, Miquel lifted her away as if she were no more than a handful of dust. Once again controlling her until she was a lifeless doll, he stood looking down at me with an expression I could only define as disappointment.

"Luckily you're not a Creator," he said softly. "If you were, if every lovesick fledgling could make others like us, it wouldn't be long before the world was full of lovesick fledglings."

"You *owe* her!" I snapped, baring my fangs in a purely animalistic gesture.

My outburst surprised him. He lay Valerie down on the sofa, took a step toward me. "It's different for you now, Stefan," he said, holding out his hands in an effort to make amends. "And while it's true you'll love every mortal you encounter simply because they *are* mortal, you must try to see that the life I've given you carries far more responsibility than anything you've known before."

He was arrogant. He was self-righteous.

And, worst of all, he was right. I didn't want to believe it, yet I saw the truth in the air between us, a tangible intangible which gave me another glimpse of the thing I'd become. Mortals were little more than food. They would live and they would die and that was that. The *real* philosophers and the real artists were the vampyres. Miquel was Goethe. He was Machiavelli. Nostradamus.

He was art and he was history. He and others like him. Others like *me*.

But he shook his head with a sad sigh. "You misunderstand me, Stefan. Yes, we have a responsibility to our own kind, but also to *them*," he stressed, indicating his rag doll love with an expression that would have broken a human heart. "Perhaps we are the artists and the philosophers, but where is our inspiration if not within *them*?"

I couldn't bear to look at him just then, for he was a house-of-horrors mirror showing me my own future. Worse, I couldn't bear to have *him* look at *me*, so I jumped up off the floor, dizzy and blood-drunk, and fled into the lush grounds beyond the house.

The night was thick, damp, still as a crypt. The black angel watched, marble feathers trembling in cold October wind.

There in my Creator's garden, crazy for this woman I did not know yet loved more than my own life, I talked incessantly to lifeless statues with hollow eyes and thought erratic thoughts. *Is Aunt Carolyn pushing up daisies this year or did they plant tea roses over her head for a change? Does it alter the balance of nature when the dead are planted in boxes and the worms can't suck their bones clean? What is a fetus but a sucker of blood, attached to Mother Earth's womb? Where do the stars hide during the day? Matches are comets in a box, waiting to bloom. Oh where oh where has my sanity gone? Oh where oh where can it be?*

I giggled and danced with my shadow for a time before sliding to the ground against the stone wall at the edge of the garden. Miquel had stolen my mind when he stole my life. And though it occurred to me to bolt into the street and run, I understood more than ever how true the words of the poet really were. *'You can never go home again'.*

The choice was made. Forever. And ever. And for ever.

I was a vampyre now, and there could be no going back to the man I'd been before.

Rain hibernated overhead, sleeping in thick black clouds. The darkness was cold and alien on my skin and a large grass spider skittered over my hand. I looked toward the house, hoping Miquel would come looking for me, cursing myself for the needy thought.

With the taste of Valerie's blood still sweet in my mouth, I cried myself to sleep, fervently praying the sun would find me there.

CHAPTER NINE

"If I thought you really wanted to die, I'd be disappointed," Miquel said, leaning against the wall next to me. Bejeweled fingers tangled in the grass, and my impression was that he'd been there for quite some time. His long legs splayed to the sides like stilts akimbo, feet bare and wet with dew, disheveled hair falling in his whirligig eyes.

For that one moment, when a cicada was singing and the scent of jasmine hung heavy in the air and the statues were looking down on us with tears from the sprinklers in their eyes, Miquel wasn't some larger-than-life myth or a miscreant night Christ looking for souls to possess.

Flesh and blood, a tall figure in a wrinkled tux with the tie dangling limp and the sleeves pushed up, he struck me as a little boy playing dress up in his father's old clothes.

Vampyre, my thoughts whispered, trying to believe it, trying not to. *Immortal vampyre...*

I stared at him, listening to the silence that had fallen like the empty space between individual seconds. None of it was real. How could it be?

"Ah, but define reality, Stefan," Miquel challenged, bringing into words the very nature of my thoughts. "What is it that makes the rain and the song of the cricket real, yet tells you vampyres can't exist?"

Scattered stars peered through pauses in the storm, campfires on the shores of heaven set ablaze by lost souls denied entrance to paradise.

"Why won't you change her?" I asked, ignoring his philosophical questioning and bringing it down to something entirely selfish. "If you really believe mortals are our muses, why won't you change her?"

It took him awhile to answer. "Valerie has nothing to offer to

100

this life, Stefan—nothing to bring to the gene pool but a towel from the gym. Beauty isn't enough, nor is intellect alone. And worse, my friend, immortality has nothing to offer her aside from a continuation of her *mortal* life—no growth, nothing *more* than an extension of what she already is. Eternal stagnation, if you will."

Unconvinced, I scoffed. "Isn't that all any of us want—just to go on living? Who are you to make that kind of judgment?"

Looking up at the clouds, Miquel breathed softly. "To survive as a vampyre, you must be willful, shrewd, and a bit insane to begin with. You must be capable of evolving into something *more* than a long-lived human, and since your blood will eventually mingle with that of every vampyre everywhere, you must bring something from your mortal life to enrich the whole of us—a song, a debate, a book or two, or at least a strong point of view— something that transcends time. Valerie loves life, but she doesn't have the stamina for an eternal battle with death. That alone disqualifies her."

The fact that the sadness in his voice was genuine didn't excuse him his callousness.

"Bastard," I repeated, drawing in on myself and slamming that telepathic door in his face again.

"You can't understand it yet," he said without anger. "You can't understand in a single night what it's taken me twelve hundred years to learn, but we're elitists by necessity. If I were to transform every mortal who wanted to live forever, the world would belong exclusively to vampyres—mostly ignorant, complacent ones who would be as terrified of an original thought as Neanderthal Man was terrified of fire—and where would we be then? No," he concluded, shaking his head with a breath of resignation, "to be a vampyre you must first be more than the sum of your *human* parts."

"*Arrogant* bastard," I amended miserably, running my tongue over the sharp points of my fangs. It was a sensual feeling I indulged repeatedly while waiting for him to kill me all over again.

But my insolence didn't bother him in the least. He just sat there against the wall, entirely unconcerned when the sprinklers brought a spray of mist to settle on his hair like tiny fallen stars. A long while passed, maybe an hour, maybe more. Vampyres had time to kill, and a single conversation might last for months, even

101

years.

And so I waited, stubborn and brooding. But when it became obvious that Miquel was far more skilled at the game than I, I heard myself muttering, "I want her. I want her to live forever, goddammit!"

Finally, with some amount of compassion, Miquel looked me up and down as if coming to some dark decision. "I will make you a promise, Stefan."

"A promise?" I asked, bitter and suspicious but also foolishly hopeful.

He studied me as if trying to decide whether or not I was ready to hear it. Then, in a tone that told me he was genuinely trying to lift my spirits, he said, "If you come upon a mortal who moves your soul and mesmerizes you with their very presence, I will bring them into my blood and give them to you as a companion—."

My head jerked up as if I were a silly schoolboy, but he motioned me to silence before I could tell him I wanted Valerie to be that companion and I wanted her right *now*.

"—*if*," he continued sternly, "you still feel the same obsession five years down the road."

My heart sank.

"You're thinking like a mortal," he said, trying to assuage me with a smile. "To a vampyre, five years is but a couplet in the collected works of Shakespeare. Try to understand, Stefan, it isn't Valerie who's bewitched you. It's her blood. You're smitten with the life she's led, not with the soul behind her eyes."

My wrist smarted where I'd bitten it, my spirit shattered because I truly was powerless. I could only glower at him and wail with desperation, "But don't you *love* her?"

Now he turned to look at me. "Ah, yes—love," he murmured as if altogether disillusioned. "Believe me, you're better off without it."

"What do you mean?" I snapped.

He went back to gazing at the clouds. A few fat drops of rain began plopping around us. One splashed over his cheek. Another landed on his nose. If he noticed, he never let on.

"More wrists have been slashed in the name of love than for any other reason, Stefan," he murmured, his tone so lonely and desolate it could have broken the stone hearts of the statues standing nearby. "Mortals live for love and die for love, but what is it, really? Can you hold it in your hand? Can you place it on the mantle amongst your other mementos?" He scoffed and locked away, full of acid.

With eternity stretched out in front of him, perhaps he had reason to be despondent if he didn't believe in love. But then it struck me that perhaps he *couldn't* love. Perhaps none of our kind could love.

My stomach knotted.

"Not to worry, my friend," he said in response to my horrified thought. "I haven't robbed you of your ability to love, though when a few centuries have gone by, you may wish I had, for the problem with vampyres is that we love too deeply, and when we lose the thing we love, it destroys us all over again."

Once more, he fastened me with those magical eyes. "I've died a hundred times, Stefan—each and every one of them for love—and the hell of it is that I'm still alive, and this virus you call love always manages to infect me again whenever I believe myself finally cured."

As much as he could be philosophical or seductive, he could also be lachrymose and filled with despair. He could weep as easily as he could laugh, and when I allowed my own stubborn shields to lower, I knew he was weeping inside at that very moment. He was weeping for love. For its beauty. For its intangible brightness. For its sting that was fatal to the soul yet mercilessly left the body alive.

Without ever shedding a tear, he was weeping for all his mortal loves lost to death and for those not yet born. He was weeping because he didn't love Valerie enough and because he loved Dimitri so much it scared him, and because he'd made the young servant, Donny, against his will, but he'd made him in the name of love because love itself had driven him to an act of madness.

But most of all, Miquel was weeping because he really did love *me*, and because my anger was every bit as tangible to him as any physical attack. Being a vampyre, he needed me to need him. Being a Creator, he needed love more than any other creature on Earth.

It was a feeling I knew all too well from being a father, but I didn't want him to love me. As he'd already pointed out, love was a virus, highly contagious, and my immune system was shot.

I cringed, hugging my arms to my bare chest, shivering. The rain came faster, angel tears in free-fall burnished gold by the tiny lights ringing the driveway.

"You ungodly bastard," I said one last time.

It was all crashing down around me—the reality of it, the horror of it, the taste of it still in my mouth. There was no going back, no undoing the spell, and now my executioner was killing my soul with love just as he'd killed my body with a kiss. I couldn't look at him as I cried out, "I despise you! God in heaven, how I *despise* you, Miquel!"

After a brief but unendurable silence, he reached out and rested his hand on top of mine.

"The sun will be up soon," he said, ignoring my outburst as he twined his fingers through mine and rose gracefully to his feet, an imposing silhouette against a grim sky. "You'll feel stronger after you've slept."

I didn't move, just sat there on the ground while he tugged at my arm in an effort to get me up. A covert glance at the horizon made me irrationally angry. Someone had cracked the obsidian egg of the night and light was leaking in at the fracture. It caused me to wince, made me grieve for darkness lost.

"There will be other nights—an eternity of them like a banquet table spread with stars," Miquel promised, his hand steady in mine.

His words comforted me. And because the sky was brightening, my body rose on instinct and I made no effort to untangle my fingers from his as we walked back toward the house. I don't recall when I stopped weeping, nor do I really know why I was carrying on at all. It just seemed natural—a further shedding of my mortal thoughts in the form of scarlet tears.

As we passed through the courtyard where the black angel stood watch, I pulled away from my Creator, stuffing my hands into the pockets of my jeans. The house stood open in silent invitation, yet I stopped beneath the portico, looking toward the silver varnished horizon as if the dawn might save me somehow. But I found no comfort, and the light stung my eyes to punish me for my sins.

"Stefan?" Miquel said quietly, standing at my back, waiting.

The storm was growing, clouds gathering, rain scraping across a slate gray sky like static on an old tv.

"I don't want to sleep with you," I muttered, wanting to hurt him.

Miquel only patted me on the back. Then, leaning so close I could feel his breath on my neck, he whispered, "I don't recall asking you to."

Without waiting to see if I would follow, he disappeared into the house, where the fireplace had gone dark and the candles had burned away and the shadows had convened like disciples waiting for his return.

My heart broke all over again.

*

After Miquel left me there with only my fatally injured pride, I came inside and wandered around until I found what appeared to be a guest room. Sparsely furnished, with only a double bed, dresser and desk, it was tucked away behind the staircase and seemed a reasonable place to lick my wounds. I lay on top of the thick green comforter, staring at the ceiling fan contrasted against a dark, wood-beamed ceiling. The *whop-whop-whop* of stark white blades stirred the damp air, mixing some magical anesthesia, but though the potion left me tired, I was unable to sleep.

The huge house was still, a sanctuary but also a tomb. Occasionally, the floorboards creaked above my head, yet I could think of no good excuse to go looking for Miquel. For awhile, I thought of Valerie, wondering when she'd left, trying to imagine her day-to-day life, knowing I might never see her again.

And yet, as if giving credence to Miquel's contention that she was only an infatuation, she was already fading from my thoughts. Had her hair been auburn or blonde? Were her eyes green? Blue? I couldn't recall anything but the taste of her blood and the addiction of her memories, and for that I didn't like myself.

Frustrated that sleep wouldn't come, I got up and began pacing until my restlessness led me into the hall. Because the sun had been up for more than an hour—concealed by the shutters which automatically lowered at dawn—my strength was gone. And yet, like a child testing its limits, I crept to the kitchen and cracked open the door. And even though the muted sunlight playing on a rain-dappled lawn neither burned me to a crisp nor blinded me for all eternity, it did fill me with a tremendous despair.

In the light of day, the black angel was just a statue, and the other plaster souls in the garden seemed far too stark and gray. Colors blended to enhance the evening couldn't translate to a morning canvas, for the night was dead now, slain to reveal flaws mercifully hidden in the dark. The sun exposed all the wrinkles and resignation in mortal faces, and now the play was in full swing with its honking horns and its joggers on the street and its sharp-edged dayshine stage where so many things seemed to matter so much.

I could look for only a moment before the intense spiritual pain forced me to shut the door.

Surely, this wasn't what Man was meant to be—compartmentalizing his life into office hours and lunch hours and coffee breaks and PTA meetings and sex with the spouse penciled in for 11 o'clock Thursday night if both parties agreed in writing and neither had an early meeting the next morning.

There was no time just to *be*, no time to let life happen because they were so busy *planning* their lives. In the rush-rush-run-point-click world of the brave new world, Man's soul was the last thing on his mind, and if he ever wanted it saved, he'd download a self-help book with a 12-step program from some would-be guru on eBay.

That was life.

And though it saddened me deeply—the ragged edges of the sun that cut the night in two—I made my way back to that lonely room beneath the stairs, tumbled into the bed with the pillow clutched to my chest, and slept the sleep of the dead.

CHAPTER TEN

Donny couldn't recall how long he'd lain in bed, waiting for death as if it were an old friend. Strong, the doctors labeled him when he'd still had doctors, when he'd still had insurance.

HIV. AIDS. The Plague. Whatever they were calling it this week, it sucked. At 19, he'd contracted it from a needle at the hospital where he worked, yet before he reached 21, he'd be in his grave, a dead virgin pushing up wildflowers that were illegal to pick. It was so goddamn pathetic it made him want to puke. Or maybe that was the drugs.

So when he'd looked up the night before to see Miquel standing over his bed, all he could do was laugh at the irony. Then cry. Then blither incoherently. That was the worst thing: the dementia.

He didn't want to die and he didn't want Miquel to see him like this, but that created a paradox, for he <u>had</u> prayed to die before his mysterious friend came back to visit him again. He'd hoped the older man might grieve a little, maybe put flowers on his grave. He'd lived the last few months with the fear that the handsome lunatic had contracted the disease through their mutual fetish for bloodletting, but he'd had no way of contacting him to find out. That was Miquel's way: no phone numbers, no commitments, no strings.

It had been that way since they met. It had been that way last night, too. What had they talked about when Miquel came stealing through the door of the run-down apartment as easily as a minor theme stole through a song? He was shocked to find Donny so close to death, that much he remembered.

> Shocked to the pale,
> shadow man behind the mourning veil.
> Where does he go when he ain't around?
> Other lovers, fresh blood, small towns.

Donny wouldn't live long enough to write the lyrics. Still, he found it amusing that Miquel had finally confessed the secret he'd been concealing for more than two years, the secret which explained why he'd never asked for sex, but only a little drink of blood now and again.

Miquel was a vampyre.

That was good for a laugh, though the laughter brought a spasm of coughing that left Donny weak when it finally subsided.

Vampyre says the light in his eyes
is just my funeral pyre
burnin' my soul to Hell
while I'm still alive, barely alive...

"If you want to live, the only way to do it now is to live forever,"
Miquel had told him, grim and sullen as he picked up the bottle of AZT
and turned it over in his hand. He rambled about how he shouldn't make
the offer, how it was a decision to be made in sound body and mind, that
anybody would do anything to escape death when they were staring it in
the face. Then his voice had softened. His eyes had gone tender, and though
it had to be just another hallucination, Donny could have sworn he saw red
tears splash over long black lashes when Miquel said something about
breaking all the rules and tearing the scythe out of the reaper's hand one
more time.

He hadn't understood all the words, for they weren't the usual
prattle he was used to hearing: "You can beat this disease, kid." "God
moves in mysterious ways." "I'm sorry, so sorry, so sorry..."

Well, Miquel certainly didn't say he was sorry. Instead, he'd
paraded around the room, a wild animal swearing at God and railing at
death as if it were some intimate personal rival. Miquel insisted death was
fatal to body and soul, assured him there was no heaven and no hell, and
gave him 24 hours to make a decision: live forever or die to oblivion,
nothing in between.

Now the 24 hours were up, the clock chewing up passing time like
lost souls in its tick tock teeth.

When the apartment door opened to let in a crack of light from the
hall, Donny rolled to his side, clenched his eyes tightly shut against the
image of Miquel in a pale ruffled shirt, and made his decision.

"No more games. Just go away and let me die in peace."

Taking a deep breath, hoping it would be his last, he tried not to
imagine what the volunteer from Mama's Kitchen would think when she
found his body stiff and cold in the morning.

But death didn't come. Instead, the weight of another man settled
on the bed when the well dressed fiend crawled underneath the sheets,
taking Donny in his arms from behind, rocking him and cradling him and
whispering, "Ssshh. Ssshh, little one."

For a few moments, it was like old times. Donny curled into the
spoon-fashion hold, craving the keen edge of the bite that would loose his
blood into the other man's mouth. But the arms that held him were gentle

now, and the perfect, precious pain didn't come.

"No, I won't hurt you this time," Miquel said, responding to a thought Donny didn't recall speaking out loud. "The world has given you enough pain, so just relax and we'll do what we've always done together, only this time I won't stop. I'll put you to sleep with a kiss, and when you wake you'll be well again forever, sweet baby... forever."

Despite how cruel this game was—for Donny knew he wouldn't be getting better ever again—he smiled a little and closed his eyes. Snuggling deeper into Miquel's arms, foolishly hoping to hide from death there, he listened to a nonsensical song from childhood rattling through his fevered mind.

'Girls, squirrels, witches fly!' He whispered the rest aloud: "If you kiss me will I die?"

Miquel held him with real affection, muscular chest rising and falling. Donny couldn't remember how long it had been since anyone had embraced him like that, and the solace of human compassion was far more addictive than any drug.

"You're already dying, my love," Miquel said, though his words didn't seem cruel. Resting his chin on Donny's shoulder until his breath became a soft wind, he added, "But if we take your life my way instead of God's, I promise you it won't hurt—at least not very much, nor for very long."

Donny didn't believe a word of it, but because he <u>wanted</u> to believe he had a chance to live, he let himself play in the fantasy as time wove itself around them for an hour or two.

He dozed—safe, warm. Miquel's cologne smelled of better times and the rustling of his shirt as his hands stroked up and down Donny's body was a lullaby of finest silk. Cool lips kissed at his shoulder, and the lean shape pressed hard against his back was relaxed and calm even when the familiar fangs raked suggestively over his neck.

So many times before they'd done this odd dance. So many seductions that ended in the kinky bloodletting. Donny's hands clenched on the sheets, his breath coming quicker, his illness blessedly forgotten for a brief time. His body even hardened, and he wondered as he always wondered now that his life was so near to its end: Will this be the last time I feel this way? Will this be the last time another person touches me? Will this be my last night on Earth?

He didn't <u>really</u> believe Miquel would do it—not this time, not when The Plague was a living entity in the room, a stench of pills and puke, despair and impending death. So when the sharp teeth cut deep into his neck, the shock of it launched him to instantaneous awareness. His heart seized and, wrestling around with the last of his strength, the breath caught in his throat, causing him to gasp.

A crimson blush stained Miquel's full, dark lips, damning in its implications, for no more efficient serial killer had ever existed than the virus in Donny's blood. And now, while he himself could be no more than a few hours from death, it had found another victim to infect, another soul to steal.

"Are you out of your mind?" he wailed, scrambling away until his shoulders were pressed into the dirty wall. Lashing out, he tried to shove the other man away, a feeble effort. "For the love of God, what have you done?"

But Miquel didn't budge, eyes feral and frightening. "I have no great love of God, my friend, for look what He's done to you." His voice was full of secrets, peril. He held his arms open, an invitation that was really a command. "Come to me, Donny. I know you can't really understand what's about to happen to you, but if you can trust me, your submission will make this easier for both of us."

What terrified Donny was how much he wanted to crawl into those outstretched arms as he'd always done, how much he longed to give up his blood to this crazy fiend who liked to think himself some creature of fable and folklore.

"Don't you understand?" he wept, sickened and horrified by the sight of his blood on the other man's mouth. "Goddamn you! God-fucking-damn you, Miquel! This isn't a game anymore! I have AIDS!"

Miquel only smiled that wicked, sinful smile which had first brought Donny to his knees. "Don't _you_ understand, my baby? _I_ am the cure."

The rest was a haze. Miquel took him as easily as some ruthless bird of prey might drop from the sky to take a helpless mouse. Donny heard himself screaming and prayed someone would call the police, but even if anyone cared what was wrong with the faggot in 14-B, he realized in retrospect that the screams were only in his mind, never reaching his lips.

With Miquel holding him fierce and tight, he was forced down into the bed and held there, looking up into the emerald eyes of his destiny. He didn't _really_ want to die, but he was dead either way. Whether Miquel did it to him now or the disease took him in another day or two, he was dead dead dead and it didn't make sense to be born only to die when he still had songs to carve out of the background noise like a sculptor finding his art hidden inside the marble.

110

From that very din, he was keenly aware of the other trying to calm him as he flailed and kicked and wept like an infant.

"No, no, baby, not like this. You've never been afraid of me before, so don't be afraid now," Miquel soothed. "Just be still and stop fighting and let me have you without all this fuss. Ssshh. Yes. Ssshh. It won't be so terrible if you close your eyes—a little pinch of pain, a moment of sleep, that's all. And when it's over you'll never be sick again and we'll be together in a world death doesn't know. I promise you these things. I promise."

But because so many people had lied to him about so many things, Donny no longer believed anything. He _hadn't_ gotten better and they _hadn't_ found the cure and his friends _were_ all dead or dying and none of it made one goddamn lick of sense, least of all the notion that Miquel was some guardian vampyre angel come to give him back his life.

He opened his mouth to cry out, but before a sound broke from his lungs, Miquel's hand was pressed hard over his lips. Already winded, his chest heaved, kaleidoscope worlds spinning upside-down and wrongsideout. Angels sang in his ear, some old Beatles song.

Panic pressed close, for this was no game. And when Donny felt the second deadly sting of Miquel's fangs—sharp and hard as early winter—he was already on the verge of unconsciousness.

Though Miquel had drunk from him in the past, it had never been like this, with a pull so strong it threatened to yank the soul right out of his body. The tug of the lifeforce through his veins. The drawing. The hurt. The perfect, perfect hurt.

But also the horror and the dread, death's companions. "Let go," a skull face told him, grinning. "Let go," the reaper repeated.

But he couldn't. Not yet. Not without one last battle, one last scream to leave behind, an echo through concrete canyons and crumbling buildings. He hadn't had enough time. Not enough time to etch his mark on the planet, not enough time to scribble out graffiti lyrics to tell the world he had been here.

His head spun, heart skittering, and though he'd believed himself too frail to offer any resistance, a surge of strength that came from nowhere propelled him out of Miquel's arms and sent him staggering wildly across the room. Disoriented, he impacted with the dresser, collapsing over the dusty wooden surface to send personal mementos and pill bottles clattering to the dirty floor.

And though he didn't want to look, a cold dread lured Donny's gaze toward the dull mirror above the dresser. His t-shirt and briefs were soaked through, wet rags clinging to his body. The laceration on his throat lay open and welling, a scarlet river overflowing its mortal banks.

Unlike the tiny punctures Miquel had inflicted on him in the past, now the jugular vein was severed as if by a scalpel, and some stray bit of trivia told him he had less than five minutes before he would bleed out. Whimpering with denial that swelled from deep in his chest, he pressed his hand over the wound in a hopeless effort to stop the torrential flood.

It was silly, of course, like trying to staunch a dam break with duct tape. The floor was slick at his feet. The bed, once white, had turned red.

In slow motion, Miquel moved toward him, and Donny knew then his life was truly finished. Even if he made it to the phone, help would never arrive in time. Going cold inside, he dropped to his knees from acute blood loss quickened by the pounding of his heart.

And then the vampyre was on him again, arms closing around him and lifting him back onto the blood-soaked bed in an embrace that was unforgivably loving and tender. Miquel's weight came down on top of him, the cold steel hands pinning his wrists to the mattress.

It was over.

Their eyes locked. Donny began to pray, asking God to forgive him his sins and promising that he in turn would forgive God for the sin of AIDS. Still, all things considered, he figured _he_ was granting the larger pardon.

But he was still scared—scared because he _didn't_ believe in anything other than the breath in his lungs. He _couldn't_ believe, not when it came down to this and he could look beyond the horizon of his death and see only a barren horizon with no heaven or hell beyond.

The only meaning of life was that life itself was all there was.

"I—please—I don't want to die!" he tried to say, but the words came out as a whispered gurgling, an unintelligible death rattle.

But because Miquel could hear his thoughts and he truly was more merciful than God, Donny felt himself drawn into the sanctuary of a trance that chased away his terror. As if drugged, his body went limp with surrender, and for the first time in months there was no pain, no fear, just a strangely beautiful clarity.

He stood apart from himself, watching as the vampyre kissed his cheek, cool tongue following the path of tears to the crimson fountain flowing at his throat. Miquel licked at the radiant river, savoring it slowly, then placed his mouth over the well and began to drink with a pull so fierce Donny whimpered.

The vampyre's body trembled, and as the light began to dim and

112

the sound of traffic receded, Donny closed his eyes and let his world end. His body quivered, a ruined temple possessed by the devil, and now the unrelenting fangs sank again into the fatal wound. The shock was so ruthless it caused him to arch up off the bed as the throes of death and pleasure coalesced into a single entity. He climaxed—hard, fast, deep—and dying was all he'd ever dreamed it might be.

> Sex is just the blood of death
> and Death himself is bleeding to death
> on the breath of city wind
> stained with the drug of lunatic love.

Miquel's suckling quickened, and now Hendrix and Holly and Morrison and Lennon were jamming in his head while Kurt Cobain wailed out lost boy lyrics scripted in dust and blood. The only real thing was Miquel: savior, destroyer, leader of the all-night band of dead minstrels.

The strange thing was feeling the vampyre's body grow warmer while his own grew colder. Stranger still was floating up to the ceiling and looking down on this act of brutal kindness transpiring on a warm bed damp with red rain.

He wept.

"I love you, Miquel," his soul said, and the secret traveled to his dying lips of their own accord. "I always have."

They were the words that would raise him from the dead, the reason he needed to live again on the far side of oblivion.

They were also the last words Donald Anthony Carrera spoke as a mortal, for when Miquel suckled their sweetness into his heart, he sank his teeth deeper into the failing flesh, lifted the ragbaby into his arms, and drained the well until the pump failed.

*

I woke with a shudder, disoriented and dizzy. Dawn had come—meaning that night had fallen—and in my flip-flop world, the purple sky beyond the open window tricked me into believing it was sunrise rather than sunset.

Oddly, though I'd never remembered my dreams much as a mortal, I'd had maybe a dozen different dreams—walking long dark streets in the rain, flying in a body lighter than air, a haunting series of erotic nightmares wherein I relived my death in Miquel's arms and my rebirth as a vampyre. I hadn't dreamt it once during my rest, but four times at least, and each time it had roused me with a jolt only to dump me into a deeper sleep before I could fully awaken.

And as if that weren't enough, now I was dreaming the servant's dreams, too.

Fighting my way back to awareness, I pushed myself up until my bare back was pressed against the cool oak headboard and my eyes were fixed on the opposite wall. Like the rest of the house, the room was papered in muted colors—faded yellow roses with falling petals and stems twined through tall dried grass. Autumn lived in this room underneath the stairs, slept here while waiting for the other seasons to pass.

The only personal decoration was a poster above the dresser. A surreal black and white photograph, it depicted five young men with wind-blown hair standing on a high mesa. Their attention was riveted to the only color in the piece: a brilliant red stone lying on the sun-parched ground at their feet. Superimposed over the bottom of the poster in graffiti style letters dripping with blood: **RED ROCK**.

Only on closer inspection did I recognize one of the young men as Donny. Red Rock, I assumed, was the name of the band he'd led.

A chilly wind crept through the window, lifting the sheer white curtains and stirring the chimes in the garden. For the first time since my ordeal began, I didn't feel fear or dread or even anxiety. As if it were still natural, I yawned broadly, stretched the muscles in my arms and shoulders until my upper body trembled, then clasped my fingers behind my head while registering the fact that I was thirsty.

But it wasn't coffee I was craving. And though the thought distressed me deeply, memories of drinking from Valerie awakened another response that had always been a traditional morning occurrence. The difference was that now, with my vampyre skin more sensitive and alive than my mortal flesh had ever been, the arousal I experienced was as acute as if I were 17 again.

My hand fell compulsively into my lap, my fingers dallying. But just as my eyes closed and I made the decision to become better acquainted with my newly enhanced body, the bed shifted—not a

114

soft rocking created by my own movement, but a sharp, quick jolt.

Startled to see the bedcovers rising up like some Halloween spook comprised of designer sheets, I leapt to my feet and staggered back from the bed, a vampyre frightened by a ghost. But just as I would have bolted, the comforter went flying to reveal the young servant about whom I'd just been dreaming.

He knelt in the center of the bed, chocolate brown hair tumbling in all directions. Painfully beautiful with his chiseled features and bare chest, he rubbed his face like a kid rubbing sleep from his eyes, then looked up to see me standing there in my wrinkled pants.

"Hey," was all he said, a lazy greeting rather than an exclamation of alarm.

I stared at him, taken aback. "I—uh... Is this your room?" Embarrassment prickled along my cheekbones—he must have seen me touching myself—but I could no longer blush or even feel heat rise into my face. Just a little tickling of blood underneath the skin. Like an ant. Or a feather. Another vestigial response from my days as a human.

He looked at me, yawning. "Yeah. You were so crashed out I didn't have the heart to wake you up, so I figured it wouldn't matter if we shared the bed for a few days." He looked away, a bit apologetic, then muttered under his breath, "Besides, sleeping with somebody helps you get through the dream."

I didn't know whether to thank him for letting me rest or get pissed off at him for crawling in bed with me. Then it dawned on me what he'd said. "A few *days*?" I repeated. "How long was I asleep?"

He got up and turned on a lamp on the dresser, a stained glass dragonfly with iridescent wings. Unabashedly naked, his body was a work of art drawn in Miquel's blood. He stood with his back to me rummaging through the closet, though I pretended to be staring at the floor when he turned and began wriggling into a pair of button fly Levis.

"You've been asleep since Monday," he offered casually, then gave a smile that showed the tips of his fangs. "It's Friday night."

I flopped down on the edge of the bed, unconsciously dropping my head into my hands. My pants were too loose and my skin too tight. I'd had a *life*, for God's sake—a car and an apartment and a cat to give me dirty looks while I sat around feeling sorry for myself.

"I want to go home," I muttered, surprised at how childlike I sounded.

The kid came to sit at my side. He put an arm around my shoulder, and without much thought I rested against him, vamping what comfort I could. That alone should have told me how much I'd changed, for as a mortal I never would have allowed myself the luxury of leaning so unashamedly on a stranger.

"You can go if you want, but it won't be the same."

Though I'd already conceded that I couldn't return to that pointless dayshine existence, I had to ask, "Why?"

"That's what I tried to tell you before Miquel changed you," Donny said after a long silence. "While you were still mortal, you could've walked away, been happy with the illusions at least."

I could only stare at him, understanding absolutely nothing.

He sighed heavily, squeezing my shoulder the way an older brother would, and this despite the fact that he appeared to be a 20-year-old kid while I was 34 and used to thinking of myself as experienced in life.

"Look, all I can tell you is that once you've seen through vampyre eyes, you can't find satisfaction in the same things anymore. The facades won't hold up, and when you see that they *are* facades, it'll make you crazy because you wish it could be real." He paused, staring out the window to watch the dew settling on the tall pines like tears of a God in whom we'd both believed not so long ago.

"Oh, we all *want* the picket fence and that lazy life in the Rockwell paintings," he went on, "but when you see how fleeting it is, you can't stand it because *you* aren't transitory anymore. It all keeps going, and there's not a damn thing you can do to stop it, so you either start running to keep up or you just sit back and watch it go to hell." After such an impassioned speech, he gave a shrug of indifference. "Immortality bites."

The familiar emptiness filled me again, but before I could comment, he patted me on the back and stood up. Every bit as changeable as Miquel, he turned to the closet, grabbed a long-sleeved shirt and shrugged into it, happy again.

"Do yourself a favor and don't think about it so much," he

suggested, cocking his head to one side. "Hey, listen, I'm going down to San Diego with Stygian, Dimitri and Bird—thought we'd do a little grocery shopping, maybe spend some time with Foxglove and Coma for laughs. They're your sisters, by the way. Want to come along?" Without waiting for my answer, he looked me up and down. "You're about the same size as Miquel, so we can swipe something from his closet for you to wear, but those pants really do have to go."

So saying, he put on an exaggerated act of being effeminate, and though I'd known he was gay, his playing it up put me at ease. The kid was crazy—rapid-fire talk, angel choir voice, voluminous hair drowning him as he picked up a brush from the dresser and began wrestling with it.

Still, I wasn't ready to go back to San Diego and face the ghosts of my old life, so I looked up at the ceiling, wondering what Miquel was doing. Wondering who he was with. Hating myself for the thought.

"I think I'll pass," I muttered.

Donny laughed at me, then turned back to the closet and snatched a pair of Reeboks. "Suit yourself, but the maahstah's not home," he advised with a Renfield accent and an evil wink that told me he could read my every thought.

Sitting down in the middle of the floor, he began rolling on a pair of socks. "He always takes off to the desert after he creates a new vampyre. It helps him get his head together—you know, get his strength back." He grinned suggestively. "Dimitri says you took a lot out of him."

He was enjoying knowing more about Miquel than I did, and though I tried not to let it bother me, it did.

"What did you mean when you said sleeping with someone helps you get through the dream?" I asked, not really meaning to speak.

Donny hesitated, fingers tangled in his shoe laces. He looked at me askance, his head lowered as his entire demeanor changed, and a gust of wind whipped through the window to send his hair flying again. "Miquel didn't tell you?"

His very tone—one of accusation and dread—sent shivers down my arms, raising the hair at the base of my neck.

This young man who'd been friendly and outgoing

suddenly reverted to the intimidated creature who'd peered out at me from the shadows of the stairwell the night Miquel made me a vampyre. Drawing in on himself, he actually appeared to wilt and go taut all at once.

"I guess not." I was awkward, not sure I wanted an answer to the question: "Tell me what?"

For nearly a full minute, he didn't move. Then, with a grim determination, he got up and leaned against the door frame, his compact athletic body silhouetted against the dim light polishing the hall. "You don't just die in his arms *once*, you know."

All the world stopped. "Wh-what?"

Face gaunt against the black shirt, Donny hunkered down into his hair. In his eyes, anxiety mingled with an emotion that had no name, yet an emotion I knew all too well. I'd had my first brush with it while drinking from Miquel's body the night I was made— love and hate precisely equal, with no center line to divide the two. Hatred reserved for one's murderer, spiritual love and erotic lust reserved for one's personal savior.

It was a paradox that could drive vampyres mad, as I was about to witness—the first of many times I would watch this sensitive young man plunge headlong into lunacy because there was simply no way to unite such conflicting emotions.

Without any ado whatsoever, Donny began to rant.

"You'll dream it every night for the rest of eternity," he told me, folding his arms over his chest as his lower lip began to tremble. "It's been seven years since I was made—not long, I know—but not a day goes by that I don't dream it. Not a single day!"

His fury became a tangible wind brought to life—napalm and liquid nitrogen caught in a common tempest—and though the brush on the dresser was well out of reach, it flew to the floor with a clatter and slid beneath the bed.

"Hell—I mean *hell*!—I know he didn't want to hurt me when he did it to me—he was trying to save me and I'll always love him for that just like you'll love him for saving your life and hate him for killing your little girl—but he cut my fucking throat with his teeth, Stefan! Jesus Christ on a solid gold cross! I didn't know he was a vampyre—I mean I didn't really *believe* it! And all that blood—all that fucking blood running out of me and there was nothing I could

118

do but crawl into his arms and let him finish it, let him turn me into—into—*this*!"

Frantic, crazed, he tossed his hands in the air, both middle fingers flying up in a well recognized fuck-you to the universe itself. "Well, so what?" he snarled, baring dangerous fangs as he howled up at the ceiling, at the sky beyond, at God Himself. "I mean—so fucking what? We're damned anyway, and it's kinda like Milton said: better to reign in hell than serve in heaven!"

Turning his head away, Donny slid to the floor with a thud! and sat staring out into the shadowy hall with his fist crammed in his mouth to staunch his sudden weeping. Then, in the barest of whispers—rapid-fire and with his eyes clenched tightly shut—he confessed, "Every time I dream that fucking dream, I'm dying all over again, but I can't stop loving him, Stefan! He's the devil himself, but I'm so in love with him I know it's going to tear my soul right out of my body one day! God *damn* him for making me love him like this! God *damn* him!"

Physically stunned by the intensity of his passions, especially when the floor gave a shudder and a music box on the desk began playing *Over the Rainbow*, I staggered backward. With his telepathic shields shattered and my own not yet fully developed, it was all I could do not to get sucked into the psychic maelstrom.

I wanted to grab him and hold him and tell him it would be all right, but I also wanted *him* to do the same for me—mainly because I couldn't imagine reliving my death every time I went to sleep. The horror was that it had already begun, and in retrospect it made sense that I'd dreamt it four times, for I'd apparently slept four days.

"Why?" I said, mostly to myself. "*Why* do we dream it every night?"

Donny gave a little snort. "Stygian says it's the price of immortality—having to die every day we live." A pause, then: "Don't tell him I told you so, but I think he likes it. Sometimes he takes naps just to *make* the dream come."

I was barely listening. I would die in Miquel's arms every night until time itself came to a stop.

Suddenly, eternity seemed an eternity long. Just as suddenly, it didn't seem nearly long enough, though I detested myself for the thought which should have appalled me but was instead more seductive than any other thought I'd ever known.

My lip curled, and for an instant I was wanting to kill Miquel. And yet, when I thought of *my* dream as compared to Donny's, I wanted to overwhelm my maker with appreciation for the gentleness he'd shown me. If he *had* severed my jugular vein, I never knew it and never saw it and for that I would be eternally grateful.

I loved him. I despised him.

Not knowing what else to do, I moved to the door and slid to the floor next to my immortal brother. Then, because he was my Blood and I could feel his despondent heartbeat in my own veins, I took him in my arms, rocking him until his breathing evened out and he fell into a light sleep devoid of any dreams.

CHAPTER ELEVEN

"Miquel calls it the Sadness," Dimitri explained as the limo sped down I-15 between San Bernardino and San Diego. He sat at my side with his elegantly pale hands folded in his lap, wearing a pair of crisp designer jeans and a white shirt. "It happens sometimes—a melancholy fear that settles in the blood—usually to those of us who are made against our will, or to those who were touched by the wings of death in their mortal lives as Donny was touched with AIDS. Fortunately, it's not fatal, but when it does rear its head, the best thing you can do is stay out of the way, for it _is_ contagious."

Entire cities were etched on the windows—full-size models of suburbs and fast food joints and gas stations dotting the landscape as the road wound through the flat, dark terrain. Other cars passed by us, wind-up toys driven by Barbie and G.I. Joe across a stage that was as separate from me as any fantasy world I'd ever created as a writer.

I barely heard Dimitri's words, for I had been drawn into the magic of the night itself and could scarcely keep my soul from flying out of my body as Miquel had warned it might. In the front seat, the tall, thin Jamaican known as Bird drove with one hand on the wheel and the other hanging out the window, where it played dive-bomber in the slipstream of the wind. Dreadlocks of varying

120

colors—blond, bronze, black—spilled over the back of his seat to nest alongside the headrest, the ends capped with psychedelic Fimo beads that gave a pleasant rattle whenever he moved.

But even though he wore a tux and a tall top hat that made him look like a chimney sweep, Bird was no more Miquel's chauffeur than Donny was his servant. Those were only roles they played from time to time, as much to amuse themselves as to entertain our Creator.

In the back of the limo, Dimitri and I sat on the seat which faced the front, while on the rear-facing seat, Donny leaned forlornly against a more mysterious vampyre. Strikingly handsome, with olive green eyes and long blond hair that shone like illumined gold, Stygian could have been a model for some sultry romance novel but was instead an exotic dancer at a prominent night club for women. With lithe muscles displayed in a low-cut tank top and jeans so tight they might have been liquid denim formed to his thighs, he stared out the window as the world flashed by in unrelated bits of light and color.

My first impression when he'd come into Miquel's house and taken Donny from my arms was that the two of them were lovers. Instead, Dimitri had drawn me aside and explained that Stygian was "stubbornly heterosexual", yet completely comfortable with the fact that Donny had had a crush on him for years. Whatever strange relationships existed between them, I couldn't deny that all of them were now a part of me. I'd lived my life as an only child, yet at 34 I suddenly had a slew of strange brothers.

It never occurred to me to blame them for Miquel's sins against my daughter or to treat them with anything less than respect. Although the world was accustomed to thinking of vampyres as lifeless fiends with greased-back hair and blood dripping down their chins, these young men were as unique as any mortal and as refined as any would-be James Bond.

Bird made his living as a blackjack dealer at an Indian casino near Palm Springs. Dimitri and Donny both lived at Miquel's house—Dimitri a computer wizard who dabbled in the stock market, Donny picking up extra cash as a psychic advisor to some of the top celebrities in Hollywood.

No, there was nothing clichéd about them, and had I not already known what they were, I would have been hard-pressed to believe they were vampyres.

Relaxing with that thought, I realized I'd been turned sideways in my seat, staring at the coffin in the back of the car. I wondered if I'd imagined it that first night, but it was there, and strangely compelling in a way I couldn't define. Though symbolic of death to the mortal world, it was symbolic of life to me because it was empty and would be eternally so. I had died once, and now would never have to die again.

Stygian shot me a wicked smile indicative of his evil sense of humor. "You think too much, Quilldriver. It's just a coffin—a bed with a lid to keep the light out of your eyes, you know?"

I did think too much, and I was even getting used to everybody reading my stray thoughts. Still: "Quilldriver?"

"Miquel's new scribe, baptized in his blood, 'cause the last one—a mortal—up and died," Stygian explained in a singsong voice deep with amusement. Overly dramatic, he clasped one hand to his heart. "Alas poor Dork, I knew him well."

Dimitri shot him a look, baring his fangs in disapproval. Turning to me, he said in a gravely serious tone, "His name was Dorin, and he chose to decline the kiss of our maker because he felt his passion resided in mortal blood." He gave a little shrug which said he himself disagreed. "You see, books about our kind will contribute to lessening the fear mortals have of us and go toward recreating the symbiotic relationships which existed between vampyres and humans before the coming of religion.

"In addition," he continued, gesturing passionately as he spoke, "though the lives we live and the night in which we live them might appear quite solid to you, Miquel is of the opinion that we are truly creatures of myth and mist—folklore incarnate, if you will. And while he would not expect you to embrace the concept just yet, he maintains that our existence depends as much on human *belief* in the magical world as in our consumption of human blood. To that end, it is necessary to keep ourselves in the public eye, which is why writers have proven invaluable to him over the centuries. By creating ourselves over and over in literature and film, we insure our immortal survival."

I blinked, taken aback as the road slid us deeper into the night. "Wait—are you saying we'll all just stop existing if people quit believing in vampyres? That's absurd! Nobody believes in vampyres anyway!" I chuckled, though somewhat nervously, I suppose.

Stygian and Donny were staring out the window again, mismatched marble bookends. Bird started singing to himself— *Amazing Grace*.

I chilled, wondering what they all knew.

"Is it absurd?" Dimitri asked, leaning against the side of the car and pulling his long legs onto the seat. He reminded me of a Siamese cat—sleek, lean, unpredictable. "Belief and faith are strange tools—secrets mortals keep from one another out of shame or fear." He paused, gazing out the window as his eyes went distant. "When I was a boy in a village near Piraeus, some of the old women still believed in the ancient gods. While they mended the fishing nets, they would prattle of how they had seen Apollo strolling through the vineyards in the cool of the evening, or how they had spoken with Aphrodite under the moon."

I bristled for no good reason—probably because I was jealous of the things he'd seen in his long lifetime, envious that he'd lived in a simpler time and seen the world grow from infancy to some soulless techno-dependent mutant.

"What people say and what they believe are two separate things, Dimitri," I protested. "And even if they did believe, so what? All that stuff about the gods is just hocus-pocus—man's attempt to explain his own existence."

Dimitri looked at me, entirely disapproving. "Then all religions are hocus-pocus?"

I hadn't yet formed a definitive answer, so I took to staring out at the night. Finally I muttered, "Believing in something won't make it happen and *not* believing won't make it go away. Prayer is a fallacy, faith a paper sword."

Discussing existential philosophy in a limo full of vampyres suddenly struck me as silly. I was solid and whole and I was still just a man even if I'd grown unobtrusive little fangs and drunk the blood of a beautiful woman. I wasn't myth. I wasn't mist.

"The Aborigines say we sing the world into being as we go," Bird pointed out with a flourish of his hand, meeting my eyes in the rearview mirror. His chocolate skin soaked in the light, a mocha mirror. "They believe that when we stop singing, the world stops, too. That is why I, for one, am always singing, Quilldriver." So

123

saying, he tipped his hat, smiled broadly, and began to hum.

"The Aborigines are full of shit," Stygian chimed in, never turning from the window. Headlights from a passing car reflected on his face, recreating him in bronze. "What's this 20th century trend of revering primitive cultures just because they *are* primitive?"

"Did you know, Stygian, that there are legends of vampyres in every culture on Earth—cultures completely isolated from one another?" Bird inquired.

"So what?" Stygian argued. "All that proves is latent telepathy in aboriginal cultures. And it makes sense when you think about it. If you don't have a cell phone, how else you gonna reach out and touch someone?" Then, abruptly irritable when he'd seemed thoroughly outgoing, he muttered under his breath, tossing his hands up in the air. "This is bullshit! Bird, turn on the radio—something loud—rock and roll!"

"Get fucked," Bird suggested with a grin, though his accent made it sound more like 'Geet foked'.

Stygian shrugged, unoffended. "I'd rather dance, but the ceiling's too low."

"There's a theory that we used to be telepathic as a species," Donny offered, speaking for the first time since leaving the house. He was animated and genuinely interested in the conversation—as if the Sadness had left him as quickly as it came upon him. "It was only when we developed language that we didn't need telepathy anymore—like we didn't need horses after cars were invented or like we thought we didn't need our immune systems after penicillin was discovered."

He tilted his dark head to the side until his hair hung down and splayed across Stygian's broad chest. "It's totally screwed up, you know? I mean—talk about a designer virus that hits you where you live! Hell, *everybody* fucks! I'm telling you: AIDS was a plot by the Baptists to wipe out the gay community, but it got loose from the lab and—."

"Are you gonna go on about that for the rest of eternity?" Bird snapped. "Let the world tear itself apart with whatever virus it can come up with! It's not like you're gonna die from it, so what do you care?"

"Stuff it, Bird," Stygian interrupted lazily. "He *did* die from it."

Bird just laughed. "He died of vampyre bite, Styx," he corrected, making a distinctive snapping sound with his teeth.

"Leave the kid alone," Stygian said, though his demeanor was altogether lethargic. "It's not funny and neither are you."

"Fuck you," Bird said again, hanging a middle finger salute in the rearview mirror, a contradiction to his broad grin.

"I'm not a kid," Donny whined.

"If Dimitri's three hundred, and I'm a hundred and fifty, and Bird's pushing his bicentennial, you're a kid." Stygian shot me a glance. "And so are you, Quilldriver. You're an *infant*."

"So what does this have to do with vampyres winking out of existence if Man stops believing in us?" I asked, my head spinning again. I had the distinct impression that these philosophical discussions were the norm for them, arguments that erupted out of the ether as a way to pass the time.

They all turned to look at me, but it was Dimitri who spoke—quietly and eloquently, unscathed by all the fierce passions flying loose in the limo.

"One evening, when I was still a boy in my village—"

"Here we go again," Bird complained, sighing dramatically and throwing his hands up in the air, ignoring the steering wheel in the process.

"I love this story!" Donny protested, and elbowed the driver's seat to silence Bird's objections.

Stygian rolled his grass-green eyes, worshipping his own silence.

"—I followed some of the old women down to the sea," Dimitri continued, ignoring them all as he fastened his eyes on me alone. "I was young—"

"—bored—"

"—bored, and had little else to do. And as I had overheard the women whispering in secret about a beautiful goddess they were going to see that very night, I thought to prove to myself once and for all that it was only a bunch of foolish—"

"—bullshit—"

"—prattle based on old folklore. At any rate—

"What does that mean anyway? At *what* rate?"

"Shut up. I want to hear this."

"You've heard it a dozen times."

"*I've* heard it a *hundred* times!"

"—while the old ones were walking along the shore between our village and the next, I saw a young girl approach them and begin talking to them, dancing for them with her skirts flying wild on the wind and her hair loosed to her thighs as she told them mystical tales of Olympus. While I hid amongst the shadows—"

"'Amongst'. Don't you just love how that word gets tangled in your fangs and makes you sound like a fag?"

"Fuck you, Bird! Shut up, goddammit! And don't use that word!"

"Amongst. Amongst. Amongst."

"—it became obvious that this girl could really have been a goddess. She was the most magnificent woman ever born and as she talked with animation and passion, the old women seemed to grow stronger—more vibrant, potent—as if they absorbed some of her youth and vitality just by being in her presence. Their backs, bent from working so many years with the nets, began to straighten—"

"He's on a roll now! Preach to us, Brother Dimitri!"

"Say amen!"

"—and in the moonlight, it actually seemed that the wrinkles on their faces began to smooth. They *believed* in her, you see! And by virtue of their own belief in myth and magic, they became stronger within themselves—"

"Hallelujah, brother!"

"Hosanna!"

"—and their infirmities healed. One of them, long-widowed, even married again."

Here Dimitri stopped, looking at me with an intensity that had shrunk the world down to hold only the two of us. I scarcely heard the comments of the others, nor noticed the movement of the car. "So what happened?"

He smiled wistfully. "These meetings with the goddess went on for many months."

"—until they were burned at the stake as witches—"

"That's a different story, asshole."

"Oh, sorry."

"The old women were heard laughing and singing at all hours of the night, sometimes until dawn itself came!"

126

"But then..."

"But then one day a messenger from our neighboring village came telling of the death of a beautiful young girl," Dimitri concluded sadly. "The goddess, it seemed, had thrown herself into the sea. Without realizing the good she had done with her pretenses, she took her own life to atone for the charade."

"Ah, shit, after all that, are you gonna to tell me the bitch was just a liar?"

"When the old women of my village heard this and realized she wasn't a goddess at all, they fell into fits of weeping and reverted to their former misery within the span of but days. They died in spiritual poverty, alone. Their belief and their faith had recreated them and restored their lives, you see, but the lack of it just as quickly destroyed them."

I started to say something, but Stygian spoke instead. "That's a swell story, Dimitri, but I think it *disproves* your point instead of proving it."

"In what manner?" Dimitri inquired with scholarly interest.

Stygian shrugged his broad shoulders. "Well, if you're trying to say that mystical beings are existentially dependent on the beliefs of mortals, it would be a better story if the old crones *should* have stopped believing in the goddess. And in her despair, the girl just folded herself on the wind—you know, like that *Star Trek* episode where Apollo was all maudlin because nobody wanted to herd ghosts anymore."

"*Goats*," Donny corrected adamantly, elbowing the older vampyre. "Nobody wanted to herd *goats*! Jeez, how the hell would you herd a ghost?"

"Whatever," Stygian conceded easily. "Goats, then."

"Hey!" Bird chimed in. "That's where you got that story, ain't it! You stole it from *Star Trek*, Dimitri! Damn! You shit! You had me going!"

Dimitri just looked at me with an expression of long-suffering. *They mean well*, his songbird thoughts explained.

Aloud, he said, "I merely meant it to illustrate that what we believe determines the way our lives unfold—whether we are vampyres in the modern world or old women by the sea in Greece. When faith fails, lives are shattered, perhaps even entire cultures."

"Maybe you should leave the parables to our ungodly father,

Dimitri," Bird suggested, watching us in the rearview mirror as he drove on into the night.

"I still think you've got it backwards, Dimitri," Stygian maintained. "You really should have had the goddess off herself because the old crones quit believing in her—not the other way around. That'd work better."

"But that isn't the way it happened," Dimitri insisted, surly.

They all looked at one another with complete seriousness. Then Stygian chuckled melodically, as if laughter were his best friend. Even Donny lifted his head and grinned. He seemed to blend into Stygian, as if the curves of one's body had been laser cut to match the other's. The sight mesmerized me, for I had never seen two creatures who fit together more perfectly than this. They shared the same heart, I'm sure. Certainly the same blood sang through their veins. Miquel's blood. Dimitri's. Bird's. As time went on, mine would undoubtedly flow through them, too, just as theirs already raced through my heart to make it beat forever.

We were Blood.

We were Family in a way I had never known. Though I'd loved my wife, we never shared a belonging such as this. And while a part of me had gone to creating my beloved Stephanie, even that gift of a child did not have the same telepathic impact of *this*—for these men had made me immortal every bit as much as Miquel had made me a vampyre.

Stygian's blood stained my heart with his easy laughter and his intense passion. Bird's irreverent soul darted through my veins to make me smile. Donny's angst and melancholy whispered through my dreams. And Dimitri's philosophical spirit tickled my mind to keep me always wondering.

For awhile, I sat in silence, awestruck, humbled.

The road was unfamiliar even though I'd traveled it dozens of times in my mortal life. But now nothing was the same, for the physical world had taken a giant step backward while at the same time coming into sharper, colder focus.

In the beat-up truck pacing us on the right, two teenagers fairly writhed with carnal thoughts, and as they glanced at our car and wondered who might be looking back at them from behind smoky glass, I could all but taste the lust coursing through their hearts. They still had a wonder about life, so much that I wanted to roll down the window and shout at them to embrace it and suckle it like mother's milk, for there was no more potent drug on Earth than awe itself.

I wanted to tell them, *'Live forever!'*—but in reality I could only stare out the window and reflect their wonder right back at them. Fate had put them there at that moment, yet in all probability I would never see them again.

They were transitory, random miracles.

For that reason—the sacrosanct embodiment of Now—it was spellbinding and sad when I brought my lips to my fingers and blew them a kiss for luck.

But when I looked toward the other side of the limo, I was struck by the pall of grief coming from a distant bedroom in the midst of an otherwise innocuous housing development. What startled me as much as knowing which house was exuding such grief was the realization that I knew everything about it: a woman barely 33 had been diagnosed with breast cancer that very afternoon and would not live past the end of the year. The irony shattered me, for while I was an infant vampyre contemplating the centuries that would create eternity, a young woman with three small children had less than 4 months to live. My throat tightened. My eyes misted.

"You're being maudlin," Dimitri pointed out, pulling me from my reverie. "The mortal world isn't yours to save. They choose their lives and they choose their deaths, for it's as Miquel so often says: all realities are self-created when you really stop to think about it. Still, the fact that you can see these things so clearly should tell you something about yourself."

"What do you mean?" I asked, dazed.

He inclined his head toward the window, but the suburb and the terrible sadness were already fading as the car sped on. "You feel the pain of the world or the gladness it can generate. You're an empath."

"An empath?"

Dimitri nodded, crazy eyes studying me. The green one reflected the light, glistening. The blue one drank light in, darkness embodied. I had to look away from him for an instant, for suddenly I was reminded of how this had all come to pass. I had fallen into those eyes and under his spell, and now the world was full of dolls and false front buildings like a Hollywood set.

"An empath feels everything soul deep," he told me. "That's why you were getting broody over whatever you were sensing out there in the night. Empathy is one of the rarer powers—it doesn't happen often, but a writer could ask for nothing better. You communicate with emotions, ideas. You communicate with pretty words and the generating of passion in others.

"Facts are beside the point to empaths, so be aware of that," he cautioned. "The only problem is that until you get your bearings, you're going to be on an emotional roller coaster. Everything you see is going to make you feel something profound, and if you're not careful, you can get sidetracked for years sitting in a cemetery listening to the songs of the bones like Adam does."

"Adam?" The name alone made me cold inside. I couldn't have said why, except that perhaps I *was* an empath and subconsciously reacting to the other vampyres around me.

"Miquel's pet pest," Donny muttered, never lifting his head off Stygian's shoulder.

"Jealous," Bird pronounced, grinning as he shook an accusatory finger at Donny in the rearview mirror.

They sounded like boys. Sons of Neverland – lost boys lonely for love. Lonely for Miquel.

The mere thought of him made me tremble. My heart beat a little faster. My mind turned soft and red warm, a shade that precisely matched the burgundy sofa where he'd taken my life and awakened me to immortality with a kiss. I could still taste it on my tongue. I could still feel his lips whispering bloodsongs into my mouth.

Donny turned his head, his eyes meeting mine. He winked devilishly to let me know he heard my darkest thoughts, and though I was petrified that he would blurt out my shameful musings for a quick laugh, he only grinned and told me with a look that my secret was safe with him. Of course, I had no reason to think the others weren't listening to my mental blather as if it had been broadcast on the radio. But if they were, they never let on, and for that I had to commend them. Gentlemen they were, whether they would ever admit it or not.

Dimitri inclined his head toward Stygian and picked up where he'd left off before. "So as I was saying, you're an empath,

Stefan. Stygian's a tracker. Bird has future sight. Donny's a siren and a weather witch. I have the siren gift, too, but mainly I'm a dream king."

At this, Stygian laughed with a fair amount of sarcasm. "Yeah, right." To me, he added, "That's a myth even among us myths. Dimitri thinks he can crawl inside other vampyres' heads and make the dreams go away—you know, *that* dream—but I'm telling you, he's lying. The only one who can do that is Miquel, and then only if you—." He stopped abruptly, and went back to staring out the window in mid-sentence. "Forget it. I don't want to talk about it."

"And then only if you're sleeping in his bed," Bird chimed in, finishing the thought. Catching my eye, he added, "Our beloved Stygian can't admit that he would ever do such a thing, but you may rest assured we've all shared bed and body with our Creator and we've all enjoyed it shamelessly because we can't help ourselves. We love him and we hate him, and we'd kill one another if we could just to avoid the competition for his attentions."

"Bullshit," Stygian muttered to himself.

Empathizing with him, I was monumentally uncomfortable. And because I felt his uneasiness, I said something that was thoroughly stupid and I said it without thinking.

"I'm straight, too."

An awful silence fell. Then Dimitri laughed out loud— tossed his head back and howled, actually. Donny looked crestfallen and clasped a hand to his breast—little shit.

Bird snickered. "We all were." A pause, then: "Once upon a long time ago."

"Not all of us," Donny protested. "I was gay even before I met Miquel."

"You croaked before you could find out what you were," Bird argued good-naturedly, brushing him aside with a gesture. "Just another dead vampyre virgin."

"Biiirr-rrr-rrrd!" Donny whined, his siren voice earsplitting.

"What're you bitching about?" Bird asked philosophically. "It's kinda sexy if you think about it—the eternal virgin."

"Wh-what do you mean: *'were'*?" I managed, my voice threatening to crack.

Bird was back to humming to himself. Donny was sulking.

Stygian wasn't talking. And Dimitri was selectively deaf.

Before I could pursue it any further, the limo pulled onto an off ramp and we were swallowed up in the neon glitz and glitter of San Diego—the Gas Lamp District near Horton Plaza.

Donny pressed his face to the window like a child and even Dimitri leaned forward for a better look. The city was an entity, alive and teeming with Friday night antics of the well-to-do mortal world. Women in elegant black dresses waited at the entrance to the Lyceum for the opening of a new play. Locals in belted shorts and long-sleeved shirts browsed fashionable antique shops. Couples walked hand-in-hand, lazy silhouettes cut from the cloth of flesh and blood.

Bird pulled into a couple of parking spaces normally reserved for cabs, shut down the engine, and leaned back in the seat as he met my eyes in the mirror.

Confused, I looked out at the night and the milling crowds. "What're we doing here?"

Stygian grinned, sending chills through my stomach. "Grocery shopping, Quilldriver. Only the food's free and you don't need a cart."

I would have blanched had I not already been pale as death itself.

"Ooohh!" Donny exclaimed, pointing animatedly to a couple on the sidewalk as he grasped Stygian's arm with enthusiasm. "Those two! Right there! The black guy in the 501s! You can have the girlfriend, I want *him*!"

Stygian tousled the kid's hair as if by some previously agreed upon signal of approval, and before I could say a word, they flung open the door and disappeared on the heels of their prey. Horrified, I started to call after them, but Dimitri placed a hand on my arm and warned me to silence.

"The night is out there, Stefan," he reminded me, his demeanor beginning to change as he looked to the window beyond. Hunger shone in his eyes, the way it had when he'd cut my hand at the convention and kissed the blood away.

Then, before I could ask him anything more—where we should meet again, what I should do, how to go about these peculiar things—he, too, was gone, a shadow in designer jeans blending into the crowd. I turned to the driver's seat, but Bird had disappeared as well, the only indication he'd ever been there his tall top hat left on the seat.

The night was out there.

*

The events of that evening were a blur, set apart in parentheses, not belonging in the rational flow of time. I prowled the streets of San Diego, a man obsessed and possessed. Everything was new yet all things were incredibly old, part of a molecular chain that had existed since before time became any part of the cosmic equation.

Mortals were drawn to me just as I had been drawn to Dimitri and Miquel before my transformation, and though I was squeamish at first, I soon discovered that the art of hunting was an "art" only insofar as picking and choosing which victim was more desirable at a given moment.

Victim.

It hardly seems the right word, for as I had already ascertained with Valerie, the act of feeding truly was a symbiotic joining, each new experience more fulfilling than the last. In exchange for the blood I received, my mortal vessels became drunk on pleasure itself, on the erotic thrill of bloodletting that hit their senses like some roller coaster climbing to the stars and then falling again.

I didn't know *how* my vampyre powers worked. I only knew they *did* work. I didn't have to make a conscious decision to mesmerize my prey, nor deliberately will them to forget the painful pleasure that was intrinsic to the blood dance. Instead, as I drank from more and more of them—spiriting them away into shadowed doorways where we would appear as any couple stealing a kiss—I began to suspect that the trance which fell over them was some natural occurrence over which neither party had any conscious control.

The hardest thing was that I really did fall in love with every mortal who came into my arms. And though my instinct was to suckle them to their death—not from any desire to harm them, but because their lives were so sweet and perfect in their temporal simplicity—it took only a conscious thought to remind myself of

133

Miquel's warning. *'Any of us can kill, but only the best of us can not kill'*.

Though I wanted to hate this thing I had become, it was as if I had been destined to be a vampyre. This peculiar new life *was* my path instead of some wicked fork in the road I'd taken by mistake. It wasn't only the pleasure that made me begin to accept it all. It was the *totality* I experienced during the act of feeding—the memories people carried around in their veins that made them unique and divine and altogether desirable no matter what shell they wore to conceal their airy souls.

The wino woman leaning against a dumpster behind a bar was as delightful on my lips as the conceited college cheerleaders hanging out in front of a trendy nightclub, wanting to be seen and admired. And, indeed, if I'd had to choose between them, I might well have chosen the drunk for the *life* she'd lived that had nothing to do with physical beauty.

For a long time, I wandered, bewitched by the sights and sounds of the city, drawn to the sharp essence of humanity as moths were drawn to the gas lamps flickering in this all-night banquet of souls. Music filtering through the open doors of a dance club was the heartbeat of the city, carried by the wind through the veins and arteries that were really streets and alleys. The night was alive, never quite solid because there was no known way to capture shadows in a bottle or echoes of laughter in a box.

The city was mist, chimera, just another rickety scaffolding of another play in which I was a rogue actor. There was so much I wanted to learn, and the only creatures who could teach me were these mortals milling around on the stage, never suspecting what a grand illusion it all really was.

As I passed through an alley, a pretty young waitress sneaking a cigarette behind a coffee shop looked up at me and smiled. When I drew her into my arms and eased my fangs into her neck to bring her blood swelling into my mouth—*sweet-leather-copper-earth-raw-heart*—the rapture that overcame us caused me to cry out, and I clutched her to my chest as if she were my lifelong lover. Her name was Carla. That's what her thoughts told me as her body climaxed uncontrollably, and the rest I stole through the stream of her bright red soul, the animus that was her life...

—*the Boyfriend was smoking crack again and dipping his dick in the girl from the downstairs apartment, so when Carla came home and found them together, it wasn't as difficult as she'd thought it might be to take the little .22 from her purse and splatter the walls with Boyfriend blood and Teenybopper tears. The silly little squealer ran naked out of the room and into the hall. Carla let her go because she had cellulite on her pudgy thighs and that was punishment enough, but she'd been running ever since—truck stops and car washes and whatever greasy spoon was looking for a graveyard girl who didn't mind "paying some attention to the boss" for a few extra dollars—*

After I left Carla, I came upon Zinna—a beautiful girl barely 16, yet already selling her body on the streets for four years. Oddly, the moment our eyes met, I had the feeling she knew *exactly* what I was, and that she truly did want me to have her blood. The thought unnerved my nerve, for I could not help recalling what Miquel had said of my Stephanie and how she had sought him out to end her pain.

I almost let Zinna go. I almost ran. But when I grabbed her to me—her firm, high breasts heaving against my chest as my fingers tangled in her hair and I bent her head back to expose her throat—the thirst left me floating in the sea of her essence as I was invited inside a part of her crippled soul no man had ever violated.

—stumbling down the porch steps, she screamed and pitched forward into the driveway, scraping her arms and legs on unforgiving asphalt. She didn't even know the bastard she was running from. Jake? Jack? It didn't make much difference when Mama's new boyfriend was on top of her, sweating and forcing her legs apart while he breathed Southern Comfort in her face and threw her school books off the bed. He held his hand over her mouth so she couldn't scream, and when he broke her cherry and told her he was doing it for her own good—to make her a "righteous bitch" so she could earn her keep—she cried from the pain and the rush of blood that stained the pink sheets. When she scratched his pocked face and bit halfway through his finger, he let her go just long enough to pull a knife. Four years later, she was still looking over her shoulder, and the little girl lights had gone out of her eyes—

I wept for her, my mouth wet with her pain that was the sweetest and yet the most bitter thing I'd ever known. I wept *with* her and I held her in my arms rocking her until she stretched up on her toes and gave me a kiss just below my ear.

"Crazy white boy," she whispered, holding my earlobe in her teeth. Because she remembered nothing of my drinking from her, she left me then and returned to the shadows, looking back at me once or twice as if wondering what had happened between us.

They all had secrets. Something they were running from. Something they were looking for. Something that chased them through their lives.

But as I continued wandering through streets which became more bleak and lonely as the crowds thinned, I realized I had been traveling in a direction which led me back to the neighborhood where I'd grown up. Indeed, as my feet turned a corner—miles from where the limo was parked—I came upon an empty lot where a scraggly oak tree stood, its trunk scarred with the initials of every kid who'd ever lived on that street.

Fingertips brushing the rough bark, my heart quickened as my eyes fell on the past. I even remembered the dreary December day I'd snuck out of the house, Boy Scout knife in hand, to make my mark on that tree I'd been forbidden to climb.

A shiver raced down my back, leaving me cold on a night that was unseasonably warm for October. As I stood there looking up through falling leaves, it was as if I had been thrown back in time, to a day when this had been the tallest, most enchanted tree I'd ever seen.

Tiny witches who sucked out the brains of children through their nostrils lived in the knot holes near the top, and legend said the dead branch which lay rotting on the ground had killed half a dozen ornery boys when it fell. It was the hangman's tree and the Halloween tree and the headstone tree that stood watch over the little pet cemetery pushing up weeds in an empty city lot.

Without realizing it, I leaned my forehead against the scarred trunk as if to suckle the memories it had gathered. Instead, the scent of human urine and decomposing garbage drifted up to remind me that this was no longer the place where I'd grown up. A derelict shivered against the retaining wall nearby, mumbling nonsense in his sleep. A boy in his early teens stood underneath a lamppost near the boarded up convenience store, hustling a john who pulled up to the curb in a shiny new Lexus. Sirens warbled in the distance.

The streets were deserted as I moved on, empty houses awaiting the wrecking ball. Dead weeds choked up through cracks in the sidewalks, and lawns tended with pride when I was a child were overgrown testaments to the inevitable parade of years. The streetlights, once brighter than the moon, stood like rows of skeletons with mournfully bowed heads, their cyclopsian eyes long since blinded by vandals and left to litter the street, tears of broken glass.

When I glanced up from my reverie, I found myself looking toward the remains of a wood frame house in a ghost town suburb. My chest grew tight, cold. And though the sky was just beginning to lighten, I climbed the decaying steps and stood there on the porch with yesterday courting me like a half remembered lover.

Reality and Time played hopscotch on the corner, fickle little girls whispering and giggling. Days and years tangled up together with no differentiation between Then and Now.

Across the street, Kevin and Keith Danson rode their squeaky twin tricycles in never-ending circles on a sidewalk split by tree roots. Two houses down, that Jason Haverhill brat who'd yanked my pants down in first grade stood with his nose pressed against the screen, a forlorn portrait nobody wanted for a friend. Next door, Allie Waymond played on a rusty swing, singing to herself in a voice no better than the squeak of the chains.

But all those ghosts paled as my attention was drawn back home, my eyes riveted to the mist forming just inside the screen door of that three bedroom illusion. There, a translucent shadow among darker patches of night, my mother stood in her Sunday dress with the white lace collar that shone like a crescent moon at her neck.

It was the dress she'd been buried in, yet now she had returned to a street of ruins where junkies and stray cats came to die, watching over the restless spirits of my childhood memories as she'd once watched over me. I blinked to clear the image, but even when I took a step backward and rubbed at my eyes, the vision remained. Her face was stern, and her hair—cola brown and shiny as I remembered it—was still done in a flipped under bob that went out of style in the 60s.

My heart stopped, then slammed against my ribs again when she gave me that look only a mother can give.

"May the good Lord save you, Stefan, what have you done?" she asked in a horrified whisper that might have been a distant screech of tires or the cry of a seagull swept inland by the winds.

137

"What has my baby boy gone and done with his soul?"

My chin quivered and I was five years old again, caught stealing oranges from the neighbor's tree. Quite suddenly, all my philosophizing was reduced to ash and my vampyre powers rendered inert, and all by a smallish woman in a flowered print cotton dress.

"I—Mama..." *I didn't mean to!*

But I couldn't speak, and so I just stood there with my hands crammed deep into the pockets of Miquel's jeans and my eyes lowered.

She watched me for a very long time—she just inside the door, I still on the porch, feeling unwelcome in the house where I'd grown up. Finally, as if she couldn't look on me anymore, she gave that sigh of abject disapproval all mothers keep in their repertoire, and then she turned away.

My soul, shattered too often of late, ripped and bled. "Mother?" I called after her. "Please—let me explain?"

She stopped in the shadows, keeping her back to me, then cast a glance over her shoulder, never meeting my eyes. "Your room's as you left it," she said coldly. "You can rest there, but be on your way as soon as the sun's down." A pause, then the soft command: "And say your prayers before you go to sleep."

A flash of anger struck like summer lightning.

Prayers?

How could I tell her no one was listening? How could I make her see that if anyone *was* listening, it was the same dispassionate bastard who had killed my father, her husband, before I was 10 years old, the same son-of-a-bitch who had sent her to her grave at 53, the same Jack-the-Ripper who had given Stephanie such a melancholy soul that she had taken her own life by slashing her throat on Miquel's teeth?

Pray to this bloodthirsty God who preyed on man for His own amusement? Incensed, I wanted to rail at her to open her eyes, but it was too late for her. God was done with her and now her soul slept in ruins, barred from a heaven reserved for God alone.

I would not pray to this thing. Let *Him* pray to *Me* for forgiveness—for I was the one who'd been forced to break all His rules and damn my soul in order to gain the immortality He could have handed out with a tweaking of a single gene!

My throat was tight, and as I glanced toward the kitchen where so many memories had been born, I knew the woman who'd given me life was only a wraith now, a thing of vapor still going through the motions of life just as the living went through their daily routines without much thought to why they were doing the strange things they did.

She took a broken cup from a phantom shelf and filled it with imaginary coffee before sitting down to read a newspaper long since crumbled to dust. Whether she was really there or not, I never knew, but I could have sworn I smelled fresh bacon and pancakes cooking on a stove long ago hauled away as junk. But because the sun was almost up and I knew I'd never make it back to the limo, I kept my head shamefully lowered and went inside. Without looking up, I made my way through the rubble of broken-down furniture and eventually found my way back to my boyhood room.

But the place which had once been a haven of solace now seemed terribly small, shattered by time's cruel touch. One wall had crumbled completely, the floor littered with debris and rat droppings. In a corner, the stool I'd once climbed on to reach the top shelf of the closet stood on three legs, a crippled old friend. Underneath the window, shreds of paper littered the floor, remnants of math tests and essays which had once defined a little boy's progress through a mixed up world.

None of it mattered now. I wondered if it ever had.

Exhausted as dawn broke over the horizon, I lay down on the cold, hard floor, drew my knees to my chest and curled into a tight ball on my side.

"Now I lay me down to sleep," I said to myself, and red tears swelled in my eyes because I *knew* how alone I was in the universe. "If I should die before I wake..."

Too late.

Dazed by sunlight splitting the horizon to stream through the dead tree outside a broken window, I found an old rag among the rubble and pulled it over my head in a vain effort to shut out the day.

'What has my baby boy gone and done with his soul?'

I didn't know.

With the euphoria of feeding behind me now—the euphoria that made every vampyre foolishly believe every night would last forever—I was plunged back into the profound confusion of the dayshine world where the sun obliterated any such certainty. I longed for darkness then—for a sealed vault or even a box to hide me from this light which revealed a side of me I couldn't look upon.

If the day must exist, I thought deliriously, surely there had to be a way to keep a little slice of the night hidden away, even if in a coffin. And to that end, abruptly insane with the need to be free of the sun, I scrambled to my knees and tore frantically through the floorboards with a strength I didn't know I possessed. The wood splintered in my hands, and though my flesh was undeniably of supernatural construct, the rusty nails ripped into me as I became a madman driven underground.

I wailed, pounding my fists against the stubborn cross member until it finally gave way and I fell through the floor to land in the damp dirt beneath the house. There, trembling and whimpering like a displaced child as I licked a trickle of blood from my wrist, I hunkered down in the darkness, a refuge shared by spiders and mice and a pregnant rat who stared at me with shiny red eyes.

"Goodness gracious sakes alive! Such a ruckus, such a fuss!" the rat exclaimed in my grandmother's staccato voice, scurrying a short distance away as I came crashing into her world like some interdimensional visitor from above. "But do you think it'll rain today, Brother Vampyre? Do you think the sky might finally fall and crush us all?"

Yes, I fear it might, Sister Rat, I told her without speaking. *Indeed, I do fear it might!*

Then, with the blood of mortals filling my belly and songs of the damned singing through my veins, I closed my eyes and dreamed: *Drowning. Drowning in a sea of Eternity worn by an archangel in a tuxedo—a beast with black wings who would take my life every time I slept until the nightlights of heaven burned out and time itself came to some bittersweet dead end.*

Ah, but what a delight it was to die in his unrelenting arms.

CHAPTER TWELVE

"Coma likes to gamble too much, while Foxglove prefers the more direct approach of simply conning mortals out of their money," Dimitri said, his smug smile robbing the words of their sting.

His voice was a scalpel that laid open the air, and he used it with the skill and vanity of a Harvard surgeon. "As a rule, Stefan, you'll discover that male and female vampyres have little use for one another, since our young aren't conceived in the bedroom or carried in the womb, but are often born with college educations. Indeed, once we dispense with the procreative urges which have drawn men and women together since the first horny salamanders climbed from the primordial soup, we find we have nothing in common, but that we can, on occasion, create a friendship based on our very diversity."

Somewhere on the outskirts of San Diego, I sat with Dimitri and the others behind a common ranch style house, lulled into a thoughtful silence by the scent of wild sage and chaparral blooming in nearby hills. A lopsided moon had sunk to the bottom of the pool, dragging Orion and the Pleiades down with her. Crickets cricked. Frogs frogged. Bats batted the air underneath a streetlight on the far side of an empty field, and seven vampyres sat around the gazebo carrying on a conversation as if it were entirely normal.

"You're full of shit, Dimitri," Coma commented lazily, stretched out on a towel beneath the stars. Wearing only a pair of cutoff shorts, she ran one finger around the nipple of her left breast—an absent-minded habit—staring up at the warm October night as if oblivious to anyone but herself.

"Full of himself, that is to say," Foxglove corrected with a shrug.

While Foxglove was more traditionally vampyric, with black hair and sullen eyes that might drill through a man's soul just for the sake of doing it, Coma could have passed for a mortal if one didn't look too close. Short curls more white than blonde lay close to her head, and her eyes were faded blue denim in the light thrown by tiki torches burning along the pool's perimeter. And though Foxglove was leaner, with the diminutive features of a china doll, Coma was more athletic in build, with tanned skin and a few freckles scattered over the bridge of her nose.

One was a mystery, the other an open book. So it stood to reason they'd been lovers since before Miquel happened upon them back in '68. Longing to see the world through Coma's psychedelic eyes, he'd followed her from one peace march to another, from one love-in to the next, from Berkeley to Woodstock and back again, until finally he painted the gene pool with her blood—neon butterflies and castles of ice and a wilted red rose that grew at the center of the universe, masquerading as the broken heart of God.

And yet, despite the passion that first drew them together, something was different after her transformation, just as it often was between men and women even after a conventional marriage. Maybe they drifted apart. Or maybe Dimitri was right: the schism between male and female vampyres was even more dangerously real than the rift between the sexes in the mortal world.

Now the women lived together and tried to mimic the motions of a normal life. Donny said they'd settled for one another. Stygian believed they were as happy as any vampyres *could* be. Bird didn't care. And Dimitri's only concern was that I must never divulge Miquel's whereabouts to either of them.

Father doesn't trust his daughters, someone's thoughts said to me.

And though I didn't begin to understand the dynamics, I didn't trust them either—especially in light of how the evening had first begun.

I'd been introduced to my sisters less than an hour before, and though they regarded me with initial wariness, I was made to feel welcome when I was offered a "handout"—the wrist of an extraordinarily handsome creature draped over their sofa as if he were just another part of the furnishings. Thoroughly entranced, he offered no resistance when, awkward and embarrassed at being watched by the others, I brought him to me and drank, ignoring his easy groan as my fangs dug deep into the firm muscle of his arm and his blood burst onto my tongue to dull the edge of the thirst.

The fact that Aaron was male was alarming, for as I began drawing on his veins, I experienced that same overpowering infatuation I'd felt for Valerie or Carla or Zinna or any of the others. And yet, unlike the females from whom I'd fed, whose minds followed rationally from one thought to the next, Aaron's memories

142

skipped through his life like a rock over water, carnal male chaos incarnate.

Here: —*seven years old and teasing the little magic wand to see it dance.* There: —*eyes bursting open in the night as a cry swelled through his lips and his sheets turned damp with the dew of a dream.* There: —*the weights had made his chest thicker, but he was no match against Carter's greater strength, so all Aaron could do was wriggle helplessly as the older man took him from behind, calling him, "My little slave boy."*

When my legs buckled, Dimitri pulled me away. Or perhaps the force of those prurient images caused me to stumble backwards into his arms. To make matters worse, the others stood there trying not to laugh—except for Foxglove, who tossed her head back and yowled in approval, clapping her hands together and spinning around until her tie-dyed skirt swirled into a whirlwind of seasick colors.

Mortified, I reeled away from them, catching my heel on a threadbare chair, stumbling. Yet before I could flee, Aaron caught my eye with an expression that could stop time dead, slender fingers rising off the sofa, curled question marks of bleached bone snaking toward me. When he grabbed me—*mortal flesh hot and beating with life*—I wanted to devour him utterly, to feel him fighting me even while craving the cruelty of my bite.

Delirious from blood loss, he smiled—a flash of white teeth that left my stomach fluttery and brought the thirst rearing up again in response to such physical beauty. My mouth watered, fangs tingling. His fingertips pulsed, blood skimming beneath the surface, mine for the taking. His gift. His pleasure. His coveted pain.

He wet his lips, and with the last of his strength, he lifted his arm to me, blood still oozing from the wounds my kiss had left on him. Tormenting me. Tempting the animal behind my eyes.

"Please?" he whispered, throaty and deep. "Please—I want you to do it. I need it—the hurt, too. I need it all the way down, all the way this time."

Deranged fool! Did he understand how easily I could take more than he had to give?

My body disintegrated, turning airy and light, a beast levitating to the surface.

"Do it, Quilldriver," Foxglove's voice said close to my ear, her neatly manicured nails raking down my back to quicken my desire. "Aaron's only delight in life is his love of death, so why not give him what he wants? He'll find it sooner or later anyway."

I fought—not because it was natural any longer, but because I *wanted* it to be.

"No, don't say no—please?" Aaron whispered, clutching my hand until the pulse of him was so strong it became painful against my skin. "I'll make it good. I need it... *need* it! To die inside somebody else, my blood inside you, see. Not to be so alone when the end comes. Isn't that what we're supposed to want? Not to be alone?"

Maybe it was.

The others watched, pale silhouettes. Time was waiting.

"Please?" Aaron whispered again. Clutching at me in trance madness. The smell of him hot in the air, so hot, a red crayon melting in the sun, bleeding.

Bleeding...

Just a taste, a swallow or two, the demon inside promised. *Yes, see how he wants it? Just a little drink now. You can stop.*

And then my lips were at his wrist, starved for the essence flowing through him—the fear and the hurt and all the memories that had brought him to this point.

His need becoming my need. My need evolving into action.

With a crazed snarl, I grabbed his outstretched hand, yanking it to me. But when my fangs scraped over his wrist—cruelly slicing rather than puncturing, a painful punishment for his suicidal wickedness—I once again knew that demented thrill reserved for immortals alone. His back arched off the couch, small nipples going hard through his shirt as a quick intake of breath left him convulsing with pain and elation.

His rapture brought me to my knees, a fall so hard it caused me to cry out, too. The drinking of him—slick, smooth sliding down my throat, his lifeforce inside me, my mind thinking his thoughts. My body quickening, a river swelling beyond hardened banks.

So perfect to feel him courting the succor of oblivion, welcoming it. Yes, this was as it should be. Not to be alone. I could give him that comfort. My benefaction, my gratitude.

The roar of the approving crowd, the roar that was really his heart, a tiny hummingbird, fragile and fast. So fast. Too fast.

So perfect. I drank. More of him. Yes, more.

144

I drank. Wet. Red. Yesterdays.

It was as it should be, as it had been for Stephanie, so perfect to seduce Aaron out of himself and into me, just as Stephanie had left her temporal husk to reside inside my maker's immortal temple, his veins the receptacle for her soul—

From another world, I heard a terrible cry that erupted from my own mouth, a wail so keen and fierce it shattered the trance and sent me pitching backward. As my eyes locked on the angelic face of this lost soul—this young man gazing up at me with the euphoria of a flagellist monk seductively wooing the torture of the lash—I knew I could not serve as the instrument of his damnation.

I couldn't mend his shattered life. Nor could I take it.

'...There are sacred moments in time, when a mortal will ask you to end their life because it truly is time for them to die'.

Miquel's words. Tempting me. Taunting me.

But it *wasn't* Aaron's time. He might crave the thrill of dying as much as any vampyre craved blood, but he didn't want the reality of it. Not yet. Not this time. No, not yet.

"I won't do it, damn you!" I roared to the thirst within me, to the other vampyres around me. "Don't make me do it!"

The others said nothing, magnificent fiends of alabaster and onyx waiting to see which way death would travel tonight. I hated them. I loved them. They were my blood, feeling everything I felt, everything Aaron felt.

They were vampyres, distanced from the mortal world by time and inhuman hearts beating slow and cold.

I envied them. Hated myself for envying them.

Scrambling to my feet, I shoved my way through that sea of the walking dead until I erupted through the back door. My body convulsed, sucking in the night air which was a natural but all too temporary antidote to the urges still raging within me and the horror of what those urges had almost done to a young man who was someone's son, someone's lover, maybe even someone's father.

For a long time, I brooded in silence, angry with my vampyre brothers for bringing me here. Angry with my sisters for their role in the play. Angry with Aaron for playing with death.

Angriest of all with myself.

The black bottomed pool threw my reflection up at me, giving me pause and mercifully distracting me. Leanly muscled and graceful in the tight jeans I'd borrowed from Miquel's closet, I barely recognized myself, though I could no longer deny that I was desirable, stunning even. It stood to reason that Aaron wanted me, for my transformation had provided camouflage for the modern predator—a pretty face and a hard body and the ability to throw humans into a trance that made them *want* to die in my arms.

You're a vampyre now, a voice inside me said.

But I was still just a man, at home in neither world.

Grasping my head with both hands to keep it from exploding, I snarled in abject futility, despising the thing I had become because men and women *would* be drawn to me as surely as the flesh of the night was black.

"You're thinking like a mortal again," Donny scolded, his reflection appearing next to mine in the pool's surface. I hadn't heard him come out of the house, but he put an arm around my shoulder, his cold hand stroking my bare skin the same way he might have soothed a frightened pet. "Blood is humanity incarnate. Some people are operas. Others are rock and roll."

"Aaron's an X-rated movie," Bird offered with a grin, tipping his tall top hat as he joined us. Wind flapped the tails of his tux. The beads in his hair clapped, colorful clay hands. "He's a feast of pleasure in love with the pain only a vampyre can bring—ambrosia to our kind." A pause, a shrug. "You *didn't* kill him, my friend."

"I could have." I confessed, "I wanted to."

Bird frowned, a philosophical still life. "And if you had?" He inclined his head toward the house, speaking with an indifference that comes only with age and experience. "They *all* die, Quilldriver. They aren't like us. You can't save them, especially ones like that."

The hell of it was that he was right. The hell of it was that I *understood* why Miquel had done what he'd done to my daughter even if I might hate him for it forever.

My head spun, leaving me scared of the changes still going on inside me. Already—so quickly—Aaron was fading from my thoughts, his blood going cold inside my own cold body until he was just another mortal, another dance in the long dark night, another drink from another fountain of eternal youth.

"Exactly," Bird said with an easy chuckle. Now he put an arm around me from the other side until we were a macabre family portrait on the black leather skin of the water.

A few moments later, Stygian ambled out and stood looking down at that picture, leaning his head on Donny's shoulder. His lips were red when he smiled, and I couldn't help picturing him drinking from Aaron's junkie veins just as I had done. It stirred me, such an intimate sharing. It bound me to my brother, that living red river which had fed us both.

Suddenly trembling, I stared at my feet, lost. Donny held me closer, a comforting shadow stored in a compact body. In a few minutes, Dimitri and the women joined us outside, and though my uneasiness lingered, none of them ever spoke of the incident again. While we sat watching the stars fall and listening to thunder rumbling in the east, we told tall tales of our days as children and then we began walking through the quiet residential neighborhood where windows glowed like golden rectangles and the scent of pink geraniums filled the air.

On my left, Donny was a silhouette in a trench coat with his hair trailing behind him on the wind. On my right, Foxglove was my feminine shadow, her arm crooked through mine as if we were clandestine lovers too long apart. The others sauntered nearby, a step ahead or a step behind as we strolled dark streets, our very nature making us always restless and driven to prowl the night.

On one street, Stygian shared a jogger with Donny before they left the man dazed on his own doorstep. Dimitri took an executive coming home late from work, their silhouettes dancing beneath a streetlight's misty bloom. Foxglove and Coma seduced their way into the car of a man who wore a black cowboy hat but had probably never been on a horse. Bird and I watched it all—he a natural born voyeur, I still gorged on Aaron.

And as the seven of us moved through that sleeping neighborhood with its red tile roofs and its glow-in-the-dark Halloween decorations mocking us from every window, it was as if I could look into each one of those middle-class homes and know far more than I wanted to know about the people living inside.

Empathy, Dimitri had called it.

There was the little girl in a corner room who always wore green flip-flops and lived in her autistic world where Daddy came to visit late at night and made her feel things she didn't like to feel, things that hurt. There was the bank manager juggling two separate affairs while his wife was pregnant with their fourth child. And there was the middle-aged fat lady writing letters to her sister in Vermont, weaving romantic tales of a fiancé who never existed and never would.

They all had their stories, and all those stories had sad endings. But we were apart from it—this incoherent, disconnected swarm of life that made up the human hive. It all seemed so random, yet I couldn't help thinking there was something I was failing to see, some common thread that might one day cause it to have cohesion.

Surely happiness existed somewhere. God was more than man's myth. Death wasn't the end of life.

There would be answers.

"I envy your infatuation with philosophy, Quilldriver, this need you have to look for meaning in things," Foxglove told me as the streetlights sprinkled vampyre shadows over neatly clipped suburban lawns. With her arm through mine again, she rested her dark head on my shoulder. "I'm only sorry it won't last."

Though I'd given up on my brothers ever calling me anything but Quilldriver, it irritated me when Foxglove did it. She read my thoughts easily, yet kept her own shielded, hidden. Because of that, I didn't like her.

"What makes you think it won't last?" I asked, clipped.

She patted my hand as if I were a foolish child. "Existence is its own answer, my dear. There's nothing more. If you go around trying to understand why mortals do all the crazy things they do, you'll end up as crazy as they are, and then where will you be but forever crazy?"

"Stars above, Foxy, do we have to get into this again?" Coma asked, tossing the words over her shoulder from a few steps ahead. "If Miquel's new scribe thinks he can find meaning in any of this, more power to him. Hell, he might surprise us!"

"Then again, he might not," Foxglove countered, shooting me a smile that wasn't the least bit friendly. "No offense, but wiser men than you have tried and failed."

"Wise men will always fail because they think they already have the answers," Stygian interjected nonchalantly. "It's the fool's journey that's worth watching, Foxy."

"Guess I'm not into sitcoms."

Bitch! The thought came from Donny, an injection straight

148

into my mind. He moved closer, his body pressed protectively against my side as we passed a string of plastic pumpkins beaming snaggle-toothed grimaces into the night.

"Why do we always end up prowling around this yuppie infested neighborhood debating ideology every time we come to San Diego?" Bird inquired, his shadow on the road a study in elegance that was incongruous with his complaining. "Eternity's a terrible thing to waste on mediocrity, Foxy. If it's grocery shopping you want, let's hop in the car and cruise up to Hollywood Boulevard."

"I want Stefan to meet Casey," Foxy replied, shooting me a wink. "She's—"

—*a vampyre lover*, Donny provided, unnerving me with his ability to sing thoughts so easily into my head.

"—a vampyre lover," Foxy concluded, unaware. "You see, Stefan, there are a few people on this wretched mud ball who still believe in vampyres and who long to become as we are. To that end, they lie awake at night and call us with the tears of their splintered souls." She paused, overly dramatic and clearly disgusted. "Simpletons," she sighed.

"Simpletons?" Stygian echoed from a few steps ahead. He turned around and began walking backwards, his hair a halo of gold dancing on his shoulders. "What's simple about wanting to live forever, my pretty sister? You *begged* Miquel for it. We all did, one way or another."

Foxglove curled her lip. "Do you *really* believe any of us would have chosen it if he'd been truthful from the beginning, if he'd told us what would happen?"

"He did tell you," Stygian said with an easy shrug, though his voice had taken on an edge of irritability. "I was there."

"You were stoned, Styx—magic mushroom tea brewed in the veins of hippies as I recall," Coma countered, laughing a little.

"He told them," Stygian assured me, adamant.

"Didn't," Foxy argued. Then, like a little girl: "The bastard just wanted to fuck me. That's the only reason he made me. Maybe he loved Coma a long time ago, but it was *me* he wanted to fuck."

Donny laughed out loud, clearly repulsed by everything Foxglove said or did, everything she was. "Conceited little bitch, ain't ya?" He looked her up and down with a sneer that stole his innocence and revealed the danger just beneath the surface. "The last thing Miquel would want is to fuck *you*! You're so stuck on yourself, there's no room for anybody else in there anyway!"

I thought Foxglove would strike the kid, for she stiffened to the point of rigidity, and all of a sudden everything was out of control.

Stepping around me, she jabbed her neon blue fingernail into Donny's chest the way a bully on the playground might do. "He made *you* out of pity, you self-righteous little snake!" she hurled, jabbing him repeatedly. "And that's what's wrong with you—you're a goddamned mortal in a vampyre's body! You can't tell your ass from a hole in the ground or blood from shit, which is why your fucking little nose is always brown!"

Donny snarled, smacking her offending finger aside. "Touch me with that thing again and I'll bite it off, Foxy," he warned. "Why don't you drag that 10-inch dildo out of mothballs and put some new D cells in it, and maybe you'll feel better, you dried-up old tampon! You *wanted* to be a vampyre, goddammit, so live with it!"

"You weren't even there!" she snarled in his face. "Miquel lied to us and he tricked us and now there's no going back! And if I ever get my hands on the son-of-a-bitch, I'll—"

"Oh, do give it a rest, Foxy," Bird suggested, interrupting with an air of long-suffering patience. To me, he added, "The truth of the matter is that our unholy father disowned Foxy when she tried to steal a pint or two of that magic stuff flowing through his veins—."

"That's a lie!" Foxglove shrieked.

"Isn't," Stygian shrugged, kicking at little rocks on the ground, distracted.

Almost unconsciously, I glanced at Coma, and as our eyes met in the darkness of that deserted street, she quickly looked away. Oddly enough, it was *her* reaction which told me everything I needed to know. Foxglove was the liar, and not entirely sane as a result of whatever had happened between her and Miquel.

"C'mon, baby," Coma said to her lover, trying to soothe her anger as an owl hooted from atop a nearby telephone pole. "It was a long time ago, okay? We can't bring Nathan back, so there's no point to all this." To Donny, she bared her fangs and added, "Thanks a lot, you little asshole."

"I'm sick of her blaming Miquel for her own bullshit! We'd all be dead if it weren't for him, but all she ever does is bitch!" Donny snapped, staring the women down. "Christ—it must be fucking awful to go through eternity with PM-fucking-S! Fuck, Coma! Get the bitch a fucking Midol junkie to sink her teeth into!"

Coma might've smacked him, but Stygian got between them, shouldering Donny aside and elbowing him to silence.

Whatever the dynamics between them, Coma relented and went to Foxglove, but the other woman twisted away. Her chin was trembling as she turned those haunted eyes on me, poked me in the chest with that same sharp fingernail, and said in a cryogenic voice: "Nathan was Coma's little boy, Quilldriver. He was eight years old when they diagnosed him with leukemia and he was ten when he died. You can figure out the rest."

My heart broke despite her hostility, despite her madness.

"Look, Foxy," Stygian said with an easy gesture of his hands. "Miquel couldn't save Nathan—."

"Bullshit!" Foxglove spat. "He's a fucking Creator, Styx!"

"It doesn't matter!" Stygian maintained in defense of our maker. Frustrated, he threw his hands up in the air. "It can't be *done*, Foxy, and that's the ugly truth! Kids can't survive the change!"

"The truth?" Foxglove sputtered, incredulous "What the hell would you know about the truth?" Then, muttering under her breath, she turned and ran back in the direction of the house, the scent of her rose perfume all that remained.

With a look that warned the rest of us not to interfere, Dimitri went after her, and the last I saw of them that night was their silhouettes underneath a streetlight. Foxglove's head was on his shoulder, her chest rising and falling as she wept and he soothed her with little sounds that never made it back to where the rest of us awkwardly waited on the sidewalk.

I expected Coma to follow after them, but instead she came up to me and put one hand on my arm—shy and tentative and not at all like her lover.

"If you ever write about us, don't judge her too harshly, Stefan," she said, almost apologetically. "She did try to steal Miquel's blood, that much is true. But she did it trying to save my boy's life." She paused, her eyes cold blue stars, fallen. She was lost, every bit as much as I was myself, and now her voice lowered until

151

only I could hear her. "When you see him again, tell him I still think about him, okay?" *Tell Miquel I still love him, Quilldriver. Tell him that?*

Filled with a foolishly human need to pacify her pain, I asked gently, "Won't you be coming to the Gathering? You can tell him yourself."

To judge by the psychic bombardment from Stygian, Bird and Donny, one would have thought I'd just pissed in the Pope's holy water. There was a shuffling of feet, a clearing of a throat. And finally Coma shook her head.

"We're not part of the Family anymore, Stefan," she told me with a shrug, tears in the corners of her eyes. "Oh, I suppose Miquel would let me in, but Foxy's been exiled forever. And where she's not welcome, I don't go."

Before I could get my foot any deeper in my mouth, Stygian went to Coma and put a reassuring arm around her shoulder. Like a loving older brother smoothing over the younger sibling's *faux pas*, he whispered something into her ear—something that made her smile contritely and dab at her tears with her sleeve—and then he walked her back to the house.

The rest of us stayed on the sidewalk. A calico cat watched from the window of a nearby house. Bird's head was lowered. Donny played an imaginary guitar, cool blues to comfort us.

"Bitch," the kid said at last, the word an ice sculpture wearing Foxglove's face.

So there we stood, going nowhere. Perhaps in that way, we weren't much different from our mortal counterparts—running in circles, starting out on wondrous quests, getting sidetracked along the way, wondering what the hell went wrong.

CHAPTER THIRTEEN

After we left Foxglove and Coma, Dimitri insisted on dropping me off at my old place so I could gather up my belongings, and though I protested being left at the drab apartment complex at 3 a.m., I knew it was something I had to face alone.

The streets were deserted as the limo pulled away, lifeless grey arteries of an atrophied world, the only sign of life a stray dog sniffing garbage cans on the sidewalk. I became mesmerized by the wretched beast—one wild thing studying another—yet it soon became obvious that this bedraggled mutt who limped on one hind leg was more scavenger than predator. Unable to turn over the cans to free their putrid treasures, he gave a keen yip of exasperation, then cocked his bad leg and pissed profusely on the object of his frustration.

For that, I had to admire him.

Though I'd envisioned disappearing into the underworld of this uncanny vampyre existence never to be bothered with mortal concerns again—a romantic vision filled with angst, appealing to us all in some way—practicality forced me to concede that I would need my bank books and my credit cards unless I wanted to be acting out that fantasy in lonesome alleys or ruined buildings.

To earn a living, I would need my computer. Vampyre or no, I would need clothes and shoes and my car which had turned up in the parking lot even though I'd left it at the hotel in Los Angeles. Charlie's handiwork, I suspected. Her way of telling me she'd known I'd come back even though I'd sworn I never would.

Odd, how quickly things could change.

Not so long ago, I'd written all of it off as props. Now I was back to looking at those props as if they were the most important things in the world. Money, transportation, vocation.

Of course, I didn't really need any of it. Worse, I could see now how easily those material possessions could become anchors— petty things to keep the body distracted and pacified so the spirit wouldn't go wandering off in search of greater quests that might overturn society's status quo.

What *was* behind that veil? And why had Man created a society that demanded his soul in exchange for a few silver coins at the end of each indistinguishable week, a society that robbed the best years of his life only so the society itself could be served?

As a vampyre existing apart from the flow of linear time, I could not help but ask these troubling questions—questions I'd fought *not* to face when I'd been mortal, questions that nonetheless assaulted me when I opened the door to my old apartment and was forced to look back on my own life.

I didn't know who I was. Worse, I wasn't even sure who I had once been.

When I turned on the lights, the first thing I noticed was the tv staring at me with its dusty visage, a window to entire worlds of complacency. The sofa had a permanent indention in it, and the coffee table bore scars which were really water marks from too many bottles of cheap wine. Books with my name on the spine collected dust—drivel I'd once thought profound—and the computer which had been an extension of my thoughts sat forlornly in the corner, its glass eye blinded by a plastic hood.

Displaced in my own home, I moved to the back room where my single bed stood like some eerie testament to the laws of chance. When I'd left the apartment—hassled and harried as I dashed out the door on my way to the convention—it never occurred to me that I might never return.

Just as Stephanie had left our hotel room that fateful night, I had left home with the certainty of coming back to this place, this room, this frozen moment.

And yet, life was chance and chance was entirely a matter of luck, so perhaps it stood to reason that I'd left this apartment as a man and returned as a vampyre who now stood next to the nightstand clutching the only thing that had any real substance.

She stared up at me from a frame of tarnished silver, her eyes too pale for the blue-black hair that outlined her face, her lips downturned into a sadness that begged for help even though I'd been too blind to see it. I wondered fleetingly if I would look at this same photograph a thousand years hence and ask who the girl had been. How much could the physical brain hold before it would begin to shed memories like a snake shedding old skin?

For nearly an hour, all I could do was stare at her, burning her sprite-like face onto my mind's eye, for I knew a day would come when this photograph would crumble back into dust.

Time, a fickle artist, had a habit of erasing its best work.

The very air exuded coldness—a sterile scent of impermanence that inhabited bus stations, taxi cabs and cheap apartments. All the clocks had stopped. And though I knew a power failure had caused the digital heart of time to blink, I preferred to take the symbolism literally.

Time *had* stopped.

Since I'd been transformed from a mortal to an immortal, even my body had ceased most of its usual functions. I had not relieved myself, nor felt any need to do so. Other than the blood of mortals, I had neither eaten nor drunk.

And for the first time, I was struck with the realization that, now and forever, I would be 34 years old. I would not change even though everything around me might crumble into ruin. Nations would come and go. Men would land on distant planets as Neil Armstrong had landed on the moon when I was a little boy. Giant redwoods would grow from saplings and die of old age and the stars themselves would dim into mere legend as the world became more populated, more overrun with manmade light designed to chase away the night.

I would live forever.

One day when I wrote of the blue whale and the white tiger, mutated humans with computer chips in their brains would say they were only fantasy, just as vampyres and faeries and all things magical, once accepted as fact, were perceived as fantasy now.

I would see the world end—at least the world I'd always known.

I sat down heavily on the sofa in the living room, my eyes fixed on the VCR and the winking red eye of time.

12:00

12:00

12:00

"Forever now." I mused to myself, entranced. "Forever midnight."

Dingy green curtains hung lifeless over dirty windows, pleated wrinkles on the face of mother night. In the air around me, particles of dust swam in the pale yellow glow cast by the overhead fixture.

My shadow was tacked up on the wall with a dozen nails which had once held paintings belonging to former tenants, and as I sat there with my elbows on my knees and my head in my hands, I said a benediction for the man I'd been before—the stranger who'd lived in this apartment without ever noticing how awful it was, the fool who'd cast that same shadow on that same wall as he sat mourning the ashes of his life because he'd forgotten how to live.

I said a prayer—to a God in whom I wanted to believe and couldn't—for the unsalvageable soul of Stefan London.

He was dead, after all, and a vampyre had crawled inside his skin and reanimated his bones, packing his belongings in old grocery sacks and ragged suitcases.

Another night was drawing to a close, silver light seeping in at the crack between worlds. Because I couldn't make the drive to Miquel's house before the sun would steal over the horizon, I snatched the mattress off the bed and wrestled it into the closet.

Yawning as I lay down in the darkness, I thought of Foxglove and Coma, though it seemed I'd met them years in the past instead of only hours ago. Time was a peculiar gravity now, heavier in some places than others.

Weary, my eyes closed.

Almost immediately, images flashed: a beautiful boy underneath the stairs who tried to warn me. A foyer of mirrors and roses. Stained glass angels mourning their dead. *'Driftwood, Stefan. I am driftwood'*. A bloodstained kiss, lips to lips.

Sleep edged closer, for the night was calling me back even when day was scratching at the horizon. Behind my eyes, Miquel was waiting in a tux.

> *Now I lay me down to bed*
> *With the devil inside my head...*

But just when sleep should have taken me, I sensed another presence in the room, as if it had stolen in on the wind or crept under the door like an early morning fog. Bolting upright, I peeked through the crack where the sliding doors met.

There, next to the nightstand, Miquel stood sequestered in shadows which followed him even in daylight, holding my daughter's picture in his hands as if he belonged here. Unaware that he was being watched, he ran his fingertips across the glass as if to caress her face, and in his eyes I saw genuine pain.

156

Who do you dance with now, little girl? And where does life go when it ends?

His thoughts came as clearly as if he'd spoken aloud, and while my initial instinct was to leap out of the closet and beat him to death—not caring that killing him would destroy me, too—now more than ever I had no choice but to believe he really had cared for her.

In the very air, I could *feel* that love.

He had loved her as I had loved Aaron, but he'd loved her more. Enough to end her pain. Enough to comfort her with the serenity of death itself.

For that, I hated him all over again. For that I loved him all the more.

But when I scrambled to my feet, Miquel tensed sharply, dark head lifting like an animal sensing danger. I never saw him move, yet before I had any comprehension of what had happened, he was standing behind me inside the closet, one arm around my chest to hold me still while he clasped his other hand firmly over my mouth just as I squawked, "Hey!"

"Keep quiet, Stefan," he whispered against my ear, so soft I barely heard him.

Keys rattled in the lock. The front door opened, shut again. Footsteps crunched over the living room carpet. I squirmed in Miquel's embrace, disturbed by his physical closeness.

Be a shadow among the shadows, his mind instructed. *Move between the molecules of space and time where mortal eyes cannot see.*

I hadn't a clue what he meant as I gazed out the crack where the doors met, expecting to see the building supervisor or even some would-be burglar. Instead, my heart thundered when I heard a woman's humming—*I Want To Know What Love Is*—and Charlie came sauntering into the room with a pitcher of water for the scraggly fichus tree.

Miquel stiffened just as she halted in mid-step, her eyes fixed on the box springs left akimbo on the Hollywood frame. Her humming stopped, and I actually felt the goose bumps lift up on her arms as apprehension zinged through her chest.

I expected her to bolt, but Charlie had never been one for girly-girl dramatics, so she set the pitcher down, turned, and perused the room.

157

"Stefan?" she called cautiously, her gaze falling on the closet.

What stunned me was her perfect beauty. Though I'd known her since we were children, I had never looked at her through eyes that saw more than the physical shell. Her aura glistened, a warm sunset on a summer afternoon, red and salty.

"Stefan?"

When I heard her voice for the second time—a tuned bell pealing a note of human love in its purest form of friendship—I was so drawn to her that I completely forgot Miquel's presence. My mouth opened to reply, but before I could make a sound, he placed a restraining hand on my arm and hushed me to silence with a nudge of his elbow in my ribs.

Then, his mouth against my ear, his voice not a voice but a preternatural whisper, he warned me, "If you care for her, stay still as death, Stefan, for if you drink from that sea in her veins, the affection you feel for one another will compel you to drink it all, and even I might not be able to stop you."

The thirst cared nothing for reason.

Perceiving Miquel only as an obstacle, I almost turned on him as I had when he'd kept me apart from Valerie. But Charlie started toward the closet, and a sinking feeling in the pit of my stomach held me motionless—like a little boy about to be caught with his hand in some forbidden cookie jar shaped like an apple in the Garden of Eden.

Miquel's mind laughed at my dread.

"You're a vampyre," he reminded me, "will-of-the-wisp to mortal eyes, a shadow in an old closet. Bend your thoughts to the night and she will see only the things of the day."

His words had two effects. They confused me utterly and they stirred me against my will, for they were spoken straight into my soul as my maker stood there with his lean body pressed against my back and his lips moving over my neck.

But before I could ask him how to accomplish this task he had set for me, Charlie stood in front of the closet, golden head tilted to one side with curiosity. My nostrils twitched when I caught the scent of her, and the craving to have her in my arms rose up like some demon that never slept.

"Stefan?" she said for the third time, and put her hand on the door.

Fog, smoke, penumbra! Miquel's mind intoned, some magical incantation. *Be!*

The door moved, one inch, then another. I closed my eyes, but I'd misplaced my faith and there was no one left to pray to. An instant later, the closet door flung wide. Squinting, I winced, but once again Miquel placed a hand over my mouth.

In his telepathic heart, amusement tickled.

There, I told you! She sees only an unpainted wall and old clothes. Nothing more.

But Charlie's eyes were boring into mine and I could hear her heartbeat like a jungle drum. My mouth went wet with need. All I had to do was reach out, ease my fangs into her throat, and take the blood. She was my friend, I rationalized, not at all rational. She'd give it to me if I asked. She'd let me have her even if I didn't ask, if I couldn't.

But then, unexpectedly, Charlie laughed and covered her mouth with her hand, her face flushing with the very blood I so craved.

"God, Stefan, I'm really sorry," she said, clearly abashed, unaware of the danger she was in. She took a step backward, repeating, "I'm really sorry! Uh—I'll just let myself out—I mean—I guess this is *really* a case of being in the closet. Shit—I shouldn't have said that! You should have told me you met somebody!" Then, because she was more flustered than I'd ever seen her, she said to Miquel as if we were at a cocktail party, "Hi, I'm Charlie Weathers—Stefan's friend?"

She started to offer him a handshake, then just as quickly crammed her hands into her pockets.

What a sight we must have been. She'd always regarded me as some eccentric writer with a few screws loose, yet here I was in the closet with another man who had one arm around my chest and one hand clasped over my mouth. Why she didn't think I was being assaulted, I never knew.

Miquel's astonishment was like a physical entity that fluttered its wings against my mind. Curiosity surged through him, followed by a hunger that matched my own. Indeed, had he not been holding me so tightly, I would have placed myself between him and Charlie—not only because I was protective of her, but because I knew her well enough to recognize the look in her eyes as

159

instantaneous attraction to the handsome ogre.

"You can see us," he said, not a question.

She looked at the vampyre as if he were daft, laughing nervously. "What? Did you think you were invisible?"

At this, Miquel stepped around me with the poise and charm of any European gentleman. "My apologies for startling you, Ms. Weathers," he murmured, and I swear he coaxed his accent to the surface as an accomplice in his bid to seduce her. Then, offering his hand, he beamed a radiant smile. "I am Miquel Kaliq Constantine, but I would be pleased if you call me Miquel."

While Charlie saw only the outward bravado of a would-be swashbuckler—made all the more convincing by the loose fitting white shirt, crisp black pants and the priceless jewels he wore so flagrantly—I saw into his heart and knew how deeply troubled he was that she actually *could* see us.

And, like any cornered animal, Miquel was dangerous.

When Charlie flushed, he brought her hand to his lips and kissed it, his fangs so close to her wrist I was instantaneously rattled from my shock. Scrambling out of the closet despite the extreme discomfort of daylight crawling along my face and arms like ants preparing to bite, I gathered my wits and went back to the business of being a writer.

"Mr. Constantine is my new European publisher, Charlie," I lied, shooting Miquel a warning glance which he must have interpreted as the equivalent of the fly giving orders to the spider. "We've been working on a new project, and in an attempt to settle a point of disagreement, we were enacting a scene from the book when—."

But Charlie wasn't listening. Instead, as I prattled helplessly, her expression changed from embarrassment to confusion to complete and undeniable fascination.

She wasn't just looking at me. She was looking *into* me, and the things she saw were not the things I wanted her to see.

"My God, Stefan, what's happened to you?" she half whispered, her voice sending chills along my spine. In her aura, a thousand thoughts danced at once, and though it broke my heart to see it, she was afraid of me and took a step backward to confirm it.

I tried to laugh it off, but I was no actor. "Look, Charlie, I..." But what could I say that wouldn't sound absolutely ridiculous?

My voice fell away when Charlie's eyes clouded with hurt and accusation. Like a dagger, it wounded me, for she had seen me through my marriage to Laurie, the birth and death of my daughter, my divorce, and the aftermath and ashes of everything I had ever been. Yet now, she stood there looking at me as if I truly were a monster.

Time clicked and rattled, not knowing what to do until Miquel spoke.

"If you are her friend, Stefan, honor her with the truth and trust her to see that your heart and soul haven't changed, but only your body," he suggested, giving her the same smile that had been my downfall. "For certainly, if she can see us at all after my will pronounced her blind, she is not a woman who will swoon in the presence of truth."

Charlie was staring at me all the time he spoke. "Stefan?" she said again, a two syllable indictment that had been my name.

I reached toward her, but instead of coming to me as she'd done since we were children, she stood deathly still, looking first at me, then at Miquel. In slow motion, her hand raised to her mouth and the blood ran from her face as if finally sensing the danger it was in.

She knew *exactly* what we were, and though I might have expected a hundred different reactions, all she did was suck in a little breath that sounded like an old house creaking under stress.

When she did make a move to flee, Miquel took control even before I knew what was happening. Reaching out to grab her arm, he spun the web of his trance around her, capturing her will so quickly and easily it was frightening.

"Ah, Ms. Weathers, I'm afraid I can't let you leave just yet," he said in a voice that was seductive and gentle and not at all threatening.

Charlie's eyes widened—that moment when a person sees the truck bearing down on them a split second before the impact—but before she could react, she was already captured by the vampyre's magic. She swayed on her feet for a moment, putting a hand to her chest, and then she simply collapsed into Miquel's outstretched arms.

It was that quick, that simple—and with a woman whose stubborn, earthy will was stronger than any I'd ever known.

For a split second, I believed she was dead—until a sigh parted her lips and she seemed to bend into the curves of Miquel's body. He lifted her easily, placing her on the mattress inside the closet the way a child might put a doll to bed for the night.

And though he made no move beyond that, a thousand horrific possibilities flashed through my mind as I saw him poised above her.

Believing he would take Charlie's life to protect himself—for she *had* seen his face—I swung wildly when he straightened. And though my blow grazed past his ear, glancing off as he evaded my assault, he caught my arm and bent it backward until I was certain even vampyre bones could break. His eyes bored into mine, and when he shoved me in the chest to send me flying against the wall, the force of his will hit me with all the energy of a train wreck.

"What on Earth is wrong with you, Stefan?" he growled at me.

Everything. No one thing.

I scrambled to get up—filled with rage and fury I didn't comprehend—but Miquel stopped me with the full brunt of his telepathic fury, slamming me against the wall for the second time without ever lifting a hand.

Whether it was self-defense or whether he'd finally had his fill of my unpredictable madness made little difference.

Addled, I slid to the floor.

It was worse than any physical blow, for it was the very *essence* of Miquel's anger, the root of his power, the source of his mystical abilities.

Must I strike you dead before you see I mean you no harm? his thoughts howled, incredulous and betrayed.

But because he was a vampyre, it was more than any idle question. He *did* strike me dead, smacking me down with his will as easily as a mortal might have swatted a gnat.

He killed me in his mind, the shock of it leaving me limp. The miracle was that I survived at all, though I do believe his reaction surprised him, for we were like two school boys fighting over a girl. Only later would he reveal that I was the only vampyre he'd ever made who could arouse his fierce temper so quickly.

I had driven him mad and now the damage was done.

I couldn't look at Miquel, for in that moment when his

162

shields fell and his thoughts were an open book, I knew he not only didn't love me, he didn't even like me.

With a posture of defeat, muttering something in Greek, he went to sit on the box springs with his feet wide apart and his head in his hands.

"I never want to hurt you, Stefan," he said to the floor, his voice low and tired. "But neither do I want to see you hurt by this world, and surely you must know what's at stake if your secret should become known."

"She's not somebody you can have!" I snapped, angry all over again despite my physical incapacitation. "I won't let you hurt her the way you hurt Stephanie!"

He didn't even look at me. With a sigh of resignation, he got to his feet and moved to the door, where he stood silhouetted against the brighter light from the other room. Head lowered, shoulders slack, he didn't move for nearly a full minute. Then, slowly, he turned toward me with a look I would have given anything never to witness.

His eyes were ancient, and for the first time I witnessed his true age—all the weariness and all the pain of a very long life, all the hurt and frustration any parent feels when a child turns on them.

"In another instant she would have bolted, and then I would have had no choice but to kill her—for while it's true that the police would not concern themselves with a madwoman prattling about vampyres, it is also true that someone somewhere *would*. And though you might find it difficult to believe, there are still people in this modern world who have devoted their lives to hunting and destroying our kind.

"So you see, Stefan," he concluded, looking me squarely in the eye, "what I did, I did to save her life, and to protect you and Dimitri and all the others. When she awakens, she will remember nothing." He gazed at me with dismay, despair that tore me asunder. "Would that it could be as simple to heal this rift which divides you and me."

He honestly didn't understand why I could hate him as much as I loved him, and if anything might make me forgive him one day, that's what it would be: his honest naiveté.

"You killed my daughter," I said at last, wanting him to

know why things were the way they were, why they had to be that way.

But the way he looked at me told me _I_ was the one who didn't understand.

"It's not something I would change even if I could, Stefan," he said with an unwavering conviction. "You see, what I did was right, necessary even. Had Stephanie gone on living, she would have gone on suffering. Wounds of the soul never heal, not even with a father's love."

He truly believed it, and that took some of the venom out of me.

"You aren't God," I mumbled, numb inside.

"No," he agreed, his voice barely audible. "I am only the instrument of His will, and _that_ is the Hell the Heavenly Father has bestowed on me. _If_ He exists, He has given me the curse of knowing when mortal pain is too much to bear, and the gift of being able to put an end to it. It's in my nature to do this, you see, and if your God is out there, who else but He created my nature?"

His words struck me with an appalling ring of truth. With the power of life and death in his hands, Miquel could create immortal angels or take mortal lives, and perhaps the wonder was that he could do either and still remain sane at all.

Who was I to judge him? He was more myth than man, not really human at all, and finally seeing that is what shattered my soul when he turned and headed for the door. His thoughts lingered, however, and though he never meant me to hear them, they were as tangible as a physical blow.

I would give you back your mortal life if I could, Stefan, he thought, driven to hopelessness by my hatred. _I would filter your blood from my veins and mine from yours and it would be as if it never was and the poison would be gone from us both._

And then he was gone, the door closing with a terrible echo of finality.

It was another minute before I could move again, and even then the anguish in my heart and the pain in my body caused me to wince. Worlds bounced away from me, rubber balls.

He was gone, all right. Not only from the room, but from _within_ me. The place inside me which had been so keenly aware of him was suddenly empty.

164

My maker had abandoned me.

I could have my life back. I could live in this apartment and go about my business as I'd always done, even if I might have to take a night job and sleep during the day. I could go bowling with my friends and sit on the couch watching reruns of _Gilligan's Island,_ and maybe even buy a place of my own and spend my weekends watering the hedge to keep my fundamentalist neighbors from looking too closely at my illumined eyes.

If nobody noticed the drug dealers on the corners or the pimps cruising the streets or the suffering that drove men mad, why should anybody notice a vampyre living in Escondido?

I stared at bland walls, drinking the emptiness from the inside out. Yes, I could have my life back.

Or I could finally start to live.

It was a scary choice, for going through the motions of life would always be easier than living—running on a track as opposed to carving my own path. And yet, I'd had my fill of tracks and plays. A puppet, once free, couldn't put on the strings again, and so I scrambled to my feet, sucking a hard breath into my lungs.

Charlie looked so young and vulnerable as her chest rose and fell in the rhythms of trance sleep, and for an instant I wished I _could_ be human again. But some awful awareness said we were lost to one another forever, inhabitants of two different worlds that only overlapped when vampyre teeth sank into human flesh and blood was spilled.

Because I knew what I would do if I stayed a moment longer, I turned to leave. But my eye caught a glint of silver metal on the nightstand and a chill slid through my spine, paralyzing me all over again.

Stephanie had begun to smile.

The photograph which had always seemed so grim had altered, as if it had been replaced, and as I stood there with my eyes gone wide and my immortal heart hammering wild inside my chest, her head turned toward me and her ghost began to speak.

"Don't you see?" she said, more vibrant than she'd ever been while she was alive. "I'm finally where I want to be, so blow me a kiss and go find your life. You were made for something bigger than grief, something better than bitters! You were made to be a vampyre and that's totally cool! Now go, Fang Daddy! Run, run,

run for your afterlife, and leave your hatred behind! Even the devil needs forgiveness, but before you can forgive him, you've gotta forgive *me*, ya know?"

Then, like the turning of a page or the closing of a book, the frame flew off the nightstand and tumbled face down on the floor.

I knew then what she'd been trying to tell me all along. *'Before you can forgive him, you've gotta forgive me'.*

She'd left me, too.

Stupefied, I stared at that fallen photograph, my jaw slack, my eyes misting with red wet tears.

She'd actually left me! Deliberately. Willfully. Without remorse or saying goodbye, without asking Daddy's permission. She'd walked out of the room that night, she'd never come back, and for that I had despised her since the day she died.

I hated her for dying! Every bit as much as I hated Miquel for taking her life, I hated *her* for giving it to him!

My throat tightened. The only analog clock in the place stared back at me from the dresser. Time wouldn't wait any longer. If I wanted a second chance at my second chance, it had to be now or never, for something told me Miquel could disappear from the world in ways that went far beyond walking out the door.

'...you've gotta forgive me...'

I didn't know if I could, but I leapt off the floor and went chasing after the devil with the intention of begging him to teach me.

CHAPTER FOURTEEN

It took every ounce of control I possessed not to scream when I burst from my apartment and into that dayshine vista ruled by the sun and peopled by automaton executives driving identical Prius hybrids. At first, still in the shadows of the building, I was able to pretend some facade of normalcy as I passed by an elderly couple on the balcony; but when I rounded the corner and confronted the sunlight glinting off of whitewashed stairs, I began to wonder if I would explode into a storm of flames and burn to ashes on the spot.

Hugging the shade, my body pressed against the building until the rough stucco dug into my back, I was forced to accept on faith that the sun could no more kill me than the night could kill mortals. Dragging a deep breath into my lungs, I bolted down the stairs two at a time until I was once again in the subterranean parking lot, where my past life had been packed into the back of a Chevy.

I fumbled in my pocket for the keys, shaking fiercely by the time I yanked open the door and leapt into the driver's seat, my lips mouthing words disconnected from my mind. "Make it stop, for the love of night, make it stop! Mother, I didn't mean to! What if I'd married you, Charlie, what then? What you must think of me, Miquel, how you must hate me. Yes, Stephanie, I think I can forgive the devil if somebody will make it stop! Stop! Stop! *Stop!*"

"It", I knew, was the day. The curse of seeing things far too clearly. Trees which were mysterious and skeletal by night were only dead trees in the daylight, killed by man's neglect. Windows that glowed magically golden when illumined from within were only dirty panes of glass when lit up by the sun.

The day was a thief, a cheap criminal robbing the world of magic.

It might not kill, but I had no doubt it could drive me mad, so I jammed my foot down on the accelerator, cranked the key in the ignition, and gave a yelp of surprise when the car lurched forward to bump the building and rattle my fangs.

The elderly couple, now in the parking lot, clung to one another and stared. The engine died. The shock jolted me back to my senses, and though I continued babbling to myself, I put my foot on the clutch before turning the key again.

Screeching out of the parking lot and into the sun, my eyes frantically scanned the streets for Miquel, but other than the stray dog I'd seen earlier, the sidewalks were altogether devoid of life. Instinct told me my maker had left on foot, but what the hell did I know of instinct?

Sun glinted off the hood of the car, admiring its own reflection. Storm clouds on the horizon talked in low, rumbling voices, promising rain. I rammed the garbage cans, deliberately spilling their fast-food blood for the urban scavengers.

In the rearview mirror, my eyes reflected wild animal panic, filling me with the fear that any mortal who looked on me during the day would see me for what I was. Indeed, people in other cars turned their heads, pursed their lips into a frown, gawked. And though they inevitably went back to gazing straight ahead—pretending not to see what they didn't want to see, divinely ignorant—I couldn't help thinking their complacency was only a clever ruse to lure me into some hidden trap.

Paranoia choked me and I considered running back to my apartment, yet I knew Miquel would be long gone by then.

I would give you back your mortal life if I could.

How he must despise me.

My foot pressed harder on the gas and, fishtailing around a corner, a reckless pulse of relief assailed my chest when I saw him sauntering down the sidewalk as if he were only a man out for a morning walk. Though he kept to the shadows of old buildings, I couldn't begin to understand why he wasn't affected by that hideous day laser which seemed intent on cutting open my skull and scattering its insane contents.

With blood rushing through my ears like a choir of insanely chanting monks, I cut across three lanes of traffic—horns screamed and a woman cursed—and skidded to a stop right next to him.

At first, he seemed entirely oblivious, but when he turned that stately head and saw me in the car, the devil turned pale. Before I saw him move, he was opening the driver's door and shoving me toward the passenger's seat as he slid under the wheel.

"Are you mad, Stefan?" he asked without any pretense at gentleness. "Move over—*quickly!*—before the sun eats a hole in your head! Barely a week old and you think you can challenge the day?

What were you thinking?"

In another instant we were streaking through side streets and narrow alleys in a manner reminiscent of Luke Skywalker's flight through the Death Star. Indeed, had I not already been dead, I would have feared for my life.

"What were you thinking?" he chastised sharply, over and over. "What in all the scattered worlds were you thinking, Stefan? There—grab that jacket off the back seat and cover yourself! Hurry!"

His panic unnerved me and I quickly did as he said, snatching up my old raincoat to cover my head and upper body. I did feel sick—feverish, nauseous. My head spun like a carnival ride, colors peeling away at the edges to reveal duller colors beneath, each hallucination melting into the next.

"But you thought I said you told me little doses of sunlight you said rain wasn't any more harmful, I'm sure you said. And I needed to find you because I had to say I wanted to tell you I'm sorry and will you let me try again and forgive you and you forgive me? Might not work but gotta try Stephanie says."

To my addled brain, this made perfect sense, but when I saw the trepidation in Miquel's eyes—normally emerald, now black with worry—I could only stare at him as my world began dissolving into a tapestry of blood red threads that were really the veins and capillaries behind my eyes.

On the moldy oldies radio station, Neil Diamond belted out *Lay Lady Lay*, and as a writer, I still had the presence of mind to be offended. I snickered into my hand, peering at Miquel from underneath the coat.

"It should be Lie, Lady, Lie, but maybe Neil thought he'd sound Cockney. Poetic license, I guess."

"Don't talk, Stefan," Miquel told me grimly, and I tasted his grief as if it were flavorless water when I needed the healing salts of blood. "Just be still. Be still, my baby, and think thoughts of the night."

I liked it when he talked to me that way, but even the sun wasn't sufficient to drive away the memory of how it had felt when he'd killed me in his mind.

"Mad? You hate my heart and broke it in two."

He didn't answer. Maybe he didn't understand. Maybe he couldn't.

Seeing Miquel in daylight was uncanny. He didn't look like a vampyre, but what was a vampyre supposed to look like? Blond and muscular, like Stygian? Black and skeletally thin, like Bird?

All I knew was that I was seeing history itself. He was magic and mystery and madness.

I hated him.

I loved him.

A fat little angel flew in the window and sat on his shoulder, preening its downy wings like a cat preening its fur. But when it caught me looking and turned its golden head to smile, I saw that even angels had pointed teeth and eyes keen as any wolf. Jealous, it curled its lip at me.

"He's mine now. You blew it, Steffy-bud," the mischievous angel proclaimed, and wrapped its wings around Miquel's head to blind him as he drove.

At the same moment, Miquel brushed his hair away from his eyes, inadvertently knocking the angel out the window with his elbow. I laughed, especially when I saw the impish little fiend hanging onto the radio antenna in proper cartoon fashion, its chubby cherub body standing straight out from the car like a flag.

"Use your wings," I said to the silly creature. "Fly away—be gone!"

Miquel grasped my hand in a firm grip that nonetheless shot his worry straight into my heart. "Hold on, Stefan," he told me, trying to sound calmer than he was. "Just hold on."

His body was so tense the veins stood up on his arms, thrumming with blood more than a thousand years old. Beneath the thin cotton shirt, preternatural muscles flexed, and when he made an abrupt turn into a parking lot, the raw power he exuded caused my senses to spin. Practically leaping from the car, he bolted around to the passenger's side, flung open the door, and lifted me as if I weighed nothing at all.

My arms went automatically around his neck, my face burrowed into his shoulder, where the scent of his cologne lulled me into an easy trance.

At last I was home.

"Can you stand?" he asked, already striding toward a new high-rise hotel.

Directly above our heads, the little angel flew, strumming its silly harp and singing a love song that was picked up and carried away by a passing truck.

I didn't answer. Couldn't.

"Stefan?" Panic gripped him, bouncing around inside my mind. "Answer me!"

Tilting my head upward, not quite understanding his anxiety, I saw the fang teeth sharp and wet in his mouth, and it made me giggle like some bewildered harlequin.

"You bit me," I mused, suddenly amused. And my soul fluttered, a sheet in the wind trying to wriggle free so it could fly away from the sun forever.

He just looked at me, tiny red tears in the corners of his eyes. He faltered in his stride as the automatic doors opened and a chilly wind rushed out to greet us. I thought of the skylight in his house—the fearsome angel carrying his fallen comrade home to the clouds.

"I'm sorry, Stefan," he told me, his voice coarser than I remembered it.

I didn't want him to be sorry. And so I lay in his arms and wept as if I really were his baby.

Outside the building, the pesky little angel sat naked on the red curb, its tubby little cheeks in its tubby little hands as it sulked.

Death was a spoiled brat.

*

Once we were in the suite with the blackout drapes drawn and the cooling system blowing pseudo winter in the air, Miquel lay me down on the king-size bed and snatched up the phone. At first, I thought he intended to summon a doctor, but then I heard him ordering two cheeseburgers and a couple of Cokes, and since it struck me as funny to think of the vampyre king with catsup on his lips, I began to laugh.

But when he returned to my side, sitting on the edge of the bed and looking down into my face, the world went still and a cold weight settled in the pit of my stomach.

"Can you trust me, Stefan?" he asked, gravely serious as he squeezed my hands to hold my attention. "Can you trust me now when it matters so much?"

His aura said that I'd die if I didn't, but the last time he'd asked for my trust, I'd died anyway. It seemed, then, that I had little to lose. "Yes," was all I could say, and that barely a whisper.

He caressed my forehead, his thoughts creeping into my mind. *Don't leave me so soon, Stefan,* he was thinking, though aloud he said, "I'll make you better, my friend." Then, like a vow to lure me back from the dead, he swore to me, "And I will never break your heart again."

I swallowed hard, my eyes misting. But before I could reply, something began tapping on the window as if looking for a way inside, and this despite the fact that we were ten stories up.

"He's out there!" I gasped, delirious as my head jerked toward the source. "He's followed us!"

Miquel shook his head as if understanding what I meant, as if he, too, had seen the angel. "It's only the rain, Stefan. We've sung to the clouds to conjure it here—Donny, Stygian, Bird and Dimitri— a storm of the night that survives even in the light, blinders for the sun."

What he really said, I do not know, but those were the words I heard. My body ached, my skin feverish. My lungs burned—

—and fire raced along the ceiling, an animal feeding on rafters and wood shake shingles that comprised the roof of my tree house. My mother was screaming and my father was shouting for the neighbors to call the fire department, and the dog was wailing that keening sound that always meant real danger. Heat licked at me, orange tendril serpents' tongues, and though the trapdoor stood open, I was frozen with my back against the flimsy plywood wall.

"Dammit, Stefan, jump!" my father yelled, some ten feet below, his arms outstretched to catch me. But I couldn't move. Smoke had sucked my lungs dry and turned the world into a black cloud with a taste for little boys. "Jump or you will die!" The fire wrapped silken umber arms around me and children with wings whispered in my ear, promising that in heaven I could play with matches all I wanted. But they had glowing coals for eyes and hypodermic needles on the ends of all their fingers, and so I jumped, screaming, and landed in my father's arms as—

—a cold cloth was pressed to my forehead and the fire receded enough to let me breathe. My eyes wouldn't focus when Miquel slid an arm around my shoulders and helped me to stand, slowly guiding me into the bathroom. Mercifully, the room was

172

without windows, dark save for a single candle burning on the vanity next to the sink.

Where Miquel got the candle, I do not know. Perhaps he manifested it from thin air or found it in the drawer, or perhaps he carried candles in his pocket the way mortals carried loose change or ticket stubs from last week's movie.

My reflection over the sink stared back at me—wild-eyed and sick from exposure to the sun—though I quickly lost interest in my doppelganger when Miquel began removing my clothes.

This didn't seem strange, so I stood there and let him do it, too dazed and disoriented to protest or even ask why.

The shirt went first, peeled from my back like skin from an apple, and then the pants were slid down my hips. I'd worn no underwear—the sensation of being inside my maker's borrowed jeans too stimulating to dull—and though I tried to explain this to him, he only patted my hand and told me to save my strength.

When I stood naked before him, I felt no shame. Indeed, there was something innocent about my nakedness, so when he came and lifted me into his arms—how I craved clinging to his neck as if he really were my father and I still a little boy—it never crossed my mind that he intended to put me in a bathtub filled with ice water.

A cry tore from me, but as Miquel knelt at the edge of the tub with one hand on my chest to keep me still, he lay a finger across my lips and hushed me as a parent would hush an hysterical child.

"Be still now and let the water do its work, Stefan," he said, the cadence of his voice easy and comforting. "The day has had its way with you and the sun has eaten your reason. You're safe now, but you have to let me take this pain away so you can find your soul again before it slips away altogether."

There were no physical burns, I knew. The burns were internal, in the blood, racing through every cell.

Deranged, flailing madly with that pain, I tried to fight him off, but my strength was gone. I wailed, cursing summer and the color yellow. But as I fought, the ice slushed around me, cold water flowing over me, exploring me intimately.

It whispered in my ear, telling me it loved me and suggesting we consummate our affair with a long, slow fuck at the

173

edge of death itself.

I grabbed at Miquel, eternal driftwood, for it seemed I would drown in that sea of knives and needles and surgical lights exploding behind my eyes. The pain was like nothing I'd experienced before—bright as a psychedelic mushroom's eye, sharper than vampyre teeth—so perhaps it stood to reason that time refused to budge so the suffering could indulge itself thoroughly.

I lost consciousness—once, twice. But always when my eyes opened, Miquel was at my side, holding me in those baptismal waters until the fight went out of me and I began to float somewhere beyond the boundaries of my normal perceptions.

Day became night.

In one instant, I would be keenly aware of my body, how the ice was kissing every inch of me with lips so cold they were no longer cold, but hot instead. In the next instant, I could only focus on the ministrations Miquel was providing as he bathed my face and head until my breathing came easier and I no longer saw the foreboding tapestry of exploding veins and wilting capillaries whenever I shut my eyes.

In the candle's flickering glow, every movement came in slow motion, strobing leftovers from some 1960s hullabaloo dance joint that lived in his memory and not at all in mine. I drifted, lulled toward precious winter where the sun was a stranger and the dayshine world did not know my name.

I was vaguely aware of Miquel standing up at one point, studying his reflection over the sink while he waited for the waters to work on me. There was a sadness about him, a melancholy that had something to do with his own lost innocence, his own lost soul. It was that vague, restless sadness adolescent boys feel in late summer, when the first nebulous scent of autumn comes creeping down the street, the woeful longing that settles in the stomach when the winds shift with promises of red leaves and gray skies and cheeks turned pink with cold that wasn't quite there yet, but close, so close it could almost reach out and grab you.

Miquel was autumn's prince, but more than that, he was the thorn-crowned king of winters yet to come, the physical embodiment of something that couldn't exist, yet did.

"You're completely delirious, you realize," he said with a self-conscious smile. "I'm a man, just like you."

174

But while I lay there in that tub which might as well have been filled with the healing waters of Lourdes—for only now did I realize those waters were pink, laced with blood this terrible angel had spilled to heal me—I saw him both as man and legend sharing a single body that wasn't large enough to accommodate all the sorrow and all the secrets and all the pleasures he had known.

Ice slowly melted. Time slowly passed. I lost track of reality.

"What do you thought about?" I asked, confusing my tenses and confirming his observation that I was out of my mind. 'I mean now. What were you to think about?"

He turned from the mirror, looking at me as if trying to decide whether to answer.

"I was remembering our dreams," he said at last. Now his expression became contemplative, and he leaned against the vanity with his arms folded over his chest. "You see, Stefan, while it's true you must die in my arms every time you sleep, it is also true that I must take your mortal life whenever I go to my rest, and in that way we are always linked." He gave a sigh, deeply sad. "As the years go by, there will be times when we're apart, perhaps for centuries at a stretch, sick to death of one another's company. But even if we are separated for ten thousand years, we will still be joined by the dream of the night you were made."

He looked away then, turning darker, sorrowful. "When I no longer dream of you, I will know you are dead."

His words scared me, and in retrospect I do not believe he meant to utter them aloud at all.

"I don't want to die." It seemed sacrilegious for an immortal to think such things, yet I knew I *could* die, and if I did a part of Miquel would die, too. Having only my own nightmares with which to contend, I didn't envy him the responsibility of being a Creator. "Do you dream of all of us? Every time you sleep, I mean? Dimitri, Donny? The others?"

He nodded almost imperceptibly, tilting his head to one side and studying me. "Do you despise it, Stefan? Do you despise me?"

Floating in my winter world where all things were right and good, I told him the only truth I knew. "You gave me eternal life. And today you saved my life again."

"I almost killed you today," he replied somberly, voice clipped with frustration. "I never should have left you in anger, and

I should have explained what I meant by small doses of sunlight. A glimpse of it through a window. A narrow shaft of it through which you must dash on your way somewhere." Pushing the ragged hair back from his eyes, he perused me with a respect I didn't deserve. "Still, the fact that you did it is remarkable. I didn't challenge the sun until I'd been a vampyre for a hundred years. You have incredible strength, and if you survive this—which I am determined you will—you will emerge stronger still."

His praise meant more to me than anything, but all I could do was grin like an idiot. Then I remembered it again, that awful aloneness I'd felt when he left me. But there was an even worse aloneness when I realized I would lose him again. And again.

If it existed in the racial memory of humans that their time on Earth was limited, so it was in the racial memory of vampyres that no love would last forever, even if it might repeat itself time and time again, a cycle of pain and pleasure, hurt and healing, coming together and tearing apart that would go on for an eternity.

I wasn't sure which scared me more—the transitory existence of mortals or an infinity filled with such terrible love.

"Stephanie's schoolgirl eyes say I have to forgive her for leaving me, but I'm not sure I want to think I really don't know how," I blathered, my words coming out inside out and upside down. "I mean, it's not you I gotta forgive—well, that, too—but you don't want me anymore and she's gone, too. How do you forgive a little girl's ghost or acquit the devil who's really a vampyre? Love always loses itself, runs away to the carnival out there by the sea."

Miquel gave me a smile that said he understood. Funny, since I didn't myself.

"Time heals, Stefan, and time is one thing you do have," he told me. "The things it can't heal are the things you simply have to forgive, or the things you must accept as being unforgivable." He paused, then seemed to decide only in that moment: "What I have done to you is unforgivable, and now we will both pay for my arrogance forever."

It sobered me instantly, awakening a passion for life I'd believed forfeit. "What's unforgivable is human suffering, Miquel. What's unforgivable is that Stephanie's awareness of her own mortality drove her to take her own life—it's what drove her to you that night. She couldn't live knowing she would die. What's unforgivable is that death exists at all and that I didn't see it in her eyes."

The pain Miquel exuded was tangible, the words he spoke profound. "For that, Stefan, you must forgive yourself." A long pause, then: "You have to love yourself again, my friend. You have to love yourself as I love you. Only then will you be free of all this terrible grief."

This took me completely off guard.

I looked down into the haunted eyes of a damned man who stared up at me from pink water.

"How can you love me?" I asked my own reflection.

But it was Miquel who answered. "You're part of me now. I chose you for love. I chose you to be immortal, not to be tormented."

The candle burned lower, flickering in the draft from the air duct. Colorless wax dripped over the edge of the vanity, hot icicles melting on white tile floor, the blood of light itself.

Finally, as if sensing the conversation had taken some dangerous turn, Miquel gave a mischievous smile and shrugged one broad shoulder. "And besides, even when I might not like you, at times when I might want to turn you over my knee and throttle you soundly, I never stop loving you, Stefan."

That was the best thing anyone could have said to me. But before I could pursue it—these strange feelings awakened by his erotic threat—he turned toward the mirror with a sigh and brought the discussion back to where it began.

"But about the dream," he insisted, looking for answers in his own eyes. "Does it drive you mad knowing you'll dream it from now until the end of everything? It drives Donny mad, you know. I fear the Sadness may destroy him yet, that he'll simply refuse to wake up one day." He paused, his voice falling lower, coarser. "That's why he doesn't have a vampyre name yet."

There was no comfort for that kind of grief, that kind of fear.

"If eternity demands a price, a dream is a small one indeed," I offered, though my lips seemed out of sync with my voice. Because a secret was all I had to give him, I said, "Besides, Donny loves you too much to die—so much he's afraid it's going to rip his soul right out of his body. That's what he said. That's what I know I think I heard him say I know I did."

The water laughed at me, tiny ice cube hands applauding

my idiocy against the side of the tub.

Miquel lifted his head ever so slightly, a reflection studying me from inside the mirror. "Really? He told you that?"

When I nodded, surprised that he was surprised, a measure of gloom left him.

I was running one hand through the baptismal pond, creating tiny wakes that trembled with a soft *zzzhhhbb-zzzhhhbb* against my fingertips while I marveled at the candle's many faces in the water. At one point, one of those reflections lit on the tip of my manhood, a golden butterfly flickering as it sat drinking water from my skin. When I touched its illumined wings, the butterfly grew larger, a wondrous metamorphosis.

Fascinated, I stroked it gently, lovingly.

Then I saw Miquel watching me. Our eyes met and the vampyre in the looking glass smiled, fang tips gleaming.

Without words, he turned to face me, and before I understood what he was doing, he began unbuttoning the loose fitting shirt which had made me visualize him as a pirate at my apartment. Somewhere in the back of my mind, that Stefan London tensed, but the naive creature in the tub could only watch, transfixed, as my maker let the white cotton ghost slide off his shoulders to lie at his feet, its only protest a quiet shush as it fell.

Oh. So this was how it would happen.

The waters soothed me with his blood and I wasn't afraid.

He truly was a sculpture escaped from the artist's hand, brought to life by alchemy. Smooth as priceless marble, his pecs were dense mounds heightened by brown aureoles—the flat male breast from which he fed his vampyre children—his shoulders and arms so perfectly developed he barely looked human at all.

When he saw me looking at him, he gave a confident smile to assuage the embarrassment that came upon me. *You can look at me, Stefan*, he was thinking, arrogant and modest at the same time. *I'm a vampyre, remember? And when you find pleasure in something you see—even if what you see is me—that pleasure becomes mine as well, a synapse we share like blood itself.*

His words awakened memories of Valerie, that first time taste of finest wine drawn from a mortal tap, the flavor that grew sweeter when offered to me on Miquel's lips in the form of a kiss that had ended too soon.

In the water, beneath my inquisitive fingertips, the butterfly spread his fiery wings, yearning to fly.

At the same time, Miquel unfastened his leather belt. Long fingers manipulated the shiny gold buckle, causing it to catch the light and send it bouncing around the room. He eased the crisp linen trousers down his thighs, leaving them on the floor beside his fallen shirt.

Naked, he met my eyes as he stood leaning casually against the vanity, then gave an easy shrug that said I was welcome to indulge my curiosity.

He was my Creator. He was an immortal.

I could not help myself.

With the sleek lines of a puma and a mystique he wore like a second skin, he was beautiful in ways I'd never imagined when I'd first seen him in torn blue jeans. His legs were made for stalking his prey—the long, lean muscles of a man who had walked a thousand dirt roads over the span of a thousand years. A flat, muscular plane made up his stomach, and though I'd halfway expected him to have no navel—further proof that he wasn't human—it was adorned with a gold earring. In the mirror, his back was carved of shadows, his buttocks rounded like an athlete's.

His only physical flaw was the jagged scar that ran from the right side of his belly down toward the pubis—the cut which would have ended his life had a vampyre not come upon him and breathed eternal life into his veins. Curiosity made me wonder about his past, about the man who had created my Creator, but he told me with a thought that it wasn't something he cared to remember, at least not now.

It occurred to me to stop there, out of common decency if nothing else, but I sensed that he wanted me to admire him, and so my gaze fell on his genitals.

From a triangular thicket of black curls which lay jealously close to his body, his manhood rested on firm testicles the same olive dark as the rest of him. Partially erect—enough to suggest arousal but not so much as to flaunt it—the broad tip dipped to his thigh, brooding under its own weight.

And though it unnerved me to realize his beauty aroused me, I could no more deny it than I could have denied that the water in which I floated was cold.

It made no difference that he was a man or that I was.

It was *Miquel* I wanted—the soul behind the predator's eyes, the spirit inside this extraordinary body.

I started to speak, but he motioned me to silence, then came to the edge of the tub and knelt there. Dipping his fingers in the water, he dripped it over my forehead, causing me to smile when it ran down the bridge of my nose and rained onto my chest with a distinct *plopping* sound.

"You seem to be feeling better," he commented, his eyes scanning the full length of the tub, the full length of me.

It thrilled me to have him look at me in that way. I was a vampyre, too. I could *feel* that look. So when he leaned over until our faces were barely an inch apart, I closed my eyes and drew a sharp breath, expecting a kiss. Instead, he placed one hand behind my neck and drew me closer still.

"Come to bed with me, Stefan," he whispered against my ear, catching the lobe in his sharp fang teeth. "There's something I want to give you."

He would kill me yet.

He slid his arms around my back to help me and I held tight to him as he wrapped my body in a plush white towel. My physical weakness disturbed me deeply, and though I made a genuine effort to stand, I sagged against him and would have fallen had he not caught me.

My legs were wet paper, my heart so slow I could not hear it at all.

Panic found me. Was I dying?

"It's just the sun's legacy," Miquel reminded me, looking at me with that dangerous, secretive smile. Then, bending to my ear, he added in a rough-cut whisper, "Come now, my baby. Let's get into bed and see what it will take to make you well again, yes?"

Oh, yes.

But when he led me from that candlelit room and my eyes fell on the shadowed bed, I stopped in mid-stride, thinking I was hallucinating. Though the room was typically hotel-sterile, the young man in the middle of that bed was far from standard issue.

No more than 18, he lay atop the dark blue comforter, long legs curled to one side, chest moving in the easy rhythms of a trance, eyes glazed as he looked at me. Yet what caused the breath

180

to catch in my throat wasn't only his dark beauty or the realization that Miquel had mesmerized him into this ethereal submission, but the fact that he was naked and clearly aroused even in his unnatural stupor.

Panic darted through my stomach, and only Miquel's embrace kept me from retreating. Urging me toward the bed, he spoke softly against my ear, as if any sound might awaken the boy from his erotic dreams.

"His name is Sergio," the vampyre told me, "and he is here to give you back your strength." Gesturing toward him with an elegant motion of one hand—a gesture that undoubtedly deepened poor Sergio's trance—Miquel added, "Take him as you would any mortal, my friend, for he has been waiting for you all his life."

Though I wasn't sure what he meant—except that he believed every action was prearranged by nature somehow—it made little difference when I looked at the boy and the hunger rose up within me. My legs, already weak, trembled. My mouth turned wet and my tongue grazed over my fangs to test their sharpness.

Sergio paled at the look in my eyes and a soft whimpering came from his throat.

Even if I'd wanted to disregard Miquel's command, it would not have been within my power, for instinct told me this was what I needed most, this was the thing that would make me whole again. I could smell the creature's arousal, that dangerous titillation of youth which knew no common sense. His eyes were pinwheels, picking up the light and spinning it in all directions, and he was every bit as out of his mind as I was myself.

Instead of dreading what was to come, he wanted it. He wanted *me*.

But he wasn't sure what either meant and that made him want it all the more—a lunatic desire that fed on mystery itself, building and growing as he looked first at me, then at Miquel, then back to me again.

Whereas Aaron had been a perfect stranger—pure male carnality in love with lust itself—Sergio was a banquet of sensual innocence, already sworn to me in a way I couldn't begin to understand. He was mine. He always had been.

Mine. Yes. Mine.

Without realizing how I came to be there, I found myself on

the bed with him—a living thing who pulsed with wild heat and concupiscent fear and thoughts so sensual they could only be written in blood with a black feather pen. His body strained as I gathered him to me, and when his arms shot around my back like a drowning man clinging to his rescuer, his heartbeat hammering against my chest was the drum that called the demons to feed.

The man I'd once been stood aside and watched, studiously taking notes, properly appalled, secretly envious. Outside, rain scratched at the window while thunder chuckled, deep grey laughter that shook the building.

"What's going to happen?" Sergio whispered against my ear, barely able to breathe his excitement was so great. "What are you going to do to me?"

No words could tell the boy what I was going to do to him, so I showed him instead. Grabbing his wrists and forcing him down, I covered him with my body to still his erotic thrashings, and before he could say another word, I sank my teeth into the apex of lean neck and tan shoulder.

The jet of blood that rushed up into my mouth shocked me in its bestial clarity, and before I realized what I was doing, I drew my head back from the bite and grabbed him again with my fangs—higher up on his neck—drawing his blood for the second time while my own body convulsed and swelled beyond its boundaries.

When he started to wail—a sound that began as a yelp of astonishment and rose to an acute warbling of fear and the reality of pain that wasn't at all like the fantasy—Miquel appeared on the other side of the bed and stifled his cries with a kiss that stole the poor thing's breath away. Beneath me, Sergio writhed helplessly, twisting and turning as I began drinking as I'd never done before, drawing hard on his veins and forcing them to yield up their feast of nourishment and memories still in the process of being made.

The Beast opened the door the same as anyone else, but that's where normalcy ended. As Sergio stood there with his serving cart, he fought the certainty that he was about to faint—a sensation that intensified when The Beast gestured graciously toward the dark interior of the room.

"Uh—room service?" Sergio gulped, and pushed the cart with its one squeaky wheel inside.

The Beast smiled at him, closing the door. "Ah, yes, I've been waiting for you, Sergio," the older man said in a voice rich with a Greek accent, glancing at his name tag as he spoke. (Only later would Sergio realize he hadn't been wearing the name tag at all).

Instantly enamored with the other's charm and poise, Sergio let his imagination start to play—a game he indulged whenever an anonymous door opened to reveal a special prize. Usually, he would go through the motions of a polite conversation, hold out his hand for a tip (often imagining that the beautiful woman would give him her black lace panties or the handsome man would place a lambskin Trojan in his hand and look meaningfully toward the bed), then he would be on his way in reality even if his mind spent the night being duly instructed in the fine art of physical love.

If he turned out straight, no problem. If he turned out gay, so what? He just wanted to be <u>something</u> before his 19th birthday.

The weird thing was that the fantasy had never reached out and grabbed him. He remembered looking into The Beast's eyes, and the next thing he knew, he was falling through some dark tunnel where graffiti spray painted in red dripped down the walls, spelling out his name in blood.

"Surrender to me and I will show you heaven on Earth," The Beast promised as he peeled off Sergio's clothes and let them drop on the floor. "Oh, it might hurt a little when you pass through the door of manhood, but a diligent creature who seeks to master pleasure shouldn't object to a small amount of pain, no?"

After that, Sergio was lost. The Beast had held him in his arms, even kissed him as he put him down on the bed—a long exploration of tongues that left him hurting with forbidden need, a boy's secret desire for an older man who wore that honed edge of masculine danger like an unconcealed weapon. But The Beast had left him then, disappeared into the bathroom while Sergio lay on the bed, wanting to touch himself as he did at home, yet unable to do so because it would have been far too much effort.

So when The Beast emerged with The Other—both gloriously naked and unquestionably aroused—Sergio began to believe he was dreaming. And though he hadn't expected The Other's kiss to be so brutally demanding and hurtful—that sharp, quick cut which made him weep and writhe shamelessly beneath the older male body—he was forced to admit that the pain was every bit as mysterious as the pleasure once he was able to bend into it and let it take him flying. He knew he was bleeding, though it didn't seem important at the time—some peculiar ritual, some rite of passage only revealed to a boy at the moment he reached *adulthood.*

It was okay that they held him down. Maybe that was how it had to be—especially since he did panic when The Beast rolled him onto his side and pressed the full length of that cruelly hard body against him. Sandwiched between the two of them, flying higher on blood loss than any homegrown grass had ever taken him, he cried out again when his body was exquisitely violated and he knew the hellish euphoria of what it meant to become a man in another man's arms.

He would have screamed if he'd been able—for the hurt was like being cleft in two—but The Other covered his mouth with a hand that was unnaturally cold. Consciousness threatened to leave him, and when The Beast began taking him in earnest—a hard, slow thrusting that brought tears to his eyes for knowing he was finally a man—all Sergio could do was lie there and take this wicked punishment which was surely sent as sweet reward for his unconfessed sins.

The suckling at his throat came harder, faster, and under the pressure of The Other's demands for his blood, Sergio winced as colors exploded behind his eyes and he began dividing into two separate and unique beings. One was air. The other substance. One was mist. The other matter.

Once friends, they were strangers now.

The Beast's unyielding arms closed around him, prison doors made of flesh, and Sergio felt his body further breached when feral teeth clamped down on his neck on the opposite side from where The Other still fed. At the same instant, The Beast drove deeper into him, filling him with a rush of intimate male tears and whispering into his mind, "It's time to let it all go now, Sergio. Time to close your eyes for the last time and look upon the face of heaven."

Sergio screamed—the torturous rapture of Christ spilling his blood for humanity as he hung on the cross—though no sound left his lips. Instead, as his own pleasure swelled and burst, he understood that this was why he had been born all those years ago. Not to become a Navy pilot as his father wanted. Not to chase after the secrets underneath a woman's skirt and sire children. Not for any purpose other than this—to sacrifice his blood and his mortal soul so that another creature could be fed and healed.

Filled with the realization that he had been here for a reason, knowing that reason was now wondrously fulfilled, he did as The Beast suggested, closing his eyes and giving up his spirit into The Other's suckling mouth. There, silk-soft-sliding, he was swallowed whole into perfect oblivion as—

184

I jerked my head away and gasped in the breath of life just as my body entered a strange release. Convulsing, my back arching until I was certain the top of my head would touch the soles of my feet, I thrashed in the throes of a sensual seizure that knew no boundaries and threatened to toss me out of my body once and for all.

Miquel tried to calm me, gathering me in his arms and rocking me as I convulsed again and again, racked with shudders so violent I could not speak as I flew higher, further, higher still.

A wet red mass—the universe as it was born, the womb as it spit me out into the world. A flash of lightning on a primeval shore and a tiny monkey, no bigger than a rat, running helter-skelter through snow-white sand, proclaiming that he was late, late, late. Firefly eyes in trees tall as skyscrapers, souls of the unborn, waiting for the cosmic soup to cool.

I groaned and clutched myself at the apex of mortal creation. Reborn, I wept. And then the convulsions began all over again, contorting my body until I was certain my bones would break under the stress.

Miquel's arms tightened, holding me, protecting me from myself. "Ssshh," he whispered, rocking me. "Easy, my baby, just go easy until the little fire finds its place inside you and settles down to rest. Easy, now. Easy..."

But there was nothing easy about it.

I'd taken a mortal life—an aphrodisiac so potent it threatened to kill me, too.

And though I could not transmit this knowledge to any human being, it wasn't murder at all, but the consummate perfection of true vampirism—predator and prey acknowledging one another's purpose in the universe, sharing the mutual exhilaration while nature wrote the inevitable script, and finally joining together in the most intimate way of all as one devoured the other utterly.

Sergio wasn't dead. How could he be dead when I could feel his very lifeforce so vital and alive inside me?

It wasn't what I wanted to believe. Killing wasn't what I wanted it to be, for now I understood.

'Only the best of us can not kill'.

I'd swallowed an immortal soul as if it were priceless wine

185

aged to perfection in a vessel of mortal clay, and now 'the little flame', as Miquel called it, was hammering and zinging through my veins until I was certain I couldn't contain it at all.

"Ah, but you must," my maker said, reading my thoughts, "for it's the fire that will heal the sun's damage and give you back your strength. Don't fear it, Stefan, just go where it leads and you'll see what I mean. There... like that... there. Yes. Oh, yes..."

Hearing the passion in Miquel's words, I convulsed again, an orgasm that had nothing to do with sex, ripped from the deepest part of me and ejected with a guttural groan. My head thrashed, my body writhing against Miquel until I felt his arousal as intense as my own. Vampyre that he was, he felt it all through me, and though I wanted him to take this pain-pleasure beast away from me, I knew it wasn't within even his power.

This was a ride I had to take alone.

Finally, inside me, the little flame found its resting place and ignited—somewhere between heart and solar plexus—and when I convulsed again, Miquel had to smother my lips with a kiss to prevent me from screaming. His mouth was wet—wet with the warm, red blood of a dead man who had given his life so I could go on living. That flavor was sweet on my maker's lips, not bitter as I might have expected, and I craved it so much I shamelessly opened my mouth to him, inviting his tongue to slip inside me, to feed me.

We kissed like lovers, mouths sparring and fighting, and though I understood he was doing this to distract me from my need to cry out with the agony of rebirth, it was nonetheless thrilling to feel the sharp edges of his teeth as they grazed over my lips and he moaned softly into my mouth.

He held me chest to chest, abdomen to abdomen, man to man, rocking me to calm me, kissing me to silence me, calling me his baby as he wrapped one long leg around my thighs and ran those fine-boned hands up and down my back until my terrible thrashing began to subside.

Though unseasoned with men, I wanted him in all ways, and I believe he wanted me as much; but when I pulled him to me and awkwardly tried to assault him with another kiss, his soul smiled at me, asking if it wouldn't be best to wait for a more welcoming bed we wouldn't have to share with a dead man.

Odd, to think of Miquel as squeamish, but I do believe he

186

was.

I was in and out of reality for awhile, back and forth between life and death as I traversed thresholds of experience for which no words exist. In one instant, I would truly believe I had found God out among the scattered stars. But in the next instant, I would realize the stars *were* God and there was nothing more beyond that. There were a thousand discoveries like that one—that any truth could always be contradicted by another truth, a higher truth, or simply a different perspective on the original question.

If heaven existed, I never saw it, yet I firmly believe Sergio went there because he was a good and decent young man, and because he himself believed that's where he should spend eternity. His soul was infinite, after all, and the spark I'd stolen from him was minuscule in comparison to the vast All that he was.

I flew beyond my body and danced on the face of the moon and played chess with Shakespeare (losing miserably), and my perceptions expanded and bloomed far beyond my physical capacity to hold.

Then, when I could go no higher and even the angels flew away to rest, I found myself lying in Miquel's arms, trembling and speechless, transformed and resurrected in a way I never would have chosen, but in a way I would not undo even if I'd been able.

At last, I was truly a vampyre.

At my side, a young man lay still and lifeless, and while I could mourn him intellectually, I knew that what I had done was not evil because it was done for the sake of survival. And to those who would call me a monster for thoughts so cold, I would remind them that the meat on their table comes from a living creature and the wolf who devours the rabbit is less of a monster than the man who picks up a rifle and kills the wolf for sport.

All of us are predators.

With true reverence, I bent my head to young Sergio's lips and left a kiss upon his cool mouth; and in the sanctuary of my thoughts, I thanked him for crossing my path when and where he did and I told him I would guard his little flame well and keep it always burning.

A sigh of contentment slipped through the dead man's lips and his corpse began to smile.

And though I couldn't begin to understand what was

happening, the room was suddenly filled with a soft golden mist that enveloped the bed and turned the world to fog.

When the haze lifted, Sergio was gone.

CHAPTER FIFTEEN

We'd been heading north on the freeway maybe fifteen minutes when Miquel finally admitted he didn't know where the body had gone. "There are some questions that have no answers, Stefan," he said, his eyes fixed on the road as he drove into the night. One muscular arm was draped across the wheel of my old blue Camaro, the other he rested on the open window.

"I'd like to hear your opinions anyway," I insisted. "What do you *think*?"

He gave an easy shrug, watching me from the corner of his eye as wind tossed his hair around and oncoming headlights illumined the angles of his face.

"He was a perfect soul—not really mortal at all."

I was turned sideways in the seat, knees drawn to my chest. As we sped along, the car's frame squeaked from time to time and trees became a poorly lit blur.

Too much had happened for me to assimilate any of it, and his analysis only set my head to spinning again. When I tried to think of the golden mist that had seemingly taken Sergio to some literal heaven, my mind wandered instead to memories of Miquel undressing by candlelight, an equally profound vision. But when I tried to concentrate on that image and surrender to my carnal impulses, I would discover myself pondering the disturbing recollection of how it had felt to consume a human soul, the very act of which had apparently propelled me into the next level of my ongoing metamorphosis.

What Miquel had said, therefore, troubled me deeply.

"He was mortal," I maintained sharply, not looking at him. "He was someone's son, someone's brother." Somewhere, a father would mourn him as I still mourned my Stephanie.

"Perhaps," Miquel said in a tone of concession that really wasn't a concession in the least. "But how can you be certain his existence wasn't merely an illusion? Do these relatives exist in the

188

physical world or only in Sergio's memory? Or is it possible that his memory *was* his physical world, and when he left the mortal plane, an entire universe perished with him?"

I was in no mood for metaphysics. "Yeah, right," I muttered to myself, and began running one finger through the dust that had gathered on the dashboard.

"So querulous you are, Stefan," he said with a little laugh, then reached across the console to rest a hand on my arm. 'Has it occurred to you that perhaps Sergio was sent to you? Not just because you were so near death that only the taking of a human life could save you, but perhaps he was an emissary as well—proof of something."

Chills raked along my arms. "Proof? Proof of what?"

Miquel pulled his hand away and went back to gazing at the road. "If I have learned nothing else in the time I have been on this Earth, Stefan, it is that the mysteries far outnumber the mundane aspects of life. Indeed, it's only when we stop appreciating the riddles that life truly does become tedious. That's what kills mortals — far more than speeding trucks or guns or cancer—it's boredom, pure and simple."

Maybe he was right, but I wanted a concrete answer, so like any spoiled child I maintained my argumentative stance. "What does any of this have to do with what happened back there?"

His eyes were polished green agates, filled with mischief, ripe with wisdom. "You needed a miracle and a miracle occurred."

I was back to rolling my eyes. "God doesn't make miracles for our kind."

Miquel laughed at me, a portrait framed against the window, painted on a backdrop of blurry suburbs. "Why must miracles come from God alone? Who's to say you didn't create the miracle yourself, that your handsome young savior wasn't a miracle you manifested in your delirious need to be saved from the angel of death who was circling over your head? Oh—don't look at me as if to say you don't know what I'm talking about, Stefan. I saw him, too—in your mind if nowhere else."

I took to staring out the window, but all I could see was Sergio's face, his dead eyes fixed and lifeless, lips smiling at some secret wonder I would never share. In my chest, the little flame flickered. I gnawed my lip, close to weeping.

Sensing my despair, Miquel sighed softly. "Ah, Stefan, don't you see? Man has become so accustomed to asking God for things that he forgets his own powers. People have grown so used to looking for handouts they've forgotten how to hunt. They've turned their back on their survival instincts without ever realizing that, *if* their God exists, He gave them their predatory nature so they could survive without always begging for His help."

He shook his head with a short, ironic laugh. "It's like the story about the young monk who finds himself at the pearly gates. God asks why he's there, since he should have lived to be a right and proper 95. The monk replies, 'Our ship sank in the deepest ocean and I prayed for your angels to deliver me from the sea, God. So when the rescue boats came—three in all—I told them to be on their way, that I was waiting for angels. I never lost faith, but the angels never came and finally I drowned, and now I really must ask why you didn't send them after all'. At this, God could only scratch His head and wonder why He'd created Man to use such a small portion of his brain. In His sadness, He looked at the monk and said, 'Foolish human, who do you think was driving the boats?'"

Maybe Miquel had a point, but I refused to smile. "But all that proves is that the monk was still at the mercy of God to send the boats, regardless of who was driving," I countered, particularly quarrelsome.

"On the contrary," Miquel disagreed. "It proves that the monk was religiously stubborn and foolishly difficult—not unlike a young vampyre I once knew. He was so busy looking for angels that he turned his back on the real miracle: that he could be found at all in such a vast ocean, and at night no less."

I shot him a dirty look. "You never said it was night."

His lips twitched, fighting a smile. "At deepest midnight— *and* in a terrible hurricane!"

When he finally looked at me straight on, I stubbornly tried to hold onto my stubbornness, though I finally buckled and laughed a little, throwing my hands up in surrender. It surprised me—how good it felt to let go of my anger, to toss it out the window and watch it bounce along the side of the road with the rest of the litter.

But my amusement quickly faded as the night settled around me, turning me philosophical again. "But if Sergio wasn't mortal, what was he?"

190

"Ah," Miquel murmured, "that's the question, isn't it? That's the question that will keep you asking more and more questions, and perhaps that's what Sergio was as much as anything—a savior angel masquerading as a mortal virgin who was really the male muse you've been chasing all your life."

Even when I could follow Miquel's logic, it left me dizzy. But before I could reply, he turned his head and pinned me with a stunning stare.

"*You* are the real miracle," he told me, sending a new wave of feeling washing over me. "Would that you could see it. Would that you could see what I see."

But I couldn't.

My head ached, but it had nothing to do with my bout with the sun. It ached because there was no solace. There was no silence behind my eyes and now I did not believe there ever could be.

That was what this transformation was all about. It wasn't about becoming some night prowling creature who drank human blood anymore than becoming a Buddhist was about eating rice. No, this was about the awakening of the mind into a far more immense world. It was the realization that the things men looked upon with mortal eyes were only a fraction of a much larger painting still in progress by some covert artist who worked on canvases comprised of vast galaxies and tiny headstones in time-lost cemeteries and the limitless human heart that was the keeper of all miracles and mysteries everywhere.

I liked to think Miquel had seen that painting in its entirety, though I doubt even he had been so privileged or he would have given up living long ago, his journey completed.

Something was out there, just beyond our ability to perceive, but whenever it seemed I might catch a glimpse of this higher truth, it slipped away, gaseous and ungraspable. And yet, whenever I gave up in a fit of fury and stopped chasing after it, it would sing to me from the shadows, calling my name with its siren voice, promising there would be answers if only I would turn that next corner and keep up the chase.

It was maddening.

"It was like that for me at first," Miquel commented, his voice edged with a hint of melancholy.

He was more open to me than he'd ever been, yet the mere

act of looking at him made me hurt for things I couldn't understand. And so I stopped looking at him and turned toward the window.

Distant houses, illumined rectangles that were only coffins for the living, called to me with their stories, but I closed my eyes and ignored all the tears and all the laughter out there in the world. The car lulled me, a safe cocoon. Wind flashed through the windows, rearranging my hair with curious fingers, cold as death.

I was in the night womb now, my entire body a phallus, primal. Darkness caressed my skin, massaging me in its tight black sheath, welcoming me home, telling me that, ironically, it would be Halloween in a few minutes.

Deep within me, something stirred, a feeling I hadn't experienced since I was a boy. A thrill born of fear. A taste of magic that lived inside a jack-o'lantern's orange eye. Suddenly I was restless, hungry for blood. Sergio was in my arms again, a ghost writhing.

"If he wasn't mortal, why did his blood taste warm on my tongue?" I insisted, not meaning to speak. "If he wasn't real, why were his memories so sharp?" I never opened my eyes, mesmerized by the whine of tires over asphalt.

"You already know the answer to that."

"But I don't."

"Ah, but you have opinions, don't you?"

"Why don't you just tell me?" I was in no mood for semantics.

"My truth and yours might not be the same," he reminded me. "Doesn't it make more sense to trust what you feel inside your own skin?"

"Inner truth is subjective," I argued.

"You want external validation of your reality, then."

My eyes opened. "Maybe. I think we all need that, to one extent or another."

"If you believe that, are you not merely trading one social reality for another, one trap for the next?" He paused, fingertips caressing the steering wheel and causing me to envy its black plastic flesh. The night was his lover now, the road their bed. "Perhaps the crime is when we try to explain magic with mortal words. Trying to interpret what happened to you with Sergio is rather like trying to explain an Aborigine to a computer, don't you think? It demeans the Aborigine and confounds the computer, which isn't capable of listening in the first place."

He was tilting my reality again.

Trucks lumbered up and down the steep grades of the lonesome highway, some barely moving, others brightly lit projectiles, all of them just props in the script. Why was *that* man in *that* truck on *this* road at precisely this moment in time? Why wasn't he ten feet further down the freeway or a mile back, or for that matter why wasn't he born a hundred years in the past instead of Now, and was he really alive at all, or if I met him would he be made of plastic mannequin flesh with watercolor eyes painted over the windows to his marionette soul? What was I to learn by being here Right Now, or was everything random in the end, just a crazy vegetable soup thrown together with spoiled leftovers from other places and times?

Not so long ago, I'd been a man in his run-down apartment trying to decide whether to feed the cat chicky-liver-chunks or birdy-wirdy-stew. Now, suddenly, I wasn't even in the same world.

I was a vampyre having a conversation with the vampyre who'd made me, and when I wasn't thinking of ways to kill him, I was thinking of ways to woo him.

On the side of the road, jackrabbits nibbled at dead grass, eyes wide and wild with the fear only prey could know. "Maybe the real trap is that we're alone inside our own minds," I offered, remembering Aaron. *'Not to be so alone when the end comes'*, he had said.

Maybe that's all any of us wanted.

"But you *aren't* alone any longer," Miquel pointed out, and sent a thought fluttering through me to prove it. It was mischievous and it tickled and it bore the scent of him, but as he'd already said, attempting to explain that kind of magic with words was silly. "You feel me within you, yes?"

The question was an erotic novel unto itself, a temporary distraction from my misery. "Yes."

He gave another shrug, a quirking smile that showed a fang. "Then we're not entirely alone."

I went back to looking out the window, recalling the conversation our minds had had back in that hotel room: when I'd told him with a thought that I wanted him (without really knowing what that meant), when his soul had given a laugh and suggested we wait to consummate our feelings (whatever they were) in a better place at a more appropriate time (but would that time ever come?)

Was I to believe that conversation was real? And if so, was it as valid as if we'd spoken aloud, or could it be written off as nothing more than passing thoughts, not binding?

"Any reality is as legitimate as you perceive it to be, Stefan, whether it involves an angel in a hotel room or a conversation in your mind," Miquel said. And because he wasn't one to cut me any slack, he shot me a suggestive smile and added darkly, "And what can be more binding than a thought? What could be more honest than the words we say to one another without ever speaking out loud?"

Oh. *Bastard*, I thought.

Yes. He was laughing inside.

For a long time, I said nothing. Dead grass covering craggy hillsides moved like a restless brown sea, eventually giving way to the rock-littered hillsides in a sparsely populated area on the outskirts of San Bernardino. Jagged mountains scratched at the sky, foreboding pinnacles blotting out the stars. In the distance, a ghostly light moved through the darkness, perhaps a motorcycle on some dusty road or an old miner still looking for a fortune in gold even though he'd died a hundred years ago.

The air turned colder. Traffic thinned. My skin prickled.

Miquel said, "You're grown quiet, my friend." *Was it something I said or something I only thought?*

Shivering, I pretended not to hear his teasing. Finally, like a coward, I asked in a completely disinterested tone: "Where are we going?"

He just laughed and shook his head with an overly dramatic sigh, switching on the radio and turning the volume up loud. As if on cue, the opening strains of _The Monster Mash_ came blasting over the airwaves, the DJ howling like a demented werewolf to shake me from my trance.

The clock on the dash read 12:01.

"It's Halloween, Stefan," Miquel replied evasively, taking an off ramp that would lead up into the foothills—a roundabout way back to where it all began. "Your brothers and sisters will be at my

194

home by now, and the sooner we join them, the sooner you'll officially be one of us."

I blinked, shooting him a dubious look. "'Officially'?" I repeated, my stomach knotting.

If Miquel heard me, he never let on.

CHAPTER SIXTEEN

When Miquel pulled into the circular driveway and shut down the engine, the sense of homecoming as I looked toward the house was overwhelming. Candles burning on the sills of every window brought a feeling of comfort, and the little creek gurgling through the gardens soothed away the tension that had been building in the car.

But it wasn't only the physical nature of the place. It was the secrets the house held, the things it symbolized. It was the eccentric estate on the outskirts of civilization that mortals passed by on their daily commute, never giving it a second glance, too caught up in their own petty affairs to imagine what mysteries were guarded by an ivy dragon with security cameras for eyes.

It was a haven for vampyres, hiding in plain sight.

Getting out of the car, I stood drinking in the wonder of my new life, *feeling* alive when I knew I'd been going through the motions before.

Tiny white lights at the edge of the cobblestone path hurled grass blade shadows at my legs. The air had grown fat on jasmine. In the rolling yard beyond the driveway, the black angel courted his stone ghosts.

I was mesmerized by the night, so perfect and undisturbed that the Milky Way stretched out above me, a veil of misty clouds blown by solar winds.

Moving closer, Miquel stood at my back and slipped his arms around me, resting his scruffy chin on my shoulder as he followed my gaze. Despite what had happened only a few hours before, I tensed in response to such intimacy, but before I realized it, I covered his hand with mine, my fingers entwining with his.

My eyes closed, my body relaxing into him as it had done the night I was made.

In my mind, I felt him smile, though it wasn't melancholy as it so often was.

"Ah, Stefan, if you can always remember how you feel right now—this gentle act of surrender which gives you power instead of stealing it from you—the nights ahead will be filled with wonder instead of pain."

Something in the way he said those words both calmed and chilled me. But when I opened my eyes to ask what he meant, I was startled to discover another vampyre standing in front of us, his approach so silent I never heard his booted footsteps even on the cobblestone driveway. Instantly rattled, I stiffened and straightened, extricating myself from my maker's embrace.

The newcomer looked maybe 25—which meant nothing, of course—with curly blond hair that caught the light from the windows and reflected brighter than the source. Delicately handsome and slight in build, the black linen pants and black silk shirt made him seem smaller still, and while the leather trench coat added an illusion of greater height, it also strengthened the impression of a lanky, willow-thin boy.

But one look at this "boy" told me he was frail in the same way a brown recluse was just a harmless little spider.

"So tell me, my friend," he said to Miquel with a waggish smile that was sinister somehow, "is this the new scribe your lost boys have been talking about ever since I arrived? What is his name, do tell? And where did you find him? And what makes you think I won't steal him away to my coffin and keep him all to myself for a century or two, or at least for the rest of the week?"

He looked me up and down as if I were some curio on an auction block and then, to top off his rude intrusion, he had the audacity to wink, hair whipping around his head like a golden halo stolen from some religious painting.

I might've been offended if his behavior hadn't been so ridiculous, but I had no chance to react as Miquel gave a short laugh and went to greet him. What surprised me was how different they were. Even in jeans and a simple gray shirt, Miquel was a portrait of poise and elegance, dark and somber and tragically beautiful. The other struck me as rough around the edges, lacking in style and refinement.

They embraced like old friends long apart—perhaps not

196

surprising for vampyres who could have been separated for centuries—but when they kissed one another on the lips, lingering longer than friends would have dared, it occurred to me to go inside so I wouldn't have to observe this intimate reunion of which I was no part.

But Miquel broke away and came to slip an arm around my waist.

"Stefan, may I introduce you to Adam—the most unusual vampyre I have ever known, and one I would advise you to beware of at all times," he said with a smile, gesturing toward the other with a graceful motion. To Adam, he hastily added, "Do try to be polite, won't you? Stefan is barely a week old, and all this talk of stealing him away to some dreary coffin with only you for company is bound to be unsettling. It unsettles me, after all, and I've known you for a century."

"Almost two, old man," Adam corrected with a sigh. Then, turquoise eyes flashing, he extended his hand and offered a smile that was, in a word, dangerous. "I'm Adam—but you may call me Adam."

Now I remembered the conversation with Dimitri and the others on the way to San Diego. No wonder they didn't like him.

But before I could introduce myself in return, the little bastard pulled my hand toward him, bent his head, and ripped the fleshy pad of my middle finger, drawing blood.

"Hey!" I squawked, taken completely off guard.

It happened so fast it stunned me—especially when the obnoxious creature drew on the cut, swallowing greedily before I could yank my hand away. Outraged, I curled my lip and would have struck him had Miquel not pulled him away and made himself a barrier between the two of us.

But Adam only grinned and gave a sheepish shrug. "Sorry. Bad habit," he confessed, peering out at me from behind Miquel's back. The look in his eyes and the fresh blood on his lips said he wasn't sorry in the least.

"I doubt it," Miquel commented, but I could tell he was amused, even if I most certainly was not.

For a few moments, they looked at one another—lovers, rivals, friends, perhaps even enemies. I couldn't be sure.

Then, as if to distract my attention from his outrageous

behavior, Adam took on the impassioned persona of a bad actor delivering a Shakespearean soliloquy, becoming even more outrageous.

"But can you fault me for desiring a sample of the feast you've so painstakingly prepared, good sir?" he asked of Miquel. "A crumb, a morsel, a tiny taste on my tongue to quench this gruesome hunger? Why, look!" he added, gesturing passionately toward me as his eyes went kaleidoscope mad and the wind snapped at his leather coat. "The echo of mortal life still paints his cheeks with sunrise, but you've made him a vampyre, m'lord, and soon that blush will fade as the rose fails in foulest winter! So how is it you deny me this fleeting repast, my beloved old love? How can you keep this precious carafe with its sweet Bordeaux all to yourself when your brother is perishing in the desert, doing your bidding at Drycreek?"

So saying, he collapsed to his knees at Miquel's feet, one hand to his heart, the other clutching my maker's shirttail in a pose reminiscent of the leper crawling to Christ.

Now I understood. It was really quite simple.

Adam was insane.

Miquel just shot him a reproachful look that nonetheless turned to a grudging smile. "I'm not your brother, and you are hardly perishing." He took Adam's wrist, helping him to his feet. Then, with a look of concern, he turned to me. "Are you all right, Stefan?"

Embarrassed that he thought me so fragile he even needed to ask, I snapped, "It's nothing." But I'd stuffed my finger in my mouth to dull the pain, so my words came out muffled.

Sensing my annoyance, Adam leaned against my car and folded his arms over his chest, pinning me with an ice blue stare.

"I'm not going to apologize for biting you and I'm not going to tell you I won't do it again," he said, stern but not unkind. "I don't have time for a bunch of polite prattle where everybody says one thing and means something else. Blood doesn't lie."

He licked the stain of me from his lips. Then, more compassionately, he decided, "You're a good man, Stefan. You might even make a good vampyre, but you really do need to lighten up a little." Tilting his head to one side as he studied me, he shrugged and amended, "A *lot*."

198

Before I could tell the arrogant ass what I thought of him, Miquel interceded, placing a hand on my elbow to stop me from doing whatever I might have done in anger.

"Stefan has had a difficult time adjusting to his new life," he explained easily. "For the moment, I think the best thing would be to find him a place to rest, something to eat."

Only when Miquel said this did I realize I was hungry again—not only for the nourishment blood would provide, but for the high, too. Embarrassed by my need though it was entirely natural, I looked away from both of them, kicking at little rocks in the cobblestone, a lost child.

"Deep thoughts run silent," Adam commented with a softer tone of voice that said he was trying to make amends.

I looked up to find him studying me. "Excuse me?" I said, unconsciously baring a fang at him.

"Adam can't read your thoughts," Miquel explained. "His blood doesn't travel your veins, so he has no access to your mind."

This surprised me.

Adam was a vampyre, but what kind of vampyre was he?

*

"That boy—that man—that *thing* is a Creator?" I stammered, incensed as I paced back and forth.

Miquel had escorted me to the room underneath the stairs, and there I'd been abandoned with Donny while my maker went off with Adam, the two of them reminiscing about triumphs and tragedies that happened long before I was born, their footsteps and easy laughter leaving me behind.

I stewed for awhile—raved, actually—when the whole time my mind kept replaying the events in the hotel, the conversation in the car. Surely Miquel had been making overtures to me, but when I was finally prepared to acquiesce to a side of myself I'd never acknowledged and greatly feared, he was off with some offensive little finger biter who was, in my opinion, a disgrace to all vampyres everywhere.

"If I ever doubted it before, now I'm sure!" I howled, causing poor Donny to cringe. "There *is* no God, goddammit!"

Sometime in the middle of my rant, Stygian had come in,

and now my brothers sat shoulder to shoulder on the bed while I paraded around the room like a wild man, my bare feet crunching through the textured pile of thick burgundy carpet.

Beyond the window which looked out over the thicket of trees at the rear of the estate, the grounds were dark. The wind had stilled until even the chimes had fallen quiet, and other than an owl hooting in the distance, the night was mute.

The silence really did roar, so deafening it could only be the death scream of every creature who had ever lived. I scuffed my feet as I paced, trying to drown it out.

"I don't know what you're carrying on about, Quilldriver," Stygian chastised, leaning against the headboard with his knees drawn to his chest and a video poker game in one hand. "It's not like any of us get to vote on what we bring to the gene pool. Nobody made Miquel or Adam Creators, they just are—same as you're an empath and Donny's a siren and I'm a tracker. Luck of the draw, you know?"

"I'm not so sure about that," Donny disagreed, tossing his hair over his shoulder. "I mean, Adam created himself, so it could be argued that he chose to make himself a Creator just like he chose to make himself a vampyre." He tilted his head curiously to one side. "Has anybody ever asked him?"

Stygian grunted, jabbing his index finger at the gizmo in his hand. "That would involve talking to the little shit." He grimaced. "Damn, should've held the queens."

I was so self-absorbed that their exchange slipped by me. Then, just as I was about to spit out some new and highly creative profanity, Donny's words sank deep and hard.

"What did you say?"

Wide brown eyes stared at me, unblinking. Stygian looked up from his game, which had begun chirping and playing _You're In the Money._ It was one of those awkward instances where they thought I already knew something I didn't know at all. Finally, Stygian switched off the toy, never glancing down to see what electronic booty he'd won that couldn't be held in his hand.

"Adam's a self-made immortal?" Donny revealed with a cautious shrug, though his statement came out as a question.

His words left a cold knot in the pit of my stomach. "What— _exactly_—is a self-made immortal?"

200

"You mean aside from the ultimate in mental masturbation?" Stygian replied, nudging Donny with his foot.

This caused Donny to snicker, and I was reminded of two ornery boys sharing a secret to which I was not privy.

"No, please. What are you talking about?" I pressed, standing at the foot of the bed as the breeze picked up and brought a honeysuckle chill dashing in from the yard.

Gradually, the amusement faded from Stygian's green eyes until he said in all sincerity, "Adam couldn't live with the idea of dying, so he cut death out of the picture."

Because I had a feeling I was about to hear something I wasn't ready to hear, I sat down on the edge of a chair that faced the bed.

"The story goes that he used his own mind to remove any hint of death from his body—it doesn't exist in his reality," Stygian explained as if reporting nothing more important than the weather. He clasped his hands behind his head until the muscled biceps stretched at the seams of his faded denim shirt. "I guess it's like those people who walk on hot coals without getting burned. Mind over matter—hocus-pocus mumbo-jumbo."

"It's way over my head," Donny confessed, slouching onto one side and propping his chin on his hand. "But Adam believed that death couldn't touch him—right down to a cellular level." He shrugged. "Kinda like people who cure themselves of cancer or those Buddhist monks who can levitate."

"Nah, that was Kwai Chang Cain," Stygian insisted.

"Asshole," Donny chastised, one delicate hand flying out to smack the older vampyre in the chest. To me, in all seriousness, he added, "Miquel says everything in the world happens in the six inches of space between your ears, so if a guy can make himself walk again when the doctors say he should be driving a wheelchair, who's to say Adam couldn't make himself immortal with a thought?"

I could only stare back and forth between them, expecting them to jump up and start laughing at me for falling for their prank. When it became obvious they weren't kidding, I muttered, "But Adam *is* a vampyre, isn't he?"

"Yeah, but he was immortal first," Stygian muttered.

My mouth was dry, my skin pulled too tight.

"But if he was already immortal, why would he need to be a vampyre at all?" I stammered, flabbergasted. "I—if he really *did*—if he really *could* transform his body by some sort of self-willed transmogrification, why would he even *want* to be a vampyre?"

"Maybe he likes it. Some of us do, you know," Donny said, offended by my incredulity.

"Besides, even the strongest belief can collapse under stress," Stygian added. "Faith falls apart whenever God does something we don't like, you know? Adam figured the only way to be sure he was immortal was to go through the motions, the ritual."

I was afraid to ask. "The ritual?"

"Miquel fed Adam his blood."

"Then he *is* like us," I decided, confused.

Donny shook his head, curling his legs underneath him. "You don't get it. Miquel never drank from Adam. Only Adam drank from Miquel."

"Adam never passed through death," Stygian clarified, his tone saying I should have figured this out long ago. Then he repeated, "Little shit."

"He runs Drycreek," Donny offered.

"Drycreek?" I echoed, remembering Adam had mentioned the word.

"Some hole in the road town out in the middle of the desert," Stygian explained. Then, snickering, he added, "Little shit's paranoid—thinks the world might end tomorrow night—so he's got himself a farm out there."

At my blank stare, Donny grinned. "Not turnips and broccoli, Stefan. A *blood* farm—lust junkie survivalists. Some vampyres do stuff like that—hoarding food, I guess you'd say."

I felt ill. Suddenly, I was out of place and altogether out of my league, and I wanted nothing to do with any of it. I didn't want to think about a colony of humans whoring their blood and their precious mortal lives to the likes of Adam. I didn't want to consider the ramifications of a man who could make himself immortal with a thought, for it meant everything I'd ever believed about the nature of human existence was a lie.

I didn't even want Miquel.

I believed that with all the fervor of a monk believing in God. For all of maybe five seconds. But then the bottom dropped

202

out of my stomach again and the devils running up and down my spine sank their cold metal teeth into my conviction and ripped it asunder.

My screwed-up psyche chased itself in circles while Donny and Stygian looked at me as if I'd gone daft.

"Oh, God," I said to myself, and dropped my head in my hands as the world spun out of focus. Here we were, talking about self-made immortals and the very nature of life and death as it related to human perception, yet all I could think about was Miquel.

He obsessed me. He'd *possessed* me.

It was that demented, heart-stopping need young boys can feel, that sense of needing another person so much it seems the whole world might end.

Suki Parker smiled at me from across the biology room, a radiant smile that could stop the earth's rotation. And though the stench of pickled frogs was enough to chase romantic ideas from any rational being, I fell in love so hard that I hit my head in the crash and completely lost my mind. Believing something was wrong with me for my inability to eat and the empty ache where my heart used to beat, I lay in bed at night writing bad poetry, convinced I would die if I couldn't have her, though I wasn't even sure at 12 what "have" really meant. In reality, of course, we never even spoke—for she probably never smiled at me to begin with and was only squinting in the formaldehyde-frog fumes, and I'd built my castles so high that any possibility of rejection held me prisoner in the tower. So at the end of the school year, we went our separate ways without ever consummating that indescribable love affair we had between one second and the next on a hot September afternoon.

But the hurt I'd felt then was a scratch, a mere flesh wound. Miquel had bitten me to the blood, to the death, and the only thing I knew for certain was that I certainly wouldn't survive *this*.

"Oh, God!" I said again, and worlds of fantasy came crashing down around me.

Not around me, exactly. They fell *on* me.

And suddenly I was crushed beneath the realization that I hadn't become a vampyre for any great idealistic purpose. Certainly I had no delusions of going back to college for my PhD in order to pursue great literary endeavors, nor did I deceive myself into thinking I'd done it so I might faithfully record the passing of future history. I hadn't done it to improve the human condition, nor to strengthen this mythical vampyre gene pool I kept hearing about, nor had I done it strictly to outwit death, as Adam had seemingly done.

No, it wasn't for humanity.

It wasn't to search for God.

It wasn't even for immortality itself.

Selfish little bastard that I was, I'd done it all for *love*. I'd done it to be with Miquel, to follow him as any disciple was driven to follow their savior. I'd done it hoping he might one day feel the same about me and—*damn him!*—I'd done it because he made me fall in love with him the first time he took me in his arms and drove his teeth into the bright red stream of my grieving soul.

And though one might think that naming the disease would ease the symptoms, a dreadful chill fell over me when I realized I didn't just love the son-of-a-bitch. I was *in* love with him.

I was in love with a vampyre.

I was in love with my god who might well be the devil.

I was in love with another man.

I didn't know if that made me a gay religious fanatic or irrefutably insane or both.

"Both. Neither," Stygian commented with a lazy smile. He'd heard every lunatic thought rattling through my mind, and though I never saw him move, he was at my side, a hand on my shoulder lending support. "Luckily, you'll live—maybe even long enough to figure some of it out." A pause, a chuckle, then: "Ain't eternity grand, Quilldriver?"

I lifted my head and looked up at him, a perfect vampyre in a flawless body. I envied his strength, his age.

"Huh?" It didn't get any more ineloquent than that.

He reached out to mess my hair. Because it had grown longer since my transformation, it fell forward over my eyes, providing a veil that muted my view of the world. If I'd glanced in a mirror just then, I would have said I looked more like some frayed Armani model than a 34-year-old writer.

My metamorphosis wasn't done yet, and as if to confirm that thought, that crazy-in-love-thing made my stomach drop again, and I had to put my head back in my hands to keep from falling off the chair.

"Oh *God!*" I fairly wailed.

Stygian just laughed and began rubbing my shoulders. "Look, the truest statement ever made was that love hurts, and as a vampyre you're going to have more than your share of love *and* hurt. It's only a problem if you try to handle it the way you did when you were mortal."

I blinked, feeling truly schizophrenic.

"Forever's too long for monogamy to be anything but a fantasy, and the words 'till death do us part' ain't in the vampyre phrase book," Stygian replied enigmatically. Then, at my continued confusion, he sighed heavily. "You can love Miquel and you can hate him, but you can't own him."

"Take it easy, Styx," Donny said from the bed. "Stefan's still a baby." To me: "No offense." Then, back to Stygian, "Besides, you followed the *maahstah* from one side of the Earth to the other and back again for a hundred years before you finally settled into your skin."

Stygian's brows lifted. "Who told you that?"

"You did!" Donny flopped back on the bed, hands behind his head, one foot crossed over the other knee. "Gods, if you're this forgetful now, what're you gonna be like when you're as old as Miquel?"

"He'll always be older," Stygian insisted. "I mean, by the time I'm a thousand, he'll be almost two thousand, so... how could I *ever* be as old as he is?"

Donny just groaned, rolled his eyes, and sighed heavily.

Discreetly, Stygian winked at me to prove he wasn't the dumb blond he sometimes pretended to be. It was just a game he played to distract the younger vampyre from his bouts with the Sadness.

That was love, I thought.

Donny picked up Stygian's poker game and started jabbing at it with one finger, ignoring us both while I sat there staring at them from behind my hair.

They reminded me of an old married couple though they weren't even lovers. They would be some day, I thought. I didn't know how or when or why it would come to pass. I only knew it would, and the knowledge was a comfort somehow. It calmed me when nothing else had.

My brothers would become lovers.

Stygian's head tilted to one side. "You think so?"

I didn't yet have the selective telepathy the older vampyres used, couldn't direct my offbeat mental jabbering to one while shielding from another. I started to apologize, but he waved off my embarrassment and sat on the floor, leaning against the foot of the bed.

"Bird's been saying the same thing for years." He gave a quick glance over his shoulder to where Donny was occupied with the poker game, oblivious to us. Then, with a wistful smile, he shot me a mental picture of the kid sleeping in his arms as the horrific blood dream of the night he was made came and went. Straight into my mind, like a wind scented with laughter and early apples, he added, *I can think of worse people to spend a piece of eternity with, you know?*

Stygian was the embodiment of what a vampyre could be. Unobtrusive, he was strength in silence, power in laughter, contradiction in action.

I had to admire him.

As our thoughts tangled, I wanted more than glimpses of his obscure past, more than flashes of a blond buccaneer balanced on the mast of a tall ship while tropical winds blew hot across the bow. I wanted to know why his voice in my mind had an island accent, and why he liked to pretend an almost casual disinterest in Miquel when the fire behind his eyes said he was as lovesick as the rest of us.

"Eternity gives you the comfort of knowing nothing really ends, Quilldriver," he replied in response to my unspoken thoughts. *I once lived an entire lifetime with Miquel. I will again.*

Mortality was no longer chasing us. Maybe life and love didn't have to be matters of now-or-never, but matters of now-and-forever.

There was *time*.

But before I could say anything, Donny lifted his head and shot me a quizzical look, responding to the silence that had fallen in the room while Stygian and I conversed in telepathic shorthand.

"What?" the kid asked suddenly. "Did you say something, Stefan?" His innocence was enviable.

Trading conspiratorial glances with Stygian, I shook my head. "Nothing," I told him, feeling better just being with them,

being accepted as one of them. "Go back to what you were doing."
But Donny tossed the game aside, rolled to his feet and padded over
to the window. Framed against the night, he seemed to glow, his
masculine beauty so flawless he might have been an alabaster
carving.

"I don't know about you two, but I'm starved," the young
vampyre said. Then, smiling so wide his fangs glistened, he inclined
his head toward the horizon and the glow of the city in the distance.
"What say we go see who we can scare up for dinner?"

So much for his innocence.

CHAPTER SEVENTEEN

When Donny, Stygian and I emerged into the shadowed
grounds at the rear of the house, I was amused by the thought that
we were just three young men out for a late dinner. The fact that the
main course would consist of blood served from a living host and
dessert would be bittersweet mortal memories suckled through a
stolen embrace no longer seemed as macabre as it had in the
beginning.

For better or for worse, I was slowly settling into the thing
I'd become.

The winds had quieted, yet our emergence into the night
awakened them again, and as a gust swept down over the sloped
roof to stir the willows, I experienced a strange quickening. It made
Stygian laugh, though it was no longer the lighthearted chuckle to
which I'd grown accustomed, but a dark-natured sound which told
me his thoughts were as red and primal as my own.

His prey would weep with pleasure tonight.

Mist brushed my cheek, a phantom's caress. Overhead, the
sky was spilling its popcorn stars, the black bowl so full that some
had to fall to make room for others still being born in all that vast
nothingness.

"Falling stars are vampyre hearts, thrown down from
heaven with the trash," Donny said, following my gaze. "Spare parts
of leftover angels."

His words chilled me, for they gave me a peek at his soul—
always searching for lyrics in the background noise the same way

writers quested after stories in the fog.

We followed a fieldstone path winding through the gardens, where I noticed unfamiliar cars parked near a side entrance. A sleek white Corvette with the vanity plate 'BADREAM' caught my eye, as did the beat-up VW bug with Grateful Dead stickers covering the rear windows. All in all, there were at least 15 vehicles—from pickups to sports cars, from vans to a couple of motorcycles.

The Gathering, Miquel had called it.

But much as I was curious about these other vampyres, I'd never been one for family reunions. The polite conversation and concealed warfare were trying at best, an awkward attempt at social courtesy by virtual strangers.

"So—our newest, babiest brother is one who prefers a few close friends over a roomful of stuffy acquaintances," Bird's melodic voice sang from a few feet behind me. "I, for one, am delighted. New blood or not, these little get-togethers are a dreadful chore sometimes."

When I spun around, it was to find the Jamaican in a stunning white tux that made him stand out against the night like a lanky, long-haired ghost. His thoughts said he'd just come from the casino where he worked near Palm Springs, his formal attire a requirement as much as a choice. He tipped his top hat, then handed it off to Donny, who immediately plopped it on his head and took up the role of a mime, pressing pale hands against imaginary cages.

Weird harlequin brothers. I adored them.

"You're just getting old and set in your ways, Bird," Stygian accused, the two of them embracing warmly.

When they separated, however, Bird became somber, shooting me a glance to include me in the conversation while Donny frolicked nearby. "Foxy came in to the tables tonight," he said to Stygian, grim. "She had that little lust junkie on her arm and she was showing off her fangs again."

Stygian stiffened, and as if in response, the wind sent a flurry of leaves skittering across our path.

Donny took off Bird's hat. "Bitch," he muttered.

Stygian was holding his breath. "Did you talk to her?"

Bird shook his head, beaded dreads spilling over his shoulders, windchimes in their own right. "She cleaned out a couple

208

of old farts in the poker room before the tribal cops asked her to leave." A pause, then: "We never spoke, but she made sure I saw her."

"We should just *do* the cow," Donny grumbled, sneering dangerously as he made a slicing motion across his throat.

Though I'd known there was bad blood between Miquel and Foxglove, I hadn't realized how deep it flowed until I saw the worry and, indeed, the real fear in the eyes of my brothers.

I started to say something, but it was at that moment that I glanced up to see Miquel and Adam emerging from the house.

"Shit," Stygian cursed under his breath, following my gaze. Quickly, quietly: "Don't say anything about Foxy. No point giving him something else to worry about until we know what's going on."

Since Stygian was the natural leader, none of us argued.

At first, looking at Adam and Miquel from a distance, they could have passed for any two young men engaged in conversation beneath a porch light where moths flickered like fairy dust and bats flitted about in pursuit of insects. And yet, under any closer scrutiny, there was something about my maker that transcended words and defied explanation.

While he stood there waiting for Adam—who was digging in his pocket like the class clown, looking for his car keys—there was something otherworldly about him, some somber and bleak mystique that went far beyond the fact that he was a vampyre. It wasn't only that he was a Creator, for Adam, despite his blunt charm, had no such higher charisma.

They didn't seem aware of our group—which fell into a hush as soon as they appeared—and only when Stygian muttered, "Little shit," under his breath, did Miquel glance over at us.

Even at a distance, it seemed his eyes met mine, and when he moved toward us, I experienced a rush that left me light-headed. Dressed in a white shirt and the same falling apart jeans he'd worn the first night I gave up my blood to him, he was a three dimensional hallucination with a gold cross in one ear and ragged hair still damp from the shower.

Just seeing him again left me anxious and awkward and sick to my stomach, no better off than I'd been when he had sucked the life out of me and replaced it with his own immortal blood.

"Since it can't be the flu, it's gotta be love, and you've got it bad," Stygian whispered, leaning close to my ear.

I elbowed him to get him off my back, my face prickling with embarrassment.

"Ah, Stefan," Miquel said as he drew up next to us, his demeanor so relaxed I could almost believe him free of concerns. "I was just wondering what you were up to. Tell me, have you fed yet?"

It seemed irreverent, him asking so casually if I'd driven my teeth into pliant mortal flesh to indulge the most intimate of pleasures. "Uh—we were just on our way out," I stammered.

But he'd already turned his attention to the others. "Bird! Is it my imagination, or have you grown taller in the night air?"

While Adam stood a few feet away, watching with amused disinterest, the changes that came over my brothers were fascinating.

Bird, whom I was used to thinking of as impervious to the world at large, actually seemed to float above the ground when he went to embrace Miquel, resting his head on our maker's shoulder and drawing a sharp breath that left no doubt as to what he was feeling. Indeed, the erotic shock of their exchange was a psychic elixir no vampyre could have ignored, and because it had become natural for me, I suckled the stray energy as if it were human blood.

Miquel moved to Stygian, drawing the blond into a loving hold that bespoke a long past, a longer future. And though Stygian always made such a production of his manly-man Chippendale-esque facade, those false-front walls collapsed entirely when he was caught up in Miquel's arms. His body relaxed utterly. He even whispered something into Miquel's ear, and though I never knew what he said, Miquel's easy laughter told me it was probably some amorous suggestion.

But when our unearthly father opened his arms to Donny, the kid stood there holding his breath, the ghosts of their past circling one another. For an instant, they were back in that crummy apartment, Miquel at war with death, Donny at war with AIDS, the casualty of that final battle the trust that had existed between them when bloodletting was an expression of love instead of a gateway to immortality through which the kid was dragged kicking and literally screaming, a vampyre made against his will.

And yet, when I saw in Miquel's eyes that all-encompassing

210

love only dreamt of or hidden in books, I had to believe love would eventually find a way to heal the jagged scars which were reopened every night in their dreams.

"Please?" Miquel said, the rings on his fingers catching moonlight as he held out his hands. "The memories are only paper demons, you realize. They can't hurt you."

I thought Donny would flee, but when Stygian gave him a little nudge, he acquiesced and moved awkwardly into Miquel's arms, though he stood like a man waiting for the axe to fall, his eyes clenched shut, body taut as a bow.

But as Miquel held him—his ecstasy when Donny came to him a feast he laid out before us in the air—the kid's shoulders relaxed and he offered no resistance when our maker pulled his head down on his shoulder.

They swayed together, dancing to music only they could hear, and though I felt like an unintentional voyeur, I could not take my eyes from them even when Miquel pushed Donny's hair aside to reveal his neck.

Before the kid even knew what was happening, Miquel's sharp fangs eased into his throat to release the bright red stream of his blood. Stiffening in surprise, whimpering as he tried to lift his head, Donny struggled, yet he was no match for Miquel's strength.

Of all the others Miquel could have taken, of course he chose the one who feared him most.

At my side, Stygian winced, whispering, "Oh, shit."

Bird turned away and began humming to himself—_Stairway To Heaven._

Adam checked his watch, impatiently tapping his foot— little shit.

I could neither move nor breathe as I watched them together—Donny beginning to yield as his arms fell limp at his sides and his head dropped back like a mortal fainting from blood loss, Miquel drawing harder on his veins as their breathing synchronized.

My body tingled from the inside out. My soul was scratching at its cage, demanding freedom.

I'd seen Miquel feed on Valerie the night after I was made. I'd watched him drive his fangs into Sergio while the three of us rode carnal death together in a rented hotel bed. But to observe this sacred exchange between two vampyres was more than I could bear, and when Donny's fingers curled into fists and his feet left the ground as Miquel lifted him into his arms, I had to look away.

The feelings emanating from them could have cured terminal illnesses or built a timeless empire. Love, lust, fear, dread, shock, surrender—a cocktail of blood aged for centuries in casks of immortal veins.

What caused me to open my eyes was when Bird stopped humming and Stygian quit muttering, "Oh, shit," to himself, and an eerie hush descended. Miquel lifted his head away, lips painted red, eyes pinpoints of emerald brilliance. He kissed softly at the wounds, tonguing the little incisions closed as he lifted the ragbaby into his arms to keep him from falling.

Donny moaned deliriously, semiconscious at best, arms dangling from his shoulders like a dead man's. His breathing was shallow, eyelids fluttering, and with his head thrown back, his hair nearly swept the ground.

He turned his face into Miquel's chest, and the picture they painted was one of some unholy disciple receiving Christ from the cross and carrying the corpse to the tomb.

As if to complete that illusion, Miquel turned to lay the young vampyre over Stygian's outstretched arms. Then, looking up at me as he surreptitiously licked the last of the blood from his lips, he gave me a smile as dangerous as it was compelling.

The bottom dropped out of my world, and before I could do anything at all, he brought me to him as he had each of my beautiful brothers. My heart thundered as if I were mortal still, and I wondered if I, too, would feel that ghastly sting which was both good and evil, slavery and emancipation.

I closed my eyes and waited, but even though Miquel bent his lips to my throat and lingered at the apex of neck and shoulder—a cruel kiss for what it promised—the pain never came.

After everything that had happened between us—life and death behind us, forgiveness still in the balance—the monster had the gall to toy with me?

"Damn you!" I whispered, looking beyond him to the black angel in the courtyard with its empty arms outstretched toward the night. *"Damn you!"*

But when I tried to wriggle free, suddenly disgusted by the

whole wretched mess, he only yanked me tighter to him and placed his mouth against my ear, his breath still sweet with Donny's lost boy blood. "Oh, my dearest Stefan, don't you know the cat always plays hardest with the mouse that protests most?" A pause, a scraping of fang teeth over my ear, then, matter-of-factly: 'I'll have you tonight, you see—heart and soul, body and blood. When the night is deepest and the house is dark and still, I shall take you away to my coffin bed, and there I shall finally have you."

But even while I was praying for salvation from this devil, I knew there could be none.

When Miquel abruptly released me and took a step backward, our eyes locked and warred, and I was standing at some mystical crossroads once again. I could give in to him. Or I could go on fighting him.

Because he was a vampyre, he needed me to love him. But because there was still some part of me that remained human, I needed him to love me in return—and I wasn't at all sure he did.

I wasn't sure he *could*.

But when the door of the house opened again and I broke eye contact to glance toward the source of easy laughter, the moment was lost, the crossroads behind me as time rushed forward to fill the void in my soul.

Underneath the porch light, four young men and two women emerged. Vampyres. Like me. Not like me at all.

Dimitri was among them, and when he looked up to see us, he gave a polite nod, but none of this other group approached us. Instead, like substance turned to shadow by an alchemist's command, they disappeared into the night, hunters indulging a quest for blood.

For a moment, I wondered if they'd ever been there at all, for they moved so swiftly and silently that I was reminded of a dream where the sound man and the director didn't always work together, where a lover's laughter was only owl song, where a black plastic sack blown through empty streets was really a vampyre.

But when I glanced toward Miquel, I found myself alone with Stygian and Donny instead. My maker had vanished with Adam, the scent of their cologne all that remained. Donny stirred, a music box doll with jerky motions, coming back to life. "'m hungry," he mumbled into Stygian's shoulder. "Is it Montana yet next

Monday?"

"You're delirious," Stygian pronounced, rocking him as a father would rock an infant.

Driven mad, I ran for my car and sped off into the night alone.

*

For the remainder of that night, I roamed the dark and dismal streets, asking myself over and over what I'd been thinking when I'd crawled into Miquel's arms and surrendered my life to death forever.

The roller coaster had dropped again, and with it any sense of hope had fallen out from under me. One minute I craved this wild ever afterlife where blood was wine and night was day and even the pain of rejection was the most exquisitely beautiful pleasure. Yet in the very next second, I would have traded it all back to Monty Hall for one more chance to live the life I'd left behind the curtain—not because I'd been happy or thought I ever could be, but because I'd once clung blindly to some illusion of emotional security which now eluded me.

I found myself in the suburbs, where the last bastion of middle class life played out on stages set with Ethan Allen sofas and Berber carpet, those places where the play could carry on as if the world really were Mayberry RFD, those matchbox homes with old-fashioned red metal tricycles inside safely fenced yards, and the distant barking of a pedigreed dog, and the his and hers Priuses waiting in the driveway for the new day to begin.

But because my vampyre nature compelled me to be forever searching for something—*anything*—with meaning, I eventually sought out the seedier side of town, the flipside of those picture perfect neighborhoods, the ghettos and barrios where crumbling warehouses and abandoned factories served as headquarters for gangs, where the tinkling sound in dark alleys wasn't windchimes but footsteps plunging headlong through broken bottles, used syringes, splintered lives.

Shadows moved behind me, stalking me, following me. But whenever I spun around to confront my would-be assassin, I found only a skinny cat bolting through the street or a piece of trash blown on metallic city wind. Stray thoughts were the only things that found me, persistent pests demanding recognition.

'More wrists have been slashed in the name of love than for any other reason, Stefan'.

My footsteps on the cracked sidewalk quickened, and I ran as I'd run when I was human. Storefronts flashed by me, pawn shops and sleazy bars bleeding the stench of beer, and an X-rated theater with its windows boarded shut, a casualty of the digital revolution.

'Driftwood, Stefan. I am driftwood'.

I slowed, not even winded after miles of sprinting. Unafraid of the night because my heart would beat forever, I sank to the ground in a stranger's yard and listened to the mewing of newborn kittens in the garage. It made me smile, especially when the exhausted mom cat purred loudly in deference to the pair of birthing her young.

'The problem with vampyres is that we love too deeply, and when we lose the thing we love it destroys us all over again'.

And that set me running again, Nikes slapping dew-damp asphalt, fists clenched until I rounded a corner and came to a standstill. Beneath the tarnished halo of a flickering streetlight, a man teetered on drunken legs, telling himself in hushed mumbles the story of the three bears and counting on his fingers to make sure he got it right. When our eyes met, his jaundiced dementia told me he didn't have long to live. Worse, I knew he knew it, and so I wept in silence at the irony which had chosen me to live forever and him to die before the age of 40. What was the difference between us? Why was the nature of nature that all things must end?

But even when I lured that man away from his lamp post and drove my fangs into the pallid flesh of his throat, the answers didn't come. He had no memories to give me, his mind blank as if he really were a hollow actor in somebody else's play.

Fed, but hungrier than ever before, I wandered, wondering if I myself were only one more prop in Miquel's black comedy.

'Forever's too long for monogamy to be anything but a fantasy'.

Probably true.

'And I will never break your heart again'.

But he *had* broken my heart again, and surely he would do it again and again. And so I ran in circles, chasing my soul through that city-within-the-city whose name I did not even know. When I stopped to catch my breath, I once again sensed a presence at my back, eyes watching me, ghosts following me on little currents of wind, running along the power lines strung chaotically above pitted streets.

But the sidewalks were barren and even the stars had closed their fiery eyes, the sky a misty gray canvas. I stretched out with my expanded senses in an attempt to get some fix on this thing shadowing me. But no matter how many times I tried, it remained elusive as winter's smoke.

The only thing I knew was that it wasn't human, for no mortal could have kept pace with me as I bolted through the night, running from fears I could not name, stalked by something I could not see, hounded by love I could never hold in my hand.

For awhile, I wondered if this were all some erotic nightmare from which I might soon awaken. But no matter how I fought to hold that hope in my heart, the reality of my transformation shattered my fantasy whenever a mortal came near.

And they *did* come, drawn to me by occult gravity, seducing me to seduce them, demanding by their petulant stares that we each play the role laid out for us by fate. Puppets, they were, even to the point of acknowledging their function as prey and placing themselves in my path to prove it.

But regardless of how sweet or rancid the blood that jetted past my lips in pursuit of a thirst that could never be satisfied, the one thing my victims had in common was that each and every one of them was a lost soul searching, endlessly searching, for love.

That's what it was all about. That was the theme of the play—just one more silly love story.

When they weren't in love, they were looking to fall in love. When they *were* in love, they were terrified of losing their love. It drove them in circles. It drove them out into the night, where their angst conjured vampyres to feed on their sorrows.

It drove them mad—just as it had driven me.

The thought gripped me with cold metal hands, shaking me.

I knew then that nothing had really changed. I had gone from mortal to immortal, from human to inhuman, from man to myth—but inside me, nothing at all had changed.

Stefan London had merely traded one obsession for another

when he traded mortal grief for unrequited love.

I wasn't like the others. I could never be Dimitri—all refinement and grace and passions under strict control. I wasn't Stygian, with the patience of the ages carved into his eyes and the enviable ability to sit back and wait for tomorrow's headlines. I couldn't be like Bird—a loner aloof from it all until Miquel came along to shatter his serenity and bring him to his knees. I couldn't even lay claim to Donny's poetic insanity that often left him melancholy but always gave him the strength to keep searching for songs in the noise.

They were all the things I could never be because they were whole unto themselves. I wasn't sure I ever had been.

As a writer, I was a channel—a conduit through which the lives and dreams of other characters passed on their way to the paper. And though I'd always longed to live those fantastical lives instead of only writing about them, I was no longer sure I had the endurance for it; for when all was said and done, I myself was hollow inside—an empty vein waiting for the next rush of human blood to fill me with memories I'd never made for myself.

The understanding of these things didn't come all at once. Rather, it had been building in bits and pieces when I found myself back at my car just as the first honed edge of morning sliced the horizon.

Man or vampyre, writer or character, the sun had taught me respect. I would need a place to rest, and quickly.

On one corner, a rats-and-lice flophouse calling itself The Presidential Hotel had sprung up out of the ground like a redbrick blight. On another corner, an abandoned church had begun its slow but inevitable deterioration back into the earth, the ground littered with debris from the last earthquake.

The irony seemed altogether fitting, so I made my way across that dreary street at the crossroads of skid row and dawn, entering the church through a broken window that looked out over a tiny, bramble-bound cemetery. To my disappointment, I didn't burst into flame, nor did the ground open up to swallow me when my feet touched the floor. Church or no, it was just a building, another ruin in a world of ruined stages.

The floor was littered with used condoms, the walls tattooed with graffiti. Shards of stained glass sparkled beneath boarded-up windows, colorful tears of angels who'd long since flown away.

Trembling and soul sick, I sank down onto a cold wooden pew and wrote my name in the dust, looking for an identity I'd long since lost if, indeed, I ever had it at all.

Above the choir loft, a larger-than-life painting depicted Christ sitting on the banks of the River Jordan. His feet disappeared beneath the water which was, in reality, the baptismal pool, half full of stagnant liquid which had collected from a hole in the roof. Compassionate brown eyes looked out over a congregation of phantom sinners, locking with mine across a crumbling altar scattered with the tangible despair of Man's lost faith.

He had broken my heart, too.

"I believed in you," I said aloud, my chin trembling, my soul unsalvageable.

But what caused me to cry out in alarm was when the man in that painting stood up, walked down off the wall, and came up the center aisle as if he were flesh and blood instead of faded, two-dimensional acrylic paint. Never taking his eyes from me—though now the mercy was gone from him completely—he mesmerized me with a trance not even a vampyre could break, then sat down on that dirty pew and rapped me on the side of my head with his knuckles before I could even think to flee.

"That's what's wrong with this world," the Savior told me in an androgynous voice that was incongruously gentle. "Everybody's so busy believing in *me* that they've quit believing in themselves! Christ—that is to say, *My Self*—if I'd known it was going to turn out like this, I never would have let that puny little centurion sink the first nail. I thought I was making a point—you know, weaving a bit of subtle allegory about self-sacrifice and self-enlightenment into all those stuffy historical texts—but leave it to Man to take everything literally and start looking for heaven among the stars even when I've given him Galileo and Hubbell to prove it isn't out there! Give them books, they eat the covers. Who's surprised?"

So saying, He shook his head and gave a deeply troubled sigh while I cowered, wide-eyed and unable to move.

"I—but—you—."

"Oh, do be quiet and let me think," He chastised, leaning back on the pew and using the bench in front of us for a foot rest as He folded His arms over a muscular chest. "You're what finally convinced me, you realize. You're what finally convinced me that everything I've ever said or done is all for naught—parlor tricks to confound the primitives who aren't looking to learn, but only to be bedazzled!"

He paused just long enough to look at me with a fair amount of disgust, then reached up to scratch His beard the same way a confused mortal might scratch his head. "I lead you to the fountain of forever and let you drink your fill, but now you're carrying on because love's the disease as well as the cure! If it's not one thing it's another, eh, Stefan?"

"I—I don't understand!" I blurted out, halfway expecting Him to strike me dead.

"You *wish* I would strike you dead, and that's what's wrong with you!" He informed me with great enthusiasm, reading my thoughts as easily as the vampyres. "You've wandered through this entire book—for you *will* write a book, as does every fool who believes he's stumbled over a vague truth—but you've wandered through this whole book moaning and weeping endlessly for the things that have been done *to* you, when the simple truth is that you could take control of your life anytime you want! Remember Dorothy? Ruby slippers? No place like home?"

Terrified, I began to prattle. "I—don't—can't—."

"I really thought you were going to grasp it," He added, rapping me up the side of my head again to shut me up. "I thought you had an honest-to-Me chance back in the first chapters, when you were rattling on about man taking responsibility for his own afterlife! But did you ever really get it? Of course not!" He exploded, throwing His hands up in the air. "It's so much easier to sit around feeling sorry for yourself, yanking the wings off the fairies and whining 'he loves me, he loves me not'!"

I said nothing, and only two things kept me from fleeing: the fact that my body was paralyzed and the belief that I truly was insane at last.

"And that's another problem!" He railed at me. "You're always worrying about your precious sanity, as if hanging onto it is some great accomplishment! Hell—one of my better literary creations, by the way—hasn't it dawned on you that a large percentage of writers and damn near all the prophets have all been several steps around the curve—."

"—bend," I edited automatically, not meaning to speak. My excuse was that I was addled from being smacked twice, and not at all tenderly either time.

"Whatever," He agreed with a shrug. "Slang's always been difficult for me. I thought I got rid of it with that Babel incident, but give it just three thousand years and here it is back again. Now where was I? Oh, yes—I was just about to tell you what an ass you've been.

"Look at what you're doing right now, for example—cowering like some scatterbrained mortal when in reality you're a vampyre—a black angel in your own right, philosopher extraordinaire, keeper and fiend of mortal dreams!

"Stand up to me! Tell me what you think! We're going to be having these conversations from now till doomsday, so stop weltering and behave like the mystical thing you are! God—that is to say 'Father!'—how I crave someone to talk to who can look me in the eye over dinner instead of staring at the table mumbling prayers of unworthiness while the food's getting cold!"

He hesitated as if he expected an answer, but I had no idea what to say to Him, and I didn't dare tell Him He seemed to be doing just fine talking to Himself.

"Just say what's on your mind," He suggested. "And don't forget to phrase your answer in the form of a question."

I stared, my jaw slack. So He laughed and elbowed me in the ribs, causing me to grunt.

"Sorry, couldn't help it, but I always wanted to be a game show host. Just a little half-hour slot called, oh, maybe _Run For Your Life_, where you throw a bunch of people in a maze and have this guy with a scythe chasing them. Of course, the ratings probably wouldn't hold up, since the fools would all gather in front of the tube to watch themselves, which means they'd quit running all too soon and die of their own complacency. Ah well. I suppose that's what I get for allowing the paradox to create itself in the first place."

He sighed dramatically and ran His fingers through His hair. "But back to you. The problem with you is that you're so afraid of failing you set yourself up to fail just so you can say I told you so. Self-fulfilling prophecies are the easiest to realize, after all, so if you build a bridge and then knock it down just to prove your prediction that it would fall, does that mean the bridge was destined to

220

collapse in the first place, or did you change its original destiny?

"That's why I was always fascinated by the noninterference directive on *Star Trek*—not any of those self-righteous spin-offs, but the *real Star Trek*. You know—Kirk, Spock, Bones? Half naked women running around saying, 'I'm frightened, Captain'?'

I nodded stupidly, finally realizing that the fallacy of religion was that God Himself was mad as any hatter.

"Good," He hurried on, seeming oblivious to my thoughts or choosing to ignore them. "My point is that you've got these guys on a spaceship with absolute power at their fingertips, but whenever they come upon some third world dirtball hanging in the void, they can't interfere. Oh, the planet may blow up in the next ten minutes, taking with it the cure for every disease known to man and the answers to all his spiritual questions, but nobody wants to beam up the primitives because the noninterference directive says they don't have the right to play God!

"Christ—My Self, that is—what's playing God any *more* than refusing to get involved? Hasn't it occurred to you people that there hasn't been any direct heavenly interference in the affairs of Man in over two thousand years? *That's* the noninterference directive—the noninterference directive *is* playing God! It's sitting up there in the clouds *watching* it all go to Hell just to see if it *will* go to Hell! And just to make *sure* it goes to Hell, there's this thing called temptation. Now what kind of odds does that leave for these poor mortal bastards crawling around on their bellies whining for forgiveness for the very weaknesses with which The Old Man created them?"

He paused just long enough to take a breath, then quickly concluded: "Personally, I've never been a fan of predestination, but I'm only one vote on a three headed Siamese triplet. To me, free will is so much more interesting, but I'm starting to think Man doesn't want free will anymore. I mean, really, why would you read a book if you knew in advance that everybody dies horribly in the end?"

I looked Him squarely in the eye and dared to ask. "Why would *you* __write__ a book where everybody dies horribly in the end?"

He stared at me as if trying to decide whether or not to smack me again, and then His lips curved into a little grin. "Touchè, Stefan," He conceded. But then, with great passion, He stressed his point home. "But don't you see that the book can end any way you want it to? You rewrote the ending, didn't you? So the question becomes: what do you do now that you've got forever to play with? And—so help me, Me—if you say you've decided to move into some drab hovel and write children's books just to hide from love, I might let the moon fly out of its orbit and smash this whole infernal ant farm! I don't need a lot of provocation, you know. Just ask Noah."

Insane or not, I had a feeling he meant it. But before I could say a word, He stood up and stretched his muscles like a man getting up after a long night's sleep. Then, standing directly in front of me, He leaned down until our faces were only inches apart, framed by a curtain of His holy hair.

"Now that we have that all straightened out, Stefan, I really must be going," He said, his breath a whisper of icebergs and the veldt and the dark side of a Jovian moon.

"G-going?" I stammered, staring helplessly into His painted acrylic eyes. "Why—where are you going?"

He just shrugged and jutted His chin toward a door which had been long boarded shut. "It's time for a haircut, some new clothes. After that, maybe I'll take in an old Bruce Lee movie or go appear in another holy tortilla somewhere in Texas. Who knows?"

With that said, He leaned in as if to kiss me goodbye. And though I was shaking so hard the pew had begun to rattle, all I could do was close my eyes and allow it. He *was* God, after all.

But what brought me to my senses was when He took me in His arms—an embrace as intimate as a lover's—and the barbed points of His fangs sank quick and deep into my throat to bring my blood flowing. He suckled harsh and fast, drawing so hard it felt as if my veins would collapse under the stress, but while I'd once dared to wonder if the Holy Redeemer had been a vampyre, certainly I'd never believed it.

Now, I *couldn't* believe it.

"Jesus Christ!" I screamed, horrified, thrashing to tear myself free of the pain that nonetheless sent my body into an instant paroxysm.

But when my eyes flashed open, my arms flailing madly as I sucked in a rasping breath, the person bending over me wasn't the Holy Savior at all, and the teeth attached to my throat didn't belong to the Vampyre Jesus but to a fat albino rat with glowing pink eyes.

Bolting upright on the pew—though I had no recollection of

222

lying down in the first place—I hurled the Son of God away from me to impact with the wall, where He slid to the floor amidst broken glass, His filthy body convulsing in death, His pale white muzzle painted red with my blood.

When my eyes focused, I realized it was Stygian standing over me in the darkness, one hand to his mouth to conceal his amusement.

"What the fuck are you doing here?" I snapped, disoriented and miserable. "How'd you find me?"

He looked at the dead rat, then at me.

"Finding you was easy," he said with a lazy grin. "I expect convincing you to come back will be the hard part. But since I'm not taking no for an answer, why not come along quietly so I don't have to fuck you up."

Though he was trying to be lighthearted, my instant reaction was to shake my head as visions of Miquel went rattling through my soul.

Outside the church, night had fallen again, and the distant sound of sirens was rivaled only by a clap of unexpected thunder. Wind whistled around crumbling headstones in the tiny cemetery, turning down the death beds. Rain scratched at the roof.

"I'm not cut out for this, Stygian," I told him, leaning forward to rest my elbows on my knees. "To be a vampyre, I mean. Hell, I'm a writer, not even a very good one. That's all I've ever been, it's all I know how to do! Tell Miquel I'm sorry."

He just rolled his eyes. "You're still wet behind the ears," he reminded. "And it's not like you can go back to the way things were before. Even if you never see Miquel again, you'll still be a vampyre and you'll still be a writer. The only difference is that you'll be alone."

I wasn't listening. Instead, I was staring at the wall at the front of the room, which was lit by a shaft of gold from a streetlight sputtering in the storm.

A chill crawled down my spine, causing my back to straighten as every nerve jangled.

"What?" Stygian said, nervously jerking his head around to follow my gaze. "You're giving me the creeps."

I stood on legs that trembled, unable to take my eyes off that wall as my hands gripped the bench in front of me for support.

"The painting," I mumbled to myself. "Look at the painting!"

Stygian stared at the wall, not seeming particularly impressed. "Yeah, so? Looks like some high school kids painted a creek and some grass on the wall. What're you, an art critic?"

I was shaking my head frantically. "No—you don't understand! I—don't you *see*? Christ came down off the wall—I mean—He was there—in the painting!"

But He wasn't there now.

Stygian just looked at me. "Whatever."

He couldn't understand, of course, and nothing I could say would change his mind. I had to believe God was more than a rat-bite hallucination, so I chose to believe Christ really had walked right out of a bad painting in a ruined church and strolled out into the world looking for a haircut and a new pair of jeans.

Maybe, like the rest of us, He just wanted to fit in.

"Well?" Stygian prompted when I'd been standing there for several minutes. "Are you coming or not?"

"No, I..."

But when I caught a glimpse of the floor—where a trail of wet footprints led from the baptismal pond and *through* the boarded up door—a profound chill caused me to understand that I no longer had the luxury of self-pity.

'...if you say you've decided to move into some drab hovel and write children's books just to hide from love, I might let the moon fly out of its orbit and smash this whole infernal ant farm!'

Stygian was tapping his foot, nervous and impatient as the storm sent another clap of thunder to rattle the roof.

"Well?" he said again, ill at ease when the lightning flashed to reveal the ruin around us—the broken pews and rat-eaten hymnals littering the floor and the puddles of water starting to collect here and there from holes in the roof.

Taking a deep breath despite the very real fear gnawing at my gut, I knew I couldn't take the easy way out.

"Let's go home," I said, though I wasn't at all sure what that word meant.

My big blond brother embraced me fondly and healed the bites on my throat with a quick and gentle kiss.

At my insistence, we buried God in the little cemetery behind the church.

CHAPTER EIGHTEEN

The black angel wept.

When we arrived back at Miquel's house, I still wasn't certain what I would be facing, so I chose to remain outside after Stygian went indoors. Another sallow statue, I stood in the courtyard for a very long time, searching for guidance inside lifeless stone eyes bleeding tears of midnight rain.

My clothes became soaked, clutching at my body. My hair hung in wintry strands.

Once, I felt eyes on the back of my neck, but whenever I turned to look, I found myself alone.

The wrought iron gates had been closed, the ivy dragon's red eyed surveillance cameras gazing out over an empty road where rain fell through an orange cone scooped out of the darkness by a streetlight. Windchimes beneath the eaves sang muffled wet melodies.

Embracing the night, I hugged my arms to my chest, though my vampyre body had no natural heat to warm my hands even when I tucked them underneath my arms. Cold, alone, I became preoccupied just trying to make sense of the puzzle pieces that were all that remained of my life.

Miquel had taken Stephanie's life (though he claimed she would have died anyway); and my mother had sent me to my room to pray for forgiveness (ashamed of me for what I had become); and I had stolen Sergio's life to save my afterlife (but was he ever alive to begin with?); and the Vampyre Jesus had bitten me to the blood and told me to stop running from love lest He drop the sky on us all; and Miquel was there inside a house of wallpaper angels, waiting to turn my world upside-down again.

I could run, but only in circles. I could never hide, for the monster I was hiding from lived behind my own eyes.

Or I could surrender.

The wind stilled, and as the eye of the storm passed overhead to show off a secret canvas of stars, the rain paused.

'Even the devil needs forgiveness, but before you can forgive him, you've gotta forgive me'.

Stephanie was smiling at me again, spectral hands reaching across time and death, suddenly grabbing me and pulling me through a keyhole to a phantom carnival at the edge of the sea. From there, we passed through a weekend at her maternal grandmother's house where we'd both been in hell, comrades in misery. Then we were off to a hundred conventions where she'd served as my guide and my inspiration. Finally, like some modern-day ghost of Christmas Past, she brought me to that crossroads moment when she stood silhouetted against the brighter light of the hotel's hall, the last night of her life.

"I'm going downstairs to the costume ball, okay, Daddy?" she said, her face obscured by her own shadow.

Had she grown taller since that afternoon? When did her hair go from chestnut brown to midnight black? I wanted to cry, for she'd turned into a young woman when I wasn't looking. An eerie feeling came over me. I knew I was losing her. "Sure you don't want to stay here with your old man? They're showing <u>Men In Black</u> *on the convention channel."*

She was a black cutout—penumbra, echo, shade. "I'm kinda restless." Here she paused for effect and, with the inflection of Kier Dullea in <u>2010</u>*, she eerily whispered, "Something's going to happen, Daddy—something* <u>wonderful</u>*!"*

She knew what was out there, what was waiting for her. And because she knew, she calmly closed the door behind her and went out to find her destiny.

I never saw her again.

"I forgive you, baby," I whispered before I realized what I was saying.

It wasn't a conscious choice, but this was, quite simply, the moment nature had chosen for my grief to end. I knew it had when I felt the swelling behind my eyes and real tears spilled over my cheeks—not tears of blood, but warm, salty, human tears, the last of their kind, the last I would ever shed.

Something inside me relaxed, a tension I could not have named leaving me through the soles of my feet, a group of muscles that didn't exist going slack. There was no earth-shattering revelation, no hand of God reaching down to lift the burden from my shoulders.

There was simply peace inside myself.

When I looked up from my daydreaming to find Miquel a few feet away—backlit by candlelight pouring out from the house just as Stephanie had been backlit in that hotel doorway—I even managed to smile.

"Didn't your mother teach you to come in out of the rain, Stefan?"

Though a distinct melancholy lingered in my heart—the loss one feels when giving up any longtime companion, even grief itself—I gave a soft chuckle.

"Afraid I'll catch my death of cold?"

This caused him to laugh. "Hardly. I seem to recall killing you once already so we would never need worry about death again."

The little fangs grazed over his lips when he spoke, and I was struck again with the realization that he was a mystical creature, alien to the mainstream world, god and devil in the same shiny wrapper.

It didn't seem possible, especially while he was standing there solid and whole in a ruffled silk shirt that fluttered in the wind. His bejeweled hands glistened, long fingers pushing shaggy hair from luminous eyes. With even his aura polished like an ominous blade, he was Death dressed to kill.

No being on Earth could have resisted him.

"Why did you choose me?" I asked impulsively. "There are thousands of writers in the world. Why me?"

He placed a hand on my elbow, encouraging me to walk at his side as he began to stroll through the grass. Drops of water collected on his shoes, flawless diamonds.

"You might not like the truth," he cautioned. "Sure you want to know?"

I wasn't sure at all, but I said, "Yes," all the same.

He was silent as we moved into the darker regions at the rear of the house, our footsteps echoing dully on the wet cobblestone path that wound through the gardens. Jasmine painted the air sweet. Mourning doves, roosting in the trees, fluttered, startled by our approach.

Miquel walked with his hands clasped behind his back, his head lowered. Finally, on a narrow wooden footbridge that crossed over the creek, he stopped, leaning forward to rest his elbows on the railing. Almost unconsciously, I mirrored his stance, looking down at our reflections in burnished black water.

My left eye was a quarter, my right a penny. I wondered

who had come looking for luck in a vampyre's secret gardens, and how much they'd found for 26 cents.

"I did it for her," he said at last, lacing his fingers together in front of him as a gust stirred the chimes. "Your daughter—Stephanie. I did it for her."

I stared at the vampyre's reflection, never looking at the man. "For her? What do you mean?"

A pensive smile crinkled his lips. Two fat drops of rain plopped into the water, their individuality swallowed up by the greater whole.

"When I drank from her, I touched you in her mind—or more precisely, she showed you to me," he replied after a long silence. "You know what I mean. You don't just drink from their veins, but from their hearts, their entire lives, all of it. We're their immortality in a way. We take them with us forever."

I'd never seen Miquel hedge before.

"Yes, I know," I reminded him. "Please—go on."

For awhile, he stood there looking down, his ruby cufflinks reflecting up like glowing red eyes that blinked whenever another drop of rain disturbed the glassy surface.

"I offered her eternity, Stefan," he told me, reverent and calm. "She would have made a splendid vampyre, with all her sullen contemplations and her diary filled with poems of a young girl's suffering and her soul dyed black to hide the scars on its edges."

He wasn't being cruel, only truthful. That's who Stephanie was. And though I never could have admitted it before, she *would* have made a good vampyre. A better one than I, certainly.

"And?" I dared to ask when he fell silent.

"She didn't want it." A gesture of dismissal, a long pause, then, more quietly, "At least she didn't want it for herself."

Reflections wouldn't do just then. I needed reality, rough edges and all, so I turned my head sharply to look at my Creator.

"Stephanie told you to do it to me?" I whispered, unconsciously holding my breath. "She told you to make me a vampyre?"

He nodded almost undetectably. "I swore a promise to her that I would."

"But—*why*?"

228

He lifted his head, more than a thousand years of secret pacts and hidden agendas in his eyes. "She loved you more than her own life, Stefan, so much that she wanted you to live forever." He tried to smile, though it was filled with sadness. "In many ways, my friend, she believed she'd created me out of the ether—not only to end her own life, but to save yours, to preserve it forever."

Maybe I should have hated him all the more, but I couldn't make myself feel it. For a long time, I just looked at him as lightning flashed in the west, brightening the horizon then plunging it into darkness again as—

—*Stephanie's scream awakened me at 3:38, and because Laurie was passed out on the living room sofa, deaf to all but the voice of Jack Daniels, I ran down the hall and into my daughter's room alone. The storm had knocked out the power. I stubbed my toe on the bedpost in the dark.*

"Dammit!" I howled, hopping on one foot, wading through inky blackness to which city dwellers are unaccustomed.

When the lightning flashed, I saw her folded in on herself in the corner of the bed that met the corner of the room, clutching a purple-faced, tuxedo clad, green-caped toy known as The Count from Sesame Street. *Despite the terror in her eyes, I had to laugh at the kid, huddling in the dark with her teddy vampire when most girls would have preferred a bear or a dopey looking dog. Not Stephanie. The baby dolls and the frilly dresses were laid to rest in the back of the closet. Barbie was the enemy. Werewolves and trolls were her friends, gargoyles her guardian angels.*

When I sat on the edge of the bed, she scurried into my lap and threw her tiny arms around my neck.

"What's the matter, punkin?" How small she was, how frail. "Bad dreams again?"

"They say they have to leave me, Daddy," she wailed, her face buried in my neck, tears soaking through my night shirt as her words fell out in a landslide tumble. "They say I'll grow up and not need them anymore and they have to go away and never see me again 'cause only little kids believe in magic! So they said they're going away, but I'll think they were just my imagination 'cause that's what grown-ups believe and if I'm gonna be a grown-up I've gotta believe it, too. But I don't wanna grow up, Daddy, not if they're gonna leave me—Mr. Boo and Red Jo and Master Fang-Fang! Daddy, oh, Daddy, don't let them leave me 'cause I won't even remember them and I don't wanna grow up if this is what it's like!"

And she clutched at my shirt and sobbed until I felt her tiny heart shatter to pieces right there in my arms.

"Nobody's going to leave you, punkin," I told her, but I knew it was a lie. How do you tell a 6 year old that they <u>will</u> grow up? How do you tell them they have to take their place in a society far less real than the one behind their mind's eye? How do you tell them childhood ends and invisible friends get left behind in dusty cardboard boxes filled with broken toys? So I lied. "Nobody's going to leave you 'cause Daddy won't let them, okay? We'll catch them in stories and hold them in books so they can never get away. I promise, punkin. I promise."

She sniffed and snuffled while heaven threw lightning bolts around the city, and finally she fell asleep on my chest with a stuffed vampire clutched in the bend of her elbow.

She believed me, and for that I never forgave myself.

I never left her side that night. And though I don't remember dozing off, I dreamt of a dark-haired faerie priestess named Red Jo who flew in through the window and sprinkled glitter under my nose. Her dress was a blue columbine, freshly picked, her floppy hat a tiny violet. She hit me on the head with her little magic wand—no bigger than a toothpick, for she herself could have slept in the palm of my hand—and all the while she kept insisting in her shrill katydid voice that I had to grow up, too.

"But you never did," Miquel surmised.

I blinked to clear my head, then lowered my gaze and went back to looking at my twin who lived at the bottom of the creek. I was dizzy. My reflection wasn't. My heart was a hammer, beating too fast. His was the serene patter of raindrops.

"*Is* that why you did it?" I asked, barely above a whisper.

Miquel's watery clone nodded, and I knew he was about to reveal some profound secret, something I should have guessed much sooner.

"All vampyres are children, Stefan," he said at last, a little bit wistful, a little bit glad. "Stephanie knew that. And she was right about something else, too: you have to believe in magic." Then, looking with eyes that saw through me, he quietly concluded, "Of all the mortals and all the vampyres I have ever known, none have believed in magic more than you."

His words broke me in half.

"I believe in nothing." Heaven was a ruined city on an ancient map, another Atlantis, lost. God was an albino rat, dead and buried.

But he only slipped an arm around my shoulder and leaned

230

close enough to whisper in my ear, "Ah, my dearest Stefan, don't you see? The nature of magic isn't that you find it, but that you're always *looking* for it. And the nature of vampyres isn't that we prowl the night thirsting for blood, but that we truly do have the time to quest after magic, the secrets beyond each new horizon."

Oh, how I wanted to believe him! But vampyres had no such comfort. *'When you die again, it will be to oblivion and it will be forever'.* Miquel's words, the night after I was made, a poison arrow straight into the heart of my faith.

I turned sharply to look at him, bitterness finding my tongue. "But the nature of irony is that *our* search can never go beyond *this* life? The price of immortality is abandoning any hope of heaven?"

Miquel gave a soft sigh. "Of course," he said as if I should have known all along. "But look at it like this: if heaven exists at all, surely it is a haunted house, Stefan, and who is the owner but the greatest serial killer of all times?"

My eyes closed. "You could be wrong."

He quirked a smile, shrugged a shoulder. "Precisely. If you didn't think so, the magic inside you would be dead and you could be as happy-go-lucky as any mortal puppet plugged into the collapsed veins of modern religion."

He paused thoughtfully, running the tip of his tongue over the tip of his fangs, an absent-minded mannerism.

"So it seems that the nature of irony *is* its own irony, and happiness is the fast track to death," he decided at last, quite pleased with himself as he became animated once more.

"What are you talking about?" I muttered, not really wanting an answer.

He had one, of course. "Mortals who walk around happy all the time have lost touch with the side of their nature that makes them *want* to search, the side of their soul that keeps crying out for answers even when they've started to suspect there aren't any.' A pause, another sigh, then adamantly: "The source of magic in the human heart is misery, for misery alone is what drives a man to believe in magic, no?"

He was infuriating. "But happiness is our right, isn't it?" I whined. "Don't we *deserve* happiness, Miquel?"

He went back to staring at his reflection in the water, a

restless sage in a tux, damp groom of the coming storm. "In small doses, it's harmless enough, I suppose, but not as a steady diet. After all, how many happy writers do you know? How many cheerful philosophers and artists have found their way into history books? Van Gogh was miserable, you realize. Socrates was hardly a barrel of laughs. Byron was a love-sick sot, and certainly _Macbeth_ did not flow from the pen of a jolly man." He shook his head, quietly concluding: "And yet for all that misery is miserable, happiness is far more dangerous."

The expression on his face said he was altogether serious. I said nothing.

"Don't you see how it breeds complacency?" he insisted, gesturing fervently with his hands. "Vampyres have earned their dreadful reputation because we shun such foolish contentment, Stefan! It's the thing that will kill us quicker than sunlight, for it's the one thing that will ensure we abandon the search for meaning and settle into utter boredom and blissful tranquility. A contented man has no reason to look for happiness because he thinks he's already found it, you see."

"Maybe he has," I offered, needing to believe it. "To some people, happiness comes from the simpler things of life: a family, good friends, growing old with someone you love."

But Miquel waved this argument aside with a sweeping motion of one hand. "Illusions, my friend," he assured me, "as you should know best of all."

"Oh?"

"You don't write because you're happy any more than a true artist paints out of boredom," he pointed out. "Did you know Michelangelo once said that painting and sculpture had ruined his chances for happiness, that he would have been better off had he hired himself out to make sulphur matches?

"Oh, Stefan, he wasn't looking for peace in the marble anymore than you are looking for it in the words you string together to form stories. If he'd been a happy man, David would be a grinning idiot and God would be wearing mouse ears on the ceiling of that little chapel! Oh, I don't doubt that mortals can experience moments of elation, but that isn't real happiness, is it?"

"Maybe it is," I said, for I felt he really did want an answer. "Happiness is different for each of us, Miquel."

232

"But what about you?" he pressed, running his fingertips through drops of rain which had gathered on the railing to eavesdrop on our conversation. "Can you say in all honesty that you've ever been really happy?"

I was starting to squirm again. "I was truly happy on the day I was married," I said, meaning it. "And on the day Stephanie was born—*that* was real happiness."

"Ah, but listen to what you're saying," he insisted, perhaps as desperate as I was myself. "On the *day* this or that happened. Days are fleeting!"

"Nothing lasts forever. Not even us." I wasn't being argumentative, but I felt constrained to point out: "You said so yourself."

"Perhaps there's no such thing as true immortality, for even the sun will burn out one day," he conceded. "But barring such cataclysm, we *can* live forever. There are other worlds, other quantum dimensions. When we're done searching through the rubble of *this* universe, we'll simply go some place else."

I had to look him in the eye again, touched by the very misery of which he so casually spoke. "But what's the point?" I asked. "If your contention is true—that happiness doesn't exist except in the search for it—why should any being *want* to live forever?"

He smiled again, relaxed and entirely radiant as the rain began falling a little faster. "There are other things besides happiness."

"Oh?" I prompted, mainly to see what he'd say.

"Love, for one," he ventured, a casual offering.

I glanced away, watching the storm scratch at the mirrored skin of the creek.

"I went into the city last night," I told him, remembering my revelations. "And of all the mortals I drank from in an effort to quell this strange thirst, the one thing all of them had in common was their abject hatred of love. Oh, they all want it—every living thing craves it, it seems—but is it *love* they want or only to be always searching—"

And in the middle of my sentence, when I was arguing a philosophical point with my Creator, I suddenly knew what he was trying to make me to see. What terrified me was that I didn't want to see it so *clearly*.

Love was the only reason *any* of us had for living, yet it was a reason that had absolutely nothing to do with happiness.

Love was its own exegesis, the illusion which was its own reflection in an endless hall of mirrors. Reason enough for death, reason enough for immortality. It was the only meaning to life, yet the meaning itself was fleeting as quicksilver, incapable of being held too tightly or for very long.

I would live forever, addicted to love, searching for the cure which was the addiction itself.

I blinked, suddenly dumfounded. But I went right on arguing, never missing a beat, because this unwanted apocalypse horrified me with its very simplicity.

"—oh, yes, they all crave this thing called love, but I'm beginning to think it's not the noble pursuit it's cracked up to be, considering what it does to mortals."

Miquel placed a hand in the middle of my rain soaked back and gave a little laugh, a little sigh. I knew he'd heard my every thought. "Only to mortals, Stefan?"

Our eyes met in the water. Raindrops gathering on his hair caught the light, airbrushing a silver halo above his head. I couldn't breathe when I remembered what this fallen seraph had done to me, when I thought about what he was going to do.

"Love terrifies me," I confessed as if to a holy man, the very words choking me, paralyzing me where I stood.

The black angel smiled at his own reflection, preening his wings with vampyre teeth. "Good," he pronounced easily. "Then there's hope for you yet, my friend."

And with that, he took me firmly by the arm and led me in out of the rain.

CHAPTER NINETEEN

The house was terminally still, lit only by guttering candles, and though I'd expected to find dozens of vampyres gathered here, my first impression was that Miquel and I were alone. The stained-glass angels some two stories above us were somber and dark, poised in flight, waiting for lightning that didn't come to illumine their path. No music stirred the air, the tall speakers silent while oil paint eyes watched from priceless works of art, keeping their eerie vigil over the dead of night.

Only when a phantom moved on that burgundy sofa where Miquel had taken my life did I realize Dimitri had been waiting for us in the darkness. He stood when we approached, his face a grim plane where shadows had gathered, his blond hair a shocking contrast to his maroon shirt, his hands so white I thought at first they were gloves.

"Ah, Dimitri," Miquel said warmly. "Would you be so kind as to take Stefan up to my bedroom and see if the spirits have manifested something for him to wear?" He smiled darkly, placing both hands on my wet shoulders as he moved behind me, his breath a gust of wind against my neck. "Once he's cleaned up, the two of you join me in the underworld, no?"

"Underworld?" I repeated, my nerves jangling at the use of this word as much as at his physical closeness. But when I turned to glance at him, he had already vanished into the shadows, leaving me alone with Dimitri.

The vampyre boy—it was hard to believe he was my oldest brother—shot me a wicked grin.

"Oh, Stefan, how I envy you this night," he sang to me. His green eye sparkled with devilment, his blue one a void blacker than a black pearl.

"What did he mean—the underworld?" I pressed.

He shrugged. "Best not to ask too many questions," he cautioned, inclining his head toward the stairs. "Now—are you going to be a good baby vampyre and take your bath, or must I rough you up to get you motivated?"

His words were so incongruous with his normal comportment that I had to laugh, which was, of course, his intention all along. But as I followed him up the stairs, where a scent of great age and melancholy lingered, my amusement faded to an almost brooding contemplation.

Entering Miquel's bedroom, I was again struck with the unique beauty—trees that seemed to grow out of the floor, walls the color of cobalt dusk, the white satin bed in the center of a room which looked more like the realm of a prince than a vampyre. This place truly was dreamlike, not at all like the rest of the house, but set apart in the same way fantasyland was set apart from the real world.

Anything was possible here.

In this room were interdimensional doors leading to the far side of imagination and the left hand of time. In this room lived Camelot and Shangri-La and Lemuria. Here, candles burning on the sills weren't just candles, but dragon eyes peering in from another place and time. The wind that lifted the sheer curtains wasn't only a storm-driven breeze, but the fresh breath of some island night where pirate ships sailed the high seas and vampyres were still courted by humans looking for immortality.

This was where magic was born, or at the very least where it slept.

Dimitri inclined his head toward the archway leading to the bath, giving me no time to sort it all out. "Come," he said, long-suffering. "The night is young, but growing older as you dawdle."

As we passed into the dressing area—a separate room with a large open wardrobe on one side and two heavy oak dressers—I was instantly enthralled with the bright silver mirror covering one entire wall and stretching from floor to ceiling.

For a moment, as I caught my own reflection, I could have sworn I saw Miquel sitting cross-legged on the floor behind me. Wearing only ragged jeans, he was a forlorn portrait with his elbows on his knees and his head in his hands, and I could only imagine that he'd raced up the stairs ahead of us and abandoned his tux for rags.

Instead, when I did a classic double take, the doppelganger vanished, leaving the mirror empty save for Dimitri and me.

"You saw it, too," Dimitri said, watching me carefully.

"Saw it?" I repeated, not sure what I'd seen.

He inclined his head toward the mirror. "He's a lonely man, Stefan, in love with a side of life that's dying all too quickly. That's what you sensed in the bedroom—the things that are lost to the world now, except in his memories, his dreams. Sometimes he sits here just looking at himself—so much that his reflection lingers even when he's not around."

"But—what is he looking for?" I asked, disturbed and fascinated all at once. 'What does he expect to ever *find*?"

Dimitri smiled wistfully. "He's trying to figure it out, I suspect. What we are—human, yet not. How we came to be here. Why we go on living while entire worlds of mythical creatures die out altogether." He gave a little sigh, then pinned me with his feral eyes, reading me as if I were a very simple book. "If you care for him at all, do what you can to love him, Stefan."

I wanted to weep for the melancholy in his voice. More than that, I sensed something that went beyond his words. A warning. A fear. But try as I might, I could not put my finger on it, and in retrospect I believe it was because he was deliberately shielding himself from me.

"You're troubled," I said, resorting to language when telepathy failed.

"For him," he said, avoiding my eyes. "I won't be with him much longer—at least I won't be sharing his bed."

This bothered me—not because it was the first time he had confirmed they were lovers, but because I'd automatically assumed their relationship was as eternal as the blood in their veins. "Why?" I blundered. "I'm sorry—I'm not meaning to pry, but—I thought..."

Dimitri just shook his head. "Because of what we are, we love one another wildly for a time, then leave one another before love turns to loathing," he explained without regret. "And while mortals would consider our relationships torturous at best, the nature of our parting is such that it will inevitably draw us together again—if not in a hundred years, then certainly in a thousand."

While the reality of it was almost too horrible to consider, I could at least understand the rationale. They could love one another enough to leave one another, and they would leave one another to preserve their love.

"Tonight at the Gathering, Miquel will choose his new companion, Stefan," Dimitri told me, then chuckled at my sorrowful expression. "Oh, don't look so crestfallen. It's not as if I'm being replaced. No, it's simply that the time has come for us to seek new paths. I'd say it's time to hunt fresh blood lest our souls grow stale, but you'd think I'm trying to be funny when that isn't my intention at all."

I started to comment, but he shook his head, abruptly becoming agitated as he tossed his hands in the air. "We're wasting time, little brother. Now—quickly—into the shower with you!"

Questions raced through my mind, but Dimitri pointed me toward the bath. "Go," was all he said, or at least all I understood. The rest he muttered under his breath, and in Greek, no less.

Having no other choice, I went into the bathroom, closed the door, and turned on the water. Miquel's cologne lingered in the corners, cloistered near the tall fichus trees and leafy philodendrons growing along the open windows. His comb lay on a narrow shelf above the sink, adorned with a single ebony hair which I impulsively stole and stashed in the pocket of my jeans, grinning nervously at my own superstitious foolishness.

But as I began undressing, I was startled by what I first perceived as another person in the room. On the back of the door, reflected in the mirror over the sink, hung an exquisite white tuxedo with a black silk shirt and red bow tie. Attached to the hanger was a small gift box with a card bearing my name. Opening it, I read:

> *My dearest Stefan,*
>
> *My tailor tells me this will fit you flawlessly and that you will look splendid in white, an odd color for our kind, perhaps, but what do I know of fashion? As for what's in the box, they are trinkets for luck and magic—gifts from your brothers. Forgive them, no? They are only children, after all, and full of vampyre mischief.*
>
> *Miquel*

Steam turned the air to fog, recreating me as my own misty ghost in the mirror. My hands shook when I removed the little box from the hanger and opened the lid. Inside, neatly folded, was a pair of black silk briefs, more accurately a G-string than any real undergarment. But far more unnerving were the other items nesting

238

on top.

The first was a gold earring the size of a quarter, which I would have worn except for the fact that my ears had never been pierced. The second was a larger ring—slightly greater in diameter than a golf ball, with the inner surface comprised of soft black leather and the outer surface a band of solid gold that caught the light to toss it in my eyes.

Frowning curiously, I couldn't imagine what it was for. But when I picked it up and held it in my hand, my body explained to me precisely where it was meant to be worn. Indeed, my manhood seemed instantly intrigued with the idea even though _I_ laughed out loud, self-conscious.

And suddenly, I was right back where it all began—in a steam filled bathroom at the edge of my wits, where there was a decision to be made that would change my life all over again.

If I put that tuxedo on—not to mention these other exotic toys—I would be climbing inside my vampyre skin forever, willfully marrying the night and holding it to me like a lover. Not only that, but I would be giving myself to another man—a once-forbidden union, yet all the more alluring because of that very taboo.

Because the decision was long since made—perhaps from the moment I was reborn in my maker's arms—I quickly stripped off my wet clothes and jumped in the shower. There, lathering myself intimately with Miquel's red glycerin soap, I threw my head back and let the hot water massage my inhibitions away as I shyly slid my wedding ring into place.

The fit was perfect.

*

When I returned to the dressing room wearing the tuxedo, I was startled to see Dimitri appear out of the shadows behind me. Feeling somewhat awkward —for my new jewelry and silk briefs were clearly meant to be stimulating—I started to say something, but he motioned me to silence with one long finger across his lips and a look that told me he knew _exactly_ what I was feeling.

Without a word, he led me into the bedroom and had me sit in a plush leather chair, and then, before I realized what was happening, he took an exquisitely sharp needle made of bone and drove it straight through the lobe of my left ear.

"Hey!"

To my surprise, though the sting was keen and deep, the gasp it brought to my lips could not be accurately described as a sound of pain. But before I could start to chase myself in circles in some attempt to understand what must simply be experienced— this erotic agony of having my flesh pierced by my beautiful brother while his fingers tangled in my hair to hold me still—Dimitri gave an evil chuckle and held up the thin white needle for me to see.

"The same delicate instrument used to pierce the tender pink nipples of Catherine the Great," he whispered with an impish grin.

"Were you there?" I asked. *Were you the one wielding the needle even then, Dimitri?*

He never told me, and that was part of his charm. Instead, he reached inside my jacket pocket to retrieve the shiny gold earring and slid it into the raw wound, fastening it with deft fingers. Finally, as if to drive me to the very edge of endurance, he bent his head close to mine and, with the tip of his tongue, cleaned away the little drops of blood left over from the piercing, his saliva healing the injury on contact.

Straightening at last, he met my gaze, licking his lips exactly as he'd done at the convention when he'd stolen the blood from a cut on my hand. His eyes were crazy again. Danger rattled through his soul, manifesting in his voice.

"Tell me, Stefan," he said coarsely, "have you had an opportunity yet to drink the blood of another vampyre?"

I shook my head, mesmerized by him. "No. I... haven't."

His smile grew. I saw his fangs.

And though I had no idea what he intended to do with me, he took my wrist and pulled me easily to my feet. Then, as we stood face to face in that candlelit room where all things were possible— two grooms of the black angel courting *him* through one another— he held out his hand to me, his palm oozing blood from a cut made with his fingernail.

"For strength, Stefan," he told me in an eerie whisper, his words raising chills. "For luck—from the old consort to the new, yes?"

The red of him. The heart of him. It glistened against his

240

palm, a magic potion that drew me as surely as heaven.

Afraid the offer would be withdrawn if I waited or looked away, I took his hand and brought it to my lips, my tongue darting out to lick greedily at the crimson gash. The sheer force of it threatened to bring me to my knees, for it was filled with the totality of all Dimitri was—the places he had been, the lovers he had known, the nights he had spent with Miquel in places and times I couldn't even imagine.

If mortal blood was an addiction to vampyres, vampyre blood was holy communion with eternity itself, a sampling of the ages, a hint of secrets only an immortal heart could contain. It came so quickly I could not sort it. There was no slow flowing of separate incidents, no memories that were singularly haunting or perfect as with Valerie or Zinna or any of my other mortal prey, but a thrumming continuity that was a voyage through time itself.

Louis XIV was there, alive one minute and dead the next, and the blood of royalty was always bitter on the tongue, especially when salted with war. And of course history wouldn't be complete without the collapse of the Mughal Empire in 1707, but who would remember it in a hundred years? Who would tend the graves of fallen warriors, once beloved by mortals, quickly forgotten by time? And Spain took Sardonia and then Sicily, and some damn thing happened—this Treaty of Nydtadt that confirmed Russia as a new world power—and nobody had the good manners to notice at the time. There was a Francis Somebody-or-other in power for awhile, and in 1752 China conquered Tibet and the world of spiritual enlightenment went to hell on that day, but now nobody thought anything of it because nobody could remember when it had been any other way, and—

Time had first begun in vampyre veins and there it would live forever.

Groaning, drawn into it as a man sucked into a riptide, I licked at the wound in an attempt to quicken the flow. But before I had even begun to drink my fill of the centuries, Dimitri drew his hand away while the wind tossed the curtains around and blew out a few more candles.

"My God," I whispered, overwrought with emotion. "*My God!*"

Beaming with radiance and just a hint of arrogance, Dimitri pressed a finger to his lips to silence me, then impulsively leaned in to kiss me so lightly I barely felt it at all.

"Not I, Stefan," he reminded me with a twinkle in his one green eye. "No, not I."

CHAPTER TWENTY

When Dimitri opened a narrow door underneath the staircase, a draft of cold air swept up to meet me. Even at first glance, it was clear that the steps winding down into the ground were carved into solid stone, the walls rising on either side of the tunnel comprised of rock. Illumined only by oil lanterns attached to the sides—a line of yellow eyes descending endlessly—this was no conventional basement.

"What is this place?" I muttered, my head still reeling, my body strangely invigorated.

Taking me by the elbow to guide me—for I really was drunk on his blood—Dimitri acted as if this were a journey he'd taken a thousand times before. But for me, the sides of the tunnel were too close, the ceiling too low. Claustrophobia made a grab for me.

Forcing myself to breathe, I inhaled a scent of earth, slightly damp but not unpleasant—the scent of a freshly turned garden in spring.

Or a grave.

Just ahead, Dimitri's boot heels echoed on the stone steps, an eerie metronome. "Miquel calls it the underworld," he said as we descended. "It's a labyrinth of caves and tunnels created by an underground river when the world was new." He inclined his head up toward the house, now some 50 feet above us. "Other than narrow crevices which vent up to the surface, the only way in or out is up there."

Feeling a little better when we emerged from the stairwell into a wider area, I brushed imaginary dirt from my shoulders as I turned around to find myself in another world.

At an apex where several tunnels converged, this underground estate opened into a massive cavern no less than a hundred feet wide, illumined in part by a phosphorescent fungus growing on the ceiling, as beautiful as it was bizarre. The whole place seemed to glow, a luminescent wonderland where quartz crystals formed random patches of ice-clear flowers, stealing the light from tall candle standards—a dozen in all and each with twelve red candles—and refracting it into colorful prisms that danced around the room like mischievous sprites.

But as odd as this alien vista seemed, what raised chills at the base of my neck were the 50 or so vampyres who stood in small groups, talking in hushed tones as if they were at some inconsequential party in a New York club.

At least before, I'd been able to tell myself it was just a fluke of nature—a few damned souls cruising around California, unconventional madmen. Now, when every head turned—intricately carved marionettes attached to a common string—this new life became more three-dimensional than it had ever been before.

Some were what I might have expected vampyres to be: stereotypically thin, pale, with long dark hair that glistened and shone. But for the most part, they were as different as Dimitri and Miquel—some blonde, others dark; some dressed formally, others more casual; some no more than teenagers—biologically, at least—others in their thirties or forties. The majority were men—at least four to one, by my estimate—but the women were every bit as vibrant as Foxglove and Coma, my sad sisters in absentia.

Maybe I shouldn't have been startled to recognize a well-known actor in the bunch, not to mention a rock superstar and a top model touted for her waifish androgyny. And maybe it shouldn't have surprised me that even these prominent people could pass for mortals. Aside from the fact that nature had given us almost inconspicuous little fangs, society really did look the other way, ignoring what it couldn't understand, and that alone was better camouflage than any trance.

It was a sobering thought.

Perhaps Miquel had reason to worry when he sat in front of his shiny mirrors, wondering what would happen when the world stopped believing in us altogether. Could we blend into mortal society and become a part of its culture, or would that very blending rob our kind of the mystical powers which separated us from that world?

After a few seconds, they went back to their individual conversations, mercifully ignoring me as I stood there in a daze.

Easy laughter erupted from one of the groups, and I picked out Stygian as the instigator. Another group listened attentively as Bird told tall tales, his top hat cradled in the bend of his elbow, beaded dreads chattering in hushed tones whenever he moved.

To my disappointment, Miquel was nowhere in the crowd, and when I turned to say something to Dimitri, even he had disappeared. I began to wander around the room, politely making eye contact and nodding acknowledgement, secretly feeling out of place even when Stygian and Bird introduced me to some of the others.

In an area that formed a natural alcove inside the larger cavern, a band had begun warming up. And though I wondered how Miquel had explained this odd venue even to a bunch of musicians who'd probably played some weird gigs, I realized on closer inspection that Donny was the lead singer, and the others, though unknown to me, were vampyres as well.

The kid looked up as if suddenly sensing me in the room, grinning as I approached the naturally raised earthen stage.

"Looking good, Stefan!" he proclaimed, eyes raking over me as he gave the thumbs up sign. Picking a steel melody with fingers that seemed liquid they moved so fast, he sang:

> "Creature of the night lost the sun,
> got drained of all his blood
> succumbing to hypnotic stress.
> But he's a vampyre now
> and if nothin' else
> he knows how to dress!"

His craziness put me at ease, allowing me a moment's laughter as I stood looking up at him. He really was extraordinary in his skintight black leather jeans and a ripped up tank top that was more rag than shirt. With his Les Paul guitar dangling from a strap embroidered with skulls, it was hard to believe this was the same kid who'd played the role of a death-pale mime-butler in that foyer where I'd first spilled my blood for Miquel, the same kid who'd gone to pieces in my arms a few days later, shattered by the melancholy of the Sadness.

Reaching out, he put a hand on my shoulder, the brother I

never had. "I was afraid you'd run off for good the other night. but I'm glad you're back. Listen—a lot of weird things go on at these Gatherings, so you kinda never know what's going down, you know?" He raised his voice to a shout as the half naked black drummer began his rousing warm-up.

It seemed an eternity ago now, but when I looked at Donny's graceful neck and saw the faded puncture wounds from Miquel's bite, I couldn't help feeling for him, especially since he seemed so eager to assuage *my* feelings.

"You okay?" I asked cautiously.

He only grinned, a look that said more than words. Then, like a shy imp who wasn't really shy at all, he ducked his head and inquired, "So—how'd you like the gifts?"

The silk G-string caressed me every time I moved. The cock ring gripped me, a jealous lover's leather hand. Now it was my turn to answer with nothing more than a smile.

The little shit tossed his head back and laughed. "Hey—we'll make a vampyre out of you yet!"

Moments later, the group launched into a hauntingly sensual instrumental that echoed through the tunnels and caverns like the heart of the Earth herself. And though the acoustics in this underground world were phenomenal, the sound would have been soul shattering even through the ten cent speaker in an old transistor radio.

It came from the vampyre heart.

It came from the vampyre soul—a familiar theme deep in the blood, music never meant for mortal ears.

For several minutes, I was spellbound by this oiled-flesh-and-black-leather band, a prisoner of the psychic energy they awakened. I wondered if my reaction were unique—if the others, by virtue of being older, had grown immune. But when I looked around to see every vampyre in the room bending toward that stage as metal filings bend toward a magnet, I knew we were all alike, kindred in ways none of us would ever be kindred with mortals again.

These were my people now, my Family.

Hearing my thought, Donny shot me a suggestive wink as his fingers made love to steel strings and set them screaming—a phrase of poetry he wrote for me in that single instant. In response, several of the others looked me over to determine what the magic boy saw in me that deserved such attention. A lip or two crinkled toward a smile when I caught them staring. Some of the bolder ones sent telepathic tendrils curling around my mind, trying to read me.

And though there was a time when I might have been intimidated, I found their envy thrilling. Meeting their eyes one at a time, I pushed my fingers through my hair and let it fall across my shoulders, remembering how I'd looked in my white tux and my scruffy face.

On the far side of the room, Stygian danced with a beautiful woman in a long dress made entirely of silk scarves, their bodies undulating in a way that told me they wouldn't be sleeping alone tonight. Dimitri had joined Bird's group and was leaning unabashedly on an older vampyre with a long silver braid that fell to his waist. In the center of the floor, others swayed together in groups of three or four, tangling sensuously around one another until they seemed to move as a single unit.

The room had become smaller. Hotter.

I wandered among them, pleasantly dazed by the sensuality of it all, ravenously hungry when I detected the sudden aroma of blood. And though I would have been appalled had I been human still, I could not feel sorry for the four mortals who had been dragged into the room, kicking and cursing, but making no sound that could be heard above the deafening music of the band.

Agitated rag dolls in mute mode and shabby clothes, they were only boys—yet they were boys in the same way a great white shark was just another fish.

My empathy awakened, both gift and curse, telling me more than I wanted to know. Jorge was 12 when he made his first kill—a drive by shooting of a 6-year-old girl that earned him his colors. Razor was 14 now, but he'd been gang banging the streets of L.A. since he was 11—a robbery here, a carjacking there, a knife assault on some tourists that left a man dead, his wife paralyzed. And then there were Machine and Motorboy—15 and 17 respectively—who specialized in burglary, rape, and dealing crack to kids in the ghetto.

Maybe I should have felt sorry for them with their baggy pants and their wild-eyed insolence, but instead a hunger I'd never felt before awakened within me.

246

It wasn't only their blood I wanted. It was their *lives*.

They were the true malevolence which vampyres found pleasing on the lips. And while some talk show shrink in a cheap suit might try to make a case for the rehabilitation of America's misguided youth, the best rehab I could think of for these 'boys" was a shallow grave where their bodies might nourish the earth.

True evil could not be redeemed.

There was no mercy in their hearts. There was no life in their eyes. They were dead already.

For that reason, I had no squeamishness when a petite female vampyre named China dragged one of the boys over to me, offering him as some macabre appetizer. Rather, when I saw the sinister rage in Jorge's cold eyes—a rage that dared me to look at him, that defied me to touch him, that challenged me to breathe his very air—I could not help but feel a rush of pleasure as I drew back my lip to reveal my fangs to him.

The antagonism left him abruptly, right along with the color in his cheeks.

For a beat or two, he just stood there, not breathing, not blinking. Then, squirming against the surly woman who easily held him captive with one hand on the back of his neck, he lifted his Nikes off the ground and began thrashing and kicking like a fish impaled on a hook.

His lips were forming words—*No* and *Please* and *God* and *Fuck, man!*—but the band played louder to drown out his screams when I grabbed a flailing arm and drove my teeth into the scarred flesh of his wrist.

His blood came easily, nectar for my hunger, for this was symbiosis, too. Nature cleaning itself up, one predator to another.

Poor thing was scared, shrieking out prayers to a God in whom he'd never believed.

Pray to the deaf ear of the devil, I said, straight into his flatliner mind. I pulled harder on his veins, so hard it had to be agony for him, so hard I could not drink quickly enough to prevent a few drops from splashing to the floor, red rain. *Pray as your victims must have prayed just before they died.*

His cries were heartbeats, rattling his blood. His curses of pain and terror were honey and I drank them down, surprising even myself. I was an empath, all right—empathic to all the lives he

247

had shattered and all the blood he had spilled for no reason other than evil itself. And though I would have relished the honor of being the one to take his life, there was a certain relief when I was gently pried away from him by a young vampyre whom I'd never met.

"Save some for your friends and cousins, yes?" the kid suggested, outgoing and friendly.

I drew a quick breath, my head jerking up as Jorge was dragged away, still wailing and considerably paler than when we were introduced. Staring back at me over his shoulder, his eyes were frenzied, for certainly he now knew he had been brought here to die.

The vampyre at my side followed my gaze, a reckless smile on full lips. His short-cropped hair was black as pitch, his eyes such a pale blue they were almost white.

"Nothing like a drink of death to make a vampyre want to kill," he commented enigmatically. "Personally, I miss the good old days—when there weren't so many laws to protect little shits like that, when they were just tied up in the woods and left for the wolves... or whatever. Ah, well, progress has its price," he sighed as a scream rent the air between one song and the next.

Then, holding out his hand, he introduced himself. "I'm Cosmo." His fingernails—long and midnight blue—glistened.

Struggling to regain my composure, I accepted his handshake, still in a daze as I realized I had desperately wanted to kill a 15 year old boy. "Stefan London," I managed, distracted.

The vampyre's eyes brightened, mirrors for the candles, and only then did I notice the scent of blood on his breath. The blood of Motorboy. On the other side of the room, Jorge writhed piteously against Stygian's great strength. Razor belonged to Bird's entourage.

Bloodlust filled the air, a potent aphrodisiac.

"Oh—the new scribe!" Cosmo exclaimed. Then, leaning closer in a conspiratorial manner, he added, "We really should talk, Stefan, for you must include my tale in whatever stories you will tell!" He placed a hand in the center of my back, pressing his side against me as if we were longtime companions—and all this while four little gangsters were being unceremoniously drained of blood, murdered. "I'll tell you the secrets these others will keep hidden from you, you see. Please—won't you join me for a time? I'd be honored if you'd accept. Come, won't you?"

When he took my elbow and urged me toward the center of the room—the band was howling an old Led Zeppelin song—I realized he was asking me to dance. And though he was what my mother might have called "cute as a bug", my take on the matter was that this bug probably had a poisonous bite.

And yet, the music pounding through these earthen veins stripped away my inhibitions, reveal a darker core I'd always denied. The blood of death was on my lips and I wanted more. My entire body had remained in a state of heightened awareness ever since I'd donned my sinful wedding ring, and perhaps in response to that very awareness, Miquel suddenly appeared at Cosmo's back as if he'd walked out of the ether.

"Cosmo, what a delight to see you," he said close to the younger vampyre's ear, though his soft-spoken words and what they really meant were clearly a contradiction.

One would have thought Cosmo had been hit by lightning, for his entire body spasmed when he spun around.

"Miquel!" he sputtered, taking a step backward. "I was just telling Stefan how honored I am to make his acquaintance. And felicitations to you, by the way, for another splendid addition to your Family."

Miquel's expression called him a pathetic little brownnoser, but aloud he said, "Of course, my friend." He inclined his head toward a group gathered on one side of the room. "But if I'm not mistaken, Adam is looking for you. Best you don't keep him waiting, no?"

Jerking his head around, Cosmo's eyes widened with apprehension. And though I hadn't noticed Adam until now, he was looking toward us with ice in his turquoise eyes. So young he looked. So innocent.

So deadly.

Cosmo fairly slunk away, never giving me so much as a backward glance after his initial come-on.

While I knew Miquel was many things, I'd never thought of him as impolite. "Why'd you do that?" I asked, sharper than intended, half shouting above the music.

Miquel sighed with exaggerated dismay. "Ah, Stefan, for a man who once earned his living through the charting of plots and schemes, you amaze me for what you *don't* see." He put his hands on my shoulders and looked me squarely in the eye. "Cosmo isn't your brother, but one of Adam's questionable creations, and I assure you he wanted a great deal more than your pleasant company. He wanted your blood, and in a few more seconds, he would have had it."

His words sobered me. "Wh-what? No—it wasn't like that."

"Oh, but it was," Miquel insisted, his face so close to mine it could only be interpreted as intimacy. His voice softened, turning seductive as he inclined his head toward the far side of the room. "Look at your brother—Stygian. Look closely, Stefan, and see for yourself."

It took a tremendous effort to break away from his gaze, but when I turned toward Stygian and his lady, the belated understanding of what they were doing caused my breath to quicken and the snug leather ring to fit noticeably tighter.

Stygian held in his arms this exquisite vampyre woman, his head resting on her shoulder, his teeth visibly piercing the pale skin of her willowy throat. At the same time, she clutched him to her in a lover's embrace, crimson lips suckling at the crest of his shoulder, where his ruffled shirt had been opened to grant her access.

"We call it dancing," Miquel said, his hands tightening on my arms. "It is an intimacy to be shared only with other vampyres, and then only with those you would trust with your very soul." A pause, then, more sternly: "Dance with the wrong vampyre and you'll find yourself dead, or worse. They can steal your powers that way, leaving you an empty vessel. They can enslave your will and bind you to do their bidding while your soul withers inside and finally dies."

I couldn't take my eyes off Stygian and the girl, so I barely realized it when Miquel pulled me against his chest and began swaying in easy rhythm with the music. His fingers were tangled in my hair, his embrace hypnotic in a way that had nothing to do with a trance he would have thrown on some swooning mortal.

He touched the gold hoop in my ear, fingertip tracing the inner edge to wake the pain god.

"Does it hurt?" he asked dangerously.

I closed my eyes as I relaxed into him, needing his closeness. Needing the strength only he could give me. "Terribly. Sadist."

He laughed easily, and that was best of all—to feel his chest rumbling against mine as we moved together on the dance floor. To my surprise, it even seemed natural, as if I belonged with him when I'd never belonged anywhere else.

Devil or no, fiend or savior, he was the price of my soul, the cure for my grief.

There were no speeches. No minister or best man. No vows to break.

Just a dance in a roomful of immortal witnesses.

Only later would I discover that this was a dance which symbolically bound me to him as his companion. Though everyone was pretending nonchalance, all eyes were on us. For a moment, I was self-conscious again. And yet, there was an undeniable thrill in being The One—the one Miquel had chosen, the one in his arms, the one with whom he would share his bed.

Oh, yes, there was a thrill in knowing they all knew it, too.

The band had segued into a slower, cool-blooded romp, and now Donny's voice cut into the night, a wordless wail too perfect to come from anything but vampyre lips.

Under Miquel's will, I drifted into some trance state not familiar to me—a sensation of being separate from myself and from the world. If my feet were on the ground, I never felt it.

Then, before I understood what was happening, he held me tighter to his chest and bent his lips close to my ear, whispering, "Just relax, Stefan. Relax and let go and let me drink your fear away so you never need be afraid again."

He took me then, in front of all of them, dangerous fangs sinking into my neck to bring my blood pouring over his lips while some of the others applauded or cheered or even wolf whistled.

At first, I thought I'd only dreamt it. But when the room began to spin and I felt the eager drawing as he tongued the vein to encourage the flow, I experienced an inexplicable euphoria that left me limp. Behind my eyes, however, entire new worlds were woven into being by neon red spiders at the center of the universe, indefinable creatures whose job it was to make the Earth spin on its axis and keep the stars lit and prevent the comets from crashing into one another in the cosmic pinball game.

This was the nature of his bite this time. This was where it took me—to a place that housed all the fairies and trolls and sprites and harpies both light and dark. It was a nonexistent place, physically real, yet built on fields of shadows by phantom hands—this dark sanctuary where nasty tempered elves sharpened their arrows and sirens practiced their songs on the decks of sunken ships and centaurs lifted their hooves to be shod by a blacksmith who was half man, half wolf.

These things I really did see—fantastical creatures who'd lived for all of time at the edge of human imagination. Maybe they were byproducts of the racial subconscious, created by Man for Man. Or perhaps they were idle thoughts in the mind of God, fantastical beings lucid dreaming the universe into existence while they waited for the program to crash or The Old Man to finally wake up and sneeze the Big Bang all over again.

Whatever they were, they whispered in my ear and welcomed me to the family, telling me without words in voices that made no sound that I was one of them now—eternal, feared, misunderstood, hated, loved, lost—a truthful illusion in a world built on lies that had become truth in the end.

I was a vampyre now, they said, and with that came a great responsibility—to instigate the fantasies of the human world, to strike fear and longing into the hearts of mortals, to caretake the night as if it were my own private paradise.

Groaning, I clung to my maker as these strange denizens painted their stories on my mind. I knew Miquel had seen them, too, and in that way, he and I were linked forever. Not every vampyre had been to this place he knew only as the Core—the center of All consciousness where mystical beings brushed wings and occasionally gathered to swap secrets of the trade.

When his fangs suddenly withdrew—the sensation an immoral agony—I was peripherally aware of being lifted into his arms and laid to rest on a bed of stone three feet above the ground. Actually an alcove cut into the wall by waters long since gone, it formed an open-fronted tomb where I was to lie in state, it seemed, an oddity for public viewing.

Time had passed. Hours, perhaps. My eyes never opened, my mind delirious from blood loss and my maker's trance. Donny sang vampyre tunes, a siren weeping love songs to his Creator on the distant shore of a wet dream.

"There's stars in my eyes
'cause you put them there
in an every-night-mare,
 tellin' me that the things we believe
grow from seeds if we don't wreck 'em
with our weedkiller beliefs
that keep on telling us
stars only belong in the sky.
I think the stars were framed, you say,
stealing cherry Kool-Aid
from my pain junkie veins.
I'm pretty sure we're all framed
and the glass is a dayshine cage
meant to keep me
from spreading these leather wings."

Faces swamed above me, blurry shadows grooming me for eternity. Someone ran cool fingers through my hair. Someone else unfastened my red bow tie and stole it for a souvenir. Adam, I think. Little shit.

A prisoner of this sacred daze, I could offer no resistance as my coat and then my shirt were peeled from my chest by hands I never saw—hands that undressed me, revealing me to the night one layer at a time until my only modesty was the silk G-string my brothers had given me for luck.

I struggled to lift my arms, but vampyres had pinned my wrists. The stone bed was cold against my bare back, the draft from deep in the earth a lonely ghost who ran silver claws over my chest just to watch the hardening of my nipples.

But whenever I thought to be afraid, whenever I tried to rise up out of my stupor, Miquel was there at my side, cruel fangs sinking compassionately into open wounds, a brutal penetration that grew more addictive each time it came.

"What—?" *What's happening to me?*

But there was no answer, and then my maker was gone.

Vulnerable, paralyzed, I wanted to weep at what I could only perceive as a betrayal—for I knew intuitively he'd left me to the others—but I could only watch with bleary-eyed fear as those hungry shadows came for me.

Inevitably, I felt an unfamiliar sting—fang teeth sinking quick and deep into my wrist while, with contradictory tenderness, a feminine hand soothed my brow. I cried out against the pain, convulsing. Then, through a mist of bright gold silhouettes that were really vampyre souls, I saw Stygian drinking from my hand while his lady held my head in her lap to calm me.

Relax, Quilldriver, his laughing thoughts said through the rushing of blood in my ears. *Miquel's new babies are always the main course. Didn't you know?*

I didn't know.

Another bite came at the bend of my elbow, and then another on the opposite wrist. At first, I tried to writhe away from each individual attack, but more and more of them came to feed.

How much blood could I give? And what would happen if they took too much, as Miquel had suggested they could?

Bird's assault was an easy piercing just above my navel, followed by a long, slow drinking that left his beaded dreads fanned over my heaving ribs. Donny's onslaught—for even the boys in the band came—was a wicked pinch on an inner thigh, an eager suckling, gentle somehow.

And still they came, shadows broken off from the larger darkness, sharp-edged. When I was certain I could stand no more, when I came to the very brink of some unfathomable chasm and looked down to see the abyss of real death, I was once again lifted and cradled against a man's chest.

But when my eyelids fluttered open, heavy as a coma, I found myself in Dimitri's arms instead of Miquel's. I curled into him with the last of my strength, believing he had come to save me from these divine fiends. But then he, too, sank his fangs into my throat as the untamed music constricted around my heart.

I was in and out of consciousness as he carried me through labyrinthine tunnels, following some ancient, sacred path known only to himself. And the whole while, he drank from me with a sense of purpose and reverence that nonetheless brought me closer and closer to oblivion.

Finally, when I could no longer hear the music, when I began to believe that silence was all there was and that life and death were the real illusions, I realized I was lying on the ground again.

My body ached. Blood trickled down my neck, my wrists. Dimitri's boot heels retreated in the distance.

Alone, I stared up at the low, cramped ceiling—this earth and rock tomb which was really the floor of the mortal world above. Red-orange light like fire glow came from all around, yet had no discernible source. The cave room was hot, yet a cold breeze wafted through, breath of the devil.

With a groan, I rolled to my side, trying to rise. But as my eyes focused, I encountered a sight that sent my senses reeling.

Though the cavern was no more than 25 feet in diameter, the entire floor was covered by what appeared to be a pool of molten rubies, the surface so smooth it would have rivaled any mirror. Clearly the source of light as it pulsed with a living luminescence, it was as hypnotic to the eye as flowing lava, and only after a moment of denial had passed did I understand this bottomless pool was filled with blood.

And yet, for all its beauty and all the terror it instilled in me, I barely gave it a second glance when I saw Miquel. A primal hallucination torn from the pages of Ovid or Goethe, he might have been a marble statue carved at the edge of this unholy lake, sitting on the side with his long legs disappearing beneath the placid surface.

It wasn't only that he was naked, chiseled body glistening with oils that gave him an iridescent, otherworldly appearance. No, it wasn't only that.

It was the enormous black wings which rose from his back and bent forward around his arms as if to form a barrier between him and all the rest of the world. At first, a hundred rational explanations shot through my addled brain: Hollywood props, blood loss illusions, a trick of the light. But in my heart—which fluttered weakly in my chest, a casualty of vampyres—I knew this was no cruel hoax.

Despite his dreadful beauty, I was terrified. He *wasn't* human.

What little life remained within me roared through my ears, for I was drained to the threshold of death by my brothers and sisters. But—*why?* Why had they hurt me? And why had this dark guardian allowed it, instigated it even?

"Miquel?" I rasped, his name containing all my questions, all my accusations.

A terrible silence fell between us, his heartbeat all but audible in the room.

"Come to me—quickly, Stefan," he said, and his wings seemed to shiver in anticipation, flight feathers brushing the surface of the pool as he yearned toward me. "If you can trust me enough to do this—this final initiation we all must endure—these red waters will fill you with vitality again, making you one with eternity itself."

A stone cold dread had settled in the pit of my stomach, growing worse as I looked at that bleak pond which held his reflection captive. Though my instinct truly was to go to him, the only way was to cross that foreboding pool of luminescent blood.

I wanted to cry. I laughed instead.

It might as well have been light-years separating us.

"I can't swim," was all I could say.

My confession surprised him, for his eyebrows rose ever so slightly. Still, he hid it well, this fear that was almost tangible.

"You don't have to swim," he insisted reasonably, but his voice had gone pale. "Listen to me, Stefan, listen carefully. In this place flows the blood of every vampyre on Earth—the same blood that now flows through your veins as well. Go to the river as you would go to a lover and trust the current to carry you across. But you must do it now—*quickly!*—before your heart stops for all time."

He might as well have told me to cut off my own head with a butter knife. Vampyre or no, I was paralyzed with dread—

—and fighting for breath as the ice broke and the black waters rose above my head, swallowing me whole. The dock at Grampa's house was old and rickety, so it stood to reason that any 4-year-old worth his Buster Browns would head straight for it the instant his mother's back was turned. But when the dry rotted timber snapped and I was plunged beneath those frigid waters, even my screams were sliced off by the demon at the bottom of the lake—the demon who pulled me down, down, deeper down into his black kingdom, filling my lungs with wet winter breath and swearing I'd never see my parents again.

But the next thing I knew, an angel yanked me away from that terrible place, and I was lying on the muddy shore, staring up at the oak tree and the tire swing and the storm gray heavens that looked far too much like that ice above me had looked when I'd fallen through the crack between one breath and the next. Grampa's face was distorted, a funhouse

256

mirror, and my mother was hysterical. "Don't you ever go near the water again, Stefan! Do you hear me? Don't ever go near the water!"

After that day, I never did.

Now, looking up at a ceiling of rock just as I'd looked up at the ice, I remembered that Grampa died of pneumonia that winter and one of my cousins found his glasses at the bottom of the lake the next spring. My mother bought a painting at a garage sale and hung it over my bed—a guardian angel looking down on two children crossing a dilapidated wooden bridge. But instead of calming me, it served as a constant reminder that little boys could drown and grandfathers could die and life was altogether finite.

"It doesn't have to be, Stefan," Miquel insisted, getting perturbed with me. "All you have to do is come to me this one last time and your life can go on forever! But it's a choice only *you* can make."

Across the divide, he opened his arms to me, wings lifting above the water, sleek black feathers reflecting the blood of the damned, so close I could almost touch them. So close.

But not close enough.

And suddenly, in a flash of genuine horror, I understood that the statues in Miquel's garden weren't his long lost mortal lovers at all, but vampyres who never made it across this final barrier. They were the failed attempts, those who had died on this forlorn shore or sunk to the bottom of the bottomless pit where even their souls had been crushed.

They were his dead children, and now I wondered how I would look in stone.

We *could* die. I *would* die.

But just when it seemed I would finally sleep without dreaming, when my head fell heavy and still against the floor, I heard Miquel stand up, his abrupt fury a palpable presence in the room.

"Damn you!" he shouted, startling me back to partial awareness with a telepathic rage that wasn't held back by this macabre vampyre gene pool. Pointing a finger at me, he began pacing wildly at the pit's edge, wingtips brushing the earthen floor with a soft *shush-shush-shush*, olive muscles trembling with wrath. "I'm offering you an eternity of wonder and all you can do is lie there and meekly let it all slip away?

"Damn you, Stefan!" he railed again. "I would save your wretched life if only I could, but the hell of it is that you have to do this for yourself—*you* have to embrace your nature once and for all time, mingling your blood with that of the ages—or I have to stand here and watch you die!"

Weak from loss of blood, I tried to ignore him, but he picked up a loose stone and hurled it at me, catching me a glancing blow on the arm that stung as it drew blood.

"Get up!" he commanded. "Damn you, Stefan, *get up* from that nothingness behind your eyes and fight!"

"Leave me alone," I muttered, hating myself every bit as much as he must have hated me. But of all the tests which could have been set for me, this was the one I was doomed to fail, and so I curled into myself, a fetus returning to the darkness that spawned it. "Just leave me alone."

"That would make it easy for you, wouldn't it?" he snarled, fangs glittering as he paced that narrow shore, seemingly as much a prisoner as I. "Well—*damn you!*—I'm not going to make it easy! What about me? What about this great love of yours—this love that obsesses you night and day? If you can't love me enough to trust me, your love is as weak as your will and perhaps you deserve to die after all!"

His crazed temper scared me, but more than that, it made me furious.

I'd died in his arms because he'd asked it. I'd challenged the sun for him. I'd taken a human life at his urging. I'd even forgiven him for murdering my daughter.

And *he* was blaming *me*?

"If you want me, come and get me!" I snapped, though my words were slurred and filled with sarcasm. "Unfold your wings and fly over here if you want my trust! Damn *you*, Miquel! Love has to work both ways or it doesn't work at all!"

And now I was shouting, too, crawling to the very edge of that ghastly gulf to scream back at him while my heart was cramping and constricting in my chest, dying.

For an instant, we stared at one another. Then, tossing his head back, clenching his fists and pounding them on the unforgiving rocks until his hands were bloody, he screamed out an unearthly wail that could be likened to no sound on Earth. It swept through the hollow tunnels, clawing at the air and bouncing off the walls as I stared down into a fathomless pool of blood.

Eternity gazed up at me, a red man in a red mirror, mocking me with a little secret: Miquel was every bit as afraid of love as I was afraid of drowning.

But as if in denial of that very thought, a shadow fell over the pool. And while I swayed on my hands and knees, no more than a few breaths from death, he raised those fantastical wings in an attempt to fly—an attempt that lifted the hair on my neck and caused me to cringe away from the onslaught.

Wind howled through the cavern, turning the glassy surface choppy, screaming through nooks and crannies as he began to flail and thrash against the rocks, a wild bird beating itself to death in a cage. Elegant feathers broke off, littering the face of the water, black tears shed in vain.

But he couldn't save me.

The walls were too close, the ceiling too low.

He could no more fly than I could swim—but the horror was that *he* would try.

"Stop it!" I screamed when the blood came seeping through the shorter feathers at the crest of his wings, turning black blacker. The sound was deafening—that soul deep wail torn from inside him, the awful thrashing stirring up a cyclone of loose dirt and red spray. "Stop it!"

But he didn't stop, for this was *his* hell. Gifted with wings, he couldn't fly.

The storm worsened, his wordless screams so shrill I had to cover my ears with my hands, and still the wail tore through me—that same cry of grief I had experienced when the phone rang in the middle of the night and a stranger told me my daughter was dead.

"Stop it, damn you!" I screamed again. "Stop it!"

Gasping as the wild zephyr ripped my world in half, I took a final breath and impulsively hurled my body into the turbulent red sea, doing it before I could think to stop myself. I honestly do not know if it was my intention to rescue Miquel from his own madness, or if, as always, my motives were purely selfish, nothing more than an attempt to escape his mournful cries.

When the thick red waters closed over me, I could think only of that icy lake, the memories sharpened by suffocation which now came again as gravity dragged me into the bloodshot eye of death. Sinking fast, I opened my mouth to cry for help, but the air was only blood. My body convulsed and the convulsions caused me to gasp and the gasping filled my lungs with more and more fluid, and the thing I feared most in the world folded over me like the heavy steel lid of a scarlet coffin.

There would be no angel to save me this time.

"I love you," I wept, though how I spoke aloud I never knew. The words brought a strange calm as I fell, and so I said them again and again, wishing I'd told him when it might have mattered, thinking of all the things I should have said and never did. "I love you. *I love you.*"

And only then, when I had nothing more to lose, did my maker's admonition echo in my ears. *'Go to the river as you would go to a lover and trust the current to carry you across'.*

Could it be that simple? Was love only another name for trust, and faith nothing more than an abandoning of suspicion and doubt, an act of not doing, not resisting?

'I've died a hundred times, Stefan—each and every one of them for love...'

Now, at last, I knew what those words meant. He had died once for each of the ghosts in the black angel's garden. He had died as a father died when a child was lost.

But I wouldn't condemn him to another eternity of grief, for I understood better than most the horror of it. So with all the strength I could find, with all the will I possessed, I actively did nothing at all. I stopped fighting. I let gravity have me. And into the void itself, I murmured the only words more significant than 'I love you'.

"I trust you," I whispered, making it my mantra. "I trust you."

Then, whether by coincidence or design, my fall was abruptly broken and I was on the bottom.

I lay on my back with my arms splayed to the sides and my knees bent toward my chest, a still statue in a silent world, looking up into a tunnel of red light as the little eddies gently rocked me to determine whether I was dead or alive.

The waters were warm and teeming with life when I stopped fighting, healing waters that washed my wounds clean, suckling the last of my blood into this greater whole and blending it with the Source. Hands that were not physical ministered to me, massaging my heart to heal its invisible fractures. Lips that had no substance whispered in my ear, telling me in an unearthly voice: *"Drink, little baby, drink us in and we will make you whole."*

And because I trusted, I drank, cradled in this peculiar womb that fed me through its pulsing red umbilical. My brothers and sisters were there—Stygian, Donny, Bird, Dimitri, Foxglove, Coma, China—distant palpitations thrumming with laughter and tears and stories that would last an ever-after-lifetime. But there were others, too, all those born of Miquel's blood and those from whose blood even he had sprung, a lineage dating so far back there was no separating it from legend.

Some were light, others dark. Some were nurturing, others envious. There were the vampyres who craved mystical knowledge, choosing to live forever in order to continue the search for physical and spiritual evolution. And there were others who preferred only the sinister side of their nature, the quest for blood, the power over mortals.

There was good.

There was evil.

There was beauty.

There was ugliness.

And as they assembled around me, they awakened me from my daze with a kiss of blood that returned my life to me.

"What do you bring us?" they wanted to know. "What treasures, what bijous, what pain or pleasure do you bring to eternity, Little-Chance-Bones-in-the-Sand?"

I understood the question despite their strange method of addressing me, and surprisingly, I even had an answer for them.

"I bring faith," I told them, and rested my case. It had to stand on its own now.

Some yearned closer. Others scoffed.

"Faith?" an Old Soul hissed. "In what?"

"Faith in anything," I replied. "Faith in love or truth or faith itself! Faith in *life*."

Some caressed me, satisfied. Others sat back and pondered.

"What use is faith to a vampyre?" one of them asked, dubious.

"Who needs faith more than an immortal?" I countered. "Who needs to believe in life more than those who will live it forever?"

During the silence, they considered this.

"False hope," one of them pronounced at last, and went away to brood. "Let him die."

"He amuses me with his angst," another argued. "And false hope is better than no hope at all. Let him live."

"Blood is our mother. Truth is our god," another said. "Faith is an illusion."

"But isn't it true that even illusion is truth, in that illusion truly exists?" still another contended. "I welcome him."

They quarreled and they bickered. In the end, perhaps they just tossed a coin.

I waited. Without fear. Without doubt.

I waited with only my faith that faith would be a sufficient gift to the gene pool—a worthwhile contribution to the Blood of the past, a legacy to the Blood of the future. Writers were a dime a dozen. They didn't want my skills, so I never offered them.

They wanted what I *was*, and perhaps the greatest miracle of all was that Miquel had enabled me to name it. I was faith, and only time would tell if it were a disease, a cure, or only a chronic source of torment.

At some point, I started to float, oddly noncorporeal as I was buoyed upward. And now, all as a single entity despite their philosophical disagreements, the others caressed me with warm red fingertips, dressing me in scarlet, chanting my strange new name over and over.

"Little-Chance-Bones-in-the-Sand," they sang, so faint and ethereal it might have been only delirium's imagination. "Little-Chance-Bones-in-the-Sand." But each time the words were whispered, the weight on my chest grew lighter as I was pushed and pulled toward the surface like an infant being expelled from the womb. "Little-Chance-Bones-in-the-Sand."

Centuries flew past me. Days went on forever.

The oldest vampyres on Earth were here—once mortal mystics who had found this pool of living Blood and drunk from it out of curiosity at first, later out of addiction to the fantastical visions it brought, finally from the realization that to drink these waters was to embrace immortality itself.

This river had four veins in the four corners of the world, I was told, and from those four veins the first four creators had sprung. Names whispered past me. Red Feather Dancing. Siobhan the Virgin. Myrrha of Karpathos. Jo'lyn the Sage.

But whenever it seemed I might glimpse their faces or capture some clandestine truth about what we really were, the secrets were yanked away like golden apples of forbidden knowledge—perhaps for no other reason than to keep us always guessing, always searching.

Physically weak, I allowed myself to be carried on the powerful currents that swept me upward through this stream of ancient souls. I drank them in, breathed them in through my lungs, absorbed them through the pores of my skin.

This was communion with the Blood.

This was sexual congress with Time.

But all too soon I was thrust above the surface, an infant weeping at the pain of birth because it could do nothing else.

At first, as I floated there in the center of that eerie lake, too disoriented even to move, I thought I was alone. Other than an occasional drop of water falling from above—condensation creating rain—there was no sound at all, no movement except for the gentle current rocking me in its red, red arms.

Gradually, my body drifted to the edge, and then I was lying on the shore, naked save for the black G-string and the gold and leather ring inside that skimpy silk basket. My wounds were healed, my body filled with new strength. And as the blood of eternity dripped from me, running back to the Source in tiny rivulets, I could only watch, mesmerized, until I was as clean and dry as if I'd never been immersed at all.

At the same time, the world resumed a normal course, and only then did I realize I hadn't levitated onto the shore, but I had been lifted out by Miquel.

He stood above my right shoulder, a priceless bronze nude with his hands on his hips, his enormous wings peaking well above his head and trailing behind him to brush the floor, his chest rising and falling in a fearsome rhythm that loosed his fury into the room. The shiny feathers were battered at the tips, frayed and beaten in places, with a smear of blood drying on the crests where he'd flailed against the rocks.

Whether an alien from the stars or a faerie lord of lore or genuinely a fallen angel, he stood there solid and real, in defiance of all the laws of nature, glowering at me with an expression which said he'd just as soon kill me as not.

Behind him, a narrow tunnel led into veins of unknown darkness, but even as a thought of fleeing crossed my mind, he raised his injured wing and clouted me like a wild bird flogging an adversary. And though I would have deserved it had he beaten me to the blood, he dropped to his knees instead, seizing me in an embrace so fierce it forced the breath from my lungs.

"You could have died!" he chastised, thrashing me again with the very wing in which he'd cradled me.

"I—I'm sor—."

But before I could begin to prattle, making excuses for my behavior, he covered my lips with his mouth, his tongue forcing its way inside and compelling me to yield. His strength said he could just as easily break me in half, and though I'd expected him to carry me off to his bed as he'd threatened earlier, there was something intriguing about the prospect of letting him have me right here.

Let the Blood watch.

Nothing else was important—not the fact that we were both male, not the fact that he had wings and I had none.

Faith said there would be answers. But for the moment, I preferred this forbidden love which threatened my soul even over the faith that had saved my life.

The tongue that flashed inside my mouth was every bit as warm and vital as any mortal kiss, and when I opened to him, encouraging him deeper, his enthusiasm was so great that he cut my lip with a fang.

I writhed when he began to suckle, and as my blood came jetting into his mouth, his body pressed hard and demanding against mine—not the delicate, sweeping curves of a woman's hips and thighs, but the steely planes and severe angles of another man. His breasts were firm, flat fields rather than feminine mounds, his manhood an unyielding column nuzzling my own, not at all shy.

It was a body to which I was unaccustomed—all sinew and bone and muscle and wing—yet one that thrilled me as none other ever had.

264

As he drew the blood from my mouth, he gave it back to me on his tongue, darting quickly between my teeth, tracing my lips with an intentional slowness that left me suffering in carnal delirium. But while the taste of my own blood was uniquely alluring, I, too, was a vampyre, and my maker's kiss was the most brutally provocative seduction there could be.

So when he tempted me with a deliberate dalliance over my fangs, I nipped the tip of his tongue and held him against my chest while he wriggled and thrashed with the shameless pain of it. And as our blood combined on the crest of that kiss, I knew why he had cautioned me against this simultaneous sharing known as dancing.

I could have drowned in him, losing myself in the labyrinth of his veins forever, a prisoner to his memories. In a single kiss, he was there for me. And though I could catch only the briefest glimpses—for it was his nature to guard his clandestine power and his past—it was as if I had been with him always—

—as if I had walked inside his skin on the far-slung shores of mainland Greece and the rocky streets on Skopelos, where he was born. I had eaten the fish his grandmother cooked when he was a little boy and listened to the tall tales his uncles told of faraway Constantinople. I had grieved with him when his brother died of cholera, and again when his mother and father succumbed a few months later, leaving him alone in the world, too young to work the ships or till the fields, too old to be taken in by an orphanage.

He cursed God for abandoning him on the day he was dragged away to the brothels in Athens, and again on the night he was forced down on a gilded bed by a merchant who plundered the last of his mortal dignity. And though the priests who gathered beneath the windows to pray for the souls of slaves and whores warned that to thrice curse God was an unpardonable sin, Miquel had again sworn vengeance against the Almighty on the day he was given over to Basil—his entire life only a souvenir to buy the emperor's favor, a trinket for the sadistic ruler's amusement—

But he turned my face away from his past, for it was dark and filled with sadness and regret. And though I was starved to learn all I could of him, he held me at arms' length, looking into my eyes with a ferocity unmatched in nature.

He would have me, that look said. Here. *Now.*

My breath came heavy as we knelt there on the shores of

that stygian pool, two demons in love with the unique agony of knowing we *were* damned, of knowing that if death did finally come for us, at least it would not consist of an additional eternity of fiery torment or worshipping some nefarious God with a heart more callous than stone.

It was, after all was said and done, a relief.

And as I looked at Miquel's face—all angles and shadows and rugged stubble—I wanted it all: the Blood and the Night and the Curse.

"So beautiful you are, Stefan," he said, an eerie whisper. Fingertips traced my cheekbones, tangling in my hair, gentle at first, then with greater authority. "So beautiful that neither the grave nor the mirror can hold you."

His wings had gathered around my back, a soft blanket but also a prison to keep me from fleeing. His body, smooth and oiled until it glistened, trembled with a preternatural passion that fell on him like a fever. His manhood strained toward me, an exquisite threat.

And though the look in those feral eyes scared me as much as anything ever had, I put my head down on his chest and turned my face into the comforting shelter of his wing.

"I love you," I told him, drunk on the scent of him, the mystery. "I need you."

My confession calmed him a little, allowing his shivering to ease. I rubbed my chin against his jaw line, rough edges to rough edges, watching his nipples harden in response. The gene pool had grown brighter as we knelt beside it, tossing flashes of light at us from time to time. I nipped at his shoulder, just above the collarbone, drawing a fine trickle of blood that caused him to groan. A taste of jack-o'lanterns filled my mouth, for he was fog and fallen stars, a wildflower grown at the edge of a cemetery.

He was pure magic, October in a man's body.

Swallowing hungrily, I drank his venom for luck, for anesthesia. I would need both.

"You love me?" he asked, abruptly tearing away the flimsy silk G-string.

I nodded, shivering. *Yes.* My mouth formed the word, but no sound came out. "Yes," I said again, and took another drink of him. Kneeling face to face, our bodies brushed, curious twins stealing a kiss.

"You trust me?" No gentler.

And now he bent his head to openly study my body, emerald eyes raking over my manhood, which strained at the bonds of its obscene wedding ring and caused me to twist and moan. As further torment, he brushed the sensitive crown with cool fingertips, feather light.

Lifting my eyes, I held his gaze, wanting him to see his blood on my lips. "I trust you."

Drawing his hand away, he smiled darkly—a vampyre with fearsome wings and dangerous teeth and eyes that had turned to psychedelic kaleidoscopes.

"We'll see," he murmured, and kissed me a glancing blow meant to tease rather than satisfy.

Cruel bastard.

Resting my head on his shoulder, I swallowed another century of him. Marco Polo and Genghis Khan were there in his heart, old friends.

He laughed at my wonder, then impulsively bit me just below the ear, his tongue tracing the edges of the cut, an obscene penetration that warned of things to come.

Dancing, he'd called it.

Dancing.

I traded him my first carnal dream for a glimpse of Marie Antoinette passing through the Parisian streets in a grand carriage. He gave me a taste of Valentino in exchange for my wedding night. And in trade for what *I* had experienced when he made me a vampyre, he gave me the view from the other side of his eyes—a gift more rare than blood.

For that one moment, he gave me himself—vampyre, Creator, angel—letting me watch my making through his memory, letting me feel for myself what he had felt that compelled him to give me the greatest of all gifts: immortality itself.

Letting me love myself as he loved me.

Maybe he would never say the words, and maybe the love he felt wasn't like mortal love, but it was enough.

It painted his lips as he lifted his head, and we traded it in another kiss.

And then, looking me squarely in the eyes to test my

conviction, he began lifting me onto him as if I weighed nothing at all. With his wings around my back for leverage, he raised my body off the ground in such a way that my legs went automatically around his waist and my hands gripped his shoulders to brace myself. I gasped, astounded at his strength.

Then, while the shadows thickened and the gene pool grew darker, he began lowering me onto his body so slowly that it seemed the most natural thing in the world. It started as an innocent prodding—the smoothly oiled peak gliding easily inside me for the first inch, arousing me so fiercely that I thrashed. And though the sensation was utterly bizarre—this keen awareness of being opened and filled as a woman must feel when she gives herself to a man—it wasn't at all terrible until the wider crown began forcing its way inside.

I drew a sharp breath, begging for leniency with a single word—"*Please!*"—though I knew he would never grant it. For regardless of my love and my faith, the pain that came as he began entering me was inevitable and necessary—a final test of endurance I desperately wanted to take even if it was a test I wasn't sure I would survive.

"Do you still love me, Stefan?" he demanded, and lowered me another inch into the fire before I could answer.

Fighting the urge to cry out, I looked him in the eye, not caring that he saw my tears.

"I love you!" I swore to him, the words torn from my throat. My hands dug into his shoulders. My legs shook, clinging desperately to his waist, for it wasn't lost on me that he could drop me—accidentally if not intentionally. Instead, he lowered me a little further onto the blade, raised me up slightly to alleviate my suffering, then let me down again, a premeditated torment. "*Mygod, ohgod* —I—love—you!"

Wetting his lips with the tip of his tongue, he smiled just a little, a portrait of mischief and evil painted in oils that left him slick, sleek. Still wet from the artist's brush.

"I'm impressed," he purred. But then, with contradictory coldness: "Ah, but do you still trust me, my friend?"

And when he voiced that leading question, he let me fall another inch or two, the muscles in his legs tightening, lifting his body up to me at the same time I dropped. A holocaust exploded behind my eyes. Machiavelli placed a bet with the devil that I wouldn't last the night.

The gene pool watched.

It was not unlike being struck by lightning—so intense it threatened to sear me in two as Miquel held me balanced between one world and the next. A sob caught in my throat, though whether a creation of unendurable pain or intolerable pleasure, I never knew.

His arms had begun to tremble. His breath came faster. His eyes were glazed.

With the last of my strength, I bent my head and whispered a promise into his mouth: "I trust you, you ungodly bastard!"

So *because* I trusted him, it stood to reason that he let me go, his arms slowly relaxing as the hands which had held me above my fate relinquished their hold. He drew a quick breath, barely audible, and his body rose up to meet me.

My eyes went wide with the ache of it, searching his face for guidance, for courage.

I found mischief instead.

And love he wouldn't speak aloud.

"You bastard!" I whispered, still in shock. "Damn you!"

He only laughed. "Too late."

Fiend!

For awhile, we didn't move—he in a modified kneeling position, me straddling his lap, filled with the hard edge of him. Then, when he lay back on the shore, I followed him down until he was on his back and I was impaled above him.

We rested together for several minutes until he began an easy rocking motion. His wings lay at his sides. His hands wandered lazily over me. A relaxed fist captured my penis, gripping and releasing in a slow rhythm until I began rocking, too.

Making love with him was nothing like I'd imagined it would be. If I'd expected him to be tender or foolishly romantic, he was demanding instead. But if I'd expected him to be cold or ruthless, his actions were always tempered with consideration for my feelings, even if he liked to pretend otherwise.

When he took my hands and pulled me down against his chest, I was drawn to the blood still flowing at his shoulder. And as his fingers tangled in my hair, bringing my lips to the wound and encouraging me to feed, I knew there could be no greater ecstasy than this. When I sank my teeth into the same tiny holes and began suckling at the source of my immortality, he returned to the cut he'd made on my neck, and we made love as vampyres and as men simultaneously.

He lifted his hips and drove deeper into me, looking up—

—*into Dimitri's eyes as they shared physical love for the first time in the belly of a ship bound for the New World. The boy was young, tender as fresh grass, but he rode the harsh crest of man-to-man sex as if he'd been doing it all his life, begging for more and taking it when it came.*

I opened to him willingly and—

—*my newly reborn body, chocolate brown and strongly muscled, lay face down in the sand, licked by the warm island waters of Jamaica. Miquel was draped across my back, a malevolent voodoo doll with his teeth sunk in my shoulder as his body slid sharply inside me and rattled loose a grunt of pain. He laughed, of course, saying, "Hush, little Bird, now don't fight me. After this terrible deed is done, it will never hurt you again, and we will be together always in the night, no?"*

Suckling intensely on my throat, he withdrew that dull blade just enough to torment me, then stabbed quick and deep as—

—*he claimed the proud pirate princeling in a weather-beaten house on the shore of Key West. This was a wild one, Miquel knew—made in a hurricane that was still blowing itself out—so he wasn't surprised when a howl of disbelief burst from the baby's lips in response to being taken from behind. "Damn you, Miquel!" Stygian wailed, thrashing beneath the vampyre's unrelenting body as angry winds ripped away the shutters for a peek inside. Of course, there was a knife in the top of his boot, but he never made a move toward it. And when Miquel turned him loose—their bodies joined only at a single sinful apex—the blond only knelt on the disheveled bed, begging for mercy that was delivered in the form of a swift, violent penetration. "Damn you to Hell, you monster!" But in the silver mirror illumined by intermittent lightning, Miquel saw his Brer Rabbit grin.*

I remained poised above my devil, looking down into his face as I—

—*willfully sacrificed myself onto his phallus to finally be rid of the label 'virgin' that had followed me even into death. "Ah, sweet Donny," he whispered, sinking deep as I choked back the cry in my throat. "I thought you were afraid, yet now you come to me in the night. Surely you knew what would happen?" Straddling his hips as my body swallowed the cruel length of him, all I could think was that this was the immortal beast who had rape-made me a vampyre on the shiny side of a Concrete Blonde CD. This was the cure for AIDS. "I wanted you to be my first," I confessed, and rode his rhythm until he suffered that familiar seizure and pulled my head down to his chest—*

—telling me, "Drink, my baby, drink deep and together we'll live forever and I will love you always."

I cried with rapture, for this was the closest thing I'd ever known to a religious experience. It wasn't only that he *said* he loved me. It was *feeling* that love through the blood dance and knowing it was real—his love for me, for my beautiful harlequin brothers, for the night, for life itself.

More, it was the knowledge that, one day in the future, he would share *this* moment—our moment—with some other newly made vampyre, a fledgling who would be as terrified and insecure and inexperienced as I was myself. One day in the future, I would be a legend, too.

As my body spasmed—a potent throbbing that grew worse when he seized me with his teeth and began drawing on my veins so hard it seemed I would turn wrongsideout—I felt the echo of release in him as well.

And for those moments, we achieved some euphoric state only imagined in fictional accounts. For those moments, we really were one entity, joined so deep there was no discerning where one ended and the other began, so deep we were no longer alone inside our individual minds.

I was making love to myself in two bodies with only one immortal vampyre soul.

But because we could never be permitted to keep such pleasure, never allowed to tell the mortal world such tales, I lost consciousness just as we traded a final crimson kiss where—

—*enormous black wings rose above the world, blotting out the* stars.

CHAPTER TWENTY-ONE

I died of vampyre bite, not once but twice. The dream found me as it always had, as it always would.

It was evening of the third day when I woke to find myself naked and alone·in Miquel's bed, and only after I'd climbed into my jeans did I remember the Gathering and the gene pool and the angel with his fearsome wings spread above me as we made love.

I thought I'd imagined it, those macabre images ripped from darkest fantasy. But as I scurried down the stairs, shirtless and barefooted, I found Donny, a perfect silhouette against the dim yellow light shining through from his bedroom.

"So—did you do it?" he asked boldly when I came up next to him. He wore nothing but a towel and a sharp-edged grin that left no room for wholesome interpretation of his question.

"*You* bit me," I reminded him, poking his bare chest with an accusatory finger.

Becoming the mime, he drew a tenderly exaggerated picture of two people entwined in a passionate kiss, and though it could have been out of line under other circumstances, it was shockingly erotic when I recalled the images I'd seen in Miquel's mind— memories of the first time he'd held *this* little vampyre in his wicked embrace.

Abruptly, Donny's phantom lover left him and he turned to me with a shrug, pronouncing the specter, "Fickle." He looked me up and down, a lopsided grin revealing his fangs. "You did, didn't you. You made it with the big guy."

I didn't deny it, for he could read my mind anyway, though it was to his credit that he didn't. It was strange, knowing we were bound by more than blood now. We'd both died in Miquel's arms and risen up as immortals.

We both knew the horror of him.

We both knew the intimacy.

Donny wrinkled his lips. "Are you gonna get all mushy and philosophical again?"

Maybe I had been gearing up for it.

"So where is everybody?" I asked instead.

The shadows were still, the candles dark. Other than the lamp in his room, the only light came from outside, a golden glow tossed up from tiny bulbs illuminating the grounds. The creek gurgled softly past an open window while the chimes gave an occasional murmur of bamboo and shell and minor-tuned metal. A scent of jasmine crept inside.

"Stygian's still asleep," he said, looking over his shoulder toward the bed. "Bird went back to Palm Springs—he said to give you a big kiss, but knowing you, you'd hate it, so we'll just pretend."

He really was weird sometimes. "Okay," I agreed, laughing.

Visibly relieved, he hurried on. "Adam and his bunch went back to Drycreek last night—good riddance—and China, Sprite and Puma all left about an hour ago. Dimitri and Briar—he's the big sexy one with the silver braid—are in the guest wing, sleeping off a hangover from those little gangsters, and—."

"Donny," I interrupted, "what I'm trying to ask is if you've seen Miquel."

"Oh!" he exclaimed, chagrinned. "Have you tried the den?"

Thanking him, I quickly crossed through the great room and knocked on the tall door that led to a part of the house I hadn't yet seen. While I waited for an answer beneath stained-glass angels now more meaningful than ever, my eyes were drawn to that burgundy sofa where two worlds had collided such a short time ago.

For an instant, I thought I saw myself there—all willowy and trembling and awash with grief and dread as I waited for a vampyre to come down the stairs to take my life—yet when I blinked, my mortal ghost disappeared, leaving me alone with the acute realization that I wasn't the same man anymore.

Stefan London really had died.

His down-to-Earth persona had been traded for long hair and a scruffy chin, his wedding ring for a cock ring.

What unnerved me was that I didn't know who to feel sorry for—the dead man or the living dead—and quite suddenly I was lost, not at all sure who I was.

Mercifully drawn from my daydreaming when the door opened, I looked up to find Miquel wearing the same ratty jeans he'd worn the night we met. And yet, he seemed smaller somehow, swallowed up inside a white poet's shirt that was too big for him.

It wasn't my imagination. The magnificent ebony wings were gone, the black angel demoted to a vampyre who could easily pass for a man.

I understood none of it, wasn't sure I ever would.

"Ah, Stefan," he said with a smile. "I was beginning to think you'd fallen into a coma from which not even a kiss could awaken you."

His touch on my shoulder was natural, putting me more at ease as he led me inside and closed the door.

The room was more a library than a den, with tall shelves holding books, magazines, old newspapers. A scent of aged paper, binding leather and printer's ink filled the air—pure perfume to a writer—and in the center of the floor was a long reading table, its dark legs carved with vines and delicate flowers.

A lamp with four fluted globes that were actually the screaming glass lips of cast-iron gargoyles sprayed the table with frosted light, leaving the rest of the den in shadows. Two tall leather chairs sat on one side, one threadbare from so much use, the other almost new; and with a thick Oriental rug against the hardwood floor, the entire setting looked like something out of a Dickens novel.

My eyes were drawn to the table, where a hardbound leather diary lay open, filled with Miquel's handwriting. My heart quickened, a few lines of poetry jumping out at me.

> *I keep the stars in my coffin,*
> *only letting them out at nite.*
> *Sometimes, sadly,*
> *they fall.*

And, on the facing page:

> *My veins are full of melted wax*
> *pilfered from cathedral altars*
> *and witches' windowsills.*
> *Flame is my heart*
> *to keep the blood flowing.*

Had these words been written only moments ago or centuries in the past? I didn't know, but the loneliness and the power captured in those images lingered around him, deepening his mystique rather than explaining him.

Feeling like an unintentional voyeur, I allowed my eyes to continue on around the room. But aside from the alluring comfort of this windowless chamber—Miquel's private retreat—the thing that stood out was the polished mahogany coffin on the far side of the room.

It sat on a raised platform with three steps leading up to it, making no apologies for its imposing presence. Deeper than most coffins, it was carved with stars and a crescent moon, and lined with tufted red satin that was as decadent as it was unusual.

A cold dread fell over me, and all I could do was stare at it—this harbinger of death, this symbol of the grave.

When Miquel caught me looking, he placed a hand in the center of my back. "At times, the only peace a vampyre can find is here, for the stray thoughts of mortals will follow you wherever you go—*except* into a coffin."

My heart had grown heavy, yet it was more than the casket disturbing me. Reality did a back flip just when I thought it had finally stabilized. My old world was gone. The new one had no sun.

What color *was* daylight? Was it white or yellow or orange like a child's first finger-painting? I didn't remember.

Miquel made a wordless sound of acknowledgement, as if my melancholy were familiar to him. He led me to his well-worn chair and encouraged me to sit, while he took the one not broken in.

It occurred to me as I sank into the contours left by his body that I *was* formed in his image—vampyre begetting vampyre—and when I looked up at him, it was all I could do not to weep, overwhelmed by an onslaught of emotions that fell on me from nowhere.

Leaning forward in his chair, he took my hands, squeezing gently. "The Sadness is the disembodied devil that haunts all of us," he said in response to my thoughts. "Once you've drunk the Old Blood, you're vulnerable to the moods of the gene pool. One might say these feelings come when the part of you left behind down there is particularly morose, lonely. Fortunately, if you don't indulge it, it passes quickly."

A cold emptiness had settled in my solar plexus, and even when I looked at Miquel with all the wonder he could inspire in me, that somber darkness lingered—not grief or even depression, per se, but a loneliness that went beyond being alone, a mourning that could not define what it was mourning.

In reality, I believe I was feeling eternity itself—infinity stretched out in front of me like a dirt road that went nowhere and everywhere all at once.

"What *are* you?" I asked impulsively. "What are *we* that we should live forever when everything else will die?"

His eyes strayed over the spines of a thousand books, perhaps searching for the answer to my question there.

"I don't know," he confessed at last, then just as quickly waved those words aside. "Oh, I could give you answers that would satisfy you on some mundane level—I could tell you that we're a separate race born when the first vampyres drank from those four scattered pools and went out to create more like themselves—but I can't tell you what we *are* anymore than I can tell you what mortals are." Then, with a degree of irony, he added, "That's the mystery, isn't it?"

His words offered little comfort. "When I was down there on the bottom of that pool, I felt that there *are* answers, that there *is* a higher truth."

His eyes brightened, pinpoints of green. "Oh, there are answers. But if they were the same for all of us, surely some fool would have discovered them by now and written a book, no?"

"Maybe they have," I ventured without much thought, oddly detached. "The Bible, the Talmud, the Koran?"

He was contemplative, troubled. "Answers for mortals, perhaps. Not for us."

I studied him in silence for a long time, marveling at the contrast of black hair to olive skin, the tiny fangs that glistened in his mouth.

"What do you see, Stefan?" he asked presently, not defensive or self-conscious, but genuinely curious.

I wasn't sure myself. "What really happened the other night?"

He gave a short laugh. "Surely someone must have explained the bats and the beasts to you by now, my friend." .

His levity made me smile, though my amusement was fleeting. Standing up, I began to pace in front of a tall wooden shelf lined with Camus and Nietzsche and Jung, Thoreau and Wilde and

Rumi—some men's answers, other men's questions.

Miquel just watched me, sitting there with his hands in his lap. He was paler than I remembered, his normal vitality diminished, his walls clearly weak.

He hadn't fed recently.

"It happens when the wings come," he explained hesitantly, distracted or maybe even embarrassed. Then, meeting my eyes as he came to some private decision, he added, "But so we may clear the air of the matter, I will tell you this: I do not know why they come, nor can I predict when they will come. I've sometimes thought it's when I'm troubled or deeply touched by some event in this eternal night, yet at times when I *am* disquieted or injured or even in love—the cruelest injury a vampyre can suffer—the wings may not come at all." A pause, then: "I'm sorry I can offer no more, but that is, sadly, all I know."

Indirectly, he answered the question I'd been afraid to ask, for inquiring about a man's wings seemed terribly personal, intimate even.

"No more intimate than making love," he murmured, reminding me we had few secrets now. Then, haltingly, "Does it disturb you?"

I smiled, leaning against the bookcase with my thumbs hooked in the pockets of my jeans and a wind from the air duct playing across my bare chest.

"It probably should. I mean—I'd never considered myself gay—but, no, I wanted it. I wanted you—the two of us together that way." The memories of it filled me: him pulling me to him, the way he'd held me, the way he'd taken me. "It was right." *I love you.*

Saying the words aloud when they were real was almost impossible, but I know he heard me anyway.

His eyes sparkled, lips twitching to create a smile. "Gender has very little to do with love, especially to vampyres, Stefan," he reminded me. "But, actually, I was referring to the wings. Do the wings disturb you?"

I couldn't help being amused at myself. And though his question took me off guard, I knew by looking at him that he'd given up plenty on account of those wings. Lovers had left him. Friends had turned on him.

Even vampyres, it seemed, were afraid of the things they

didn't understand.

"No—of course not," I assured him. "As a mortal, I might have found it unnerving—men don't have wings as a rule. But you're a vampyre. *We're* vampyres." I was prattling, making no sense. My head hurt from too much input, and though I rubbed at my temples, it brought no relief for a pain that wasn't physical.

Miquel sighed, eyeing me critically. "We're going to be together for a long time, you know. It would help if you could relax with me. Now, what is it you're trying to say?"

"Why not just read my mind?" Though I didn't intend to snap, I heard the edge in my voice. Annoyed, I folded my arms over my chest, then unfolded them again. My skin was on wrong. My hair hurt.

"I'd have better luck reading tea leaves or Chinese alphabet soup," he said without apology. "You're wallowing in your own chaos, creating it." He paused, softening his accusation with a smile. "Let it go."

Maybe he was right. I took a deep breath, then another. After a few minutes, I looked up and said the first thing that came to mind.

"Will it happen to me? Does it happen to all of us? The wings."

Leaning against the end of the table, he was a portrait painted over black rose wallpaper.

"It first happened when the Crusaders were ransacking Constantinople," he explained darkly. "It was December in the year 1204, and though I had encountered murmurings among other vampyres of a group of us who possessed wings, I never believed the rumors until it happened to me."

He spoke of lost centuries with such familiarity that it raised chills on my arms every bit as much as the image of his first angelic transformation.

"Were you afraid?"

He smiled softly. "Perhaps—but I was far more afraid of religious fanaticism than the wings which took me away from the war. Take a man's money and he'll cut off your hand. Take his wife and he'll put you to death. Ah, but threaten his fragile beliefs and he'll subjugate the entire world, destroying it if necessary, in the name of God."

He fell silent, struggling for a lighter tone that didn't come at his bidding. "All I can tell you is that I have been alive for almost twelve hundred years, and during that time, the wings have come to no other vampyre I've ever known. In that way, I believe I am unique, and though I might occasionally long for another like myself, it is not a curse I would wish on anyone else." Reaching out, he picked up a strand of my hair and let it fall through his fingers. "I do not believe it will happen to you."

I didn't know whether to be relieved or disappointed. We were different, he and I. I had no wings.

All I could say was, "I'm sorry," though it wasn't what I meant. "It doesn't matter, you know. But—why does it have to be a curse? My God—when I first saw you on the edge of that pool, you were beautiful!"

"Beautiful?" he repeated, snarling over the word. "Such beauty is hardly practical."

"And being a vampyre is?"

"It has its advantages," he replied darkly, and started to turn away.

I grabbed an arm before he could flee, surprising even myself with the passion I felt for this man.

"Don't you see?" I said, feeling the pulse in his wrist as a slow and steady drum. When I thought of what he was, how he had turned my world wrongsideout, I blurted out pure blasphemy. "You can do what God Himself can't—or won't! You can give eternal life to mortal Man! So—*yes*—you *are* different—but thank heaven and hell that you are, because if you weren't, Donny and Dimitri and all the others would be dead!"

But then, with a terrible coldness that frosted his voice and reached its icy hand inside my chest, he reminded me, "And your daughter would still be alive."

It hurt—not because I believed it was true, but because I needed so desperately to believe it wasn't.

"No, Miquel," I said quietly. "Stephanie would still be dead and my soul would still be dying, and in that way there would have been two deaths instead of one. You saved me because she wouldn't let you save her, and if it takes ten lifetimes, I'll prove to you that you're not the monster you think you are."

"No?" he said, never raising his voice. "If not a monster,

what then?" But he didn't wait for an answer as his mood abruptly darkened. "Do you remember those four boys the other night?"

When I realized he wanted me to reply, I nodded. "Yes."

"I'm the one who went into the city and plucked them from their lives as easily as mortals would pluck apples from the trees, you realize," he stressed grimly. "I'm the one who brought them to the Gathering and, ultimately, I am the one responsible for their deaths."

When I started to interrupt, he held one hand up to stave off my questions.

"They did not die easily, I assure you—not in a pleasant swoon from the euphoria of blood loss—but screaming and in terror, in pain too horrible to imagine," he continued with a dark passion that caused the lamp to flicker and a book to fall from the top shelf—_A Brief History of Time._

"Despite what I've said to you before, Stefan, I _am_ a murderer—in this case, a murderer of children—and the horror is that I neither regret it nor would I change it if I could."

The night we'd met, I might have agreed with his self-analysis. Now, I couldn't see it—not in his splintered heart, not in his ragged denim soul.

"A killer, perhaps, but hardly a murderer," I disagreed, going quiet and calm inside. I wouldn't reach him with anger. It had to be with intellect, with love—the same love he'd shown to me more times than I deserved. "What was it you said the night you gave me this life? 'Is the coyote evil because he kills? No, he is only a hungry coyote, capable of compassion'."

But he glanced away, looking at his dusty books. An index finger brushed faded leather spines as the silence gathered around him, a grey shadow who knew him well.

"Compassion," he repeated, rolling the word over his tongue. "I have none."

"Don't you?" I asked, remembering the evil I'd felt when I'd taken Jorge to my lips. "Can't you see that you chose those little monsters _because_ of compassion? Maybe you took four lives, but how many more did you _save_ by removing the cancer from the body of society before it could kill again?"

He only scoffed, filled with sarcasm. "The needs of the many, Stefan?"

"The laws of nature," I countered. "You said it yourself: God made you what you are. And—*just maybe*—He put you at the top of the food chain for a reason: because you have the wisdom to know you *are* cruel and the compassion to use that cruelty when it's called for."

At this, his lips quirked and he gave a theatrical sigh. 'I said *if* there is a God."

"Semantics," I pronounced, irritated that he ignored my impassioned speech to criticize the syntax.

"Words," he corrected. "As a writer, I should think choosing them carefully would be a priority."

"Sometimes what the words express is more important than the words themselves," I argued, becoming heated. "It scares you to think you *aren't* a fiend, that you *do* have a conscience!"

He went back to his well used chair, sinking down into it, folding his arms over his chest. I'd ruffled his wings whether I could see them or not.

"If this pseudo-new-age-mumbo-jumbo rationalization is what you need in order to reconcile your world, so be it," he told me. "But I assure you, my so-called conscience is controlled by my hunger and not by any deeply rooted moral convictions."

Stubborn ass.

"Then why did you make a point of teaching me *not* to kill?"

He muttered something in Greek—probably an incantation meant to strike me mute—but his magic was weak because he hadn't fed.

"Well?" I pressed when he didn't answer.

He met my eyes with a controlled ferocity that really was frightening. "Has it not occurred to you that death is a messy affair, Stefan? On the face of the Earth, there are approximately fifteen hundred vampyres—a small and elite society when compared to our mortal counterparts. Yet if each of us were to leave a trail of corpses littering the streets every night, it wouldn't be long until we were hunted down and destroyed.

"It's happened before," he added sternly, pointing a finger at me. "We've been hunted practically to extinction more times than I care to remember, countless of our numbers slaughtered in ways that would sicken your soft and civilized stomach. Vampyres with history in their hearts and magic at their fingertips—massacred by ignorant, pious fools! *But*—"

To stress his point, he got up out of his chair and started pacing, his aura turning to hot coals that could ignite at any moment. "*But*—while I've lost friends and enemies alike to these vampyre hunters, it's always been when we've become too arrogant for our own good, believing ourselves gods with the inherent right to choose life and death for mortals."

"Sometimes, somebody needs to decide such matters and carry out the sentence without mercy," I reminded him. "Sometimes society won't protect itself—or can't!"

Looking right into my eyes, he said with complete calm, "Then perhaps it *should* fall, no?"

"No!" I shot back at him, though I had to wonder if he were right, if it had gotten so big and complicated that the fall was inevitable. But I refused to accept that, so I thought of an argument and fought to make it stick. "What I'm trying to say is that society is as much our problem as anyone else's. If it falls, so do we."

"The affairs of mortals should not concern you, Stefan," he cautioned. "If this society falls, another one will rise in its place."

I wasn't so sure. "And what if the whole thing collapses—all of it—every last human being on Earth?" I postulated. "What if—?"

"What if a comet slams into the planet tomorrow?" he interrupted, then went back to talking to himself in Greek. Finally, he tossed his hands in the air, emeralds and rubies throwing lamplight around the room like fireflies scattering in the face of his wrath. "You enjoy your chaos," he decided, flustered. "You thrive on it and even find ways to make it contagious! Now leave me alone! Go away and leave me in peace! Go play with your brothers or find some mortal blood to drink or write an essay in honor of your misery! But leave me before you drive the both of us mad!"

Overly dramatic son of a bitch.

"You're trying to change the subject," I observed.

"I'm not!" he insisted. "I'm simply not going to talk to you! Now—*go!*"

"No," I said, though now it was my turn to be calm and his turn to rail.

Spinning toward me, he curled his lip in disgust, revealing his fangs. For a few seconds, we just stared at one another, and though my instinct was to flee from the fury I read in his eyes, I

282

stood my ground. Maybe he would finally kill me. Or maybe he would send me away for good. But I was *not* going to go skulking off to lick my wounds just because he ordered me to leave.

"You're a misguided fool," he pronounced quietly.

"And you a fallen angel who's lost his wings," I decided. "Who needs one another more than the two of us?"

His eyes flashed fire at me. He snarled. "I could break you in half."

I wrinkled my lip, reminding him I had fangs, too. "Your compassion won't let you."

Finally, like two ornery boys in a staring match, we both started to grin, but I found a special satisfaction that *he* was the first to laugh out loud. Afterwards, of course, I laughed, too, and though it didn't solve the impasse we'd reached, it did break the tension.

When he returned to his chair—each of us looking away at the same instant—he gestured me to join him, and because I admired the rules of his dangerous games, I sat down.

"You realize, of course, that neither of us will give an inch in our mulish beliefs," he said to me. "You're stubborn as a blood stain, and that's another reason I chose you."

At this, I had to laugh. "Beliefs? I don't know *what* I believe!"

"Precisely," he agreed, hiding his smile behind his hand "And if you weren't in such constant turmoil, you would hardly be interesting. It's the fact that you know nothing—that you willingly accept Chaos as your god and Bewilderment as your patron saint— that makes you valuable. Not only *can* you argue both sides of any given concept, but you can be counted on to do so with angst ridden conviction! I could have hoped for nothing better in a scribe, though as a companion I suspect you're going to be an insufferable pest."

He had an uncanny knack for delivering praise and damnation in a single breath, and I wasn't at all sure which way to take his words.

"Which proves my point precisely," he commented with an affectionate snarl that was actually an ironic laugh. "That's why the Old Souls named you Little-Chance-Bones-in-the-Sand, you know."

I didn't bother asking how he knew what I'd heard in my drowning delirium. "What do you mean?" I asked cautiously, still smarting from the use of the word 'pest'.

He gave a nonchalant shrug.

"Bones-in-the-sand is the name given to mortals by the Old Souls. What they were saying to you when you were reborn from the gene pool is that you have little chance of surviving as an immortal because you are still, for the most part, bones-in-the-sand." He chuckled softly to himself, shaking his head at my look of perplexity. "Stick-in-the-Mud would have worked just as well."

I might've kicked him if I'd had the nerve, but in reality I was deeply hurt. "Glad you're amused."

He shot me a nasty frown. "Oh, don't go getting all indignant again. Obviously, if I agreed with them, I never would have made you a vampyre to begin with. Call yourself Chance and wear the name proudly, for in the grand scheme of things, you probably have a better chance of keeping your soul than most of *them*, for the simple reason that you aren't afraid of error *or* chaos."

Because I wanted to believe him, I tried to let it go. Secretly, I think I liked the name. Chance. Stefan London was dead. Chance had stolen his afterlife and taken his place in the mirror.

Yes, I decided I liked it. Rebirth. The new self emerging.

Miquel sat there, saying nothing as he ran one fingertip around the frayed edge of a rip in his jeans. And I suddenly realized he was scared, too.

The night he'd taken my life and given it back to me, he'd seemed so confident, so sure of himself that his determination and poise had made me less afraid. When he'd sat on the edge of the gene pool, naked and otherworldly, I'd thought there was nothing he couldn't do, no secret he didn't know, no soul he couldn't steal.

He was a mystical being, after all. He *should* have all the answers.

Drawn from his reverie by my thoughts, he looked up with an expression that reached so deep inside me I thought I would not survive.

"Don't you see?" he said, his torment a tangible presence in the room as our eyes met. "Perhaps I've given you eternal life—or some illusion of it at least—but I can't define your soul for you. I can't even define my own, nor am I even certain I have one after all the things I've done."

I went to him, putting my hands on his shoulders even when he tried to wave me off. As I'd noted before, he was changeable as the wind, arrogant and all-knowing one minute, lost and insecure the next.

"The fact that you can question the things you've done should tell you your soul's alive and well," I reminded him, leaning close to his ear as he so often did with me. And because it felt natural to touch him, I closed my arms around his chest and let my hand slip inside his shirt to stroke the flat plane of his chest.

At first, it seemed he would reject my advances, a prisoner of his own reclusive misery. But then he began to relax, and in another minute, he reached up to grasp my wrist, holding me with those long, slender fingers until it was almost painful. I think it was hard for him, for he was normally the one offering strength and solace, the one nurturing the rest of us. Accepting something in return—even this intangible strength I so wanted to give him—did not come easily.

We said nothing for a long time, he in his chair, me leaning over him with my cheek resting on top of his head.

I'm not sure how it all started, except that I kissed him once on the corner of the mouth—an almost absent-minded gesture for comfort—but the next thing I realized, we were together on the floor underneath the reading table. Our jeans were tangled on the arm of his chair, and though he'd managed to keep his shirt, it was open and pushed down from his shoulders.

He captured me in his arms, pulling me down on top of him until the full lengths of our bodies were pressed against one another—chest to chest, abdomen to abdomen, blade to blade—and in his embrace, I was protected and crushed at the same time.

Camus looked down on us from the top shelf. Kierkegaard gathered dust to throw at us, rice of the ages. Freud analyzed the situation from his leather-bound couch. Nietzsche proclaimed it all illusory because he hadn't thought of it himself.

And I didn't give a damn about any of them.

When Miquel kissed me—never with tenderness but always with a fierce and needful yearning—all I knew was that I wanted it to go on forever, this warring of tongues that left us writhing and twisting on the rug. I worshipped my maker with my mouth as if it were something I'd done before, taking the length of him onto my tongue and suckling. His hips pitched, hands digging into the floor as he called out my old name and my new name in the same breath.

285

This time, he showed me nothing of his past, nothing of his other vampyre children who were my brothers and sisters now, nothing of other lovers he had known throughout the centuries. Rather, Miquel gave me himself there on the floor of his private sanctuary—the honesty of his cries of pleasure and the sincerity of his lust that was expressed by his head thrashing from side to side until his hair fanned out to create an elegant black halo.

He gave me his compassion, tangling his fingers in my hair as I suckled this rigid male nipple; and he gave me his love in the form of a scream that burst from his lips when his climax swelled on my tongue, beating like a mortal heart.

But because he was a vampyre and not a man, the essence that fed me was mystery and misery and smoke from the fires in other peoples' chimneys. It was a drink of *him*. It was the blood of soldiers dying on the battlefields of Lucknow and Bull Run and Nicosia. It was the tears of witches burned at Salem for sorceries only imagined. It was the sweat of the martyrs whose causes had been lost to time and passing history.

It was all the things he'd done, all the things he'd seen, all the truths he'd gathered. It was the true seed of the vampyre's existence—dark and somber and yet filled with the clandestine power that could create eternal life.

And though I was eager to give him something as profound, I could only whimper like a child pulled from the nipple as he lifted my head and encouraged me to lie at his side. His arms went around me like a vice, fangs scraping over my ear as he whispered breathlessly, "Let me taste it on your tongue, Chance. Feed me that kiss of life from your own mouth."

Groaning, delirious—for I *was* the vampyre Chance now, and no longer a man at all—I kissed him hard and deep, not hearing his words as arrogant, but as a plea. He wanted to see himself as I saw him—and *that* was the greatest gift I could ever give him.

Because it was who he was to me, I showed him the demon who had stolen my last mortal breath, and I showed him a little boy in his father's tux, sitting in sprinkler rain in a garden of stone vampyres. I showed him the imp with a conscience who had taught me not to kill, and the imp without a conscience who had instructed me in the taking of young Sergio's life.

But most of all, I showed him the black angel who had stolen my immortal soul, wrapping it up in softest down and spiriting it away to the night, where it would live forever.

He gasped and writhed, and though his ferocity was intimidating, I experienced a deeply carnal satisfaction when he slid down my body, a serpent coiling, preparing to strike. When he took me in his mouth—*cool damp prison with dangerous teeth for bars*—I thrashed against the rug, beating my fists on the floor.

I cried for mercy, not really wanting it. I begged for deliverance from the devil, though I was thoroughly damned.

I lifted my head and looked into his crazy eyes as he was devouring me, and when he smiled that terrible smile—scraping his fangs over the swollen flesh until we both tasted blood—I twisted my fingers in his hair as I was seized in a crisis the likes of which I'd never known.

How is it possible to explain the sensations of which a vampyre body is capable? Suffice it to say that it was more than any ordinary climax, a cresting that could best be likened to plunging down some mammoth water slide in the dark—stomach falling out from under the body, head spinning, breath coming hard and fast, up being down and down being up, gravity lost.

Finally, lifting his dark head, he wet his lips with the tip of his tongue, stealing away a final trace of my blood from the incision made by his wicked fangs.

"Jesus Christ," I whispered, then thought better of praying to an albino rat in the throes of passion. With as much of a smile as I could find, I amended it to, "I love you."

With his head resting on my thigh, Miquel kissed the softening edge of me to paint his mouth red again. At the same time, his saliva sealed the tiny wound, healing the little cut until there was no evidence it had ever been there.

"I know, my friend," the devil purred, satisfied that he finally owned my soul. "I know you do."

Putting my head down on the floor, I stared up at the world, counting stars that were only dust sprites floating and flying on tiny currents of air.

*

After we'd gotten dressed, he showed me around his private library and began explaining some of the things he did to maintain his fortune. In addition to owning several apartment buildings in New York and Los Angeles, he had investments in a dozen lucrative business and Swiss bank accounts under as many different names.

Money came to him *because* he was a vampyre, he said.

"I never steal from the mortal world," he explained with real vigor. "I don't have to. As long as you give something back, humans will be lined up to hand you whatever it is you need. Keep them satisfied and you'll never want for anything, and that alone is the fine art of vamping wealth and power as well as blood."

For myself, I wasn't much interested in wealth or power, though I was forced to concede that a long life would either serve as incentive to set oneself up in a comfortable environment, or to completely disregard any adherence to a normal lifestyle. According to Miquel, a vampyre could live in the shadows of the mortal world without any home of his own, without any tangible resources, without anything but his intellect and his will.

They could inhabit empty rooms in fine mansions, attics or basements in the suburbs, or even church belfries. They could make their daybeds in the cracks beneath a freeway bridge or on the top floors of old buildings—those eerie downtown rooms with dirty windows where musty cardboard boxes gathered dust in the name of things long forgotten, where even the skeletal keys had rusted in the locks of doors never opened.

Since the mortal world chose not to perceive what it didn't want to see, it wasn't difficult for our kind to live any life we chose. More than one attorney had been called a bloodsucker with good reason, and more than one blood bank technician on the graveyard shift thrived on her work as more than just a job.

Some vampyres were fascinated with mimicking human lifestyles, Miquel said, while others chose to walk the secretive paths well away from the dayshine world. For himself—though he did enjoy his comforts and his homes in New York, Key West and Greece—he had no desire to live in the guise of ordinary men, for to adopt the human lifestyle meant adopting the rules and restrictions of human life as well. Friends. Job. Social circles. Routine.

"The living death," he called it, and wrinkled his lip as if he'd stepped in something unpleasant.

The things that called to him weren't cocktail parties or golf courses or opulent luxuries, but the somber corners of the Earth, the secrets obscured by shadows. Machu Picchu. The Plains of Nazca. Stonehenge. The ruins of fallen civilizations and the legends still living among the stones.

He'd seen plenty of the physical world, he said. What fascinated him was what lay *beyond* the normal constructs of human awareness.

He swore he'd once seen a troll go darting across the lane near Dublin, and a tiny fairy admiring her reflection in a moonlit stream in Kilkenney. He'd witnessed mysterious airships hundreds of years before the first dirigibles clamored awkwardly into the skies, and he'd spoken at length with John Lennon one cold January afternoon—never realizing at the time that the conversation took place a month *after* the man's murder.

"So you see," he concluded after we'd toured his library, "when we talk about what's possible and what isn't, it's all a matter of perception and perspective. Some vampyres would tell you there's no such thing as magic, while others become so embroiled in the sorcery of the night that they lose touch with the mortal world entirely."

I was fascinated with him all over again, and oh, how I wanted to climb inside his mind, suckling his memories into my own head. But when I became silent, he slid an arm around my shoulder, gazing at his tall bookshelf where dead men had gathered to tell their tales in dust and crumbling parchment.

"Your thoughts are written in Sanskrit again, my friend," he said after a long pause in our conversation.

I smiled to myself, distracted, a bit melancholy. "I was just wishing I could step back in time—to see the things you've seen."

"Such ambitions you have, Chance. And who's to say you won't be able to fulfill them one day, as the world changes, as technology grows. When I first became a vampyre, all I wanted to do was feed and run wild through the night—it's all there was *to* do." A mischievous look stole his handsome face. "The delightful thing is that even now, all these centuries later, it still sounds like a fine idea, no?"

I, too, had grown hungry for the things only mortals could

provide—warm blood and reckless memories of human life now lost to me forever—so when he gestured toward the tall oak doors and the night beyond, I knew he was done discussing the fairy folk and the ghosts of dead musicians.

It was time to feed and the streets were full of blood.

CHAPTER TWENTY-TWO

Miquel had initially suggested that the two of us go into the city on his Harley, but by the time we'd showered and changed clothes, we came downstairs to find Stygian and Donny playing video games in the great room, and Dimitri and Briar holed up in the kitchen. They sat staring at one another across the table, trading intimate secrets I chose not to hear, their hands resting on the polished oak surface, Dimitri's fingertips brushing Briar's wrists.

The sounds and scents filling the house were ridiculously normal: the tinny music of retro-Tetris on the computer; a scent of mixed cologne and hair still wet from the shower; a chilly breeze creeping through the window, bringing jasmine with it.

Dimitri looked up when I entered the kitchen, lips curling toward a smile which reminded me once again that he was as dangerous as he was alluring. I'd felt his sting. Not just Dimitri, but all of them. They'd sipped me into their veins, making me part of them just as I'd become part of them when I'd drunk from that macabre pool far beneath the earth's surface.

Family.

"Ah, what a delight to see you again, Stefan," Dimitri sang to me, his siren voice as otherworldly now as the first time I'd heard it. "I'm most curious: did the gene pool give you a vampyre name, or has it been left entirely to chance?"

I glanced at Miquel, but he'd wandered into the great room.

"Actually my name *is* Chance," I told Dimitri, ignoring the ruckus as Donny and Stygian erupted into an argument over their game.

Donny was claiming Stygian used his vampyre powers to influence the controls. Stygian maintained his innocence and called the kid a sore loser. The pushing and shoving of fists against chests was undoubtedly just an excuse for physical contact, a charade

290

designed to get Miquel between them, which, of course, he did.

Clever devils.

"Chance, eh?" Dimitri said, mulling the word over his tongue. "Tell me, will you use the name on the spine of your next book—the one you'll write about us all with myself in the starring role, of course—or will Stefan London be the pseudonym Chance uses to protect his vampyre identity?"

"I hadn't thought about it," I confessed. Still, using my mortal name as a pseudonym—truth in the guise of a lie to protect a deeper truth—seemed a fine idea.

"The name suits you," the other vampyre pronounced. He stood up and offered his hand, perusing me with soft brown eyes. "We met at the Gathering," he reminded me, his words and his mouth out of sync like some old Japanese movie. For though I heard English, it was another language that fell from his lips. "I'm Briar-of-the-White-Rose, but Briar will do just fine, and if you should ever need anything, know I will be happy to give it if it is within my power."

Each word had thought behind it, and though I would later learn that Briar wasn't much for idle conversation, when he did speak, it was always with conviction.

I accepted his handshake—a modified thumb lock— allowing him to draw me into a powerful embrace. Though we were approximately the same height, he was considerably larger, with a broad physique that would have done justice to a quarterback. Clearly of Native American descent, he had the appearance of a man in his early 40s, but the air of wisdom that went with great age. His silver braid was thick as a woman's wrist, an entity unto itself, a pet.

"I—thank you," I said when we separated.

His warm fervor wasn't what I'd come to expect of the vampyres, with their hidden agendas and their dangerous games and their love of practical jokes. Indeed, his openness was almost unnerving.

"Briar was a Sioux shaman in his mortal life," Dimitri explained, and only then did I realize he'd spoken his native language.

When I looked at Dimitri and Briar standing side by side— mismatched though they were in both stature and aura—I didn't need my empathy to tell me they'd become companions. They looked like two different breeds of cat who'd shared a canary, Briar with his easy satisfaction that resonated like a pleasant note of music, Dimitri with his deceptively innocent mannerisms which nonetheless projected a haughty arrogance he wore so well.

And yet, I knew he was wondering—wondering if Miquel and I had shared physical love, wondering when and where and how it had happened, wondering how long it would be before *he* was Miquel's companion again. And I was wondering, too. Was he hurt? Did he resent me? Or was I still trying to put mortal expectations onto immortal relationships?

I wanted to say something—something that would tell him I intended to keep the promises I'd sworn the night he'd carried me through that underworld labyrinth to my fate.

I *would* love Miquel. I would do whatever I could to end his loneliness.

But whatever we might have said to one another was put aside when our maker appeared with Donny in tow. The kid looked pale and scared and downright nervous in Miquel's shadow— normal, in other words. I glanced around for Stygian, but before I could ask what had become of him, the warble of steel belted radials over the cobblestone driveway gave me my answer.

As the five of us stood there, Miquel shot me a look that could have ended worlds—a look of heat and passion and hunger, a look that told me I belonged to him and he to me.

Aloud, he only said, "All things considered, perhaps the car would be more practical than the Harley, no?"

I was so euphoric on the drug of love that I wanted the others to come along—as witnesses, as friends, Family. I wanted to hunt with them in the bleak city streets and share the blood of my human prey with them on my tongue, for this was what it meant to be everlasting, to be at odds with death.

And yet, when Briar moved ahead of us and opened the door, I was inundated with an abrupt rush of feelings I couldn't place. I could have blamed it on Donny's Sadness, but when I glanced over my shoulder and saw him prattling animatedly to Dimitri, I knew he wasn't the source. I might have thought it was a lingering sorrow from Dimitri, but when he caught my eye and shot me a mischievous wink, I had to rule him out.

I could have blamed Miquel, believing him lachrymose because he'd misplaced his wings, yet the mood enveloping him was one of almost unparalleled contentment, the unholy father surrounded by his vampyre children.

Only in retrospect would I recognize the sensation as the same peculiar feeling I'd experienced a few days before—when I'd gone alone into the city and felt someone pursuing me, when I'd sensed hostile eyes on the back of my neck.

I started to say something to the others, yet their very mirth accused me of being foolish, for certainly if there had been any danger, they would have been aware of it far more keenly than I.

All I can accurately say is that the world went still just then, with every nuance coming in slow motion. The night that rushed into the foyer as the door swung open was spiced with an early fog that had rolled in to celebrate the autumn chill. The tiny lights illuminating the driveway glistened in amber haze, miniature suns out of focus. The limo was a shiny black monster with tail light eyes staining the night red.

As if in a molasses dream, Briar moved out under the portico, then Dimitri and Donny. Their laughter was warm, but the tape was dragging, the sound distorted. I followed after them, Miquel just behind me, his hand in the middle of my back a caress that would have thrilled me if I'd been inside my body instead of hovering above it.

I wanted to scream without reason.

I wanted to plant my feet and not move, for the evil that assaulted me as I stepped outside was as real as the crunch of sand on cement beneath my boots.

I shouted, "No!" without understanding why, and the next thing I knew, a stranger who had possessed my body was trying to shove Miquel back inside.

Though I don't recall turning around, my hands were on his chest, my body automatically shielding him. But he'd closed the door behind him when we moved outside, and all I succeeded in doing was slamming him against it with such a force that the wood split with a noisy *crack*.

In a sharp focus world of intensified perceptions, I was looking through a fisheye lens at my maker's perplexed face while also seeing the others' reactions. Briar had started running across the wide expanse of the lawn, his silver braid bouncing after him as he pursued an adversary I never saw but only sensed. Donny's head turned toward me in super-slow-mo, full lips forming the words, "What the fuck?" Dimitri hurled himself on top of me as I inadvertently dragged Miquel to the ground, and though he was shrieking out a series of commands—"Get inside, Chance! Goddammit—get him inside!"—all I heard was the *popopopopop-pop!* that filled my chest with gravestone anxiety.

My first impression was that it was a kid on the street with a string of firecrackers, but that was what I *wanted* to believe. And though I'd come to think we couldn't die, I was nonetheless horrified into icy paralysis when a sudden spray of blood blinded my eyes, leaving my face and chest wet.

Gunfire!, my mind provided, an idiot twin cataloguing events.

It was a blur of nonsensical events: the limo's tires kicking up dirt as Stygian slammed the car in reverse, attempting to shield us; a woman's scream as Briar dived headlong into the shadows at the edge of the garden; a dead weight crushing me; sticky wetness pouring over me from a source I could not determine; the door to the house splintering inward as Donny kicked it; rough textured cement digging into my face and arms when I was dragged inside.

Miquel's scream.

It stood alone, for it wasn't a physical scream at all. Instead, it was a slash of pure horror that burst from his soul and tore straight through me, deafening in its telepathic intensity even though his voice uttered no sound whatsoever.

Dazed, sprawled on the cold marble floor, I was vaguely aware of looking up into the mirrored ceiling of the foyer, my eyes fixed on the face of dread which was my own reflection. Donny was kneeling over me, shaking my shoulders, shouting something in my ear. Another figure came crashing through the space where the door had once been—Stygian.

"Are you hit?" Donny kept shrieking, over and over. "Are you hit? Where are you hit, Stefan?"

But my world was on the ceiling, ending faster than it had begun. I didn't know anyone named Stefan.

Blinking stupidly, I touched my hands to my chest, watching them come away red. I giggled, and—

—Old Lady Carolis was pink-cheeked pissed off because I'd dipped my hands in the red tempera paint and left my mark on Jason Haverhill's white t-shirt. When she grabbed my arm and yanked me out of my desk for "a trip to the principal's office", I was surprised that—

—there was no pain, but only a sense of unparalleled dread.

Dying didn't hurt at least, though eternity had been pitifully short and vampyre blood was thinner and shinier than first grade paint.

Immortality had sprung a fatal leak.

But when Miquel's screams grew louder in my mind, I was suddenly crawling toward him, driven by a ghastly emptiness that could only be the grim presence of Death itself. Bleak and wintry, it wore the faded grey face of a tombstone, the dank perfume of overturned earth.

"It's not my blood!" I heard myself shouting, though I have no recollection of forming the thought in my mind. "Not my blood!"

But that made the dread worse, for if the blood hadn't come from me—.

My vampyre heart stopped and— *"Ohgod, godno, pleasefuckingdamnyou!"*— I couldn't breathe.

Scrambling on my hands and knees—for the tile floor was wet and red and slick and cold—I swiped at the blood in my eyes with the sleeve of my shirt. When my vision cleared, I was on top of Miquel, looking down into a face twisted with indescribable agony.

"Goddamn you, don't you die!" I screamed, selfish to the last. "Miquel, damn you, *no!*"

Hands tried to pull me away, but I lashed out with the fury of my vampyre strength and sent Stygian flying across the foyer to impact with the wall. The vase of fresh roses crashed to the floor, a storm of cobalt blue porcelain and scarlet petals raining chaos. Botticelli angels leapt off the papered walls, ripped canvas wings dragging them to the ground.

Grabbing Miquel to yank him back from the abyss of death, I began shaking him the way a child might shake a disobedient teddy bear, shouting down into his face. His clothes were soaked with blood. His eyes, though open, stared at nothing.

And so I shook him harder, screaming louder, words that ran together in a frenzied, threatening prayer to God and the devil and any other deities who might be hovering nearby.

"Don't leave me!" I was shouting like some insane child. "Don't go, damn you, don't you fucking leave me!"

"Stop it, Stefan!" Donny was shrieking, pulling at my shirt to draw me away. "Dimitri's hit! It's Dimitri! Fuck! It's Dimitri's blood!"

The flurry of telepathic images he was projecting eventually struck me, yanking me from my frenzy just as Stygian was picking himself up off the floor.

A few feet away, crumbled and folded in on himself like some cruelly broken marionette, Dimitri lay on his side in a pool of crimson that was evaporating almost as quickly as it spilled. At first, I remained crouched over Miquel, frozen in time and space, not sure what I was looking at.

Blood poured from Dimitri's chest, turning to a thick smoke and finally disappearing altogether, a red will-o-the-wisp stealing his life as it curled toward the ceiling and through the door and up the stairs. Already, the floor was clean. My shirt was drying—not red and stained, but white. The blood on my hands had vanished.

I whimpered, not understanding at all, yet understanding all too well.

As Stygian fell to his knees, gathering the limp body in his arms, my soul ran cold when I saw the massive hole torn in Dimitri's chest by what must have been a bullet designed to explode on impact. Located precisely over the heart, the injury bled profusely while the body grew noticeably smaller in defiance of all the laws of physics or common sense. Quite suddenly, the clothes were too large, the facial features too small. The fine boned fingers which had once been so long and graceful grew shorter, tinier, thin as pencils, thin as twigs.

And all so fast. Death's dark secret: strike from the shadows, act quickly, be gone.

Death, the right-hand man of God, was an unmitigated coward.

But Dimitri was a vampyre! And though I told myself he couldn't die of something as mundane as a gunshot wound, he *was* dying.

Clearly numb, Stygian began rocking the lifeless shell which gone pale, this china doll that grew smaller and smaller while we all looked on in helpless disbelief.

Miquel stirred from his telepathic shock then, and though

his eyes were glazed and wild, he gasped in a ragged breath and clamored to his knees. Pushing me aside, he crawled frantically across the floor, the wail in his mind finally breaking through to the air when his gaze fell on Dimitri.

His mournful, wordless cry racked my body with shivers. Donny drew in on himself. Stygian began weeping.

The expression on Miquel's face cannot be described. Denial. Shock. Dread. Grief that would last an eternity and beyond.

I knew that look. And, God help me, though I loved him more than my own life, there was a mortal monster still seething inside me that took its vile revenge.

Now you know how it feels, you bastard! I thought vehemently, instantly hating myself for a malice I would not have believed myself capable of. But it *was* my hatred—the hatred of Stefan London that came boiling out of me with a vengeance.

Maybe I'd forgiven Stephanie for leaving me, but I hadn't forgiven Miquel for showing her the way out.

Maybe I never would.

He heard my thoughts—an assault of cruelty I never intended—and jerked his head toward me, our eyes locking across a world of chaos littered with rose petals and broken glass and the blood of his first made son.

I saw his heart splinter and break, and when he turned away from me, a cold steel door slammed between us, leaving me more alone than I'd ever been.

Then, with a gentleness that was heartbreaking, with a love that had survived for centuries only to end on an evening of no particular significance, Miquel took Dimitri and cradled him against his chest, rocking him as a father would rock an infant, watching him die as he'd watched him die more than 300 years before.

But now it was forever.

Not even Miquel could raise him from the dead this time.

The world had gone quiet, and though Stygian's chest rose and fell in rhythm with his weeping, there was no soundtrack. When Donny staggered through the broken door and into the night, his booted feet left no echo on the marble floor. From somewhere outside, Briar's mournful cry pierced the hymen of my quiet world, a scratch on the canvas of charcoal silence, a weeping that told me Dimitri was gone.

In shock, I lay there watching as his body disintegrated into nothingness, leaving Miquel's arms empty save for a pair of faded blue jeans and a thin cotton shirt.

'While humans may question if they will live again, for vampyres it is a certainty we do not'.

Dimitri hadn't gone to heaven or hell or any place in between. He was gone forever into the nowhere. I didn't believe it only because Miquel did, but because I felt the very essence of him leave the world—and not at all gently or willingly or graciously. He left us in anger, in shock, in total surprise.

A few minutes ago, we'd been laughing together. A few days ago, he'd pierced my ear with a needle that had known Catherine the Great intimately, yet now it was as if he'd never been here at all.

There was no justice in the universe.

There was no poetry in the night.

There was no God.

And if there were, He was not someone I cared to know. If death and grief were the price of heaven, leave the stars to mortal fools with bowed heads and bended knee.

I would not worship the creator of Death.

With the last of my strength, I went to Miquel, but he shoved me away with a ferocity that sent me reeling backward. Ignoring the warning in his eyes, I started toward him again, but Stygian wrestled me through the archway and into the great room. There, with a tenderness that surprised me, he picked me up and placed me on that burgundy sofa where my journey had begun and where it seemed destined to end.

What he did beyond that, I do not know. I couldn't move except to breathe, and when I tried to struggle against this odd paralysis, it became colder, thicker, a cage in which I was held.

For awhile, I drifted, prisoner of another vampyre's trance. Time passed, though I do not know how long, and at some point I became aware of Briar sitting on the floor next to me, elbows on his thighs, head in his hands.

My hand was allowed to move and I placed it on his arm, though I almost withdrew when his heartache washed into me.

"It was Foxglove," he said, his voice calm and measured even in his grief. "Her hatred has taken three lives tonight, Chance."

298

A cold, hard knot formed in the pit of my stomach. "Three?"

He reached up to cover my hand with his own, twining our fingers so tightly it became painful.

"By killing Dimitri, she has killed herself. When Foxglove is dead, Coma will take her own life."

It made no sense. "Foxglove?" I repeated numbly. "But— *why*?"

Briar made a small sound. "Revenge, jealousy, malice. Who's to say? She did it because fate sent her. She did it because death came into the world looking for a vampyre and would accept nothing less that the obliteration of an immortal."

The night was a ripped black shroud. My soul was an empty well, drained dry.

The clock crept toward sunrise, and just as the horizon began to lighten and the automatic shutters started closing over the windows, Foxglove's shrill scream slashed through the silence, delivering me from my shock induced stupor.

My stomach went hollow, cold. Briar flinched.

He released me from whatever paralysis Stygian had cast upon me, and together the two of us returned to the foyer to find it deserted. The splintered remains of the door littered the floor, leaving the house open to the world beyond. Dimitri's clothes, all that remained of him now, were crumpled rags, abandoned in a field of shattered glass and scattered diamonds that were only drops of spilt water.

In the east, the silver blade of morning had cut the night in two, bleeding pallid light over the garden where dead vampyres stood in solemn bereavement for their fallen brother. But worse than the terrible sorrow which hung in the air was the sight revealed by dawn's arrival.

Held in place by Donny and Stygian, Foxglove twisted and fought as Miquel secured her wrists to the black angel's outstretched hands, his actions so terse and quick they could only be described as a fit of rage. Her wild black hair flew on the wind, her head convulsing from side to side as her feet flailed a foot off the ground, her screams so shrill that the mortal world would dismiss them as the cries of a wounded eagle, a rabid coyote, anything but human.

Savagely tearing segments from his leather belt, he bound

each tiny wrist and then her feet, securing her to that macabre makeshift cross without mercy, his own eyes hollow and red with tears.

Spellbound by this horror, I couldn't move. And yet, when I recalled the emptiness I had suffered when I'd first learned of Stephanie's death, I could do nothing less than aid him in completing his grim task.

I, too, wanted to kill—not for food or to save my own life, but for vengeance. I wanted to stand beneath the cross and torment the creature who had taken Dimitri's life.

But as I started forward, Briar took my arm. "The sun's coming," he warned, casting a glance toward the east. "Neither of us has the strength to challenge the day, Chance."

But my own life was meaningless, so I twisted away from him and went outside.

Though the brighter rays of the sun hadn't yet found their way over the horizon, the morning light was punishing. It brought me to my knees when I staggered toward the garden, but my rage alone got me on my feet again, propelling me forward through dew-damp grass.

When Stygian saw me, he curled a lip to show his fangs, a warning to keep me away from Miquel. But Donny got between the two of us, a long-haired silhouette against a steel grey dawn.

"Leave him be, Styx," the kid warned. "Dimitri was his brother, too. He needs to be here."

And so the three of us stood there, unholy disciples of the black angel, lost. Gradually, we drifted toward one another until our shoulders brushed—Stygian on one side of me, Donny on the other—our grief an assault that Foxglove had to feel.

As if by agreement previously made, we began shutting her out of our reality, removing her from our lives with a thought, failing to perceive her for the vampyre she was, revealing her to the dayshine world and its sunlit king as the horizon grew brighter, warmer, deadlier.

We slaughtered her in our minds.

Vampyres thrived on community as much as blood. Foxglove would die alone, shunned, without even the company of a compassionate thought.

Only later would I learn that this was how it was done. This was how a vampyre's life was taken to atone for the murder of one's own kind—a plundering of her mind, a rape of her soul, a degradation of her spirit that would make survival impossible even if the body somehow regenerated after death.

There would be no trial, no plea bargain, no mercy, for justice was swift and allowed no appeal.

But it wasn't real somehow. It was a cartoon. A bad dream. Foxglove's scream as the sun began to crest the horizon was only the whistling of Mom's tea kettle. I'd wake up in my bed soon, six years old and with my whole life in front of me. How would I do things differently this time? I wondered. How would I change the life I'd led, or would I change it at all?

But I didn't wake up.

Miquel was entirely oblivious to our presence, for when he finished securing Foxglove's feet to the base of the statue, he just stood there with his hands limp at his sides, gazing at her twisting body with a grief so potent I could have sworn I felt the ground beneath our feet tremble.

"Why?" he asked her, his voice choked. "*Why*?"

She never did answer.

She hung as Christ on the cross, crucified by her vampyre father just as Jesus had been sent to his death by God when all was said and done. And though she fought against her bonds— demented eyes shivering in their sockets as she stared toward the dawn, body bending and pitching until bones snapped under the stress—I could feel no pity for her whatsoever.

She would join Dimitri in oblivion, and I could only hope he would forever torment any surviving fragment of her soul in some hidden dimension of existence not even vampyres could understand.

I did not remember being led back inside the house where, from the sanctuary of the shadows, I watched in horrified fascination as Miquel took a knife from the folds of his clothes and split Foxglove's throat from one ear to the other, cutting off her shriek somewhere in the middle just as the first golden rays of sunlight began searing her pallid skin. The fatal wound was made with deliberate slowness, in a ritualistic fashion that spilled her life in front of her, forcing her to watch her very soul evaporate into mist and curl up around her body on its way to eternal lethe.

The life he had given her, he took from her with a sacred blade carved of vampyre bone.

But it changed nothing.

Dimitri was gone.

*

There would be no police, no funeral. The period of mourning would last precisely forever.

"It had to be the blood of another Creator," Donny muttered to himself, pacing back and forth in the great room. "The bullet was filled with the blood of another Creator. When it exploded, it killed him instantly. Gods, poor fucker! Miquel shouldn't've cut her throat—whoring cunt! He should've left her for the sun. It would've been slower, goddammit! She deserved to burn, to see death coming for her. That's the worst, you know—the waiting, knowing it *will* come, not knowing when—."

"Shut up," Stygian said, sitting on the couch with his head hanging down until the ends of his golden hair brushed the Persian rug. "Just shut up."

Donny didn't hear him, or didn't care. "But where'd she get the blood?" he mumbled, continuing to pace. "Stygian, where'd the bitch get blood like that? What other Creators does she know? Adam wouldn't give it to her. Who would give it to her, Styx?"

Stygian ignored him. He'd re-hung what was left of the door and chased the sun out of the foyer with an old blanket tacked to the frame. Outside, the limo finally ran out of gas, sputtering to a stop in the driveway.

Silence infected the house, a lethal virus.

Briar had fallen into a dangerously deep sleep shortly after dawn and now lay in the guest room with Dimitri's pillow clutched to his chest.

When Miquel had finally come in out of the morning—pale and drawn and more sick from the sun than he would admit—he went up to his room, speaking to no one. And though I wanted to go to him, the others would not permit it, saying only that he had to grieve alone before he could grieve with us.

Now, holed up in the great room, I curled on my side on the sofa next to Stygian, looking sideways at a world that was topsy-turvy no matter what my perspective.

"When we went down to San Diego, Dimitri was kinder to Foxy than any of us," Donny mumbled to himself. "Why would she want to hurt him?"

Stygian just grunted. "She was after Miquel—revenge for Coma's kid, shit that happened a long fucking time ago." He sighed heavily, staring at the floor. "Dimitri sacrificed himself for us.'

"What do you mean?" I asked, numb.

"If Miquel dies, we all die," Donny reminded grimly. "Legend says the only thing that can kill a Creator is the blood of another Creator—not by drinking it, but like a poison arrow thing, I guess, if it enters the bloodstream."

Stygian grunted, a sound of irony. "She was trying to kill us all—even herself."

In the end, it didn't matter how or even why it had happened, for motives and methods were things of the mortal world. We had loved Dimitri. Perhaps we'd even admired Foxglove. Trying to sew up their lives with threads of intrigue in an attempt to have it all make sense was pointless.

No matter what we might learn, it would never make sense. Death never did.

Outside the shuttered window, a mockingbird mimicked a car horn while the whine of tires on asphalt brought home to me the reality of the dayshine world.

While we mourned a brother with useless speculation and questions that might never be answered, mortals were going about their business. They were running to the bank and the grocery stores and the malls, preparing for the holidays ahead. They were driving the kids to school and drinking coffee in styrofoam cups on their way to work, and in that moment, I hated every one of them. I hated the fact that the sun was out there in the streets, holding me prisoner. And I hated the sound of children's laughter pouring over a school playground somewhere far in the distance.

My muscles twitched. I wanted to run.

For the remainder of that day, I lay on the sofa, drifting in and out of nightmares, and though I dreamt my mortal death as I had every day since I'd become a vampyre, the dream had turned to a sepia wash, the colors faded, dulled. At my side, Stygian never slept at all, just sat there with his hair hanging down and his silent tears staining the rug. Donny eventually curled up in a chair next to the tv., but his fitful sleep soon got him on his feet and set him to pacing again, a corporeal pendulum moving back and forth across the room, marking meaningless time.

Whenever I woke up during that interminable day, I looked toward the stairs, but the shadows never moved. The candles were dark, the wicks cold. Dimitri's ghost did not haunt the house.

'When I no longer dream of you, I will know you are dead'.

I wept for the hollow place in Miquel's soul.

CHAPTER TWENTY-THREE

Miquel left the house shortly after dusk. I neither heard him rise nor saw him leave, but I was awakened by the lonesome thunder of a Harley, carrying him away on a different set of wings. He did not come home the following dawn, nor the dawn after that. A week went by, then another.

Months passed without so much as a whisper of denim in the shadows or a scent of his cologne. Indeed, I would have believed him dead except that the dream of the night I was made still came whenever I slept.

I cannot tell you how I spent the time, what thoughts went through my mind as I rattled around the house with only Donny and old books for company. I was empty without Miquel, and though some modern thinkers might label such relationships as unhealthy or obsessive, I cannot imagine love being anything but all-encompassing. The addiction more compelling than blood.

And yet, there came the day when I realized that I was at fault for Dimitri's death as much as Foxglove. It was she who had stalked me when I'd gone into the city that first night of the Gathering, undoubtedly following me back to Miquel's home, where she'd waited for the moment when she could do the most damage.

When this revelation crept upon me in a dream, I bolted out of bed and would have hurled myself into the noonday sun except that Donny put himself between me and the door. The guilt threatened to destroy me utterly, for only then did I recall Dimitri's warning. Under no circumstances were Foxglove and Coma to

304

know Miquel's whereabouts, and while I hadn't divulged any such secret, my ridiculous angst had created a beacon Foxglove could follow as easily as if it had been a lighthouse.

Stygian called me a fool for blaming myself, pointing out that she could have tracked any one of us to the Gathering, reminding me that she *had* appeared at the casino where Bird worked that same night. But despite his efforts to assuage my guilt, I knew in my heart of hearts she had followed *me*.

I was careless.

Perhaps I was selfish for staying in Miquel's home once I came to understand these things, yet Donny and Stygian were quick to point out that disappearing into the darkness forever would not atone for my sins. Indeed, they said, if we allowed Dimitri's death to destroy the Family, Foxglove had ultimately won her revenge.

But whenever I dreamt Dimitri's face, whenever I recalled how he had first approached me under the guise of a boy in a vampyre get-up, I knew I would never truly forgive myself. I had been the downfall of the creature who had brought me to immortality, and perhaps that was the hell in which I would be cursed to live forever.

Once, because I was lonely and foolishly hoping I might be able to keep some portion of my mortal life intact, I returned to Escondido to search for Charlie. But when I found her house on a tree lined rural street, when I saw her through the golden window playing with her little boy, when I remembered the look she'd given me after she realized what I'd become, I knew I was as alien to her now as a disembodied spirit, dead to her world.

After the first few months of isolation, I started writing a little—nothing more than notes in the beginning, then a few stumbling attempts at condensing the tale into some palatable truth that might pass for fiction. At times, I sat in Miquel's chair and frantically scribbled whole scenes onto faded yellow legal pads, only to angrily rip the entire night's work into shreds and toss the scraps in the fireplace to burn. Other times, I roamed the grounds of the estate, committing my thoughts to a digital recorder, recording over them the next night, giving up in fits of fury, coming back to take a running jump at a new false start, finally returning to the more familiar feel of my computer which I'd set up in the library.

But character motivations and plot complications weren't the problem. The problem was that the very act of writing took me back to the man I'd once been—that self-absorbed, self-righteous, self-conscious word merchant who'd buried himself in plots and turns of phrase as a substitute for living, that man who'd introduced himself as "Stefan London, the writer" without ever realizing there was nothing behind the title.

Placing my fingers on the clickety-click ergonomic keyboard again was like stepping back into that dangerous existence, that leg trap which was the undoing of so many men and women. They were doctors and landscapers and toy makers and manicurists and engineers, all of them in love with the tools and terminology of their trades. But if you asked who they *were* and compelled them to give an answer that didn't include what they did for a living, they'd give you a zombie-eyed stare.

I wanted to *live* my vampyre life instead of writing about it. I wanted to be out in the night making love with intangible shadows instead of trying to find a way to describe such things.

I wanted to *be* instead of only dream.

And yet, this was a story only I could tell, a story I *must* tell—not to please Miquel or a publisher somewhere, but to explain to myself what it had meant to be alive, how it *really* felt to die, the events which had taken me from being mortal to immortal—the process of evolution itself.

I had to confront the faith I'd lost, then found, then lost again.

But even though I attacked the book with great passion once I found a silent niche in which to secrete myself, the thing that held me back was that the story seemed predestined to have some sad ending that wouldn't really end the tale at all. I feared coming to somber conclusions that would lead readers to believe the night must always be melancholy and empty, and that the price of immortality would inevitably be counted on the fallen petals of graveyard flowers or the number of fractures in a broken heart. Worst of all, I feared leading my audience to believe that vampyres *must* long to die or yearn to be mortal again, and that eternal life really wasn't all it was cracked up to be.

In reality, there was no such moral to the tale.

Despite what I'd felt shortly after my transformation, I would not give up what I had become even for an opportunity to be human again. As nearly as I could determine, there was no particular advantage to being human—indeed, mortality itself seemed to me to be a distinct disadvantage—so I could hardly use the woeful vampyre's angst for his lost soul as the closing theme for the book.

Immortality had not destroyed my hunger for life, and my soul was very much alive. Indeed, I was finally learning to live, to take the risks I'd been afraid to take as a man, to examine and question reality intricately, to appreciate pain and pleasure equally for what they could teach.

On some grandiose philosophical level, perhaps that's what I wanted to say in those first difficult attempts at writing it all down. But on a purely personal level, all I know is Dimitri's death changed everything.

He took a part of us with him when he left the world.

Though Stygian still visited frequently, helping Donny manage the affairs of the house, his easy laughter no longer accompanied him. Briar hadn't been around at all since the tragedy, and rumor placed him somewhere in Peru, a ruined shadow on crumbling streets. Bird no longer sang. Donny spent too much time in front of the tv., his mime face long and sad with downturned lips.

For myself, when I hunted, I hunted alone, and even mortal blood was no longer as satisfying as it had once been. Instead of reveling in human joys and losing myself in their sorrows to experience their compelling pain, I took what nourishment I needed from them and nothing more. At times, I found an almost perverse satisfaction in leaving them to wonder what had stolen a few minutes from their lives, what had left them longing for something they could not touch or even name, what had left them feeling that *something* had happened... *something* between one second and the next. But... *what?*

On occasion, I even killed, taking out the garbage because I had grown weary of it polluting the streets. For awhile, Donny pretended to be annoyed with me for destroying life in such a fashion, but one hot night in August when we were strolling the footpath which wound through the gardens—each of us worrying about Miquel while pretending not to think of him at all—he confessed that he, too, had grown fond of killing.

Maybe we killed to defy Miquel for leaving us. Or maybe it

was the way we took our revenge against fate, even if it had to be acted out against nameless delinquent who had nothing to do with Dimitri's murder, but who were nonetheless killers of their own kind.

I murdered Foxglove twenty times or more that summer. Sometimes she was the 16-year-old boy giving speed to fourth graders to get them hooked. Other times she was a deviant fiend who threatened his victims with a knife, forcing them to whisper words of love into his deformed ear while he raped them repeatedly. Still other times, she was a hooker with AIDS, intentionally passing the disease on to unwitting johns, who in turn took it home to their wives and unborn children.

So perhaps we killed to assuage the injustice we felt—the injustice that had taken Dimitri from us, that had sent Miquel away, the injustice that had fucked up the entire world.

Or maybe, in some warped corner of reality, both Donny and I were trying to start a war with God.

Come down here and fight for the lives of your wayward sons and daughters, I often thought when taking the life of my bitter-blooded prey. *Come down here and stop me if you really are the God of love!*

But God never came.

The murders were a 10-second spot on the news, back-up filler to more alluring tales of celebrity scandals. A few cops took a few notes, but in the long run, nobody gave a damn about the body count on the streets of America, and that was simply that.

Time went on, and during the thirteen months Miquel was away, I slept in his bed during the day, shamelessly resting my head on his pillow to steal whatever dreams he might have left behind. Sometimes I dreamt him holed up in a cheap motel watching reruns of mindless sitcoms. Occasionally, I imagined he'd found his wings again and flown into the sun to finally be rid of his grief. Still other times, I believed he'd returned to the narrow streets of Greece, searching for a blond ghost near the harbor at Piraeus.

Weeds had crept into the gardens. The final scrap of Foxglove's dress—which had remained snagged in the black angel's fingers for months—finally blew away on blistering Santa Ana winds. On a particularly cold evening in early December, I removed the cracked leather bindings from the statue's feet and wrists, striking off his chains, symbolically setting my maker free again.

That night, for the first time since Dimitri died, I lit the big house's candles.

*

I had just stepped outside the front door when I heard the faraway rumble of a Harley, and though that sound had filled me with anxious expectation for over a year, I'd finally stopped believing Miquel was going to come roaring up the circular driveway. I ignored it altogether, therefore, leaning over the portico's white balustrade to watch the first lights of the holiday season glittering along tile rooftops scattered on nearby hillsides. Plastic Santas glowed. Nativity scenes glistened. A distant church's bells pealed eerily—*O, Holy Night.*

Donny had gone with Stygian to San Diego for a few weeks, and though I missed his presence immensely, I had learned to appreciate solitude, too. But the writing wouldn't come tonight, the voices in my head silent as the empty house.

Thick clouds hung low on the horizon, a storm contemplating the earth. A lone frog spoke from the dense foliage hugging the banks of the creek while the little stream shushed its way over rocks and tiny waterfalls.

It occurred to me to drive into the city to hunt fresh blood, but while the idea was pleasing, the reality of doing it seemed far too much a burden. An unusual restlessness had followed me since I'd risen at sunset, and the only thing I wanted was for the world to make sense.

Nothing much. Just the meaning of it all. Love. Sex. Death. God. No, nothing much at all.

Looking out over the expansive lawn, my eyes could easily discern tiny spiders weaving their silver webs in the too tall grass. I could hear the shiny conversation of bats diving in the glow of a flickering streetlight several blocks away. In a nearby house, two teenagers were making love beneath a plastic tree, their iridescent adolescent passions a virtual cacophony on psychic winds.

All these things I easily perceived, so how I came to miss the motorcycle entering the driveway and Miquel walking up the steps, I do not know.

"I've heard vampyres live in this old house," he said as he

came up behind me, his voice a familiar melody that spoke not at all of his grief. "Tell me, my friend, do you think it safe to be out in the night when such sinister tales abound?"

Spinning toward him, I almost fell down. I'd visualized this reunion ten thousand times since he'd left, but now I could think of absolutely nothing to say that wouldn't sound inane.

Catching him in my arms, I crushed him against my chest, inundating him with every image and feeling that had filled my head since he left: events; passages from the book on which I needed his input; a profoundly inadequate apology for the stray thoughts and unforgivably foolish deeds of a dead writer.

But none of it mattered now.

Our bodies swayed together with the easy motion of a heartbeat, a boat on gentle seas, a lazy metronome.

He was a vision cut from black leather and blue denim, and while he was exactly as I remembered him, he had also changed. His body was thinner than when he left, his hands devoid of jewels, and the ebony hair which had barely brushed the tops of his shoulders when we met now fell halfway down his back, sleek and wind-blown all at once.

Though his body was clean, his clothes were dirty and torn in places, his boots scuffed and worn out, his 5 o'clock scruff heavier than I recalled. And despite the fact that he was ageless, there was a wariness around his eyes that made him appear older than he had before.

Ragged angel, I thought, crazily trying to decide how I would describe his homecoming in the book. *Miquel was a ragged angel with black leather wings still dusty from the road.*

He was ratty and threadbare and frayed at every edge, a wounded lion who still had his fangs despite all the trouble he had known in more than a thousand years of being alive.

Because he was still unpredictable and dangerous, it didn't surprise me to feel the slow sinking of those fangs into my throat as he held me to him. A small moan caught me unawares, my legs going weak with the pleasure of that special pain he brought home to me, a gift from his journeys. And because I needed him more than sanity, because I loved him more than any other creature, I claimed my right as his companion by driving my own fangs into him, just above the collar of his frayed jacket.

310

His blood poured over my tongue in slick, easy waves, an ocean I'd not swum in for far too long. There was fresh grief in the salts of that cool sea, to be sure, but there was also the comforting balm of knowing Dimitri had given his life to save the rest of us.

Miquel's healing had begun, though I knew it would never be complete. Scars would form. Time and distance would allow the painful memories to fade while bringing pleasant remembrances into sharper focus. But he would never be quite the same again anymore than Stefan London had been the same after the death of his daughter.

In the spiritual nakedness of the blood dance, I tried to impart to him the sorrow and the genuine regret I felt for my part in it all, but he drank those thoughts into oblivion.

"Blame and guilt have no part in the immortal world, Chance," he whispered against my neck, imparting to me the renewed wonder he'd found out there on the road. "They change nothing. They destroy us if we let them."

It was time to live again, for that was precisely what Dimitri would have demanded we do to honor his memory. *Drink a blond and devour a brunette for me*, he would have said, winking his one blue eye. *Live forever.*

That was how Miquel remembered him. That was how he wanted me to remember him, too.

In the bittersweet feast, my maker fed me there beneath the storm clouds, I tasted the exotic spice of Santa Fe, where he had gone to look for answers he never found; and I knew the cold grey winds of a New England harbor where he had spent his summer nights searching for someone he'd never met, someone he couldn't describe.

What secrets he took from me, I was never sure. If my blood told grim tales of the men and women I'd killed during his absence, he never spoke of it. If my veins yielded up memories of the hot July night I'd lain in his coffin bed, making selfish love to my hand while trying to conjure him home, he did not let on.

I do not know how long it went on like that, how long we remained locked in the blood dance which recreated us as a single soul in two preternatural bodies. All I know is that when we returned to the prisons of our individual shells, there was a bond between us that had not existed before.

311

Without a word, without going inside his house after more than a year away, Miquel gestured toward the driveway and the Harley still hot from the road. And though I'd never ridden a motorcycle, I climbed on the back and wrapped my arms around his waist, resting my head on his shoulder to shield against the fierce wind.

While the night flashed past—sable sky streaked with amber light—I lost track of the machinations of mortal time. The only thing that mattered was the late autumn air and the leather between my thighs and the vampyre who had stolen my soul for the second time, spiriting it away on a black machine.

Street lamps gave way to scraggly pine trees, the pines yielded to tall cactus, and the entire world melted into a fog of nebulous terrain. We sped past big rigs on narrow roads and raced through tiny towns on the borderlands of Nowhere. Occasionally, other bikers pulled up next to us to share the desolate highway, but whenever the headlights of an oncoming car showed them our ashen skin and the ominous edges of our smiles, they quickly fell behind in the rearview mirror.

Throughout the ride into the desert, we never spoke, and when the bike finally rolled to a stop at the dead end of a winding road, I realized Miquel had brought us high into the mountains. More than six thousand feet below, little towns glittered like fields of fallen stars, bisected by a river of taillights which was actually the interstate slashing across the wasteland.

It was sobering.

In all that pandemonium, mortals were making love and having late dinners and living and dying, yet we were no part of it.

So far away, it was all just an imaginary world, an electric dollhouse, a diorama.

The vantage point hung over the edge of the universe, a precipice wrapped in silence that became deafening when the Harley's engine stopped. Fog whispered by, a curious mist interrupting the view, and only then did I realize we were up among the clouds themselves, trespassers in heaven.

Mortals would not come here, certainly not in the rain which was starting to fall in fat, cold drops. They were not drawn to the little breaths of smoke puffing out from so many chimney nostrils down below, but instead they were repulsed by the melancholy of the night which was sustenance to the vampyre every bit as much as blood.

Lonely though it was, cold and damp and forlorn somehow, I felt I had finally come home to a place I'd never been, a place I'd been searching for all my life, a place that had nothing to do with physical location.

The asphalt smelled wet. In the cul-de-sac parking lot at the end of the road, puddles of water undulated—black to silver to black again—reflecting the storm above, revealing the occasional star bold enough to peek through the thickening haze.

Towering rock formations rose to the left and right, sprinkled with treacherous cholla cactus and whimsical Joshua trees. Silhouetted against a pallid sky, they reminded me of demented evangelists, their misshapen arms stretched up toward heaven, their bodies often twisted or bent into arches, their spiny fingers scratching at the wind and causing it to whistle in pain.

Miquel climbed off the bike and moved to a low block wall—the only thing separating six thousand feet from sea level. Leaning forward, he rested his elbows on the railing, and when I went to his side, I couldn't avoid the automatic vertigo that came with looking down.

Far in the distance, the Salton Sea was an irregular black shadow on the face of the earth. Airplanes on approach to Palm Springs hung in midair, toys suspended far beneath us. Nearby, a coyote wailed, a keen yipping howl that called the clouds down lower.

The world disappeared again, swallowed whole by this eerie vapor that crept so close I could barely see Miquel right next to me. Foolishly, I was afraid.

"I've come to the conclusion that death isn't at all natural, Chance," he said at last, his voice deep and philosophical. And though the lights below were completely obscured now, his gaze was fixed on the distance beyond the clouds. "Oh, mystics, ministers and morticians would all have us believing otherwise—for it's in their best interest to keep death alive and well—but I'm personally convinced it isn't natural in the least."

It shouldn't have surprised me to hear him talk like that, for I'd spent the past year learning to feel precisely the same thing. Death was a disease, a virus, an enemy.

313

"Can you really be sure we don't live again, Miquel?" I asked impulsively, thinking of Dimitri and Foxglove and vampyre purgatories and paradises beyond imagining. "I mean—how can we know what lies beyond this life any more than mortals know what lies beyond death?"

He was silent for a time, looking down on blurry desert communities through a momentary break in the clouds. At our backs, wind crossed the road, an invisible broom pushing leaves and sand and icy cold.

"If there were anything beyond this life, my friend, would we fight so desperately to remain alive, damning our very souls for the privilege?" he postulated, a question for a question. "If it were natural to die, would death not be a welcomed friend instead of something to be feared?"

Universal questions, no different on a vampyre's lips than a mortal man's.

"Plenty of people would say death *is* a friend," I reminded Miquel. "The terminally ill often long for death."

"Ah, but they don't," he countered, his hair getting caught in the wind. "What they long for is an end to their pain. The problem is that death is viewed like morphine when it should be seen as cyanide—not anesthesia, but fatal poison for which no antidote exists. By accepting it as inevitable, Man has damned himself to it."

He paused thoughtfully, running his fingers through the air to see the thick mist part for him. Far below, the red ribbon of taillights undulated, a steady stream of human life flowing in all directions, chaos in action.

"I no longer believe in God," I said, mostly to myself, and for the first time I wasn't afraid to speak those blasphemous words. Indeed, it was a relief, for it meant I was finally free to live.

But Miquel only smiled, shaking his head with a soft sigh. "By those very words, you acknowledge that you *do* believe."

"What are you talking about?" I muttered, sharper than I might have wanted. "I think I should know what I believe and what I don't by now."

"Maybe," he conceded. "But I should also think you would be more careful with your words. To say you don't believe *in* God implies there is a God in whom to believe. It implies an underlying belief in a sentient creator who might be called upon to intervene in the affairs of the world." He grinned at me, teasing but also accusing. "It implies you *need* to believe, but that you've chosen to *say* you don't."

I rolled my eyes, irritable. "Semantics," I said, and once again we were picking up the conversation where it had ended the right Dimitri died. "You know what I meant."

Miquel shrugged one shabby leather shoulder. "I know what you said." Turning his head to look me squarely in the eye, he boldly added, "The question isn't what you believe—which is, in the end, entirely irrelevant—but whether or not God really exists. And if He does exist, it's a question of whether or not He gives an unholy damn about this clutter we call civilization."

Under my breath, I muttered one word, chosen with extreme care and forethought: "Bastard."

He shot me a dirty look. "Oh, there you go getting all offended again, and just when things were getting interesting. Now let's try it again." A pause, then: "Do you think God exists, Chance? Do you still need that belief to get you through your nights? It's all right if you do, but personally I'm afraid you're going to be disappointed."

Maybe he really was crazy. Maybe he wanted company in his madness and had made it his goal to drive me to that destination.

I finally had to admit, "I don't know. It's just hard to think it's all random. It's hard to think we're all alone—that someone or some thing wrote the program, set it all in motion, then just walked away."

His eyes were dangerous green flames, filled with mischief. "Perhaps He didn't walk away at all." He gestured elaborately toward the world, proclaiming with overly dramatic certainty, "And on the eighth day, He *ran!*"

He was probably right.

I held Miquel's gaze for several seconds, but I was the first to glance away, distracted with that diorama so far below. When the clouds whispered thin, headlights crept up and down residential hillsides many miles in the distance, illumined ants crawling on the surface of the hive.

"They don't know, do they?" I said to myself, dazed by the enormity of it all.

Miquel frowned. "Know?"

I wasn't sure myself what I meant. "When I was mortal, I wouldn't let myself think about death," I told him, sorting it out as I spoke. "Then, after Stephanie died, I came to look on it as a reunion that would happen one day—you know, loved ones coming together again on the other side."

At this, he gave a little sound of disgust. "The other side of what?" he asked rhetorically, then just as quickly brushed his sarcasm aside. "Those are only words, you realize—words of comfort written in the consensual script to keep mortals complacent."

He went back to staring out over the infinite nothingness of silver clouds. "If everybody believes death happens to everybody else, they accept their fate easier, not making demands on those in positions of authority, whether church or state. They stop looking for answers to riddles that supposedly can't be solved because they've come to believe they really *can't* be solved."

Now he'd lost me and I was annoyed again. "What are you talking about? Death *does* happen to all of them!"

"Mmm," Miquel murmured, evasive. "Maybe it doesn't have to."

Something in the way he said those words sent chills racing up and down my spine, and for a instant, I almost caught the darker thoughts whiplashing around his mind. But like mercury, they fled.

"Care to tell me what you're thinking?" I tried, admitting my inability to read his mind.

His lips curved, a pensive smile. "One day, perhaps I'll tell you, but not now. Not tonight." Then, as if on second thought, he grudgingly added, "Let's just say Adam has the right idea, and one of these days the two of us are going to unleash the truth about death on the world. If *he* made himself immortal with a thought, others can, too, you see."

My heart quickened, and I was reminded of something Miquel had said the first night we'd met—something about building a new garden, a new world peopled with immortals. Had he meant it literally?

"How? I mean—."

"I don't know yet," he interrupted, his tone clipped as he became annoyed with my stubborn persistence. "All I can tell you is that there are alternatives. Mortals don't have to die. They've simply gotten used to it."

The passion with which he spoke was infectious, his words mirroring thoughts I'd entertained since before finding my own immortality in his blood. But he waved me to silence before I could speak.

"Be patient with me, yes?" he asked gently. "You're like a dog with a steak—so eager to fill your stomach that you forget to enjoy the feast. Neither you nor I shall solve all the puzzles of life and death in a single night, nor even a single lifetime. That's why I made you eternal. I'll figure it out, little by little, and you'll write it down."

I knew him well enough to know arguing would do no good. Human or alien, wings or none, he was still an unmitigated son-of-a-bitch when it suited him. He had secrets and plans and hidden agendas I couldn't begin to imagine, and he teased me with them mercilessly at times, dangling them in front of me to see if I would follow.

"Bastard," I said again, not really irritated, but wanting him to think so.

He didn't deny it. Instead, turning his head to look at me, his amusement faded and he said the one thing in all the worlds I did not expect him to say.

"I was wrong, Chance," he told me, his green eyes haunted with reflections of clouds.

"Wrong?" I repeated, my stomach knotting.

He nodded almost imperceptibly, then went back to leaning on the wall with his gaze fixed on some other world.

"I was wrong to take her life," he clarified, his confession barely a whisper. "I was wrong to take Stephanie's life, to steal from her even one more moment of living. Life really is priceless, whether it is lived in great happiness or great misery, whether it is a thousand years long or only moments."

I could not have been more stupefied, for it had been much easier when he'd defended his actions with vehemence and arrogance.

For a very long time, I could not speak. When I did, my voice was unreliable, shaky, and though my words were ineloquent, they were brutally honest.

"I should hate you for it," I said, "but I can't. I tried, but—damn you!—I don't have the stomach or the stamina for hatred. *That's* what I should hate you for! I should hate you for making me love you, for not giving me any choice in the matter!"

It was to his credit that he didn't try to comfort me. Instead, he just stood there in the clouds and let me have my final fit of mourning and my silent red tears and my paradoxical conflict that might never be resolved even in the span of all eternity. He let me have my hatred, even if I had to call it love in order to keep my soul.

"It was only when Dimitri died that I realized what I had taken from you, Stefan," he admitted when I was calmer, calling me by my mortal name for what would turn out to be the last time ever. "And even though vampyres do not normally apologize for their actions—for words will always be insufficient and blood is a far deeper bond than any exchange of meaningless phrases—I want you to know that I *am* sorry."

Far below, the desert was going to sleep, for when the clouds parted again, there were less lights than there had been before. My hair was damp with rain.

"Would she have lived?" I asked, scared of the answer. I'd come to believe her death had been inevitable, suicide assisted by vampyre bite. Now, suddenly, I had to know: "*Could* she have lived?"

Sighing softly, Miquel turned around and hopped up on the edge of the wall, sitting there facing me with his back to infinity and his legs dangling like a little boy's. The implications made me dizzy, for reality was six thousand feet below.

"No," he said at last, a statement of fact. "She would not have lived."

"You sound certain."

"I am." He was silent for a moment, then seemed to come to some private decision. "I can prove it to you, though I should warn you that there are times when ignorance is a blessing for the fantasies it allows us to maintain."

My heart was in my throat, and though I didn't understand what he was offering me, there was only one answer I could give. "I want to know, Miquel. I *have* to know."

He studied me for a long time, then held out a hand to me, palm down, fist closed tight as he flinched. "It's her. It's Stephanie,"

318

he explained in response to my blank, questioning stare.

I'd stopped breathing, and as he gestured me closer, I held out a trembling hand, not knowing what to expect, surprised when his fingers opened to release a single drop of blood onto my wrist as if he'd pulled it down from heaven. Not thin and cool like vampyre blood, it was deepest crimson, mortally alive.

Warm.

It *was* Stephanie. I smelled her shampoo, heard that string of bells on the back of her bedroom door, caught a glimpse of her dancing on the wind.

"Oh, God," I breathed, and took a step backward as I looked into his fearsome eyes. "What are you trying to say?"

His expression was morose. "It's the certainty you long for so desperately, Chance," he explained, though there was a dark edge in his voice that reflected in his eyes. "If you really believe I stole her life, if you really think she would have lived, if you doubt my word and think me a killer, then take her blood on your tongue, and you'll finally know for sure."

Time froze in the icy wind.

I stared at Miquel, then at the tiny drop of blood on my wrist, already beginning to go cold. I didn't need to know how he did the things he did to believe he could do them. He had raised me from the dead to give me eternal life. He had fed me his heart, his soul. He had shown me his wings.

Now he was offering me a truth and a certainty no grieving mortal had ever known—for if I did what he was suggesting, if I took my daughter's blood into me, I would know everything there was to know about her life and about her death. I would know the secrets from her diaries and the truth about her pain and the sorrow of what it meant to grow up with a melancholy soul. I would know the awkward delight of her first boy-girl kiss and the awful anxiety of her first menstrual period. I would know what she thought about when she looked at me and how she'd really felt in Miquel's arms on the dance floor at a long-away costume ball.

But more than that, I'd know—once and for all of eternity— if Miquel had killed her or if he'd only helped her to die.

The scarlet circle glistened, sparkled. Miquel sat there on the edge of the world, watching, waiting.

Angel of life. Angel of death.

I would finally know.

But when I brought my wrist to my mouth, when my eyes closed in anticipation of the secrets contained in that lone drop of blood, I couldn't do it. My arm trembled, body shaking.

Fate was what it was, the grave the final resting place of all secrets. I had no right to exhume them even if I did have the power.

Stephanie was dead. And whether Miquel had told me the truth from the beginning or lied all along, the only thing I was certain of in all the chaos was that I did love him and he loved me.

Selfishly, I wasn't willing to lose that, too, and for that reason alone, I impulsively held my arms out to the night and let the rain wash the blood from my hand before I could change my mind.

For a long time, I couldn't look at him, so I stared at the lonesome Joshua trees and listened to their mournful tales of how the world had changed. They wanted to know about all the faraway places Harley Davidson had been and why he wouldn't talk to them as the ravens and the jackrabbits did. They wanted to know why the rainforests were dying and what Man intended to do about the fact that the salmon weren't swimming upstream anymore. They wanted to know about the blight of lights that had grown on the world below and if the luminescent cancer would soon spread to this high mountain.

I had no answers to give them.

Finally, while I stood there in that dead end parking lot looking down at my reflection in a puddle of water marred by swirls of motor oil and fractured by rain, Miquel came up behind me and slipped his arms around my waist, resting his dark, wet head on my shoulder.

"Most men would have chosen certainty even over love," he whispered close to my ear.

I cupped my hands over his, experiencing a moment of genuine serenity—my first since becoming an immortal. That was my answer, I knew. That was the only answer I needed.

"And if I'd found out something I didn't want to know?" I asked. "Eternity would be a long time to live with only hatred for company."

His scruffy chin brushed my neck, softened by rain. I felt him smile, sad though it was. "You're starting to sound like a vampyre."

Maybe I was at that.

Turning to face him, I snaked my wet arms underneath his leather jacket, secretly delighted when he flinched from the cold of my skin. When he bent his head to kiss me, I turned my face away from him, curling my lip to show my fangs until he grabbed my chin and forced me to submit.

As the storm thickened, the drizzle slowly evolved to fine white powder, a snowy blanket more suited to our kind than warmest wool or softest down.

Clouds gathered near, old friends embracing us.

It was as close to heaven as I ever wanted to be.

* * *

About the Author...

Della Van Hise is a native of Florida, transplanted to California at the age of 21, who has subsequently sunk her roots into the high desert near Joshua Tree National Park. She has not personally seen any aliens since around 1992, but there is rumored to be a secret UFO base underneath her house.

Her first professional novel was best-selling *Killing Time* - the controversial *Star Trek* novel which was recalled and re-edited in 1984. More recently, Della has written extensively in the non-fiction genre, with titles such as *Quantum Shaman (Diary of a Nagual Woman)*, *Into the Infinite* and *Questions Along the Way*. The *Quantum Shaman* series focuses heavily on the author's metaphysical explorations and experiences. If you enjoyed the works of Carlos Castaneda or Don Miguel Ruiz, you'll enjoy the non-fiction works of Della Van Hise.

In addition, Della has written professionally for Tomorrow Magazine and other prominent science fiction publications. Her most recent fiction works include *Sons of Neverland* (an award-winning vampire novel); *Year of the Ram* (a space-faring gay romance); and *Coyote* a - romantic science fiction novel combining the mystical aspects of martial arts, coming of age, and personal sacrifice.

TEACHINGS OF THE IMMORTALS
by Mikal Nyght
So... You Want To Live Forever?

The teachings are presented as brief vignettes in no particular order of importance. This is not a book you read from start to finish in a single night. It is a grimoire of self-creation, ntended to be contemplated slowly so as to be assimilated wholly. P ck it up and turn to a page at random. Where your eyes come to rest on the page is your lesson for the day. Go no further until you have assimilated the lesson totally.

The teachings are seduction as much as instruction. This is the way of The Dark Evolution.

The Ruby Slippers

The danger of the consensual continuum is that its ratural gravity exists at the lowest common denominator of human experience, and because of this it will automatically make you forget those elusive truths you've fought to learn, and before you know it you're lost in petty dramas again, sinking into the mire of old familiar scripts.

The only way to overcome this is to be continually cavorting with worlds and events beyond human experience, journeying into the unknown so that it can become known, expanding knowledge and awareness to become more than you were, bringing back from the Dreaming those secrets which will teach you how to use the ruby slippers to transport yourself over the rainbow to the vampyre wizard's secret lair.

Perception

This is the nature of reality: to be precisely what perception dictates, as solid and whole as your interpretation of it, or as changeable and eternal as you permit it to be.

It wasn't knowledge god tried to keep from Man, you see. It was perception, for perception alone has the power to destroy god and obliterate comfortable consensual realities to create unending immortality.

Take the apple, my embryonic children. Nibble its red red flesh. Open your vampyre eyes so you may finally begin to See.

YEAR OF THE RAM
Della Van Hise

Year of the Ram was described by one reviewer as... "A spacefaring gay romance full of love, angst, and longing."

Only after Star Commander Morgan Diego becomes an exile as a result of a Galaxy Corps political blunder does he begin to realize how much he valued the companionship of his second in command - the mysterious Lucien, an Alfarian who is more elven than human, with peculiar powers & abilities which begin to unfold as he, too, realizes what he has lost.

Separated by circumstance from his former life, Morgan is thrust into a world where he must survive by his wits. When he meets a peculiar little old man calling himself Kim Le, Morgan finds himself in a situation where he is required to master The Art - not only a form of human & extraterrestrial martial arts, but a way of living and being that will alter his life forever.

At the temple, he is introduced to his new teacher, another Alfarian who begins to steal his heart - a heart which is already promised to Lucien. Torn and conflicted, Morgan struggles with the world he left behind and the world he now inhabits.

Beginning to believe he may never again return to his ship and to the friends and loved ones he left behind, he is all the more frustrated and heartbroken when a new Master arrives at the temple: a man to whom Morgan is immediately drawn both mentally and physically, a man who is strikingly familiar... yet utterly alien.

Year of the Ram is a fully-fleshed novel, approximately 97000 words, with a focus on the love story and romance angle. Set against a science fiction milieu, it explores the infinite possibilities of the human and alien heart. Sexual content is explicit, though is not the primary focus of the novel.

For those who like a romance that forces its characters to contemplate the ecstasies AND the agonies of love... you will enjoy *Year of the Ram* immensely.

COYOTE
Della Van Hise

*A Novel of Love, Honor
and Personal Sacrifice...*

When River Willows is accused of a murder she didn't commit, her life takes a turn toward the sanctuary of a world existing at right-angles to our own. Combining the mysticism of martial arts and the romantic conflict of a young woman torn between two powerful men, COYOTE takes the reader on an epic journey of dangerous secrets, military cover-ups, and the infinite heart of the peaceful warrior.

———————

"So who's Coyote?" I asked, trying to ignore the effect he was having on me. "You?"

Steale laughed easily, though it did little to hide the torment behind that mask of indifference he wore so well.

"Coyote's a scavenger, Jack of all trades. The Native Americans call him the trickster - the one who brought chaos down on the world." He shrugged as if altogether unconcerned. "Original sin."

"Is that what you are?" I asked, keeping it light despite the growing knot my stomach. "Original sin?"

He kept his profile to me, eyes straight ahead as he drove. "Sure you want to know?"

I couldn't help wondering if I had cornered the coyote, or if the clever trickster had cornered me.

———————

By the author of **KILLING TIME** – without a doubt the most controversial **STAR TREK** novel ever published!

The Foundling
by Wendy Rathbone

Diego is a powerful man with a tragic past. Out on the expansive ocean in his private yacht, he discovers a beautiful and mysterious man adrift on a raft, near death. The bond that forms between them in the aftermath of Alec's rescue is one of fierce passion, though lacking in trust. Can they make it work, or will Alec's amnesia bring forth secrets so disturbing as to tear them apart? A passionately erotic love story of desire and darkness, exquisite and explicit.

I can see his struggle between gratitude and uneasiness. He is buffeted by all things new and strange. He does not know where he is from, who he is or what happened to him. He does not know me. There has not been enough time to transition between strangers and friendship.

This isolation of his is something I can identify with, but it is also a feeling no one can help him with until or unless he gets his own life back. And his memory.

If that doesn't happen, then it will take time for him to build a new life. He is polite to me, even friendly, but even a night together during a storm with his arms wrapped tight around my waist doesn't calm the surge I see inside him, the emptiness, the loss, possibly even panic. That night may have reinforced some trust in me, but so far not enough for him to completely relax.

He seeks me out, though. That's something. He sits by me at dinner when he can have any seat of his choosing. I watch him closely when he does not realize it. At dinner the following night after we had only 'slept' together, and before we go to bed again in separate rooms, I notice everything about him, how he moves, the way the air warms when he is closer to me, the dry sheen of his lips as they part for more air when he is reacting to something, or speaking, or eating.

His hands still shake. Anyone else might not notice because he keeps them clasped into fists at his sides or, while sitting, pressed tight to his lap.

I spend another fretful night alone. I dream restlessly, wild, loud and colorful visions I cannot recall at all as soon as my eyes open. All I know is the dreams leave me unfulfilled, impatient.

The Foundling trilogy is available on Amazon or directly from the author
www.eyescrypublications.com

Prince of Umberlight
Alexis Fegan Black

"If Prince of Umberlight doesn't rattle your cage, you're more dead than the undead!" **-Night Readers**

Thorn may be an 800 year old vampire, but he does not possess the ability to create others of his kind, and so he is cursed to fall in love with mortals, only to watch them grow old and die. Torn by grief, Thorn denounces his immortality and enters into a comatose oblivion for decades. When he awakens, he is no longer in London, but finds himself in a world spun into being by his own desires - a world where Time and Death do not exist, a world where it is forever autumn, where the Parish of Shadows and the River of Stars become his home. It is in this world of Umberlight that he meets Atom - an interloper into his private sanctuary, but also an impudent imp who is destined to reveal to Thorn the three dangerous elements a vampire must possess in order to become a Creator.

The Art of Brutality.
Submission to Dark Desire.
Love.

Available on Amazon or directly from the publisher at www.eyescrypublications.com

Eye Scry Publications
A Visionary Publishing Company

www.eyescrypublications.com

The door between realities
stands open a crack,
revealing the shadows still to come,
the effect of moonlight on tombstones.

-Note found scrawled
in a vampyre's diary